Also by David Ignatius

Agents of Innocence
SIRO
The Bank of Fear
A Firing Offense

THE SUN KING

THE SUN KING

A NOVEL

David Ignatius

RANDOM HOUSE
NEW YORK

FIC IGN

Library of Congress Cataloging-in-Publication Data
Ignatius, David.
The sun king / David Ignatius.
p.   cm.
ISBN 0-679-44861-6 (acid-free paper)
I. Title.
PS3559.G54S77   1999
813'.54—dc21   99-13490

Random House website address: www.atrandom.com

Printed in the United States of America on acid-free paper

98765432

First Edition

A12003425208

For Sarah, Amy, and Adi

Soyez mystérieuse

soyez amoureuse

et vous serez heureuse.

———————

—PAUL GAUGUIN,

inscription carved on the
doorway of the house in the
South Seas where he died

Author's Note

Washington itself has become so outlandishly unreal that any disclaimer about a novel set in the nation's capital should be redundant. But I would stress that this book is a work of fiction. The characters, events, companies, and institutions are products of the author's imagination and should not be construed as real. I hope several friends from college days and since will be amused by a few brief walk-on characters they partly inspired, but otherwise any resemblance to the actual flora and fauna of Washington is unintended. *The Washington Sun and Tribune* of my story has no connection with any real newspaper. Similarly, the D.C. mayor of my tale is neither modeled on nor inspired by the incumbent or any previous holder of that office; the secretary of transportation, assistant secretary of the Treasury, and other worthies inhabit a Washington only of the imagination.

THE SUN
KING

ONE

I OWE MY INTRODUCTION TO SANDY GALVIN TO THE ONE essential, irreducible requirement of being a magazine editor, which is that you have to fill the white space. Our features editor, Annabelle Paige, had quit—she called it a "resignation in protest," as if she were an aggrieved member of the President's Cabinet—because I had changed a picture caption she had written. The picture was of a woman in her sixties who was trying to defy age and gravity in a low-cut ball gown. Our features editor had written, "The always charming Mrs. Robert P. Edgerly trips the life fantastic at the Ambassador's Ball." I had crossed that out and written, "Barbie's mom? No, it's Mrs. Robert P. Edgerly at the Ambassador's Ball."

Nothing too mean about that. Some women might actually take it as a compliment. And besides, Annabelle Paige hadn't even gotten the cliché right. She was accident prone, our features editor—a blond former airline stewardess with a pert suburban accent that never quite concealed the awful truth that she was really from *New Zealand*. When she saw

the change on the bluelines, she threw a three-alarm tantrum. She called the owner and burst into tears, saying that I
was a cruel man who hated women and that she couldn't
stand to work for me one more hour, and so she *quit*. She
must have expected the owner to try and talk her out of it,
but it was the wrong day to pick this particular fight, because
our monthly magazine, *Reveal: The Social Bible of Washington,*
was in such a deep hole financially that the owner had actually been considering whether to *fire* Annabelle Paige. And
now she didn't have to. "Mmmm, delightful!" as Annabelle
would say. The only thing our former features editor could
do in retaliation was to pull the article she had written for the
next issue—a profile of a man whose chief accomplishment,
other than sucking up to Annabelle, was that he had been
named northern Virginia's Car Dealer of the Year. That left
me with a two-page hole to fill, but not with a heavy heart.

"Annabelle quit," I shouted down the hall to Pamela, my
assistant. "She pulled her piece on the car dealer." Our office
was a tiny walk-up in an old building on Connecticut Avenue.
It was a dump, frankly. Once upon a time, before the owner's
husband died, the office had been nicely decorated with attractive photographs and even a few paintings. But those had
been sold off, and the best we could do now were old movie
and travel posters tacked to the walls.

"Fuck!" said Pamela. She was a petite redhead, a recent
graduate of American University who talked as if she had
spent her life in the merchant marine. Her previous journalism experience consisted of one year on the college newspaper. "How are we supposed to fill the hole?" she demanded.

"We're closing tonight, remember? And I have a date, so if you're expecting me to stay late, forget it."

"Do you have any suggestions?" I asked.

"How the hell should I know who to profile? I'm twenty-two years old."

I told Pamela not to worry. I was working the case. I would figure out a solution. But she was already on the phone, telling one of her friends what a loser I was.

And I couldn't really dispute that. I was a tall, thin, balding man, with oversize black glasses like the kind Buddy Holly used to wear. The joke in high school was that if I turned sideways, all you could see was a straight line. People like Pamela existed in three dimensions; they took up space. But I lived in two dimensions, on printed pages. I had no mass. Just words.

NOTHING IMPORTANT IN LIFE is simply an accident. To believe otherwise would be to accept a universe in which *everything* is accidental, the random collision of billiard balls on a table, with no event connected to any other except in time and space. I've never been able to accept that randomness, especially when it involves things that matter—like my collision that day with the heretofore unseen world of Sandy Galvin. So much happened as a result of that particular carom that I cannot imagine it not having occurred. It changed my life, and his too.

So it could not have been mere chance that I called my friend Hugo Bell, the real estate snoop, for suggestions about whom to profile in place of the car dealer. And it could not have been mere chance that he had just noticed in some title records that a man had recently purchased a mansion in McLean, overlooking the Potomac River, and *another* mansion in Georgetown. Two trophy houses in one month—this was *Reveal*'s dream come true! And surely it could not have been mere chance that this multidomiciled man was named Carl S. Galvin, and that my friend happened to have his Virginia phone number on his desk.

I DIDN'T EXPECT HIM to answer the phone. The man had two mansions, after all. Why should he answer his own phone? "Hi!" I said brightly. "My name is David Cantor and I'm the editor of *Reveal: The Social Bible of Washington*. Is Mr. Galvin there?"

"What do you want?" answered the voice at the other end. "Mr. Galvin is busy." He was clipped, dismissive; some sort of butler, I thought.

"We'd like to profile him in our next issue. A thousand words, with a nice picture. His comments about moving to Washington, inspirational thoughts for the kids. Instant celebrity!"

"He's not interested," said the voice. He was about to hang up.

"How do you *know* he's not interested?" I did not relish the prospect of having to search for another profile subject that afternoon from among the limited galaxy of Washington's rich and famous.

"Because I *am* Galvin. And I don't want to be profiled by anything called *Reveal*. It sounds like a complete waste of time."

"I hate that name too," I said hastily. "I want to change it, but the owner won't let me. The magazine used to be called *Enjoy!* And that was even worse, in my opinion. I wanted to rename it *The Savant,* which is what we *aspire* to be, but the owner said no—too obscure—so we compromised on *Reveal.* But I agree, it's a terrible name. It's a good magazine, however, and it will be good for you if we profile you. I promise."

I was babbling. I was desperate. And as I said before, it was fate. He couldn't say no. I wouldn't let him.

"Why will it be good for me?" asked Galvin. There was a hint of mirth in his voice now. He was enjoying listening to my desperate pitch.

"Because we'll make you famous. At least modestly so. You're already rich, obviously, if you've bought two houses—that's right, isn't it? You did buy two houses, didn't you?—so now, presumably, you want to be famous. That's why people move to Washington. And our magazine is the gatekeeper. We tell people who they should be interested in, and if we profile you—boom!—you're interesting. And there's another reason you should say yes. We only do favorable profiles. I should probably be embarrassed by that, but I'm not. It's a fact."

He was chuckling out loud now, at my absurd begging. That's one thing in my favor as an editor and as a human being. I have never been too proud to beg.

"Come by my house tonight and we'll talk about it," Galvin said. "I'm having a little party by the river. Seven to nine. We'll see if you're as ridiculous as you sound."

"Which house?" I asked, but he had hung up. It had to be

Virginia. I was home free. Even if he threw me out of the party, I already had enough to fill the white space.

I CALLED THE OWNER of *Reveal* before I left, to make sure she approved of my plan to sub Galvin for the car dealer. I liked her better now that she was a widow. Her late husband had bought the magazine for her as a kind of toy, but she had grown to love it and fought to keep it when the estate was settled. "I believe in journalism," she told me earnestly, and she meant it, in her way. Her only rule was that we write nice things about her friends. Otherwise she didn't care, so long as people complimented the magazine at parties. Which they always did, because they wanted her to print their pictures.

People may scoff at *Reveal* now, but in its day, everybody read it. And I know why. Because in a city where everything is serious and low in cholesterol, we were a big, gooey chocolate sundae. We fawned over the things people pretended they weren't interested in—money, fancy clothes, big houses, cosmetic surgery—and we had just enough of a sneer to convey that we were *better* than that, too. I understood the rules of the game, when to grovel and when to sneer. And I never, *ever* picked fights with the owner's friends. I knew, for example, that she didn't like Jane Edgerly. Otherwise I would never have called her Barbie's mom.

"We're running a profile of a new arrival in town," I explained to the owner. "A man named Galvin."

"What does he do?" She sounded far away. I could hear the television in the background.

"I don't know. But he's very rich. He owns two mansions. And he appears to be unmarried, since he bought both places in his own name." I knew that would interest her. She was still on the rebound, looking for Mr. Rich.

There was a pause on the other end of the phone. "Is he, uh . . . you know . . ."

The owner was getting sensitive about that subject. A few weeks ago she had received a postcard whose only message was "Too many Jews!!!" I tried to tell her it wasn't our fault. The Jews were the ones making the money and going to the charity balls. The WASPs were losing it. Going to seed. Their children were staying at the summer house all year round. That was reality, but it made the owner nervous, so she had suggested a quota system for the photo spreads—a one-to-one ratio, chosen and unchosen. Believe me, it was hard finding enough dopey, pink-faced WASPs to fill out our pages. For the owner, it had become sort of an unmentionable subject, except that she mentioned it all the time. Like me, she was a secret member of the tribe. I wanted to reassure her.

"No," I said. "I don't think he's Jewish. It didn't come up, actually."

"It's all right," she said with a sigh. "It doesn't matter. Ask him to buy an ad in the next issue."

NO ONE WAS LESS suited to chronicle Washington life than I, so I liked to think, and I consoled myself with that inner unsuitability long after I had become a creature of the nation's capital.

I had come to Washington from the Midwest—a North Side suburb of Chicago, actually; not exactly corn country—but I had always felt like an outsider in the East. My father had been a lawyer, and he had assumed I would do the same, go to law school, come home to Highland Park and do the right thing. But he had actually done the wrong thing, it turned out, in terms of taking care of himself, and he died when I was in college. I wouldn't have come home anyway, but his early death made it easier to explain why I was choosing the rootless, bootless life of a journalist. I didn't want to end up like my dad, with a law practice and a country club membership and the good wishes of my friends on the holidays but dead at forty-five.

My father lived to see me go off to Harvard, which probably added to his sense of security and well-being but had the opposite effect on me. That's Harvard's secret, if you didn't know. Yale or Princeton or Stanford make a man feel good about himself, comfortable, secure in the world. Harvard deliberately inculcates the opposite sensation. You think you're smart? Well, look around, sonny boy. Smart people, wall-to-wall, as far as the eye can see. You're nothing. Less than nothing. You can't even get laid on the weekend, the way those blockheads from Yale and Princeton and Stanford do. The message is, You may be smart, but so what? You're still a loser. That's why Harvard graduates do so well in the world. They are creatures of insecurity.

And I suspect that's also why so many Harvard grads ended up in Washington. We understood the place. It was pure anxiety, one big SAT test. Everyone was an outsider here; no one really belonged—except for those aging pink-faced alcoholics in *Reveal*'s Around the Whirl section, whose fathers' fathers had gone to the right prep schools but whose own sons couldn't get in because the blood was running a little *thin.* They belonged, the pink faces, but everyone else was insecure, impermanent, newly arrived. That's what the Nigerian cabdrivers had in common with the K Street lawyers and the real estate developers and the journalistic vipers-in-waiting. None of us belonged. We were all struggling to make it. The city's esteemed, somnambulant newspaper, *The Washington Sun and Tribune,* treated us like picaresque vagrants. But my magazine, God bless it, wanted to show us the way.

My appreciation of anxiety as a lifestyle has shaped my philosophy of magazines, which I can summarize as follows: Write *about* the A's—but *for* the B's. The people who really *are* movers and shakers don't have time to read society magazines, and they don't need instruction in how to be rich and famous—because they already are. But everyone else is *dying* to know the secrets—in anticipation of the day when they too will be asked to serve as cochair of the Leukemia Ball, or get appointed ambassador to Luxembourg, or marry the twenty-nine-year-old ex-model who looks so delectable in that beaded Emanuel Ungaro cocktail dress. That was why it was so important to have the newly rich represented in our pages—so that our readers could see themselves taking that step up. They could see the real estate developer, whose biggest claim to fame heretofore had been building the big shopping mall outside Annapolis, standing next to the secretary of state, for God's sake—he and his wife looking a little nervous, but *being there,* taking that step up from B-dom to A-dom. And we were there too, as chroniclers and voyeurs.

My only real question about Galvin was whether he

was a B or an A. Was he a car dealer wanting to get his picture taken next to the President? Or was he one of nature's aristocrats—a man who truly *was* indifferent whether *Reveal* ran a story about him—and for that reason absolutely, positively the one we wanted? I knew nothing about him, other than the fact that he owned two huge houses. But I had the odd feeling you get standing by the railroad tracks, when the rails begin to hum and the birds twitter in the trees and you know, even though you can't see it yet, that there is a big train coming.

TWO

IT WAS A GOOD NIGHT FOR A PARTY—LATE JUNE, A sapphire-blue sky darkening to a soft Virginia purple as the evening fell. The azaleas and dogwoods of spring were gone, but the summer heat hadn't scorched the grass yet, and there was a lovely green on the trees, the lawns, the ferns, everywhere you looked. As I turned down Galvin's long driveway, I saw the first signs of his "little" party. Cars were parked on both sides of the drive, handsome sedans in iridescent colors never found in nature, resting on the green grass.

I had brought along our regular party photographer, a likable social miscreant who spent his evenings photographing women in fancy dresses so that he could indulge his real passion, which was playing the harmonica in a blues band that never had any concert engagements. "We should park," he said helpfully, so I nestled my gray Honda Civic in between a tangerine Lexus and a powder-blue BMW. Though we were still far from the house, we could hear the sound of the partygoers below—shrill laughs, an occasional shriek, but mostly a low, melodious chorus that seemed to bounce off the trees above and the river below.

The house came into view as we rounded a green curve. It had a handsome redbrick facade, and was simple but imposing. It might have been an Edwardian country house. A pool and gardens stretched to the right, and beyond the house a broad lawn sloped gently toward the cliffs overlooking the river. Perhaps I've seen larger houses, but not in Washington. I rang the bell and a butler answered, a real butler this time, who knew who I was and said that Mr. Galvin was out back with his guests. We made our way through a large living room that had been decorated in handsome, if eclectic, style—a fine Persian carpet, Chinese silk screens, an iconic Warhol portrait of Marilyn Monroe on the far wall. The unifying theme was that everything was pleasing to the eye, and had cost a lot of money.

As we neared the door, we saw the guests arrayed on the deck and on the lush lawn below. My photographer began taking pictures. Many of the guests were well-known Washington faces: the impish, streetwise bureau chief of *The New York Times;* the plummy British ambassador and his starstruck wife; the columnists, leaning intently toward their sources in government, several of whom looked like they could use a good cry, what with the President's troubles; and the many former government officials, now better tailored and far wealthier than when they had been in government, who had the empty serenity of people who don't have enough to *do.* There were other guests too—businesspeople you didn't usually see at Washington parties. A Nobel laureate who had founded a local biotechnology company and become rich, rich, rich. A thirty-five-year-old boy entrepreneur who had created an Internet company that the stock market now judged more valuable than General Motors; he was sporting a black leather jacket with his company name in script on the back. This was an odd party, I remember thinking. How could Galvin have gotten all these prominent people to come to his house so soon after arriving in town?

We were at something of a disadvantage, my photographer and I, because neither of us knew what Carl Galvin actually looked like. I told the photographer to stop shooting. I didn't want to get thrown out before we at least had eyeballed him. We made our way down the back stairs toward the lawn. The guests parted as we approached, and looked away blankly, as if we were tradesmen who had wandered in through the wrong door. That offended me—I belonged! I had been invited!—so I grabbed a glass of wine from a silver tray and strolled off toward the stone wall that overlooked the water. It had been a rainy spring, and the Potomac was still a surging, white-water river. Later in the summer it would slow to a dry-bed trickle, but for now it cascaded over its narrow banks, carrying silt and brush from the uplands toward the city.

The photographer sat down on the stone wall and announced that he wasn't moving until we found our man. I gazed up the slope toward the crowd of partygoers, searching for a face I didn't recognize. There was a stirring up near the house, laughter, arms extended to shake hands.

I knew him instantly. He was tall and broad-shouldered, standing nearly a head above most of his guests. He was wearing a summer suit that was draped on his frame in the comfortable, elegant way that movie stars from the 1940s wore their clothes. He was talking with the deputy secretary of the Treasury, and the odd thing was that the deputy secretary was leaning toward Galvin, straining to hear what *he* had to say. As Galvin made his point, the deputy secretary nodded in that grave Washington way, prompting the host to do something most unusual. He smiled—the broadest smile I had seen in months—as if to say, *What a night, what a place, what a pleasure!* And the deputy secretary smiled back nearly as broadly, with the self-satisfied look of a fellow conspirator. And I understood, in that moment, the essential fact about Galvin: He knew how to make people happy.

He had seen me staring at him, and he began making his way toward me, still smiling. A woman caught his arm and he turned to her and whispered something that made her laugh. Then he pointed down the hill to me and made an apology. She watched him walk away and called out something that I couldn't hear but didn't have to. She wanted him for herself. They all did.

"You must be the magazine man," said Galvin, extending his hand. It was a soft handshake: polite, nothing to prove, establishing distance and intimacy at the same time. My camera-laden friend had dismounted the stone wall and was beginning to shoot. Galvin retreated a step. "And this must be the photographer, although I don't remember anything about photographs. But never mind. What have you got to say for yourself, Mr. Editor? Something revelatory, I hope."

"Nice house," I said dumbly. He had taken me off guard. I don't know what I had expected, but it wasn't this prince among his newfound courtiers. "I apologize for bringing along the photographer, but the truth is, we *need* a photograph, and I thought it was in the spirit of my request. I just need to ask you a few questions and then I'll leave. Gratefully. I promise." I had taken a notebook from my pocket and was poised, ready to write.

He was frowning. I had disappointed him in some way. I studied his face so I would be able to describe it, in case he threw me out. He was surprisingly dark, close up, with a deep tan and jet-black hair that was cut short and sculpted to his face. It was a face that was as smooth and sharp as an arrowhead. The face, combined with that lovely draped suit, gave him the appearance of a man who had fallen out of time, from the Stork Club long ago, directly to here and now.

"Let's take a walk," he said, taking me by the elbow and leaving the photographer behind. "That way, people will assume that I know you, and that you're not just some party crasher from a society magazine."

"Sure," I said. "Let's take a walk." We were about the same height, but I felt pencil thin standing next to him. I realized that I was wasting time, being sociable. We had to close the issue that night. I needed information. "Why did you buy two houses?" I asked greedily. That was the peg for my story; I had to nail that one.

"On the record?" he queried, arching his eyebrows.

I nodded.

"The answer is that I couldn't make up my mind. One

friend told me I absolutely had to live in Georgetown. Another said I had to live in McLean. I found two beautiful houses and decided to buy them both."

"That's mush," I said. "And it makes you sound indecisive. What about off the record?" I put down my pen.

"Off the record, they were great investments. I'm going to flip the one in Georgetown and make a killing. And your article is going to help." He winked. He had just done it to me, too. We were coconspirators.

"*Use* me!" I said. "I have to respect someone who's completely unprincipled. Not a problem with me. Now, let's go back on the record. Are you planning to sell your Georgetown house after my article appears and make a killing?"

"No comment." A sweet smile, nonchalant. It was obvious now. The man was a jewel thief.

"Let's try the basics," I said, pen poised above my pad again. "Where are you from?"

He waved his hand dismissively. "My butler will give you a biography. It has all the details, or at least all the ones I'm prepared to share with the readers of *Reveal*. Where are *you* from?"

"Chicago. North Side. After that, I went to Harvard. But that was a long time ago. Now, like everyone else in this city, I'm not really from anywhere."

"Pity. I'm from someplace very particular. But we do have one thing in common. I went to Harvard, just like you. But I dropped out. Best thing I ever did." He gave me that smile again. Unforced, natural, as spontaneous as a puff of wind. When he smiled, it was as if a little spotlight had been turned onto his face, highlighting the smooth tan cheeks and the white teeth and the sparkling eyes.

"Why was dropping out such a smart move?" I asked.

"Because it gave me all this." He gestured with a broad sweep of his hand toward the lawn, the house, the guests. "It taught me to take risks, and not to listen to what other people think."

"But *how* did you get so rich?" I was writing down everything he said, but it was crap. I still didn't know anything. I needed some juice.

"It's in the bio," Galvin said. By now, I noticed, he had walked me around to the side door, away from the guests. My photographer was trotting along behind, humming the tune to "Hootchie Kootchie Man." Galvin shook my hand, thanked me for coming, apologized for not having more time. I threw out a few of those junk questions that pass for color in magazine profiles—"What's your favorite TV show?" "What's the last book you read?" "If you could be any movie star, who would you be?"—but he wasn't playing. It was all in the bio, he said.

I had one last item. It was boilerplate, but it yielded my first hint of the irregularities that were hidden inside this imposing package.

"What does the S stand for?" I asked.

"Sandburg," he answered softly. "My full name is Carl Sandburg Galvin. People used to call me Sandy in college. I was named after the poet. Never quite lived up to it, but I'm trying."

IT TURNED OUT THERE was almost nothing in the bio. I read it as soon as I got back to my car, under the dim yellow light of the reading lamp. It said he had made his money in "overseas investments." It didn't say where he was born, or where he had lived before moving here. It said he had never graduated from college but didn't mention Harvard. The only really useful piece of information was the explanation of why he had come to Washington: "Mr. Galvin is establishing a fund that will invest in a range of local and national businesses, including the media business."

HE INTERESTED ME. HE was dragging something invisible along behind him, which was giving off sparks. The general type was familiar enough to *Reveal* readers: They arrived every year in the capital from St. Louis or Phoenix, men who had just sold the family department-store chain or real estate business to set themselves up as problem solvers, party givers, candidates for ambassadorial posts in northern latitudes. They quickly discovered which schools, churches and synagogues would confer the most prestige; their wives found the right personal trainer, caterer and book club. Friends who'd arrived here in earlier expeditions of civic duty put them up for the right clubs. It wasn't all that different from the way things worked back in St. Louis, really—just a bigger version.

But Galvin was something else. He maintained the aloof confidence of an outsider; the city was paying *him* court. It wasn't simply that he was so rich. He appeared to have a different sort of ambition—not to join the conversation, but to alter it. What would make a man so sure of himself? And what was he lacking, that had brought him here? He didn't seem to want power, at least not in the usual sense of running for office or obtaining a Cabinet post. He wanted something more raw and immediate—the ability to command attention, to make people listen. But I had no idea what he would say.

THREE

THE PRESIDENT'S TROUBLES CONTINUED TO WORSEN that summer, which added to the sense of oppression and entrapment that is part of Washington in July. It was as if an impermeable membrane had been placed over the top of the city, which prevented anything from escaping: air, heat, imagination, gossip—all trapped inside the bubble with the sweltering residents. The precise details of the scandal were difficult to ascertain back then; a grand jury was meeting in secret, supposedly, to hear evidence about the President's criminal activities. Accounts of what those crimes might be varied from day to day, depending on which witnesses were before the grand jury and what news organizations were leading the chase. The general assessment of the President's situation seemed to fluctuate with the level of the stock market. So long as it remained buoyant, the consensus was that he would survive.

Not even the publication of a new issue of *Reveal*—and the wet kiss it bestowed upon Carl Sandburg Galvin—could relieve the gloomy July mood. The profile was a tidy piece of hackwork, if I do say so myself. I described the arrival of this mysterious outsider into our bubble; I sketched the scene at his garden party, the way he looked and talked and moved among his guests. We'd gotten a good photo of him too, standing on his lawn with the house and guests behind—the thinnest wisp of a smile on his face, but just enough to establish a bond with the reader and whisper: Look at me! Look at this!

I made a point of noting the many questions Galvin had refused to answer about himself, and I included comments from several of the guests. One of them, a newsmagazine writer known for his laconic, preppy asides, said Galvin had come to town to rescue his old friend, the President. A Washington hostess said she'd heard he'd been some sort of spy. A local investment banker said that was poppycock; Galvin had made his money in the oil business. He was a buccaneer capitalist, this man claimed—one of the smartest and most ruthless in the world. It didn't matter whether any of it was true, it added to the allure. All people were certain of about Galvin was that he was rich, charming and had already made large contributions to several of the capital's most deserving and fashionable charities.

Galvin himself telephoned the day after the July issue had been deposited on the doorsteps of all the right Zip Codes. Pamela took the call. I told her I didn't want to talk to him just then and to say that I was out. She got half of it right. I listened through the thin wall as she said, "I'm sorry, Mr. Galvin. He doesn't want to talk to you."

I was too nervous to speak with him, frankly. People only

call after an article is published to say that you've gotten something wrong, and I didn't want to know yet what I had screwed up. It was a purely neurotic reaction—like getting a letter that you just don't want to open and letting it gather dust on the table for a few days, until it's safe. Clearly that had never happened to Pamela. She admonished me that it was wrong to lie, even on the phone, and that I should never have told her to do so. What she actually said was that I was a "total wacko," but never mind. Pamela scared me. What worried me most was the possibility that she was the normal one.

I didn't return Galvin's call the rest of that day. I thought I'd let it age a bit. And it was too hot to do any work anyway, especially something taxing like making a phone call. So I went to the movies and sat in the back near an air-conditioning vent.

I was still thinking about Galvin the next morning when the owner summoned me. She suggested that we have lunch at the Jockey Club, which was a bad sign. The restaurant had been the hangout for a certain kind of long-in-the-tooth celebrity when the Republicans were in the White House; it was the place where Johnny Carson's ex-wife lunched when she was in town, and Ed McMahon probably would have eaten there too, if he ever came to Washington. My poor owner liked to go there when she needed to feel *substantial*. The staff fawned over you, if you were a regular and tipped well. It was obvious the owner had something bad to tell me, because she was already drinking a glass of wine when I arrived.

"We're going broke," she said morosely. I was relieved; I already knew that.

Her slender hand was gripping the wineglass a bit too tightly. She was looking around the room to make sure that nobody important was present to witness her distress. She looked especially beautiful that day, I thought. She was a slight blond woman, with a fine-boned face. Her features had been highlighted and softened in all the right ways for so many years that she made you think she had been *born* with those eyebrows, that her hair had that soft sweep when she woke up in the morning. It is the highest calling of artifice to seem so natural. Her beauty was heightened by the edge of anxiety, by the distracted, doelike look in her eye.

"This time it's serious, my dear," she said, taking a quick drink of wine and putting the glass back unsteadily on the table. "Finlandia has canceled the back-page vodka ad. Chanel is pulling its dress ads, starting in October. And the plastic surgeons have just sent me a group letter saying that unless we do a special issue on breast augmentation, they're gone too. Which leaves us with the real estate ads and a few caterers and those swimming pool builders, and that's it. Which isn't enough to pay the bills."

I didn't say anything in response, and there was a long, funereal pause as we both contemplated the prospect that *The Social Bible of Washington* might cease publication. I reached out and touched her hand. Sometimes, words just don't suffice. She gave me a wan smile as if to say, *So this is what it has come to . . . being comforted by* you.

"What should we do?" she asked at last.

"We could change the name again," I offered. "I've never been sure that *Reveal* is quite right. It's a little *cheap*. It doesn't fully convey the ambition of what we're trying to do."

"What do you suggest?" she asked warily. We had been down this road before, a few years ago. "And please don't say *The Savant* again. Because that's out of the question."

"I was thinking of something more upmarket." I paused, and not just for effect—I was trying to think of something. "How about *Lush*. That sounds rich, verdant, fructifying. Or *Moist*. Same thing, but more mysterious."

"You're kidding, please. *Lush* sounds like a magazine for drunks. *Moist* sounds like an underarm deodorant. You're losing it, David. Try again."

"Okay. I agree. Those aren't very good. How about something that would speak to advertisers directly. Position the product differently. Something like *Flaunt It!* with an exclamation point. That's elemental, right? Read this magazine, buy the stuff in it, and you can tell the world to go to hell. Or maybe *Go for It!* Same thing, but a little less intense. Or *Indulge!* Candlelight, soft focus. Or just call it *Envy!* I like that. It's in your face, unembarrassed. And that's the business we're in. We exist to make you realize that someone else has a bigger house, a younger wife, a richer husband. We sell envy!"

I paused a moment. I wasn't sure whether I was serious or pulling her leg. That was the problem with this job. It was so completely ridiculous to begin with, it was hard to know what was serious and what was a joke. "The more I think about it," I said, "the more I like *Flaunt It!* That says everything to me."

"Stop it!" she said. "This isn't a game. It's real. I'm going to close the magazine unless we can get some new money in a hurry. I take my journalistic responsibility very seriously. I know this community needs me. But I am not going to sell the house on Martha's Vineyard just to meet the payroll. I won't do it! And we *can't* continue like this."

"You're right," I answered solemnly. "Something must be done. We can't just let the magazine *die*." I told her I would make a list of advertisers we could approach. Jewelers were a good bet. We already had a special wedding issue in June, but maybe we could add an engagement issue. And the people who sold linens—sheets and towels, bedspreads—we hadn't even tried them. "September is *bedding* month!" And orthodontists! Why hadn't I thought of that before? *Reveal* readers certainly cared about straight teeth. We should *own* that marketplace. I promised the owner I would make a list of the *top* orthodontists.

BUT WHAT I WAS really thinking was that I needed an escape plan. It made no sense for me to remain on the deck of *Reveal* and go down nobly with the ship. No sense at all. And besides, disloyalty is an underrated virtue. It's the very soul of our political and economic life. Clearly it was time to think about jumping ship, but the question was, Where to go?

I had always thought it best to avoid making career plans. It seemed to me that ambition was dangerous. You set yourself a goal, fine—but what happens when you don't achieve it? You feel miserable, and for good reason. You have *failed*. Your friends have watched with silent pleasure as you've tried to climb a notch above them and then slipped ignominiously backward. They've sent you notes offering heartfelt, insincere condolences. Whereas, if you never set a goal, you never risk failure. You are blown by the winds of unemployment until you land on fertile ground, take root and flower. Or wither and die, as the case may be, but it doesn't matter, because nobody will see that you've screwed up.

My chief career fantasy, in those moments when I allowed myself to imagine that *Reveal* would not be a lifetime job, had involved the television industry. Not to become one of those robot reporters who are always badgering people about what it *feels* like to have lost a child or an election or an Olympic medal. No, that sounded less attractive even than law school or a career in gastroenterology. My ambition, if you can call it that, lay in a different direction entirely.

This will sound peculiar, even to people with a taste for the exotic, but I dreamed of working as a booker on *The Jerry Springer Show.* Though he is not widely appreciated among the mineral-water set, Jerry is the Meriwether Lewis of popular culture. He journeys each day into uncharted lands—to discover the poor child who declares, "I'm twelve and I take care of my 680-pound mom!" or to encounter the young woman who boasts, "I want to be a teen stripper!" or to unlock the riddle of "Zack: The 70-pound Baby." That last was one of my favorite episodes, actually. What mother would not be interested in the saga of an eighteen-month-old toddler who weighs seventy pounds? An adventure in parenting, to say nothing of all those diapers.

What America secretly wonders each night watching *Jerry* is: Where do they *find* these people? Under what rock, around what bend, up what hollow do they live? And I wanted to know the answer. I wanted to be the booker, the man who conducted the initial interview with Clem, the fifty-pound baby, and decided: Nope! Sorry, you just don't cut

it. We're gonna wait for *Zack*. I wanted to take the first un-
varnished look at the woman who decided to tell her
boyfriend, on national TV, that she's really a *man*. I wanted to
meet the woman who boasted, "I broke the world's sex
record!" (The magic number here, if you're not a regular
Jerry viewer, was three hundred men in a single porno
movie.) These people seemed like miracles—too good for
real life. Would they even exist if Jerry wasn't there to tell
their stories?

In all seriousness: There is nothing more uplifting on television today than *Jerry Springer*, and that includes *Mobil
Masterpiece Theatre*. The astounding revelations go on, night
after night, a pageant of the infinitely perverse and interesting ways ordinary Americans find to express themselves in
this homogenized, soulless land. The mineral-water camp is
always talking about the importance of diversity. Well, this is
diversity, by God! "I'm in Love with a Serial Killer." "I Stole
My 12-year-old's Boyfriend!" "My 15-year-old Son Wears a
Dress!" "I Married a Horse!"

This is what we have left at the end of the American century. This is our special gift. Can you imagine producing such
a show in a formerly great nation like France or Germany or
England? Of course not. They haven't the energy for it, the
gift for self-invention. They are dead cultures, while we are
alive—expectorating, excreting, mutating, evolving toward a
higher and better state. But I digress.

FOUR

PAMELA QUIT THE NEXT DAY. THAT SHOULDN'T HAVE FELT like a blow—she was an incompetent secretary, and she frightened me—but it did. She was a quicker rat off the sinking ship than I, that was the troubling thing. I was losing my touch. "How dare you?" I said when she announced this would be her last day, or morning, actually, because she would be taking a long lunch. "Hey, asshole," she responded. "Get a life!" No point really in continuing that conversation.

I called the owner and advised her that our merry band had been reduced by one—two if you also counted our recently departed features editor, Annabelle Paige. That should have pleased her—one less person to dismiss when *Reveal* went belly up—but it seemed instead to have the opposite effect. "It's the end, isn't it?" she said lugubriously. "They *know*."

"Not at all," I answered. "It's not the end. It's not even the beginning of the end. It's more like the end of the beginning."

"Please, David. I appreciate the sentiment, but you aren't Winston Churchill, and this isn't World War Two. Have you called any of the orthodontists yet?"

I had to admit that I had not. That plunged the owner deeper into despair. I was becoming concerned—I didn't want *her* to jump ship before me, too. We had to hold on long enough for me to devise an "exit strategy," as Henry Kissinger would say.

"I have a plan," I said untruthfully, playing for time. "It's something I thought of a while ago, but it's just the thing we need now, to really *cement* our position as *The Social Bible of Washington*."

"What is it?" she answered dully. It was sad, just listening to that depleted, heartsick voice. She needed to get laid. That had to be part of the problem.

"Here it is: We will *create* a member of the Washington social elite, from scratch. We'll select someone, whoever we like—that lady with the big teeth who does the Chevrolet ads, say, or one of the women who didn't get picked as honorary cochair for the Leukemia Ball—and turn her into a celebrity. First, we'll run a photograph of her in Around the Whirl, dancing at a charity ball. Next issue, we'll run a photograph of her giving a speech, wearing glasses and looking very *policy*, with people crowding around listening. Next issue, we'll write a story about how she's giving an award in the name of someone famous—Evangeline Bruce, very famous *and* dead—and we'll photograph her with all the society matrons. Next issue, we get her invited to the White House, where we photograph her with the President and write a story about her *private* advice to the First Couple, which we'll splash all over the magazine. Next issue, we put her on the *cover*—big photo, pearls, borrow a dress from Saks Jandel—with the headline WASHINGTON'S SECRET POWER HOSTESS. Then, pow! We *expose* her as a phony from nowhere and denounce her to the world. From rags to riches and back to rags, all thanks to *Reveal*. What do you think?"

The owner took a deep breath. It took perhaps five seconds for her to exhale. I had gone over the line this time. I was treating it all like a *joke*. She cleared her throat soberly. "That's idiotic, David. You are coming completely undone. You don't seem to understand that this is real. We can't continue like this. We have no money, we have no advertising, we can't meet the payroll. Without a new investor, we're finished. Do you understand?"

"Yes," I said. "Money is important. We must find money. Without money, we will not survive."

"But *where* will we find it?" It was a low moan of despair, followed by the inevitable infuriating sound of her crying. It's outrageous when women lose control like that. It's so calculating.

"Don't cry," I said. "We'll figure something out." But I knew she wasn't going to call anyone herself. Any man who had the money to bail out her sinking magazine was more valuable to her as a potential husband—screw the magazine.

"You've been so good to me," said the owner, still sniffling. "I don't deserve you." And that was true, I had to admit.

PAMELA WAS STILL AT her desk, doing her nails one last time before she walked out the door. She bugged me. "You're fired!" I said. I ordered her to leave the premises immediately, or I would call the police. Her retort, inevitably, was to scream, "Piss off!" and tell me what an idiot I was; but she left, which made me feel better. Alone in the office, I began composing my letter to Jerry Springer. How to explain the special nature of my request? I was not just another aspiring television job seeker. I had read the essays of Camille Paglia. I knew the seven types of ambiguity.

"Dear Mr. Springer," I began. "Looking back on my undergraduate years at Harvard, I think of the many outstanding individuals that fine institution gave me an opportunity to meet. James Q. Wilson, Nathan Marsh Pusey, Barrington Moore, Jr.—some of the intellectual giants who have justly given Harvard its reputation as the Athens of the modern world. Now, Mr. Springer, I am offering you an opportunity to join that select group."

No, too much like a form letter. Jerry didn't care about credentials. He was *way* beyond all that. He wanted someone who could help him stay on the cutting edge.

"Dear Mr. Springer," I began again. "I believe I can help you locate a ninety-pound baby. This kid makes Zack look anorexic. Please contact me as soon as possible, because Geraldo and Ricki Lake may also be interested."

Bingo! As I was putting the letter in an envelope, the telephone rang. "Pamela!" I shouted across the partition, waiting for her to pick up the phone—but she wasn't there. I let it ring, once, twice, three times, waiting for the answering machine to kick in so I could find out who was calling. The voice was deep, sonorous, but slightly confused too, as if its owner wasn't used to making his own calls and leaving messages. It was Galvin calling again and asking me to call him back. I didn't pick up the phone, even so. I wasn't ready yet.

But as I listened to that voice, with its slight edge of uncertainty, I concluded that he could not possibly be calling to complain about my article. That voice would have been sharper, more certain of its mission. No, this was something more benign. He was initiating the call. He was walking down my fork of the road, just as I had walked down his. What happened as a consequence could not be my fault. The man had money, he had ambition—what he lacked was a larcenous, free-spending assistant.

THE OWNER ARRIVED A few minutes later. She rarely came to the office anymore, so this was not a good sign. She looked around at the posters of Mexican beach resorts and grunge rock bands and shook her head. What was the point of owning *this*?

"I came in to look at the books," she said. "See how bad the damage is." She installed herself in the big office in the back, which we saved for state visits, and emerged after twenty minutes, looking ashen. "We owe a hundred seventy thousand dollars, including sixty-five thousand to the printer, who says he will not print the next issue unless he receives a check immediately. I don't know what to do."

"Send him a check," I said.

"But we don't have any *money*, David. We can't cover it."

"I know that. Just listen to me. Call the printer right now and tell him you're sending the check for sixty-five thousand. And send it—just as you promised—but don't *sign* it. He'll call you up and scream that your signature isn't on it, and you'll say '*oops*, I must have forgotten, I'll send you *another* check.' By that time, if we're lucky and the mail is slow, we will have wasted a week. And by then, maybe something will have turned up and we can actually pay him."

"Is that legal?" she asked, shaking her head in wonder.

"Beats me, but who cares? If anybody asks, just lie. You'll get away with it. I promise."

"But how are we going to meet the payroll?" she asked, still shaking her head. "I can't send everyone unsigned checks."

"What about barter? Why don't you tell everyone that this is catalogue month. Instead of paychecks, they can order whatever they want from Williams-Sonoma, L.L. Bean, Victoria's Secret. If they're hungry, you can throw in fruit baskets from Harry and David. Then put everything on your Visa card and presto! Payroll is paid. Personally, I want cash. But tell the rest it's barter or nothing."

"That sounds reasonable enough," she said. She was in a state of shock, I think. She took my hand. We were alone, at the edge of the precipice. It was a time for sharing. "I never loved my husband," she whispered. "Not even in the beginning."

I gave her hand a squeeze and let it drop. This could not continue much longer. The woman was unraveling. "There, there," I said. "We'll find some money."

"I got a call from your friend Mr. Galvin today," she said slyly. "He's rich, isn't he? Why don't you ask *him* for money?"

"What did he want?" I asked nervously. "He's not going to sue us, is he?"

"No, no. He was just trying to reach you. He said he's left

two messages, but you haven't returned the calls. He was afraid something terrible happened to you. I tried to find out what he wants, but he insisted on talking to you. The man is rich. *Call* him. I'm not paying you to be neurotic."

"Of course. I'll call him. I've just been so busy. But I'll do it today. Or tomorrow."

"Listen, David." She took my hand again. "If you can find some money, I'm prepared to give you a share of the magazine as a finder's fee. What do you think about that?"

She could see the sudden eagerness on my face. Too eager. "How big a share of the magazine?" I asked.

"Five percent, dearie," she said curtly. She had perked right up. She wasn't going to give away the store, for God's sake.

"Out of the question. Fifty percent or nothing."

"You monster! You're trying to take advantage of me when I'm weak. You're worse than my husband. Ten percent, and that's too much."

We settled on a 15 percent share for me as a finder's fee, with up to 34 percent going to the investor—nice trick, allowing her to keep control, 51 to 49—plus she wanted the investor to pay her an annual salary and bonus totaling $150,000.

I agreed. What the hell? It was easy to spend someone else's money on a project they'd never heard of. I reminded the owner that we still needed a cover for the next issue. Something really hot, to make an impression on our new partner: "Kiss and Tell: Top Orthodontists Confide Their Success Tips." Or maybe "Power Drapes: The Five Secrets Every Interior Designer Knows." Or "U.N. Seen Nothin' Yet:

International Diplomats' Travel Tricks—from U Thant to
Boutros Boutros-Ghali." I promised I would do some reporting or, if necessary, make something up.

I STILL WASN'T READY to call him. I walked home from the
office—not a taxing trip, since it was just two blocks up Connecticut Avenue. But I was weary just the same. It's not easy
being insubstantial; there is a desire for mass, heft, weight in
the world. I trudged up the avenue. Everything in my neighborhood had become insubstantial too—a land of coffee
bars. We'd had a real grocery store here once, called Lar-
rimer's, with the best butchers in the city. They looked like
old-time congressmen—fat and friendly, and they saved
bones for your dog. It was a food boutique now, selling coffee
beans and bottled pesto sauce. The only real things left were
the bookstores and the gay nightclubs, and a strip joint, oddly
enough—the loud, sweaty kind where men stick five-dollar
bills in the stripper's garter.

My apartment building was across the street from the
strip bar. From my living room window, I could see the strip-
pers arriving for work in the late afternoon in their blue
jeans, their faces as welcoming as a suburban shopping mall,
and the beefy men stumbling out late at night, too drunk to
be embarrassed. If my building manager knew how much I
enjoyed the location, he would have tried to charge me extra.
He was standing just inside the door when I arrived home.
He didn't like me. I had been trying for several years to move
to one of the apartments on the upper floors, facing south,
which overlooked the city. Several had opened up but I'd
never gotten one, and I was convinced the lucky tenants had

paid the old toad off. Meanwhile, I remained on one of the lower floors, facing north, with my view of the strip joint and an Episcopal church just up the street. I could hear the organist playing Bach every Sunday, and the congregation singing the great Protestant hymns, tunelessly.

THAT NIGHT I HAD dinner with my real estate friend, Hugo Bell, at a run-down Indian restaurant below Dupont Circle. It was a dark, perpetually empty place with the unlikely slogan *Romance in Dining.* "Anonymity in dining" would have been more descriptive. I liked it because it was one of the few restaurants in the neighborhood where I could be absolutely certain I wouldn't run into anyone I knew.

Hugo Bell was a shadow-dweller, even more than I. He was a black man—or, to be more precise, a honey-brown man mottled with flecks of darker and lighter pigments. His skin mirrored his soul, for he was truly a man caught between the racial trenches. I felt sorry for him, which always makes it easy to like someone—pity being the most seductive of emotions. He felt sorry for me too—a tall, lonely and highly repressed Jew who survived on a diet of envy and bile. That was our kinship.

Bell had attended a fancy private school in Philadelphia, then gone to Harvard, where we had met. He was brilliant, with an uncanny aptitude for numbers. He'd supported himself through college playing blackjack in casinos—placing what amounted to a bet on the racism of the dealers and pit bosses. They would never suspect that a black man could count cards successfully, he was convinced, and would therefore assume that he was just a lucky guy. And he won big, in casino after casino—amassing a stake of over $100,000 at one point, which to college kids seemed like a fortune.

Hugo went on to Stanford Law School, but he was too crazy with his black-white thing to work for a fancy law firm when he graduated. He felt like he was floating in a hot-air balloon and would just drift away if he didn't chain himself to something real. So he founded a title insurance company on Capitol Hill, and earned a living doing the most ordinary, low-rent real estate work he could find.

The title insurance company gave him a steady income for not much work—I mean, has anyone ever actually filed a *claim* on their title insurance policy? But he knew things. That was his revenge on the white world. He didn't want its money; he wanted to know its secrets—like the fact that someone named Carl S. Galvin had just bought two trophy houses. Bell studied real estate records the way a gambler will study the racing form at the track—looking for angles, tips, nuggets of real information disguised as mundane detail. He was an eccentric, by Washington standards, especially in the way he lurked at our racial boundaries. He would have seemed quite ordinary in Miami or Rio or Panama City, but here in the land of entitlements he gave off a whiff of danger.

I had asked Hugo to find more information about Galvin. I wanted to know as much about him as I could before my visit. "Never go into an interview unprepared," the guidance counselor at the Harvard Office of Graduate and Career Planning had advised before suggesting that I interview with an advertising agency—a deeply worrying observation that helped steer me away from the concept of career planning. But Galvin was worth the trouble.

Bell had indeed unearthed two items that, after a second Kingfisher beer, he was prepared to share. The first was that Galvin had mortgages on both houses. Very rich people arriving in the city from abroad usually bought their homes with cash, Bell said. The second oddity was that the mortgages had been issued by an offshore bank headquartered in the Netherlands Antilles. "Nothing down there but coconuts and crooks," he observed. "Nice people don't go there for mortgages."

FIVE

WHEN I FINALLY REACHED GALVIN, HE INITIALLY SEEMED uncertain why he had called me. After an agonizing pause, he proposed that we meet for lunch, leaving me to wonder whether that had been his original plan, or a face-saving substitute. I didn't care. I had my own purpose now; he was in my power as much as I was in his. He asked if I would mind coming back to his place on the river and I said not at *all*, I would be happy to revisit Tara North.

Galvin's place looked empty now, without its merrymakers. The colorful parade of parked cars had disappeared from the long driveway, and the vast house on the river looked more forbidding without the musical banter of cocktail conversation. Galvin was waiting in his study. He was dressed in casual clothes, made of the fine Italian fabrics that allow the right sort of fellow to spend a thousand dollars for a shirt and a pair of pants. He looked as handsome as ever, but there was a restlessness in his manner that I hadn't remembered. Maybe he was just lonely, communing with his wardrobe in that enormous house.

Galvin made small talk, or at least his oversize version of it. He had just come back from California, where he had been visiting a small biotechnology company he wanted to buy. The company claimed to have achieved a breakthrough in dissolving plaque in the arteries, which would allow them to treat heart disease without having to operate. Sounded pretty good to me. My father had died of a heart attack. I asked if he had bought the company. "Nope," he said. "Too expensive." That was why I wasn't cut out for business, I thought to myself. I didn't understand that everything has its price.

We ate on a screened porch, suspended between the muggy air outside and the cool blast of the air conditioner streaming through the open door. That was a Galvin touch—trying to air-condition the world. You couldn't see the river from where we sat; just the stone wall and the sudden abyss beyond. The colors of the landscape weren't crisp and distinct, as before, but a hot, hazy wash, like a watercolor painting that hadn't quite dried.

Galvin's chef had prepared a lobster salad—not the frozen rock lobsters either, but the big boys from Maine. It was served on a bed of lettuce and tomatoes so sweet and delicious that you couldn't imagine they had come out of the ground. He poured me a glass of Meursault and a half glass for himself, which he barely touched. He was nicer to me now. The taunting "say something revelatory, Mr. Editor" tone was gone; I was his friend, a guest in his house. He picked at his lobster. The gleaming silver fork looked tiny in his hand. He gave me an awkward smile, not the radiant marquee of several weeks before, but something more tentative. There was an appealing vulnerability about him now, as if he felt like a visitor in his own mansion.

"I suppose I should tell you something about myself," he said. "It was obvious, reading your profile, that you know almost nothing about me. An admirable job, given that. But still . . ."

"You wouldn't tell me anything," I answered. "That made it difficult. I could have made things up, but that would have bothered people. Not me particularly, but other people."

"I didn't trust you. In my business, people don't like reporters. They'd rather not take the risk."

"What *is* your business, may I ask? That was never clear to me."

"I trade commodities. I buy things and then I sell them. It's simple. That's why you don't understand it. And I'm lucky. That's the other thing you have to understand about me."

Looking at him, it was hard to doubt that last statement. "Luck, I understand," I said, "but not commodities. So tell me. How did you get started?"

He put up his hands, like a man backed into a corner. He had no choice. He had invited me here, for whatever reason, and now he was my prisoner. He was going to have to talk. And I think he wanted to. Part of the burden of being a big man, larger than life, is that you have to carry it all on your back; you can never put anything down.

IT WAS AN UNLIKELY story, the way he told it—a series of lit-tle successes that, as they gathered momentum, took on the guise of inevitability. When he left college in 1971, Galvin had wanted to go to Vietnam—the emotional ground zero for young men his age—but as a relief worker rather than as a soldier. He applied to an outfit called the International Re-lief Fund. He'd heard rumors that it was a CIA front, but that was nonsense, he said. They sent him to Thailand, and he spent the next year working up country aiding refugees along the Laotian border, and back in Bangkok getting stoned with friends from the embassy. His memories of that time were of the green heat of the jungle and the empty laughter of Thai girls trying to hustle his money.

In 1972 he left the relief agency and moved to Hong Kong. He lived on Lantau Island, as poor as a Chinaman, sharing an apartment with a fellow Harvard dropout. Galvin was happy enough kicking around there, writing freelance articles for an oil industry newsletter. But his friend was get-ting antsy—fearing that if he didn't get back to Harvard soon, the gravy train would leave the station without him. The friend packed up his opium pipe and went back to school, but Galvin stayed. He loved Hong Kong and had no interest in going home.

The first lucky accident came when a British friend in the commodities business suggested he join the firm. The Brit, though very stupid, was getting rich playing the futures mar-ket and Galvin thought, Why not me? He bought a new suit and pretended he knew what he was doing, and after a few weeks, he actually did. It wasn't all that hard. The essence was to take sensible risks, and to keep your nerve. It was like poker; when you had a good hand, you bet all the chips you could find; when you didn't, you folded. His first big score was in 1973, when he made a modest bet that oil prices would rise, only to have the Arabs impose their oil embargo a few months later. People thought he was a genius, and more money flowed his way. He soon found that he liked being rich. He bought himself a Rolls-Royce, ordered new suits from the tailor in the Mandarin Hotel, flew first class on airplanes—and the stack of money grew and grew. Over the next two decades, he built one of the biggest commodities firms in the world—with offices in Geneva and New York as well as in Hong Kong—but in the last few years, the business had begun to bore him. It was like having to play tennis all day, every day, forever. And there was the nagging fear that his luck would change.

"It's time to cash out," he said. "That's why I came to Washington. I want to clean up my portfolio and start something new."

He was beginning to come into focus, though I still didn't understand how a twenty-three-year-old could buy a Rolls-Royce. That was a pretty big itch, to have to scratch so hard.

"Where did you grow up?" I asked. That was always a reasonable journalistic gambit. Find out where the string began, and see if you could follow it to the center of the maze. I didn't think he would tell me much, but it was worth a try.

"Pittsburgh." He said the word carefully, in two distinct syllables, *Pitts-burgh,* as if it were too big and rough for one bite.

"What did your dad do?"

For the first time, Galvin faltered. It was his house, his porch, his lobster salad, his father. There was no reason for him to say anything. But he had started now, and for reasons I didn't understand then (and didn't understand later either, even when I thought I did) he decided to continue.

HE HAD GROWN UP in a suburb called Mount Lebanon, across the Monongahela River from downtown Pittsburgh. It was the middle of the middle class—small lots, boxy houses, a boat parked in every driveway. Galvin had hated the place, growing up. Nearly everyone had something to do with the steel industry, whose mills and furnaces lined the banks of the river. The smart kids at his high school were all boring; their fathers were middle managers at the plants, and their idea of success was working downtown at headquarters. The bad kids were interesting, but they were on a dead-end trip to the mills, or to prison. This was an area where people's idea of a big success was Joe Namath, who had played football a few miles down the river. Galvin played football too—he was big and tough enough to take the punishment. But he was heading to Harvard on an academic scholarship, and that made him a freak. The yearbook said he was most likely to be elected president; his high school girlfriend knew that once he left Pittsburgh, he would never come back.

When a man tells his story and doesn't begin with his father, you begin to suspect that he's avoiding something. But he got around to it eventually. Galvin's father worked at the international headquarters of the United Steelworkers of America. He was a sort of one-man research staff. When it was time to negotiate with the steel companies, Mr. Galvin would calculate what health benefits should cost, and how much to put into the pension plan. But he was a dreamer— that was his real vocation, figuring out how the world should work. He'd sit in his study and write memos about free health care, and free vacation resorts for working people, and free universities. Everything was going to be free, and when his inquisitive son asked who was going to pay for it, the old man would answer, "The bosses." Mr. Galvin would put his memos in a cardboard box, and when he finished one box, he would take it down to the basement and start another. He was also working on a treatise he called *The Encyclopedia of Labor,* which each year grew more encyclopedic and less publishable. His father was a professional idealist, Galvin said. He spent his whole life being disappointed.

Galvin grew up hearing his father's big ideas, and listening to Pete Seeger records and going to picnics with the Young People's Socialist League. It was a working-class bohemia—the sort of world that's pleasant to fantasize about but impossible to inhabit if you were a restless young man in 1967. When Galvin got to college that fall, he was astonished to find that the intellectual clutter of his father's basement had become stylish. Everyone in Cambridge wanted to sing folk songs and grow up to be Woody Guthrie. For a while, Galvin tried to play along with the left-wing preppies who pretended to envy him because he was from Pittsburgh and his father was a union man. But their big ideas annoyed him. He'd heard them all before; they smelled like his father's pipe tobacco. Making money, on the other hand, sounded interesting.

His father was mystified. He had never considered the possibility that his clever son would grow up to love business. He had named him after Carl Sandburg for a reason—his destiny was to speak for the hog butchers, toolmakers, stackers of wheat. The old man never realized that this was precisely what happened—that in the true American version of the tale, every hog butcher secretly wanted to own the packing house. But it didn't sit right back home in Mount Lebanon. For many years, the father had remained in his modest suburban house and refused his son's offers of financial help. But when his wife, the town librarian, slipped on the ice one winter and broke her hip, he decided that it was time to retire to Florida—even steelworkers did that—and let his wealthy son buy him a house in Sarasota.

GALVIN WANTED SOMETHING. THAT was the only explanation for this tender of self-revelation. I was curious. Part of the mystique of people like him is the sense that they don't need *anything*. But I wanted something too, and it seemed important to get my request in first, before the remains of that lobster had been cleared. Otherwise, his agenda—whatever it was—would surely overwhelm mine.

"I have a business proposition for you, Mr. Galvin," I said grandly, in the way I imagined businessmen liked to talk. He laughed, which would have discouraged a less desperate man.

"From what I hear," I continued, "one of the leading publications in Washington may be looking for a new investor. I wanted to tell you about it first, before it was on the street. I thought perhaps I could play a . . . helpful role in introducing you to the owner."

God! I was so bad at this. But he perked up immediately. The arsenal of charm was suddenly deployed. The thin smile; the hand on the elbow; the confidential voice. "I knew I had you pegged right," he said.

"The publication in question, Mr. Galvin, is arguably the most important in the city. It's experiencing some short-term cash flow problems at present, caused by an unfortunate decline in advertising. But with an infusion of capital, I believe those problems can be overcome."

"Go on!" he said, but a hint of doubt had darkened his face. "Get to the point. What publication are you talking about?"

"Sorry, but I've never done anything this *financial* before, so you'll have to bear with me. The publication I'm referring to is known, not without reason, as *The Social Bible of Washington*. It is, in fact, my own beloved but financially challenged magazine—*Reveal*."

He groaned. "Shit!" he said. "Is that all?"

That was deflating, I must admit. But I pressed on.

"I know it's not *Time* or *Newsweek*, but it's not *The New England Journal of Medicine,* either. We have loyal readers, and we have advertisers—a few of them, at least. We are unfortunately going broke, and the owner—an attractive widow, bless her heart—is looking for a new investor. And I thought immediately of you. Maybe that was silly, but it seemed to me you'd make an outstanding publisher. Think about it: You could order up humiliating exposés of your enemies and flattering pieces about your friends. We could even give you a column called 'On My Mind,' say, in which you could share some of your thoughts about the topics of the day. Plus, you'd have me as a permanent lackey and hatchet man."

Galvin chuckled at my patter. That stance seemed to please him—the jester who was willing to say anything that fell into his head.

"I like your enthusiasm, but I was hoping you were talking about *another* local publication that might need a cash transfusion. I have a strong interest in that other publication."

"Ah! The other publication. Of course. And what might that publication be?"

"*The Washington Sun and Tribune.*" He said the words respectfully, the way a mountain climber might say "Everest."

"No kidding!" I said. That wasn't much of a retort, but it was the best I could do. The *Sun,* as it was known to nearly everyone, was the dominant newspaper in town. It was the first thing the president and Congress read each morning, and as a consequence, it set the city's political and journalistic agenda. It was owned by two old Washington families, the Hazens and the Crosbys, who wanted to make enough money to pay the club dues, but not too much. The *Sun* was a *plum.* Ever since it bested the *Post* in a circulation war in the 1980s, the *Sun* had essentially been a monopoly newspaper. There was no sweeter prize in journalism, but people had always assumed it would never be for sale.

Galvin put a big forearm across the table, as hard as a crowbar. His eyes had lost the easy softness of before and had narrowed down to a sharp, insistent focus. It was clearer now what he did. He wasn't in the business of making people happy, or at least not simply that. He bought and sold things, just as he had said.

"I'm going to tell you a business secret," he confided. "The *Sun* is on the rocks. It's barely profitable. You can't see it on the books yet, but it's a fact. The two families know it— they're bickering, or so I hear—and they might consider a buy-out offer. That's why I invited you to lunch. I wanted to see what you knew about the *Sun*. Or could find out."

I sat back in my chair. A slight afternoon breeze had come up, rustling the limp leaves in the trees and blowing the bugs into hiding. Galvin was looking at me, waiting for an answer. His face was taut. You could trace a line of muscle and bone that began high on his cheek and ended in the sharp angle of his jaw. How extraordinary: He needed me.

I took off my big black glasses and rubbed my small black eyes. "What do I know about the *Sun*? I know that the Hazens and the Crosbys don't like each other very much. I know that they got into a feud a few years ago when some of the younger family members got ideas about selling their shares, but supposedly that got patched up. I know that the editor, Howard Bacon, has been talking to *The New York Times* about editing their magazine, which he wouldn't consider unless he was nervous about something. So come to think of it, I know quite a lot about the *Sun*. And I can find out more."

"How?" That intensity was still on his face. He was going to climb this mountain, and he needed help.

"I know people there. I know people everywhere. That's what I do. I'm Washington's social chronicler."

"Who do you know at the *Sun*? Be precise."

"Well, I know Bacon a little, but not very much. I know some of the younger reporters. I know the Lifestyle editor. She's a weasel, by the way—you should fire her as soon as you take over, and hire me. The person I know the best is the foreign editor. Her name is Candace Ridgway."

I couldn't tell if that name registered. He listened, but he wasn't looking at me. He had risen and was staring out across the stone wall to the opposite bank of the river, which was as thick and green as a jungle. He turned back to me.

"I don't want any bullshit. This is real. I need information about what's going on over there."

"Yes, Captain."

"Because when that ridiculous magazine of yours goes belly up, you're going to need a job."

"Yes, Captain. That is most assuredly true."

"So let's do this right." He put his arm on my shoulder. It felt heavy, consequential. "If we pull it off, you can come work for me. Lifestyle editor, comics editor. Whatever you like. You understand? This is the real thing."

We took a walk. He showed me the gym he had built himself, over the garage. It was like a little health club, with Cybex machines, a StairMaster, a water cooler, towels neatly stacked—everything except girls in spandex tights. There was a new speed bag too, hanging from the ceiling. He had been an amateur boxer in college, he said. That was what he'd liked to do when he got stoned—he pounded the speed bag.

I wasn't really listening, I have to admit. I was mind-surfing. Sandy Galvin—the man who had renounced the usual undergraduate dreams in his twenties in favor of ac-

quiring money—had decided, just shy of his fiftieth birth-
day, to take the dreamy gamble of buying a newspaper. I
didn't understand why then—and as I suggested before, I
didn't really understand even later. But from that day on,
I was his man—his spear-carrier and spy—and he was my
man too, in ways that he probably never understood, even at
the end. We had embarked on a conspiracy of mutual self-in-
terest, which offered the opportunity to create mischief on a
scale bigger than I had ever imagined.

SIX

THE WASHINGTON SUN AND TRIBUNE BUILDING WAS AN elegant metal-and-glass structure in Foggy Bottom, halfway between the White House and Georgetown. The area had once been known for its warehouses and empty lots, but in recent years, like nearly every district of fin de siècle Washington, it had become a magnet for money and power. Fifteen years before, the owners had moved the paper to this glamorous headquarters from its old home in Northeast, uncomfortably across the city's invisible but universally recognized racial boundary. The new building was their reward—their monument to themselves and their victory over the *Post*. They had hired one of the country's leading architects to design the structure, and spent far too much on it. Sometimes an unhappy married couple will do something similar—build a magnificent home in the hope that it will take their minds off their troubles, but it rarely works.

The skin of the building was gleaming in the midday

summer sun. It looked too hot to touch. I stood on the curb outside, admiring what the owners' wealth and taste had been able to create. The facade was like a piece of modern sculpture—a sheet of chrome and glass that soared gracefully into the air, like a roll of newsprint rising to the tower of one of the *Sun's* presses. It was bounded on each side by metal beams that were as black as ink. Inside was a large atrium, in which the two families had erected a museum to celebrate themselves and their good works. There was a bronzed statue of the first Hazen shaking hands with the first Crosby back in 1910, when they had bought two failing newspapers, the morning *Sun-Democrat* and the afternoon *Tribune,* and combined them; and modest pictures of their sons, who had kept the paper alive through the lean years of the forties and fifties; and a much bigger picture of the current patriarch—Harold Hazen—who with the blessing of the Crosbys had managed the paper through its years of growth. He was a shrewd old man, I thought as I stared at the likeness of him that towered over the atrium lobby—but also a vain one. Perhaps that was inevitable in a newspaper owner, but it was a dangerous trait.

I had come to see my friend Candace Ridgway, who was my most reliable source of gossip about the *Sun.* She had a reporter's knack for gathering information. She didn't wheedle or scheme for it, as I did; it flowed to her naturally, as if by right. She had recently returned from a tour as London bureau chief to become foreign editor. That was a sign, and her colleagues assumed that more promotions would follow. People talked about Candace; there was an assumption that what she did mattered. Part of it was that she was openly ambitious. She had been telling people ever since she was in college that she wanted to run a newspaper someday.

I had known Candace slightly at Harvard. She was three years older than I was and already a senior when I arrived—but she had been nice to me during the odious "comp" to join *The Harvard Crimson* and helped keep me afloat during my suicidal freshman year. I had followed her career from afar ever since, sending her fawning notes when I liked one of her stories and occasionally calling her for advice. Unlike me, she seemed to have perfect balance. Where I had bumped from job to job, priding myself on my noncelebrity, she had moved steadily upward in the news firmament. I try, as a rule, to dislike people who have been so successful, but in Candace's case, it was difficult.

Part of Candace's aura was that she was a child of the Washington establishment. What took the edge off, and made her current success tolerable to others, was the fact that her outwardly perfect life had been touched by tragedy. During the late 1960s, her father had been deputy secretary of defense. At the height of the Vietnam War, he'd had a "breakdown," as people used to put it back then. Two years after that, in the fall of 1971, he had committed suicide. I'd known about Candace's father before I ever met her. He was a symbol of The Crack-up—the end of the genteel but short-of-breath Establishment that was routed by a bunch of Asian peasants and dope-smoking college students.

Her father's death was the one area of Candace's life that remained untidy. It was the only way you understood what had made her so strong—when you saw a hint of that wound and realized the strength and self-discipline it had taken to get past it. We used to talk about it, when we were at college. We had both lost our fathers. That was one of the few things we really had in common.

Her personal life was mysterious, but so far as I knew, she had no permanent attachment to anyone or anything—except the newspaper. She was rumored to be dating an aging wonder boy who was an assistant secretary of the Treasury—we had even published a picture of them together in *Reveal,* a few issues back—but she just rolled her eyes when I asked about him. She liked to call herself the "Mistress of Fact," and that was reassuring. Part of why she was so sexy, I thought, was that it was impossible to imagine her actually having sex with anyone.

As I waited for her, a stream of people flowed out of the building for lunchtime appointments. That was what journalists did when you stripped away the nonessentials; they ate lunch. Most of the men were wearing suits, even in the heat. The *Sun* did that to people—it seemed to wrap its recruits in a kind of corporate identity and rebrand them, so they all looked and talked the same. I had observed the process with some of my ambitious friends who went to work there. The *Sun* sucked out whatever was loose and frail and particular, and then pumped in its own zero-temperature life force, and soon enough the new recruits were swollen up larger than life, dressed in their suits, ready to go out into the world and piss on everybody. I liked to think that Candace was different, that she had retained her own look and smell and sense of values, but maybe that was because I didn't know her as well as I thought.

CANDACE BOUNDED FROM THE glass palace at twelve-thirty
exactly and gave me a little wave. She was dressed in a light
green suit, the color of a Key lime pie—an outrageous thing
to wear to work! I let myself imagine she had worn it because she was having lunch with me, but that couldn't be.
She walked toward me, pushing a dancing tendril of blond
hair back from her face, smiling and extending her hand.
There was something charming and appropriate about her
self-consciousness. She knew she was beautiful. Like a
model, she understood the impression she created: the perfect ivory skin; the dewy glow on her cheeks; the supple
body.

She donned her sunglasses against the noontime glare.
They helped to mask the keenness in her eyes. That was Candace's true secret: Under the blond veil was a rock-hard
woman. Indeed, within the news business, she was known
less for her beauty (which was tolerated) than for her toughness. She'd been trapped once in Basra during the Iraq-Iran
war—after all the other journalists had been evacuated, she
had somehow been allowed to stay. And she'd written a hi-
larious diary recounting her adventures—driving to the front
in broken-down taxis; taking a four-hour bath one night
when the city was being bombed because someone had told
her the plumbing fixtures would survive if the hotel was hit;
fending off an egregious string of propositions from sex-
crazed Iraqis. She had captured it all in her diary. She was the
kind of feminist who believed that it was okay to be sexy—
that for a woman, sex *was* power. "Honestly now," she supposedly had said to an envious male colleague after securing

an exclusive interview, "who do you think King Hussein would rather talk to after a long day—you or me?"

I shouted for a passing cab to stop, and held open the door for Candace as she swung her slender legs across the seat. That was one sure mark of an elegant woman—the ability to enter a cab in a short skirt and make it look graceful. I had made a reservation at an absurdly expensive French restaurant nearby, figuring I would stick Galvin with the tab. When I called out the name of the place to the driver, she instantly sensed that something was up.

"I thought *Reveal* was broke," she said, eyebrows arched. "What happened? Have you started selling space in the photo section?"

"Actually, business is rotten—but that's a good idea about selling space. I may get back to you on that. No, I want you to think of this as a date, with your old and dear friend."

"Then let's go to a hotel," she said. "We can have lunch in bed."

That was the game she played with me—bantering about sex because she knew it was harmless. She had a way of finding the right frequency, different for everyone she was with. Some of her friends resented that, but not me. I liked being manipulated by a professional.

"How are things at the paper?" I asked when we were seated at our table. That was always an acceptable question with journalists. They really do think their work is so interesting and important that everyone else must be dying to know what it's like at the office.

"Appalling!" she answered. "I can't get anyone into Baghdad. Our New Delhi bureau chief went into labor the day the typhoon hit Bangladesh. Our Moscow correspondent says he's going to the *Times* unless we hire his wife. I'm sick of them all, frankly."

She made a dismissive gesture with her hand, as if brushing away a bug. Her nails, I saw, were freshly lacquered and buffed. That was another thing about Candace: She never let the drudgery of newspapering deflect her from the fundamentally important things, like a good manicure.

"I don't know how you put up with all the crap," I said. "You're not cut out to be a bureaucrat."

"Yes, I am," she said. "That's the worrisome thing. I'm actually quite good at it. It plays to my dictatorial side. My reporters care desperately what I think. They're so *needy*. Especially the men. I have to be careful I don't torture them."

I could believe that about Candace. She made you want to please her. A waiter came and rattled off the list of specials. None of them had any prices. I wondered whether my Visa card could handle the damage and then thought, What the hell? Spies didn't worry about credit-card limits.

"Are you still seeing the king of the sub-Cabinet?" I asked. Why was I so derisive about him? His name was Mark Pavel, and he was assistant secretary for international economic affairs. It was a very important job, I'm sure, but he struck me as an empty suit. I'd looked up his biography once, in a spasm of jealousy. He had the entire string of merit badges: Yale (his board scores must have been a bit low for you know where— too bad!); Trinity College, Cambridge, on a Marshall Scholarship; Harvard Business School; Goldman Sachs; Council on Foreign Relations. He'd done everything except live in the world.

"We get together occasionally," she answered. "He's decorative, and he has nice ties."

"You should dump him. He's a worm."

"Maybe, but he's easy. Microwave ready. And if you won't propose to me, I have to fend for myself."

Much as I enjoyed this idle flirtation, I needed to change the subject. If I was going to stick Galvin with the lunch bill, I would need to give him some information.

"How are the Hazens and Crosbys doing?" I asked. "I hear things are a little rocky."

She looked at me curiously. It was an odd question for me to be asking, but then I had the benefit of *being* odd.

"They *are* rocky," she answered. "The families are a mess. They're unhappy with the paper, and they're upset with each other. The younger generation thinks the *Sun* isn't making as much money as it should, and they're all mad at Harold Hazen because the stock price is so low. It's trading at about forty dollars—the same as it was five years ago. The biggest bull market in history, and they haven't made a penny on the family business."

"Poor dears." It was hard for me to feel sorry for rich people with underperforming assets. "How do you know all this? It doesn't sound like your normal newsroom gossip."

"It's not." She smiled coyly. "I have a source."

"Come on." I held out my hands and beckoned. "Tell David. Please. I really want to know."

"This isn't one for *Reveal*, is it?"

"Of course not. Never heard of it. This is for my novel about Washington life. Unless you tell me the truth, I'll make up something really unpleasant."

She laughed and shook her head. What a card! In her mind, I was still the skinny freshman trying to get on the *Crimson*, and desperately making moon eyes at her even though I would have been terrified if she'd said yes. "Do you *really* want to know?" she demanded.

"Yes. Passionately." There must have been something in my voice that conveyed that I was serious. I really *did* want to know.

"All right, I'll tell you, but only because you're so hopeless I know I can trust you. I have an old friend named Ariane Hazen. She's Harold's daughter. For a year or two in high school, she was my best friend. We've stayed in touch, and I've seen a good deal of her since I came back from London. She's divorced and lonely. I think she wants a friend in the newsroom, and I'm the only one she really knows."

"*So* . . ." I leaned toward her conspiratorially. "What does she say?"

"She's upset. She thinks the paper is mismanaged, and she wants changes. She's trying to convince her brother and the Crosby kids to work with her. Her father is angry. He's heard the gossip that his daughter is plotting against him, and his feelings are hurt. He knows the paper is in a rut, but he doesn't know how to change it. And he doesn't want to undercut the newsroom. That's why we love Mr. Hazen. He's old school. He takes care of us. He gets his kicks from publishing a good newspaper, not from the stock price."

"So where's it heading?" I queried. "Are the Hazens shopping the paper?"

"I don't think so. The family is still bickering. Ariane isn't sure what to do. The last time we talked, she wanted to hire an adviser to help the younger generation sort out its options. Why are you asking about all this? You're up to something. Do you have a buyer?" Her face was alive with that taunting curiosity. She knew more than she was telling—she always did. But in this case, so did I.

"*Me?* Of course not! How would I know anyone who would want to buy the *Sun?*"

She reached out and gave my hand a little pat. There, there. That was the advantage of being perceived as a loser. It made you seem harmless. People could not imagine, as they told you their secrets, that you could do anything truly damaging with them.

There was a rustle over by the door. A bulky figure with a fancy tie and a big handshake was entering the restaurant, setting off little ripples of recognition. He was greeting the maître d', stopping to chat with a magazine columnist seated at another table. The man was a former government official, now an investment banker, rumored as a possible secretary of state if the Republicans returned to power. It was inevitable that he would know Candace, and that his rolling bonhomie would soon grace our table.

"Hello, Candy," he said, giving her a kiss on the cheek. Candace introduced me, mercifully leaving out the fact that I worked for *Reveal*. This was a certified Big Guy. I stood awkwardly while they talked about Bosnia and Iraq and other subjects on which I had no opinion. Amazingly, during this odious interaction, Candace never lost her poise. She never gave him a false smile, never laughed too loud at one of his jokes. She had perfect pitch that way. She was the Mistress of Fact.

"I WORRY ABOUT YOU sometimes, David," she said after the dessert had been cleared. "You don't seem happy."

I had to pause a minute. People didn't normally discuss my private life. What was the point? "I'm sorry, but you're using a word I don't understand. What is *happy*?"

"I'm serious, David. You worry me. You have so much talent, and you're wasting it on that ridiculous magazine. As far as I can tell, you have no personal life whatsoever."

"What do you mean?" I demanded. "I have a cat. *And* I have a television set."

"Stop making a joke out of everything. It makes you seem even more pathetic. Are you seeing anyone?"

"No, of course not. Come now. Who would I see?"

I left that thought hanging in the air. Who *would* I see? And what would I do if I saw them? That problem was far too complicated to address at that moment, after a fine lunch of sautéed squab and a tasty crème brûlée. No, when it came to personal matters, the monastic approach was the most sensible. I'm told there was a saint, long ago, who spent her life picking the fleas off her unkempt body, one by one, and then, when she was done, putting them all back in the same painstaking way. And all things considered, I had a *much* better life than that.

Candace Ridgway was looking at me: the soft vellum of her skin, the hint of color on her cheeks, the full lips, the effervescent intelligence. "Who would I see," I asked, "unless it was you?"

WE BOTH HAD COLD hearts, I suspected. That was what had drawn me and Candace together. I don't mean that in the usual, cold-and-clammy sense, but in a particular way that Candace first suggested to me soon after we met in college. I thought at the time, in the portentous way that under-graduates do, that I had found the key to her personality. And oddly enough, it's possible that I was right.

I had entered the *Crimson* building on Plympton Street that day looking for her. She was my "tutor," the upper-classman who supervised my work for the paper. She was sitting on a fat, red leather couch in the editorial chair-man's office, reading a novel by Graham Greene. It was *The Heart of the Matter*—one of his bleak Catholic novels, a great book and all that, but an unlikely thing to be reading back then.

I asked her about the novel, wanting to make conversa-tion. She had a faraway look in her eye, like people some-times get when they're about to cry. My question pulled her back; she was grateful, I think, for someone to talk to. She said she wanted to read me a passage from the book. It was the part where Yousef, the Arab trader, quotes a Syrian prov-erb to Major Scobie, the despairing police chief. I looked it up again recently, to remind myself of the exact words: "Of two hearts one is always warm and one is always cold: the cold heart is more precious than diamonds: the warm heart has no value and is thrown away."

"Do you think that's right?" Candace had asked me.

I said I didn't know. I was just eighteen. I wasn't sure I had a heart at all.

"I think it's true," she continued. "When a cold heart becomes warm, it stays that way forever."

It was an intensely personal comment, but she said no more. That was the sort of remark college kids dropped on each other back then, at least at Harvard. We were all secret readers of Emily Dickinson; there was romance in the tap water. And it made me feel better about not being a demonstrative, "loving" person. Perhaps that meant I didn't have one of those cheap, warm hearts.

We went on with our appointed business, which was her critique of one of my snide theater reviews. But the Graham Greene passage stuck with me. She was obviously talking about herself, and I remember wondering at the time whether her own heart was already slow-baking with passion—or whether it was still stone cold.

HUGO BELL CALLED ME. He said he was having dinner at a Ligurian restaurant—not Italian, mind you, but Ligurian—with a friend who worked as a broker at one of the local investment firms. They had been talking about the commodities business and Carl Galvin's name had come up, and the conversation was *very* interesting. He suggested I come over right away for a nice Ligurian dessert—peaches with mulled wine—and listen to what his friend had to say. I wouldn't normally have ventured out at that hour. I was listening to music, and *The Simpsons* reruns were coming on in a little while, but this was irresistible. In dealing with Galvin, knowledge was my only weapon.

The restaurant was a noisy little place on Connecticut Avenue. Bell was sitting in a booth in the back, with a row of beer bottles lined up in front of him. His friend was a beagle of a man named Jack Liggitt. They shared an interest in jazz, it seemed. Liggitt in his youth had tried to play drums with Ahmad Jamal; but the black folks wouldn't have him, so he was stuck in between—loving what he could never fully possess. That was what he and Hugo had in common: They were both stranded.

Liggitt gave me his card, the way brokers always do, and a howdy-do handshake. He must have thought I could help him make some money. "This guy Galvin is a piece of work!" he ventured. "You know anything about him?"

"Not really," I said. I recounted what little Galvin had told me about his business.

"He left out all the interesting parts!" said my informant, who was only too happy to fill in the gaps. It seemed he had been following the fortunes of Carl Galvin Corporation for years.

Galvin had begun trading oil contracts in 1973, just as he'd told me, but it had hardly been the series of accidents he'd described. According to Jack, he had powerful friends already—people he'd met at the U.S. embassy in Bangkok. When he went to work for the commodities firm in Hong Kong, his embassy contacts had helped him—giving him tips, making introductions, steering their friends his way. He'd been working there only a few months when he got lucky. With a gambler's sense of timing, he signed a contract in late summer to take delivery of a hundred thousand barrels of Iranian crude in December at a price just above the August spot-market price of roughly five dollars a barrel. He assumed he could unload it on the Japanese.

"Talk about lucky!" Jack said. The Mideast war broke out in October, followed by the Arab oil embargo, and by December the spot price had risen to thirteen dollars a barrel. Galvin's profit on the deal was $800,000—not bad for a twenty-three-year-old dropout. Any possibility that he would return to Harvard disappeared after that. He stayed in Hong Kong for the next ten years, building his commodities business, branching into lead, tin, nickel, manganese, aluminum—even mercury. By the late 1970s, he had tired of sharing his winnings with the stodgy British firm and formed his own company. Like many speculators, he made and lost several fortunes over the following twenty years, riding the roller coaster of the market, but in the 1990s, he had become seriously rich. *The Financial Times* had estimated his fortune three years ago at nearly one billion dollars. There were whispers Galvin was overextended, but people always said that about commodities traders.

"This guy's secret is that he operates at the margin," explained Jack. I asked what that meant. Galvin hardly seemed like a marginal figure, but I was misunderstanding.

"He's always ready to do the *deal* at the margin," said the broker. "The deal nobody else will do." When nobody would lift oil from Angola after the Portuguese left in 1975, he did the business—which meant that when the oil shock hit in the late seventies, he had access to crude. When nobody would go into the Persian Gulf during the tanker war in the mid-eighties, Galvin did the business. He bought up rusty old tankers and sent them in and made a killing. Same thing with Russia in the nineties. It was wild and wooly, and most traders were scared off. But it was a perfect opportunity for Galvin.

I asked if Galvin was a crook. Jack found that amusing.

"This is the commodities business," he said. "The only crime is being on the wrong side of a contract."

The real problem with commodities, Jack observed, was trying to get out. The business was so highly leveraged that you couldn't avoid owing people a lot of money. And when the markets turned around, it was sometimes hard to cover your bets.

"I think Galvin wants out," I said, remembering an elliptical comment he had made toward the end of our lunch.

"Well, he'd better hurry," said Jack. The market was soft, and when you were playing with other people's money, you weren't a free man.

SEVEN

GALVIN WANTED TO KNOW THE DETAILS OF MY LUNCH-
eon conversation with Candace. I wasn't sure what to tell
him. It seemed unfair, like one of those tricks they play on
the guests on *The Jerry Springer Show*, when they keep the wife
backstage while the husband is telling Jerry how he's having
an affair with his wife's *sister*. But I didn't really have a choice.
The lunch check had come to nearly $150, so discretion
wasn't a practical option. And I didn't see any lasting harm in
what I was doing. It seemed to me that Galvin could only be
good for the *Sun* and the talented people there, like Candace.
But that was the logic of the hired man.

Galvin asked me to come to his house in Georgetown
this time. He said he would be selling it soon, and he wanted
to get a little more use out of it before it was gone. It was an
old town house on Q Street—not much to look at from the
sidewalk, but inside it was all creamy wallpaper and dark
bookshelves and French doors opening onto a big garden,

hidden away in the midst of the city like an emerald in a jewel box. I'm told that houses in Arab cities like Damascus and Cairo are built the same way—with a plain exterior, to avoid rousing the envy of the neighbors, concealing a palace inside.

The butler—not the same one as at the Virginia house, but a different one—said that Mr. Galvin was out back in the garden, taking a swim. He led me toward a gray slate pool, bounded on four sides by the deep green of the lawn. Galvin was swimming laps; I sat and watched. His body churned through the water, arms and legs moving together like a single muscle that created its own wake with each forward stroke, like the prow of a ship. He ignored me until he was done, and then emerged, dripping wet, looking very pleased with himself.

I handed Galvin a towel. I was one of his entourage now—like the butler or the gardener. While he dried himself and sipped a Diet Coke, I described my lunch with Ms. Ridgway. He listened mostly in silence, asking me occasional questions to steer my recollection toward the topics that interested him. When I mentioned Ariane Hazen, he smiled contentedly. Oh yes! He seemed to know all about her. She was the key, he said. She was the only one of the Hazen and Crosby children who had a head for business. If she led, the others would follow.

He pointed a wet finger in my direction. "How much do you think the *Sun and Tribune* is worth?" I shrugged, so he answered his own question. "At forty dollars a share, the market is valuing the company at about eight hundred million dollars. But that's only because it's being run by idiots. In an auction, the price could go as high as sixty or seventy a share. The question is, how could we get it cheaper—for, say, fifty dollars a share, or fifty-five."

"You're asking the wrong guy," I said. "I flunked home economics."

"It will come down to the Hazen trust," he observed, more to himself than to me. He explained that the *Sun* had two classes of stock, for takeover protection—A shares for the family, and B shares for everyone else. The company couldn't be sold without a majority of the A shares, and the largest block of stock was held in a trust for Harold Hazen's children. It had been established in 1963, and was voted by Harold and his son. Galvin said the 1963 trust was the main event.

He squeezed his big hand into a fist and grazed it gently against my chin. "Almost Golden Gloves," he said. It was odd, but he didn't really seem like the boxer type. He was the opposite of muscle-bound—there was such natural grace in his movements.

When we had finished talking about the *Sun,* I handed him the restaurant receipt and asked in my most servile voice if perhaps he could reimburse me, that being quite a lot of money and me being quite poor.

"Of course!" he snorted. "Don't be a chump." He retired inside and returned with an envelope. Inside was a check—not for $150, but for $5,000.

"I can't take this," I said. "It's ridiculous."

"Sure you can. You earned it. Let me know when this runs out, and I'll give you more."

I folded the check neatly and put it in my wallet. Who

was I to complain if he wanted to throw some of his money at me. And perhaps he was right—maybe I *had* earned it, though that was a disturbing thought. I was ready to leave, but he put his hand up—bidding me to stay a moment more.

"How did she look?" he asked.

"Who?" For a moment, I wasn't sure who he was talking about.

"Candace Ridgway. What did she look like, when you took her to lunch?"

He was studying me, waiting for my answer. "Let me think," I said. "She's very beautiful. Maybe you've heard that already, but it's true. She was wearing a pastel suit, light green—an odd color, but it suited her. She has bouncy blond hair that's always falling in her face, and beautiful skin. She's flirtatious but untouchable, if you know what I mean. What can I say? She looked great."

Galvin didn't answer. He closed his eyes as if he were trying to see her in his mind. He sat there for a long time, and it seemed like a good moment to leave, so I said goodbye and let myself out the front door. I glanced back once and saw him bent over, head in his hands, wrapped in his big bath towel. He was like a fighter getting ready for a big bout—or nursing his wounds from an earlier one, it was hard to tell.

GALVIN HAD LUNCH A few days later with Ariane Hazen. He telephoned her, out of the blue, explaining that he was an investor, new to town, who was following her company and would love to take her to lunch. She said yes instantly—she already knew who he was. Galvin said she was nervous at first—she didn't want anyone to get the idea that she was conniving with a potential buyer. She even wore a hat so that people wouldn't recognize her at the restaurant. Galvin found that promising, that she would take the meeting seriously enough to think it was something to conceal.

Strange woman, he said. So much energy, but it was blunted. That was the curse of being born a Hazen. Too many times in her life—at the moments when most people want to say "I quit," but know they can't—she had been able to bail out. She was a victim of the freedom that money provides to escape life's unpleasant lessons. The phrases *hunker down* or *gut it out* had no meaning for her. That made her a natural target for someone like Galvin.

It was clear from his account that he had put his charm to good use that day. He took her to a small Italian restaurant—a place where people brought their friends, as opposed to business associates—and he sat next to her on the banquette, rather than across the table. He told her stories about his adventures in Africa and in the Middle East years ago, when he was building his business. It's always surprising how vulnerable people are to that sort of blandishment. They don't realize what a weapon friendliness can be.

When it was time to talk business, Galvin asked bluntly how she thought the *Sun* was doing financially. Wall Street was skeptical, he said. The analysts who followed the company thought it wasn't well managed. And he confided he'd heard that circulation and advertising figures for the second quarter would be below estimates, which would push the stock price down even more.

"You know more than Daddy," she replied caustically. "He thinks everything's fine." The lid had been popped, and out poured her troubles. The paper wasn't making as much as some younger members of the family thought it should, she complained. It was coasting. Other media companies were trading at twenty times earnings—some even at twenty-five—but the *Sun* was selling at a puny twelve. That was fine for the older generation. They had everything they could possibly want, and they were living nicely on the dividends. But for Ariane and her generation, it wasn't enough. The *Sun* was their principal investment. If it couldn't match the returns of other media companies, then maybe it was time to find new management—or sell their shares and buy something else.

"What does your father say?" Galvin asked.

"He says *The Sun* is a public trust. If we're interested in money, then we should invest in Coca-Cola."

"A noble sentiment," Galvin remarked, "but not a very profitable one." He sketched an alternative vision of how the company might be run—how it might expand from newspapers into broadcast television, cable, magazines, high technology. That was the way the world worked now, he said. Disney didn't just make movies. General Electric didn't just sell lightbulbs.

He was goading her, tempting her to imagine the value that was buried inside her father's stolid public trust. But he cautioned that he shouldn't be giving advice. The family needed an investment banker—someone who could help them sort out various alternatives.

"*Please* tell me what you think," asked Ariane. "We need help, and I honestly don't know where to turn. I don't trust anyone."

"My only suggestion," Galvin offered, "is that you move soon." He warned that if the *Sun*'s current management couldn't convince Wall Street that it was ready to be more aggressive, the *Sun* would be vulnerable to a raid by people who thought they could squeeze a lot more than forty dollars a share out of the company. And once that process began, it would be hard to stop.

Ariane nodded gravely. He was, of course, telling her precisely what she already believed. That was why it seemed so profoundly true. She asked if he might be willing to meet with other members of her family, and Galvin said that he would be happy to do so. But he again cautioned Ariane not to wait too long. This was a volatile market. The *Sun* was a tempting prize. There were rumors on Wall Street that someone might already be planning a raid. Even Harold Hazen wasn't powerful enough to hold back the financial tide forever.

I RAN INTO CANDACE at the video store. She was slightly embarrassed about what she was renting, which made me curious. *Prison Gals in Chains!* perhaps? But it turned out to be *Bringing Up Baby,* the old screwball comedy with Katharine Hepburn and Cary Grant. Maybe she was hiding a secret fixation on Katharine Hepburn. The tawny aristocrat, too smart and quick for anyone but the incomparable Mr. Grant; a woman who understood that men were useful toys, to be inflated and deflated as the circumstances required.

I asked her to come have coffee with me at a Starbucks near the video store. That was all you could find in Washington anymore. In some neighborhoods, there was one on every block. They knew their market: caffeine freaks with status anxiety.

"The world is getting squishy," said Candace. "Have you noticed that?"

I wasn't sure what she was talking about.

"Things are falling apart. I keep getting these extraordinary messages from our correspondents. Do you know that property in Hong Kong is worth half what it was a year ago? Russia can't pay the interest on its debt, it's so broke. Brazil owes three hundred billion dollars. Japanese banks have five hundred billion in bad loans. Do you see a pattern here, David? Does any of this register with you?"

"Not really," I said. "It sounds bad. But someone must be paying attention."

"No, they're not. Even sensible people don't see it. People are *fools*! That's why they need newspapers." She described a project her correspondents were working on, which would try to make all this global misery interesting. But when she saw the faraway look in my eye, she gave it up, with an oh-never-mind Katharine Hepburn wave of dismissal.

I asked if she'd heard any more from her friend Ariane Hazen, and her eyes widened. "She's frantic!" she said. "Haven't you heard the rumor? Someone's buying up blocks of stock. The Hazens are in a state of shock!"

Really, now! I professed surprise. I *loved* having a secret. I asked Candace what she thought about the prospect of the paper being sold—this was her livelihood, after all. But she laughed it off—it was bad form for journalists to care too much about the business side of the paper.

She went home to watch her splendid relics on video and

try not to think about how squishy the world was becoming. I imagined her curled up in bed, watching the scene in *Bringing Up Baby* where Hepburn enters a ballroom unaware of the rip in her dress, while Grant gallantly tries to cover her bottom with a top hat. Candace was the rare modern woman who could play that scene herself. That was her problem— she was a thoroughbred, stabled with a team of plough horses.

I CALLED GALVIN WHEN I got home, thinking he might be the mystery buyer. He knew all about the rumors, but he said it was someone else. The only certainty was that a New York investment bank had gone into the market to buy large blocks of Washington Sun and Tribune Co. stock on behalf of an unnamed client. Galvin thought it might be a real estate speculator from California, but he wasn't sure. The mystery buyer was staying below the 5 percent level that would require disclosure of his identity to the SEC. But trading was so active that the *Sun's* stock had awakened from its forty-dollar-a-share slumber and begun to climb slightly in value. Ariane Hazen was calling him hourly, Galvin said, practically begging him to help the family. This was what she had wanted and dreaded: The *Sun* was finally in play, but Harold Hazen was stubbornly refusing to hire an investment banker—preferring to stay at anchor and ride out the storm.

GALVIN VISITED ARIANE HAZEN the next day. He asked me to come along—he wanted a colleague, he said, to make things more businesslike. She lived in Cleveland Park, in a Victorian house that was all turrets and porches and crenellated edges. This was where the city's limousine liberals lived—except that they all had sport-utility vehicles parked out front nowadays. You could throw a rock in any direction in this neighborhood and be pretty confident of not hitting a Republican—that's the kind of place it was. Ariane had painted her Cleveland Park mansion peach, lest anyone think she was just another footloose, unhappy newspaper heiress.

She greeted us in a black dress that hugged her large bosom. She seemed eager to talk business—even had a calculator ready on the coffee table, should we need it. It was odd that this woman in her forties had fastened her life's passion on the notion that the family business wasn't profitable enough. Making money had become fashionable, or at least acceptable, in the nineties—nothing to apologize about. And Ariane's feminism gave her acquisitiveness a benign edge. She just wanted what was *hers*.

Galvin was dressed in a loose-fitting linen suit and an open-neck brown shirt—not the outfit of a mercenary, certainly. He was carrying a manila file folder, which he handed to Ariane. "We know who the raider is," he said. Inside the folder was a document from one of the big Wall Street firms, reporting the sale of a big block of *Sun* stock. The purchaser was identified as a holding company called PalmTrust.

"I can't tell you how my associate got hold of this," Galvin said, nodding in my direction. "But it's authentic."

I turned to him curiously. What the hell? How had I become the source of inside stock information? Wasn't that illegal? An exciting thought, but I would like to have been asked. Galvin shot me a glance that said, *Keep quiet and play your part.*

"I've never heard of PalmTrust," she said. "Who are they?" Her hand was trembling slightly as she held the paper. She wanted to do the right thing, for herself and her family, but this was frightening.

"PalmTrust is registered in Delaware. The records there don't explain much. But my associate tells me the company is controlled by a prominent real estate developer named Melvin J. Wolfe, from California originally. He made his money as a 'bottom fisher.' A tough guy, people say."

He looked to me for confirmation. "That's right," I said, nodding.

"Is he really a real estate developer? That's awful! I have to tell my father. What will they do, now that they've bought all this stock?" She looked at me, for some reason.

"Wolfe's a madman!" I blurted out. "You can never tell what a man like that will do." I was getting into my role, but Galvin extended his hand in my direction, in a gesture that said, unmistakably, *Cut!*

"It's a fluid situation," Galvin said more softly. "They're just below the five-percent level. Maybe they're buying it as an investment, but I doubt it. Seems more likely that they're about to make a takeover bid."

"What should we do?" she asked. By now, she was totally in his hands.

"Start planning a takeover defense, right away. Unless you want to sell them the newspaper. In that case, do nothing."

She stretched out her arms toward this handsome man who had blown into town a few months before and had, in a short time—who could say how, exactly?—made himself indispensable to the people who mattered in Washington.

"Please," she said. "Will you meet with my family? We need help, and you're the only person I trust."

Galvin gave her a gentle pat on the back. It was such an uneven contest. He knew what he wanted, and she didn't. "I'm happy to help," he said, "but you're going to need a real plan. You can't make folks like Wolfe go away just by blowing on them."

We drove off in Galvin's limousine. I was deep in the plush velour, feet up, and enjoying my new life as a method actor, but Galvin was not amused. "Don't *ever* do that again," he said. "I don't like surprises. The next time you do that, you're fired." He had not raised his voice, but there was no mistaking his seriousness. It was unsettling. He wanted me to understand that I was his, and that he could hurt me. There are people in this world who are capable of doing violence to others. I am not one of them, so I'm slow to recognize this quality in others. But I saw it fleetingly that day in Galvin.

EIGHT

THE HAZEN AND CROSBY FAMILIES GATHERED THE NEXT morning at ten A.M. in the conference room of the family law firm. Harold Hazen must have hoped that if he hunkered down and cuffed his daughter back into line, it would all go away. But it was too late. At nine that morning, just before the market opened, PalmTrust made a public offer to acquire all outstanding stock of The Washington Sun and Tribune Co. for forty-eight dollars a share. The formal announcement added to the uneasiness in the room, as the two families struggled to understand what to do.

I had asked Galvin to let me come along, despite my over-acting the previous day. I wanted to be there, to see what cards he would pull from his deck. Galvin at first said no, but relented when I assured him that nobody would connect me with my ridiculous magazine. I doubted any of them had ever read it—they were at the top of the Washington social pyramid, after all; why would they need *Reveal*? The only reason he agreed, I think, was that he wanted an audience. I wore an old blue suit with stovepipe pants that made me look like I was walking on stilts.

The conference room was on the top floor of a new office tower that looked out over Lafayette Park and the White House. It was a handsome room, with a long marble conference table and the latest in audiovisual equipment. It was probably a mistake for the law firm to invite clients there. It was so lavish, it proclaimed that the firm was charging too much. Galvin and I sat at one end of the table, Harold Hazen and his lawyer at the other. On either side were arrayed various members of the Hazen and Crosby clans. Rather than divide along blood lines, they had arranged themselves according to age, with the parents—Harold's generation—facing Ariane and the other children. It seemed odd to call them children—they were all in their thirties and forties—but that wasn't far off. None of them had done much in the world, as far as I knew.

Mr. Hazen offered a gruff welcome and said the family would be grateful for any advice we might have. He was the sort of man who tried to be gracious even when he didn't like you. But life was backing up on him, like sewage in a clogged pipe. He had worked hard for many years, and was confounded to discover that his family appreciated him so little.

Galvin's charm, in contrast, was that he appeared to do everything effortlessly, and this morning was no exception. He looked as easy and comfortable in that office as one of the partners, and better dressed, in a trim gray suit and an ice-blue Hermès tie. The picture window was behind him, framing a postcard view of the White House. He commanded our attention, but I don't think anyone, least of all me, could have anticipated what he would say.

"I feel honored to be here with you," he began, gazing down the table at Mr. Hazen. "Your newspaper isn't just a business, it's a public trust." *Don't lay it on too thick,* I silently coached him. These people might have lost a step, but they weren't stupid.

"I make it a rule never to give advice," Galvin continued. "But if you'd like, I can help you think through your options."

"Please do," said Mr. Hazen. Heads nodded around the table.

"As I see it," he said, "you've got three basic choices. None of them is perfect, but you've got to select one and stick with it. The first is simply to accept the offer PalmTrust made this morning. That would give you a nice profit on your shares, and maybe Wolfe will sweeten it a little, to fifty dollars a share, let's say. That's your first order of business. Do any of you want to sell your shares to PalmTrust?"

The room was silent for an agonizingly long moment, until Ariane spoke up. She was wearing a simple brown dress—all business. "Come on, *people,*" she said, looking at her brother and the Crosbys. "It's now or never."

One of the Crosby boys raised his hand. He was blond and balding, with a face that looked like it had been through the washing machine too many times—a face that was a living warning that even the sturdiest families run out of gas eventually.

"I'm Andrew Crosby, Mr. Galvin. As far as I'm concerned, forty-eight dollars sounds attractive, and fifty even better. It's not enough, but it's more than we have."

"Nonsense!" growled Harold Hazen. "They would be stealing the paper for that price. It's outrageous. Let's not talk about it anymore. It makes me ill. What is option number two, Mr. Galvin?"

"Option two is to fight the PalmTrust offer as hard as you can," Galvin explained. "And you may win—if you stick together—because the company can't be sold without approval of a majority of the stock held by people who are gathered in this room. But you'll need to convince your board of directors that refusing PalmTrust is in the best interest of all the shareholders. And you need to ask yourselves the same question the analysts will be asking—which is whether you're ready to be more aggressive and unlock more of the value that's in the business."

Ariane and the other children voiced their approval of the idea that the newspaper should be making more money. "Hear, hear!" said Andrew Crosby. This was the most polite revolution imaginable.

"I will listen to any reasonable suggestions," said Mr. Hazen, looking to his lawyer for support. "But I must remind you that I still control the 1963 trust. And if I can look forward to continued support from Mr. Crosby Senior, that gives me a comfortable majority of the voting stock."

Ariane nudged her younger brother, Michael, who had been quiet until now. He lived in Santa Monica most of the time, writing screenplays that were never made into movies. "I'd be careful with the math, Pop," he said. "You need my support to vote the 1963 trust, and I'm still thinking things over."

"*Thinking things over?*" The old man was shaking his

head. "When did you all get so greedy?" You could see the hurt in his eyes. Did these people have any idea what "unlocking value" meant in practice? It meant firing loyal employees. It meant running pictures of bosomy women in bathing suits. It meant foolish contests and coupons and advertorial sections. Harold Hazen wouldn't do it. He had never run the business that way, and he didn't intend to start now.

"It's not about greed, Daddy. That's not what we're saying."

"Oh, I *know* what you're saying. You want more money— so you want to sell out now, or keep your stock and find a new CEO who can pump it up. Well, that may or may not be in the newspaper's interest, but it's absolutely none of your business. It's between me and the board of directors. Until they fire me, I report to them. So, what's your third option, Mr. Galvin?"

Galvin had been listening silently as the family members fired poison darts at each other. He paused a long while before answering—walking to the window, studying the pedestrians ambling through Lafayette Park and the sharpshooters perched atop the White House. I was beginning to wonder whether he would say anything at all, he looked so pensive and uncertain. What an actor he is, I thought. I didn't know where he was going, but I was spellbound.

"I hadn't planned to get involved personally in this fight," he began. "But you have a problem, and you need to solve it quickly or you're going to destroy a great newspaper."

"Spare us," interjected Mr. Hazen. "What's option three?"

"Option three is to find a white knight—someone who

can make a friendly takeover offer and block PalmTrust. As I listen to this conversation, it's becoming obvious that's the right answer. Otherwise, this story isn't going to have a happy ending."

"And who might that white knight be?" asked Mr. Hazen. But the look on his face showed that he already knew. All of us did, suddenly, though I would wager that no one, least of all me, had realized that he was leading us into this cul-de-sac until we were actually there.

"Please listen carefully to what I'm about to say." Galvin fixed his eyes on them, one by one, around the table. "I am prepared to offer fifty dollars a share for the *Sun*, with a premium of fifty-five a share payable to holders of the A shares who are seated around this table. That's about seventeen percent more than what PalmTrust is offering. I'm doing this because I think I can save the paper and make it prosperous again. I would like to ally with the Hazens and Crosbys. Your alternative, I'm afraid, is a costly war with Mr. Wolfe. But if you aren't interested, tell me quickly, because I don't want to waste your time, or mine."

Galvin sat down. Many voices were speaking at once, but the loudest was Harold Hazen's. "What the *hell*?" he thundered. "What kind of a trick *is* this?"

But almost as loud was his daughter's voice. "I think it's a superb idea, and I think we should discuss it, and then put it to a vote." That set off more tongue-wagging, back and forth. Galvin, only now, sneaked a glance in my direction. His face was ice cold, but his eyes were on fire.

The family lawyer suggested that now might be a good time for us to leave the patriarchs and their children alone.

They had a lot to talk about. Galvin said he needed time too, to prepare a document for the board of directors outlining his bid and specifying the financial details. Before he left, he went around the table and shook hands with each member of the family, thanking them for the privilege of meeting with him. They looked up at him with a sense of bewilderment— this powerful, dark man in his perfect suit who had fallen out of the sky. Even Harold Hazen seemed undone by Galvin's performance.

As Galvin reached the door, he turned back to them. "Do what's best for the newspaper," he said. "That's all I ask."

He didn't say a word as we descended in the elevator, and didn't open his mouth until we were out the door and around the corner. I expected a radiant smile, or even a shout of joy, but he was surprisingly cold and contained; he seemed, in fact, almost rueful. "I know I should be exhilarated," he said, "but I found that sad. It was too easy. They're nice people, but they're dinosaurs. It's time for them to get out of the way."

As we walked up Connecticut Avenue, Galvin stopped and chatted with some of the people who were strolling to lunch—White House aides, journalists, the head of a local bank, partners in the city's leading law firms. He had to stop every few steps; many of these people had been out to his house and wanted to thank him for his hospitality. He was already acting like the mayor of this little town, and he had barely arrived. That was Harold Hazen's real problem. There was an inevitability about Galvin's accession. The only question was what he would do with the power that was already flowing toward him so naturally and irresistibly.

NINE

GALVIN AND I SAT IN HIS GARDEN IN GEORGETOWN THAT afternoon, waiting for Ariane to arrive. He had invited her to come for a swim. That was a nice touch—it didn't make her seem quite so much like his stooge, and Galvin wasn't making any mistakes that day. He hadn't lost the restless energy from the morning. He had a yo-yo with him, of all things, a beautiful handmade one carved in the shape of the world, and he was absentmindedly doing tricks with it while we talked. He was surprisingly proficient.

"You don't see a lot of yo-yo expertise in the business world," I said. "How did you get to be so good?"

"The Duncan yo-yo man taught me," he said, spinning the little globe toward me in a looping arc. "He used to come by the school playground in Mount Lebanon selling yo-yos to the kids. He was a mysterious guy, drove a big Pontiac convertible, wore slick clothes. Probably he was a queer. He would teach us tricks—loop the loop, around the world. That was the biggest thing our parents had to worry about back then—that we were wasting our time learning yo-yo tricks and would never amount to anything."

He gave it a few more practice spins, and then did a trick called cat's cradle, in which he hoisted the string with his fingers so that it formed a little archway and then made the yo-yo pass through, still spinning. I was impressed. But then, everything about Galvin impressed me. Where did his energy come from? Toward what goal was it really directed? The exterior of the man was so finely drawn, but the interior was still fuzzy halftones.

"Why do you want to buy the *Sun*?" I asked. That question had been nagging at me during his performance before the Hazens and Crosbys. "What's in it for you? You don't need the money. You don't need the aggravation. You don't really know anything about the newspaper business. I don't get it."

"Walk the dog!" he said. That was the name of another trick, not an answer to my question. He spun the yo-yo down to the ground and gave his wrist a little flick, which sent the tiny globe skittering along the flagstone of his patio. He gave me a wink and put the toy aside.

"It's not about money," he said. "You're right about that. It's about journalism. Basically, I think they're producing a lousy paper and I can produce a better one. Not just more profitable, but better. How about that?"

He seemed to want my approval that this was an acceptable answer. I still wasn't convinced.

"Okay," he said, palms out. "I admit it. It's about love." He cocked his head and gave me one of his billion-dollar smiles.

I thought he was joking. "Come on!" I said. "The *Sun* is a

serious paper. All the serious people think so, anyway. It wins a Pulitzer Prize every other year. You're just a businessman. What makes you think you can do better?"

"The *Sun* is awful, and you know it! It's boring. It's constipated. It runs interminable series like "Whither Rwanda?" and "The Future of the Foreign Service." The editors are so worried about offending readers they've stopped having fun. I mean, honestly, do you read the thing? I've only been here a few months, and I'm already tired of it. The writers all sound like they have a rod up their ass. You know the first thing I'm going to tell the staff if we win? *Lighten up!*"

"What's the second thing you'll tell them?"

"I don't know. Cut back on expensive trips. Stop wasting paper clips. How should I know? It's going to be fun, that's all. Wait and see." He wagged a finger at me.

I had rarely seen him so animated. He was in stride, closing in on his quarry. But I was such a fool I didn't begin to understand how complicated his pursuit really was, and I certainly didn't see the real prize that was drawing him on.

He was still doing tricks with his yo-yo when the doorbell rang and the butler showed Ariane Hazen into the garden. She was wearing the same plain brown dress she'd worn that morning, but she'd added a French silk scarf for Galvin's benefit.

Galvin took her by the arm and steered her toward the chairs by the pool. She had brought her bathing suit in a little gym bag, but I knew they weren't going to swim. She was too excited by what Galvin had set in motion. This was patricide. They were going to oust her father, and she had the knife in her hand.

"You were magnificent this morning," said Galvin. "What happened after we left?"

"It was noisy. There was a lot of arguing, but we agreed on a few things." She explained that the two families had voted quickly to reject the PalmTrust offer. That was easy. Then, after much discussion, they had agreed that management changes were necessary at the paper. Mr. Hazen wasn't happy about that, but he would have to live with it. Finally, they had taken up Galvin's offer. That was the hardest part. Mr. Hazen was insisting that Galvin was manipulating the whole thing.

"Where are the votes, Ariane?" asked Galvin. "Who's got control?"

"We do, I think." She said it tentatively, girlishly, still not sure of her power. "My brother told Daddy at the end of the meeting that he'll vote the 1963 trust in favor of your offer. Daddy said he's still opposed, so there's a tie—which means those shares will be voted by the trustee, who's a New York lawyer. He'll do what the board wants. But I don't think it will come to that."

"Why not?" Galvin's big body moved in the chair. This was the moment.

"Because after the meeting, Mr. Crosby spoke with my father alone. The Crosbys have let Daddy have his way for twenty years, but they're not pushovers, especially the old man. Mr. Crosby told Daddy it was over. The Crosbys won't turn down an offer of fifty-five dollars a share for their stock. They can't afford to. Which means they'll vote their shares with you. So it doesn't matter about the 1963 trust. You're there."

"Then do it," said Galvin.

"What do you mean?" she asked.

"*Pull the trigger!*" he shouted. "Now! Call the question. Convene another meeting of the family tonight. The board will have my documents by late this afternoon. The directors are already being polled informally, by telephone. Do it! Don't wait. Don't let this slip out of our fingers."

"Yes, of course." She was shaken momentarily. He had frightened her with his sudden flash of temper. It was a moment when the cloak had parted, and you could see the raw power that was normally hidden. Galvin saw that he had blundered, and put one of his huge hands gently on her shoulder.

"I'm sorry," he said, instantly recalibrating his voice and manner. "I'm just so excited about what we can do at the *Sun*. I get carried away. But I mean it about moving quickly. The longer we wait, the easier it becomes for Wolfe. When will the family be getting together again?"

"We have a meeting tomorrow morning. Would that be too late?" She sounded anxious, afraid he might become angry again.

"Just right. My lawyer will call your father's lawyer tonight." He took her hand. "We're almost home," he said, giving her another kiss on the cheek. "I hope you'll never regret this."

She pulled back from his kiss this time, surprised by his words. "That's a silly thing to say. How could I regret it?" Her question hung in the air, requiring an answer. She caught Galvin with her eyes, rimmed with years of disappointment and regret, and forced him to look back.

"I'm forty-seven years old," she said. "This is the most

important thing I've ever done—probably the most important thing I'll ever do. It has to be right. Promise me that it will work."

He was wise enough not to sweet-talk her. "I can't promise you I'll succeed," he said. "But I will do my best to make the paper better and more profitable. I'm a complicated person—like you, probably—but for me, this is simple. I wouldn't let any of us take the risk if I wasn't confident I could succeed."

She studied him, holding her hand over her eyes to shield the afternoon sun. "I wasn't sure I could go through with this, so I asked my friend Candace Ridgway about you. I needed some advice, and she's smart about people."

The stillness in the garden was total for a moment. "What did Candace Ridgway say?"

"She said it was the right thing to do. She said the paper needed a change, and you looked like a decent person who would do a good job. And I trust Candace. That's why I know I won't regret it."

IT WAS OVER QUICKLY. At the end, Galvin was like a bull-fighter who plunges the sword in all the way to the hilt, so that the bull crumples to its knees even as it is charging toward him.

Galvin stayed at home by the telephone the next morning. He sent me out at one point to buy some cigarettes. He never smoked any of them, but he seemed reassured to know that they were there. Every so often he would throw his head back and laugh, or mumble some phrase of wonderment from his tie-dyed youth, like "Can you *believe* this?" or *"Far* out!" That enthusiasm was part of his secret. He hadn't lost the ability to be surprised by his good fortune.

He sent his attorneys over to negotiate final details with the Hazens and the Crosbys. Mr. Hazen wanted a severance package, in addition to the money for his stock. Galvin had anticipated this, and his lawyers had a proposal ready, which, after several rounds, was approved. Mr. Crosby wanted an extension of his consulting contract, and that too was quickly settled.

Ariane Hazen wanted a continuing role at the paper, so Galvin promised she could run its new charitable arm, The Washington Sun and Tribune Foundation. Everyone wanted evidence that Galvin actually had the money to complete a tender offer that would be worth more than a billion dollars. A senior representative of a New York investment bank was on hand to explain the complex financing, which would involve a syndicate of banks that had lent money to Galvin over the years. Under the terms of the agreement, Galvin would retain control only of the Hazen-Crosby voting stock—the rest would be refloated to the public.

Just before noon, one of his lawyers called to say that a deal was near. Galvin told him to send champagne up to the conference room, and then had his chauffeur drive him there so that he could be present for the final agreement. He had arranged for a photographer to record the historic handshake between a worn, embittered Harold Hazen and an ebullient Sandy Galvin. There was a family picture too, with Ariane gazing up at her white knight. The other Hazens and Crosbys had empty smiles, but you knew what they were thinking: fifty-five dollars a share, in cash!

Galvin went to the *Sun*'s headquarters that afternoon to meet with the board of directors. Only half of them had managed to get to Washington on such short notice; the rest were linked by conference call. Galvin and his lawyers made a detailed presentation that lasted nearly two hours. The directors asked a few questions, but from what Galvin told me later, it was obvious that the fix was in. He had several friends on the board. It turned out that he'd begun quiet conversations with them soon after he arrived in Washington.

The board authorized a brief statement that was released at four o'clock, as rumors were circulating that a new bid for the *Sun* was imminent. It said that the directors had received an offer from an investment group headed by Carl S. Galvin, and that the board's preliminary determination was to recommend that shareholders should accept it. There was a new flurry of buying, in expectation that PalmTrust would top Galvin with a revised offer of its own. But the real estate king was silent. After the market closed, PalmTrust announced that it was withdrawing its bid and would tender its shares to Galvin.

Galvin returned to the Georgetown house at five-thirty, looking tired but immensely relieved. "We did it," he said. "Thanks for your help." That was all. He wasn't a strutter in victory. Perhaps he regarded success as inevitable, and thus uninteresting.

He went upstairs to change into a fresh shirt for the round of newspaper and television interviews that was about to begin. Galvin had arranged that too. A procession of reporters marched through the living room, taking fifteen-minute slices of the new publisher. He had me in the pantry, safely out of the way, but I watched through the door as he gestured, scowled, shrugged, opined. He was the man of the hour; everyone wanted a piece of him now.

IT IS A NATURAL impulse, surely, to ask after the magician has completed a trick: How did he do it? I grant that nobody likes the kid who tugs at Grandpa's sleeve when he's doing his famous Magic Pink Ball trick and says, "Look! He's got *another* pink ball right here in his hand!" But it was my fate to be that kid, now and forever. So as Galvin was taking his bows as the new owner of the *Sun,* I found myself reviewing the events of the past few weeks, trying to understand how he had put together this invincible assault with so little apparent effort. Had I missed something?

What was obvious, on reflection, was that Galvin had planned the operation meticulously, like a military campaign. He had prepared the financial details of his offer long before that first meeting with the Hazens and the Crosbys—his touching statement that he "hadn't planned" to offer himself as white knight had been nonsense. Of course he had—he'd costed out his offer to the last dollar. But the white knight had needed an adversary to threaten the damsel. Where had the mysterious black knight come from, and how had Galvin known so much about his moves? But obviously I suspected the answer. I worked for the magician; I didn't need to look in his pocket to know that he was hiding something. I hadn't any moral qualms about it, really—these people were all rats, as far as I was concerned—but I wanted to be sure it was true.

So I asked him. That was a near-fatal mistake, as it turned out, but it was in character. I called Galvin two days after his purchase of the *Sun* was announced, as he was winding down the round of interviews, and said gravely that I needed to see him immediately about a very important matter. He laughed out loud—he wasn't used to such seriousness from me—but said I should come to the Georgetown house right away.

It was midmorning when I arrived. He was sitting outside in a silk dressing gown, sipping coffee and reading the *Sun*.

"This really is a terrible paper," he said as he saw me coming. "It's like one of those new tomatoes they sell in the supermarket—big and red and juicy, but it has no flavor. The life has been squeezed out of it—you know what I mean? It will be so easy to make it better."

"You stole it," I said.

"What are you talking about, boy? Sit down and have some coffee. Have you lost your mind?"

"You stole it," I repeated. "You arranged for PalmTrust to make its offer so that you could top it. That's how you knew so much about their hostile offer—because you had set it in motion. There never was a black knight—other than you."

"Now, that is an *outrageous* accusation," he said. "What you are describing would be *illegal*." I thought I saw a trace of a smile on his lips. "And besides, you don't have any evidence."

"Maybe not, but it's true, isn't it?" I was looking him square in the eye, something a court jester never did. "Tell me the truth. I'm not just a bag carrier. I want to know."

"Be careful, David," he said. "Opportunity is about to knock. Good things are about to happen. Don't blow it."

"I could ask the SEC what they think. I'll bet they could get to the bottom of this pretty damn quick." His self-confidence annoyed me. I didn't want him to think he could just manipulate me, the way he had done everyone else. I wanted to be in on the joke—part of the scam. He saw that, thank goodness, before we went any farther.

"Let's make a deal, you and me, right now. You won't push me about business details, and I won't push you about journalism. Okay? There are a lot of things you don't know about this transaction, and this is one of them. Do we understand each other?"

I nodded. That was as much of a confirmation as I was going to get, or needed. It was enough, for now, simply to know the truth—or what I imagined it to be.

"Good." He relaxed. "Now let me tell you another thing you don't know. I have decided to appoint a new editor for the Lifestyle section. And that is going to be my own trusted lieutenant, Mr. David Cantor."

He smiled and shook my hand. He loved bestowing presents.

"Hey, great!" I said. That was an idiotic response, but frankly, I was overwhelmed. This was the sort of job I would have dreamed about, if I hadn't foresworn ambition.

"I hope that means yes. You suggested it yourself a few weeks ago, and I decided it was a good idea. You're a troublemaker. You don't care about offending people, and that's what I need right now—a bomb thrower who has no ties to the old regime. So, do we have a deal?"

"Yes," I said, still numb. I was as happy as an unhappy person can be. There was a nagging question, then and later, of whether I had been anointed as his viceroy, or simply bought off. That was a disturbing thought—that I was really just like the Crosbys and the Hazens, and he had figured out my price—but I could live with it.

I CALLED THE OWNER that night, to tell her that I was quitting *Reveal*. I should have done it in person, but I was afraid she would make a scene, and I couldn't handle that. You'd think it would have felt good to tell her I was taking a hike after so many years of humiliation—she was still paying me just $48,000 a year, for God's sake!—but it was sad. I was all she had left. We had limped through the last issue—I decided finally to do the cover story on "Washington's Power Hairdressers." The printers were now threatening a lawsuit, after the ruse with the unsigned check. And at the end, we hadn't even been able to afford delivery for about a third of the circulation, and stacks of the Power Hairdressers issue were piled up in the offices on Connecticut Avenue.

"I have some sad news," I told the owner. "At least, I hope you'll think it's sad news. If you don't, then it's even sadder."

"What is it?" she asked in a louder voice than I expected, leading me to suspect that cocktail hour had already begun.

I couldn't just say it flat out. It was like shooting an old dog. "We've had a good run, you and I, some good times."

"No, we haven't. The magazine is going bankrupt. We have failed completely. People have stopped reading us. They don't even care anymore whether we run their pictures. How can you say that we've had a good run?"

"Well, we tried." I didn't want to get into an argument with her, and besides, she was right. The magazine was a piece of shit. "Listen, there's something important that I have to tell you."

"You want to change the name again? Fine. Call it whatever you want. I don't care anymore. *Lush, Moist, Throb, Flaccid*. It doesn't matter. You can call it *Blow Job*, for all I care."

"It's not that. I don't want to change the name. I like *Reveal*. It's grown on me. No, it's something else."

"You want to be paid. Of course you do. I'm sorry. Maybe you'd like something from one of the catalogues. How about The Sharper Image? They have nice things. Or some meat from Balducci's."

"I'm quitting." There wasn't any easy way to say it. "I'm taking another job. Power Hairdressers was my last issue."

"Oh, God!" The line went quiet. I thought she'd had a heart attack, but eventually, after fifteen seconds or so, I heard the sound of weeping. "It's over," she said between sobs. "My baby is dead."

This was even worse than I had feared. The woman was unhinged. "You can find another editor," I said. "I'll help."

The offer of charity infuriated her. Her self-pity was replaced with indignation. How dare I offer to help? That was intolerable, the notion that she might need assistance from a clod like me. She would never sink so low. "I don't want your help, you bastard. I thought you cared about journalism!"

"I do. It's just that I got a better offer."

"Ha!" she cut in. She didn't want to hear what it was. "Whatever it is, it's too good for you. I should have listened to Annabelle Paige. She warned me that you hated women."

The conversation was degenerating. "I'm sorry it's ending this way," I said. "I'm grateful for all the help you've given me. I'll clean out my office tomorrow morning."

"You're a shit!" She hung up. When I got to the office the next morning, the lock had already been changed.

TEN

GALVIN DECIDED TO THROW HIMSELF A VICTORY celebration—a black-tie dinner dance, no less—at his Virginia mansion. It was his way of announcing to Washington that its newspaper—known for sagacious editorials and worthy local reporting, but not for its sense of fun—was in glamorous new hands. The invitations went out a few days after he closed the deal with Harold Hazen. They were printed on thick, creamy paper and stuffed into massive envelopes lined with gold foil, like invitations to a wedding. There was something delightfully childlike about Galvin's enthusiasm. He had bought himself a fantastic billion-dollar toy, and he couldn't wait to show it off to the other kids.

Because Galvin had decided that I had professional expertise in the area of party giving—had I not been editor of *The Social Bible of Washington*?—I was designated as the event planner. He told me to spend whatever was needed—more than was needed, this had to be the best party ever given in Washington. I wasted a day in urgent, useless activity before turning sheepishly to my erstwhile employer, the owner of *Reveal*. I told her frankly that I was desperate—it had fallen to me to organize the party of the year and I didn't even own a tux. She was *of course* high on the guest list, I explained, since it was *her* magazine that had launched Galvin in Washington. So, in that sense, it was *her* party too. And would she—could she—possibly offer some advice?

It will not surprise anyone familiar with the folkways of our nation's capital that my former employer, who only days before had been addressing me with four-letter words, readily agreed to help. In a city of courtiers, there is only the eternal present; with each movement in the constellation of power, the past is instantly and entirely obliterated. The owner knew this, as she knew all things. She was happy to suggest the right caterer, the right florist—the right orchestra, bartender, valet parker, liquor purveyor, grocer, tent provider. Representatives of these worthy establishments scrambled to meet us and present their bids; the owner would study the quotations, demand a 25 percent reduction in price, settle for a 10 percent cut—and then hand the contract to me to sign. Galvin wandered in on one of these negotiating sessions and gave her a look of unqualified, unfeigned approval—which was all the compensation she could want.

Soon trucks began arriving at the house, unloading crates of china, tables and chairs, tents big enough for P. T. Barnum, a dance floor the size of a baseball infield, a jungle of fresh flowers and enough booze to float a battleship. Galvin observed all this activity with genial contentment. He would come in from the tennis court, pleasantly fatigued after a lesson with the pro who seemed to be perpetually on duty, and see me hassling with some purveyor or victualer.

"How many shrimp did you order?" he would ask. "Two thousand," I would answer—four for every guest. "Double it!" he would shout back. And the same with the stone crabs, oysters, caviar and smoked salmon. When I told him what each particular bit of excess would cost, he would smile happily. *What a lucky man,* his face said, *to be hosting such an affair.*

By the afternoon of the party, I was so nervous that I decided it would be wise to take some drugs. That was a vestige of my sentimental education from the 1970s—experience in the ways of self-medication. I called my doctor in search of Valium, Klonopin, cough syrup, anything!—but she was away, and her nurse cruelly refused to help—so I opted for the lower-tech but still effective brain deadener known as the martini. Thus fortified, I put on my rented tuxedo and drove my Honda out to the plantation. I was the first to arrive and gaze, with genuine wonder, on what our labors had produced.

WE HAD CREATED AN imaginary landscape. The trees that bordered the long driveway had been decorated with tiny golden lights, so that they shimmered and sparkled in the evening breeze like the pathway to an enchanted palace. At the bottom of the drive, the great redbrick house was illuminated by a dozen spotlights. The whole place seemed to be glowing, as if it had just landed on that spot from another galaxy. Inside, the house was in bloom, with garlands of fresh flowers and the supernatural colors of Galvin's art collection—to which he had recently added a phantasmal Dieben-

korn and a stark red-and-black Motherwell. But the interior
was no more than a passageway this evening, to the pageant
of color and light out back.

The wonder was that the weather too had obliged Sandy
Galvin. It was a perfect, cloudless evening in late September,
the very last trailing edge of summer—as if the gods above
had taken a particular interest in the play that was about to
unfold, and wanted an unobstructed view. A full moon was
rising to the east, over the river—perfectly round, ghostly
white and improbably large. It was too bright outside to see
the stars, but they were up there, too—one for every grain of
sand in the ocean, one for every drop of ink in Mr. Galvin's
newspaper. As I walked through the French doors into the
open air, I could hear the sound of a violin, testing a few
notes of a Strauss waltz, stopping to retune and gaily starting
up again.

The garden had been decorated to resemble the scene de-
picted by Renoir in his famous painting of an outdoor dance
in *Moulin de la Galette*. That had been Galvin's idea, and I'd
thought he was out of his mind at first. But now that I saw
the final effect, it was breathtaking. Paper lanterns were hung
from the trees and across the yard, casting a delicate play of
shadow and light. Two great tents bounded the sloping
lawn—one for dining, one for dancing. Beyond the tents, the
trees had been dotted with tiny gold lights like those along
the driveway. They twinkled and sparkled like an orchard of
Christmas trees. The orchestra was rehearsing in one tent,
and the catering staff was hurrying to the other with platters
and chafing dishes laden with food and hors d'oeuvres.

I caught sight of Galvin upstairs in his bedroom. He was

looking out through the picture window at what he had created. It was a wary, expectant gaze. He was waiting for someone. He had constructed this perfect stage, and now he
needed the players to arrive—one in particular, whom he
could see in his mind but who was still invisible to me.

TWO HOURS LATER, THE garden was full. I could tell it was
going to be a good party—people were actually drinking.
Normally, people at Washington parties made a point of
being abstemious. Drinking would mean relaxing, letting go,
taking the risk of saying something foolish or being unprepared or making a mistake. When you were drinking, you
were not working, and people in Washington never stopped
working—especially the journalists, who had become the
most abstemious and risk-averse of all. But tonight was different. It was as if relaxation and decompression were the
price of admission.

Galvin's guest list was masterful. His rule seemed to be:
Magnanimous in victory. He had invited the Hazens and the
Crosbys—not just the younger men and women whose votes
had carried the day, but the old gentlemen as well. The families had taken several tables to themselves in the buffet tent
and were accepting handshakes and best wishes with the
good manners of General Lee at Appomattox—all except
Ariane. She was making the rounds, introducing Galvin to
people he needed to know—advertisers, corporate vice presidents, loyal family retainers. He was lucky to have her; he
would need some link to the past to have any chance of suc-
ceeding.

Galvin made his way among the crowd like John D.

Rockefeller handing out dimes. Everyone wanted to talk to him. This was his party, of course, but one sensed that on this night, at least, it was also his town. In a city of transients, the newspaper was the one permanent store of value. It was the market maker in the goods that were traded here—influence, power, reputation. When the newspaper changed hands, it was like a change of government.

Striding among the guests in his French garden, bathed in the soft glow of his paper lanterns, Galvin looked like an artist's creation himself—tall and muscular, dressed in finely tailored clothes that conveyed an easy elegance, greeting the world with a face that seemed unmarked by a sleepless night or a day of worry. He was the man for this season. It's said that George Washington was an inevitable choice to become our first president because no one had ever looked better riding a horse. There was something of the same inevitability about Galvin.

I lurked at the edges of the party, looking at all the famous faces. Three justices of the Supreme Court had come, enough for a powerful dissent, at least; the Speaker of the House was here, popping out of his tuxedo like the Pillsbury Doughboy. The secretary of the Treasury arrived and departed early, looking as thin as a whippet and slightly stooped, as if bent over by the weight of all the money he had to worry about. The secretary of state came too, although she kept disappearing inside self-importantly to take telephone calls; it was rumored that she was on the way out, but who knew? The Vice President was over in the dancing tent, doing the Temptations Walk with his wife—probably the same steps they'd done when they first met at a tea dance in high school, thirty-five years before. It was deemed a credit to the man, in the current environment, that one could imagine his bouncy wife having an affair more easily than him.

And everywhere were the journalists, leaning against tent poles, sizing up the guests, talking mostly to each other (for who could be more interesting?). The President was finished, they were saying. His position was deteriorating; the polls showed it. It wasn't what he had done, but the *appearance* of what he had done, someone was saying. No, it wasn't that, someone else said. It was that he didn't appear to be truly *sorry* about what he appeared to have done. They knew everything and nothing, this crowd. You wouldn't find the journalists over by the raw bar, scarfing down free shrimp— not anymore. They made more money, in their virtuous passivity, than many of the businessmen and lawyers. And I was one of them. Why did I dislike them so?

The owner of *Reveal* wafted by, dressed in a poufy yellow dress that might have been worn by an old-time TV star like Dinah Shore or Florence Henderson. She looked beautiful, in the completely artificial manner of those olden days. She was on the arm of the former northern Virginia Car Dealer of the Year—the man we'd been about to profile a few issues back and had replaced at the last minute with Galvin. He had recently left his wife, it seemed, and was stepping out! Perhaps there were happy endings, after all.

I wandered over toward the stone wall that overlooked the river. The moon was higher in the sky now, casting a bone-white shadow on the slow-moving water. I had come there to rest. It was wearying, all this unearned status and derivative glory. People were being nice to me now, for no reason. I wanted to say something unpleasant to each and every well-wisher: *Where were you the day before yesterday, when I was a pathetic stick figure with no money and a broken-down Honda?* But I was instead shaking hands and half smiling back—already a bad sign.

Two men had ambled up to the stone wall a little farther along, deep in conversation. One of them was Galvin. He was gazing down the river toward the distant lights of Washington, sipping a glass of champagne while the other man talked. This other gentleman was seated on the wall, below Galvin. He was paunchy, with thinning blond hair and a weary look. He was probably about Galvin's age, late forties, but he looked far older. He had a big glass of whiskey in his hand and, it soon became clear, was quite drunk. It took me a moment to realize that it was Howard Bacon, the editor of the *Sun*.

"I'm too old to be polite," Bacon was saying. "I've put in too many years and worked for too many different newspaper owners. So I'm just going to ask you straight out: What are you going to do to the paper?"

"Make it better," answered Galvin. "With help from you, and everyone else."

"Well, that's a nice thought. It's hard to disagree with that. But better for who? For the advertisers, who think we're the devil? For the President, who whines every day that we're not being fair to him? For the President's enemies in Congress? For the Black Caucus, and the American Jewish Committee, and the AARP, and the Harvard-Yale club—have I left anybody out?" Poor man, he was definitely in his cups.

"Better for readers," Galvin answered gently.

"Of course, of course. Don't pay any attention to me. I've got too many miles on my tires; they're worn down, and sometimes they squeal. And I'll admit I get sick of all the complaints about the paper, yes I do. But I'll say one thing for us: We seem to piss people off in all directions, so we must be doing something right. Eh?"

Galvin frowned. "I don't get that part about how it's good to piss off all sides, Howard. Why do you think it's good for people to hate you? Maybe there's a reason they don't like the *Sun*. We'll have to talk about that."

"Sure. Absolutely. We'll talk about everything. You're the boss now. I've tried to do what I can to improve the paper, but I'll be honest: I get stuck in a rut sometimes—have trouble remembering why I got into the business. The sharp edges get worn down, the picture gets fuzzy. You know what I mean?"

He looked up at Galvin. "No, probably you don't. But for the rest of us, it's not easy. We could all use some new ideas. I just want to be sure they're good ones."

Bacon was talking in that tone of sad bemusement that men discover in middle age, when they begin to add up the accounts and see that things don't quite balance. It was a quality I had begun to notice among the fortysomethings I knew—that spacey, where's-the-rest-of-me look. But interestingly, I had never seen it in Galvin. He was still climbing, aspiring, searching. The phrase *Is this all?* had never crossed his lips. He was bored by Bacon's middle-age angst and changed the subject.

"What are people saying at the paper? The reporters and editors. What do they think?"

"Honestly, they're scared shitless. They don't know much about you, but what they have heard, they don't like. They're worried you're going to fire a lot of people, and do focus groups to create new sections   Television Today, Fun Facts from Abroad—and generally dumb it down. They like the newspaper the way it is. They're proud of it. They don't want to see it change."

"Change is always painful." Galvin put his hand on Bacon's shoulder. "I'll be honest with you too, Howard. I do have some new ideas. I'll save the particulars for another time, but I don't want to play games. I do intend to shake the paper up. That is a fact. I think it needs shaking up. And I want editors who can help me do it."

"I hear you," he said noncommittally. "Message received." Bacon stood up from his perch on the wall. He looked shattered—his face wasted by too many years of stress and booze and late-night deadlines. He wobbled unsteadily for a moment. The worst thing that could happen to a journalist was happening to him. "You will forgive me, sir," he said, "if I go in search of one of your lavatories."

Galvin watched his editor walk away and then turned back toward the house. As he did so, he saw me standing in the shadows. "I suppose you heard all that," he said.

"Yup. Pathetic. Mr. Bacon is not what I would call a titan of journalism. But I hear they've got a smart new guy coming in as Lifestyle editor."

Galvin smiled. Nothing could put him off his good mood this evening. "Never judge a man when he has a glass of whiskey in his hand," he said. "Always a mistake."

THE PARTY LASTED LATE into the night. People didn't come and go; they came and stayed. That was another Washington rarity. The usual rule here was lights out at eleven o'clock, so that everybody would be bright-eyed for school the next morning. But perhaps Galvin was rewriting that one, too.

I continued to meander; I knew I hadn't seen half the guests yet, it was such a big party. The orchestra had started another set in the music tent; they were playing old-time dance favorites—Glenn Miller, Broadway show tunes, even that waltz I'd heard the violinist practicing hours ago. Drawn by the music, I wandered into the tent. A cordon of people was ringing the dance floor, watching one couple dancing all alone. I opened my eyes, at last, and it was like a blow to the head.

Galvin was holding Candace gently in his arms, moving her with a tilt of his shoulders, a brush of his thighs. I hadn't seen her until that moment, what with so many people and my hiding much of the time in the shadows. She looked magnificent. Her blond hair was swept back from her face in a way that accentuated the beauty of her cheekbones and her graceful neck. She was wearing a string of white pearls and a long black dress that seemed to be made of chiffon, it was so light and delicate. In all my years of admiring Candace, I had never seen her look so beautiful.

The music stopped, but they remained together on the floor, talking. He whispered something in her ear and she laughed—there it was, that wispy smile of his, boyish and ir-resistible. The music resumed, and they started up again. You could see from the way they moved that they had danced to-

gether before. Her body seemed to understand his, to float
with it, like a leaf carried on a powerful gust of wind. Nobody else danced; we didn't move; we were transfixed. The
new owner of the *Sun* was dancing with the paper's foreign
editor. When the music ended, we all applauded.

I had been so stupid. Even when it should have been obvious, I hadn't seen it. When Galvin quizzed me about my
lunch with Candace, I had thought what a clever boy I was, to
be giving him such good information. When he confessed to
me that he was buying the paper for love, I thought he was
joking. I hadn't even understood when he looked down from
his bedroom window a few hours before, that the absent face
he awaited so tenderly was hers. Perhaps this entire party,
over which I had labored so diligently, had been a piece of
theater, created for Candace.

I wandered about in a daze for a half hour or so. It
shouldn't have hurt so much. God knows, I had no claim on
her, but Candace had been my only fantasy. Though I had
never spent an intimate moment with her, I had somehow
developed the lover's pride of possession—the notion that I
alone could appreciate her specialness. Yet after watching
them together on the dance floor, I knew that my claim was
entirely fraudulent and absurd. It was such a powerful feeling
of defeat; I cannot fully explain it.

It was time to go. My party was over. As I walked through
the house toward the front door, I passed the small study,
where Galvin and I had spent hours preparing for the party,
making plans for what we would do at the newspaper. The
door was ajar, and I could just see into the room. They were
sitting on the couch—not kissing or holding hands, but just

talking. I heard laughter. He was remembering something funny from long ago, and she was giggling about it. It was a sound I had never heard from her. A peal of laughter. The sound of pure pleasure.

I don't know whom I felt more betrayed by—him or her. But that was silly. I was not a real person. I existed in two dimensions only. Love was for people who took up more space in the world. But even a stick man is capable of theater—better at it, even. He can hide in the shadows; he can disappear into the crevices of other people's ambition and desire.

ELEVEN

CANDACE RIDGWAY LIVED ON A NARROW STREET IN Georgetown peopled mostly by retired diplomats and spies. Her house was a handsome three-story brick structure, with a wrought-iron staircase up to the front door and a postage-stamp garden in back. Inside, it was light and spare, with simple furniture that complemented the old floors and moldings. It was a house that could belong only to a single person—and probably only to a single woman. It was so neat, for one thing, and you couldn't find a television anywhere. But more than that, it had the crisp orderliness of a woman's home. The windows were clean, the drapes were pleated and hung just so, the rugs didn't ruck in the middle. Each object was in its place for a reason.

Above the mantel was a nineteenth-century portrait of a handsome, fair-haired woman; she wore the high-collared blouse and severe hairstyle of the period, but the painter had captured the passion in her eyes and the high color in her cheeks. Candace had told me once that the woman in the

painting was an ancestor, but it could not have been otherwise. On a table nearby rested a picture of her father and
mother in happier times. The photograph captured the New
England vision of romance, the two of them aboard a big
Concordia yawl cruising off the Maine coast, tanned and
windblown, the mother looking as if she was about to make
a wisecrack and the father already smiling.

A fire was neatly laid in the fireplace, reminding visitors
that the mistress of the house didn't need a man to keep her
warm. Set back from the hearth were a comfortable couch
and two easy chairs. Over by the stairs was a well-stocked bar,
signaling that the owner didn't need a man to make her a
drink, either. It was a congenial place to sit and talk. But it
was obvious, too, that it was a lonely room, where an unmarried woman spent too many hours reading to herself.

I had called Candace the morning after the party.
Overnight, my unhappiness had congealed into something
hard and dry. I wasn't hurt, I told myself; I was curious. Now
that I knew a little bit, I wanted to know the rest. That would
be my revenge, I had decided, that I would learn everything I
could about them. Candace must have understood the intensity in my voice, because she invited me to come over that
morning for Sunday brunch. It reassured me, I will admit,
that she *was* at home. When I had departed Galvin's fairyland
the night before, I had wondered if Candace would ever
leave. But here she was.

She came to the door dressed in white shorts and a yellow
Lacoste shirt with one of those little crocodiles over the left
breast. She was flushed; she had been in the garden, planting
her fall annuals. She suggested we take some coffee out back

and enjoy the morning sun before it got too hot. The garden displayed her sense of style and precision. The newly planted flowers formed a dazzling border, their tiny petals as bright as tropical fish.

"That was quite a party last night," I said. "I hadn't realized that you knew Galvin."

"Nobody knew. I gather we made quite a spectacle of ourselves."

I nodded. The September sun cast a delicate light on her face. There was something about it that reminded me of one of Renoir's models—a freshness as if she had just stepped out of the bath. Perhaps that was why Galvin had staged his *"bal au Moulin"*—because he too saw her as one of the women in the painting.

"Tell me about you and Galvin. I concede it's none of my business, but so what? That makes it more interesting. If it were my business, I'd already know it. But I don't, so tell me the story."

She looked at me, debating whether to answer. She wanted to talk about him, you could see that. She had unlocked something the night before, and now she wanted to let it run free. But it was a dangerous topic, too, in ways I could not then imagine.

"We're talking ancient history here," she said. "Does it still matter?"

Oh yes, I assured her. It mattered.

"We were friends in college, but it ended badly, and we sort of lost track of each other. When he arrived in Washington a few months ago, he asked me out, but I said no. Too much voltage still in the wire for it to be easy. But then everything got complicated. When people realized that he was trying to buy the newspaper, I decided not to tell anyone that we had been friends once. It felt awkward. Then he invited me to his party, and he asked me to dance, and there we were. And now everybody knows, or imagines, that we were lovers. Why do you want to hear about us, anyway? Is this healthy?"

"No. It's sick. But indulge me. Either that, or you have to remain my fetish object forever."

"How to tell you. . . ." She folded her hands and rested them against her lips. The words came eventually, like a flow of water through an old pipe.

CANDACE HAD ARRIVED AT Radcliffe in the fall of 1970. The world was coming apart that year; that was the first thing you had to understand, she said. It wasn't like today. The kettle was boiling over, and crazy things were happening. Boys from fancy prep schools were running around talking about revolution and learning to shoot guns. They would take drugs and make up lyrics like "I'm dreaming of a white riot" to the tune of "White Christmas." At the freshman mixers, under the stern portrait of A. Lawrence Lowell, people danced to "Street Fighting Man." Nobody knew what was serious and what was a put-on. The smell of sex was in the air—messy and lubricious and wonderful.

She met Galvin one afternoon in the Yard, after class. It was a beautiful fall day. He was throwing a Frisbee. Candace was sitting on a bench in the sun, trying to read Max Weber. The Frisbee game ended, and he strode over and sat down next to her. She was ready to be interrupted. When he struck up a conversation—easy and unforced, a relaxed smile on his face—it didn't seem like a pickup. He was two years older, a junior already. He called that night and asked her for a date. She should have been wary—upperclassmen were always hitting on Radcliffe freshmen, getting their names from a directory the boys called the "pig book." But she wasn't frightened of him. He had a gentle, playful manner, and a self-confidence that made him seem more like a man than a boy.

A few days later, they went to a lecture by Norman Mailer. A classic Harvard date. *The Armies of the Night* had recently been published, and Mailer was a god. But he showed up howling drunk. It was sad: He was sputtering and shouting at everybody. Candace tried to ask him a question about reportorial objectivity and subjectivity—she was so serious; she already knew she wanted to be a reporter. He took offense and started calling her "bitch" and "cunt," but she mustered her courage and shouted back—saying that he was a pig and not a real journalist at all. People started booing him after that. It was an incredible scene. Galvin couldn't stop smiling. He thought she was so cool—a freshman Cliffie, telling off Norman Mailer.

Afterward he took her to a seedy Irish bar, and they talked for a long time. She was still feeling the rush of getting into a shouting match with America's most famous writer. Everything she said came out right, and he was laughing, introducing her to his friends, calling out to the waiter for more beer. He was handsome and smart—an impossibility; those two never went together. He walked her back to Cabot Hall and they made out on the bed in her room. He didn't push it, the way a boy would have done. He waited for her to open to him—for her breasts to brush against his chest, her body to arch toward his. They didn't "go all the way" that first night— she might have let him, but he didn't push that, either.

They made love a week later. She told him to be gentle, because she was almost a virgin. He laughed and asked what that could possibly mean, and she explained that she had done it once, at the end of the summer with her high school boyfriend. He had been bugging her to put out for nearly a year, and she had finally given in, but it was a mess. He had come after about ten seconds, and he'd been so embarrassed afterward, he could hardly talk. So in her mind, that didn't really count. But Galvin knew what he was doing, and she re- membered every moment—the feel of him, the lightness in her head, the weakness in her knees. The tenderness after- ward.

This is what love is like, she told herself.

He asked her to call him Sandy, and explained that he was named after the poet Carl Sandburg. He described his father as a union official, but didn't say too much else about him. In fact, he seemed a little embarrassed that he was from Pitts- burgh. All he said at first was that he was from "western Pennsylvania." How could he have known that it was a happy escape for her to spend time with someone who wasn't from her world of privilege?

He wanted to know all about her father. Dwight Ridgway was modestly infamous on campus, as a former Pentagon of- ficial. The preppy leftists were calling him a war criminal, but Galvin wanted to know the real story. Perhaps he was mea- suring himself, sizing up the competition. Candace tried to explain what he had been like, before the war took its toll. It wasn't easy; how do you describe the man who seems, in your memory, to have held up the sky? She was his only child, so he had channeled all of his aspirations into this one life. He wanted her to be beautiful and brave; forthright and cunning. He encouraged her to take risks, and was there to catch her if she fell. It was no accident, she said, that a child's first word was usually "Dada," rather than "Mama"—for fathers were the playful ones who encouraged you to try new things. But they were also the ones who went away.

In the last few years, her father had been ailing. It wasn't discussed much at home, but Candace knew that something was wrong. He was tired; he was drinking too much; his spirit had been damaged in some way that she didn't understand. He had gone off to a hospital the previous spring, for a long stretch that her mother never explained. There had been tears in his eyes in September, when he put her on the plane for college. She had never seen him cry before.

That fall at Harvard was like a house party that stretched on for months. Nobody did much work, the campus was still too crazy. Candace and her new boyfriend went with the turbid flow: They had sex all day and night, and they took drugs. A few years later, people became a tad more cautious. They just took normal drugs, like speed and cocaine. But in 1970, a young couple could still explore the whole medicine cabinet—pot, acid, mescaline, peyote. Candace tried mescaline with Galvin—she was the sort of person who had to try everything—and she wasn't embarrassed, years later, to admit that she had loved it.

They would ingest the icky-tasting tablets in Galvin's room in Adams House. In the beginning when it was intense, they would lie in bed listening to music and watching the wallpaper melt. Sandy might put a cool washcloth on her forehead, or just blow on her cheek. Little things felt like big things; it was as if the bandwidth of every nerve had been expanded, so it could carry more starbursts of information. They would make love sometimes—very weird, very intense; hallucinating while someone was inside you. Then they would walk down to the river, their eyes popping out of their heads—everyone must have known they were high—and lie down by the riverbank and watch the clouds turn into animals. That was how she knew she loved him, because she could lie there stoned—oozing and crackling—and still feel completely safe, because he was next to her.

That was what made Sandy Galvin different. The world around him was getting strange, full of holes, but he somehow stayed as hard as a concrete block. Even his hair was still short, the way it had been in high school. People thought he must be in the business school, he looked so straight. He kept playing sports, too—intramural boxing, lacrosse, and football until his sophomore year, when he broke his ankle. He was the only attractive man Candace knew who kept his head. The reason he took drugs, she suspected, was that he didn't want to disconnect totally. It was so crazy back then. If you weren't a little crazy yourself, you weren't really there.

One weekend, they took a camping trip to the White Mountains. It was mid-October—almost Halloween. The leaves had turned, painting the New Hampshire hillsides scarlet and saffron, and it was getting chilly. They climbed for two or three hours to a high lake—ice blue, surrounded by tall fir trees that ringed the water. Sandy made a fire, and they put out sleeping bags and grilled some fish he had caught in the lake. They were so tired from hiking that they fell asleep after dinner and didn't make love, but they awoke in the middle of the night. The fire had died down to embers, and the stars were so big and bright they seemed to be just beyond arm's reach, and they made love then. Nothing ever felt so good. Sex and love, and a boundless sky. They fell asleep together in the same sleeping bag, their arms around each other—packed in so tight they couldn't move.

When they awoke the next morning, Galvin asked her to marry him. She was shivering as he proposed. The temperature had dropped overnight. There was frost on the ground. He didn't understand why she was crying.

Candace's eyes filled with tears all over again as she recalled this part of the story. That crystalline fall morning had been the beginning of the bad times. She had pulled back as soon as he said it. It was crazy even to think about getting married. She was a college freshman; she had a father who was veering erratically toward mental illness; she had a boyfriend who worshipped her like the sun and the moon. It was too much. Her circuits were overloaded, and they began to shut down, for self-preservation. Sandy didn't press her, but he never fully understood what had gone wrong that morning by the lake.

All that winter, she played the bluesy Joni Mitchell song "Urge for Going" on her stereo in Cabot Hall. It was about the anticipation of loss, the early frost that devours what's left of summer and makes us ready to depart even as we hold on. She would sing along quietly, and Galvin would put his big arms around her and give her a hug. He didn't understand, and she couldn't tell him.

IT TOOK ANOTHER YEAR for the affair to end—it wasn't until after her father was dead that they finally stopped seeing each other. I asked what had caused the final break, but Candace didn't want to talk about it. Her eyes were red; she was exhausted. It had been hard enough to put herself back in Harvard Yard that freshman year, in the arms of the man she'd loved. She didn't want to remember how it had felt when they parted. She went into her house, to be alone. How odd she had looked, I thought, when she was crying. Her lip had trembled, and all the muscles in her face seemed to go slack. The control had disappeared, but only for an instant.

She came back outside after a few minutes, apologizing. She had put herself back together—put the cap back on so quickly. I was sad to see it, for she had been quite lovely in those minutes when she had been lost in time, but I understood. She was sorry to have gotten so emotional—she *never* did that. She didn't want me to get the wrong idea. She was still the Mistress of Fact. We talked awhile about the President's troubles. She had a theory about his being the son of an alcoholic and needing to do bizarre things to get people to love him, but everyone was psychoanalyzing the President that week. It had become the national pastime, bigger even than baseball.

We ate some bagels and drank some more coffee. I told her I would be coming to work at the *Sun*—Galvin had de-

cided to fire the Lifestyle editor and had offered me the job—
and she seemed genuinely pleased.

"We'll be together!" she said. That made me feel something close to happiness—the thought that I could slink over
when I was in a particularly foul mood, gaze upon her un-
reachably beautiful body and goad her into saying something
outrageous.

She wanted me to leave, but I still had to ask the question.
That was why I had come, really, and it would have been unlike me to leave without trying to get an answer. I was at the
door before the words finally formed on my lips.

"Are you still in love with him?" I asked.

She was startled. Her head bridled back for an instant. I
knew by the look on her face that she hadn't wanted to ask
herself the question, much less answer it. "I don't know," she
said.

TWELVE

THE DAY THE DEAL CLOSED, GALVIN MOVED INTO MR. Hazen's old office. It was on the top floor of the building, with a view across Foggy Bottom to the Potomac River. When I answered his summons that morning, he was standing at the window, gazing at the line of rooftops abutting the hazy blue-gray sky. "Why is this city so flat?" he wanted to know. "It looks like someone took a knife and just cut it off. It's unreal." I explained about the height limit, which decreed that no building could be taller than the Capitol. But he was right, it did look unreal.

The plaque outside his door said SANDY GALVIN. He asked me to call him that, from now on. It seemed like a soft name for such a hard man, but he said he wanted everyone to address him that way. He was a newspaper publisher now; he could finally claim the legacy of his namesake, Mr. Sandburg. I suspected this was Candace's doing. She must have thought it would make him seem less forbidding.

The new publisher didn't waste any time. He called a senior staff meeting that first morning so that he could plot strategy with the vice presidents. Howard Bacon showed up, representing the news side; he looked better than at the party, but not much. A heavyset man strode in cracking jokes; he turned out to be the VP for advertising, Frank Moran. Also shuffling into the room were the heads of circulation, marketing, community relations and accounting. They were deferential to me, thinking I must be the big guy's hatchet man. I think they all feared they were about to be fired.

Galvin assembled them on the couches and asked each to give a five-minute report on his department. He had spent the past few days studying all the available numbers—on circulation, ad revenues, newsprint costs, labor costs and projected profitability for the rest of the year. From the questions he asked, he already seemed to know nearly as much about the paper's financial performance as his subordinates. When the vice presidents had finished, Galvin shook his head and said, "This isn't good enough." He told each of them to send him a memo by the next Monday with five good ideas for making the paper more profitable. Anyone who couldn't think of five good ideas should resign.

I had expected Galvin to go slow during his first few weeks as publisher. That would have been the prudent thing to do, especially for a new arrival who couldn't be sure where the rocks and shoals were hidden. But I had misjudged the man once again. He was like a light switch—either on or off; he didn't have a middle point. The newspaper instantly became his life—he seemed to have no family, no other job, to have never experienced the joys and miseries of running a big enterprise like this—and he was relentless in proposing new ideas, strategies and gimmicks. He embraced the institution and began to shake its foundations, just as he had promised. He seemed convinced that without such shock therapy, it would never change.

He arrived each morning at seven-thirty—the first person in the building, usually, except for the janitors and the security guards—and spent the first hour just reading the paper. He would circle articles with a yellow pen and fire off notes to people. "Loved your cops story!" "I've read that Bosnia story before!" "Why don't we cover stock-car racing?" He gathered the senior staff each morning at nine-thirty to brainstorm, and it turned out they did have a few good ideas—all except Moran, the adman, who was wise enough to understand that it was time to pack it in. Galvin called in consultants too, and asked them to review the paper's recent performance. And he began wandering around the building, dropping in on reporters, press operators, the nice old ladies who took classified ads on the telephone. The first question he asked was always the same: "How can we sell more newspapers?" He stayed late into the evening, talking to the copy editors and the night-side news aides and the pressmen—waiting most nights until the presses began rolling. Newspapers are easy to love, and it was obvious that Galvin was smitten.

He began to make changes, too—ones that people could see. The first thing to go was the family shrine in the lobby. The day after he arrived in the building, workmen began removing the statues and portraits of the various Hazens and Crosbys who had guided the paper for the past ninety years. He supervised the job in person—with his tie off, the sleeves of his white shirt rolled up to his biceps—while the laborers hauled the tons of historic debris outside to a big truck. The families grumbled, but they didn't want the memorabilia either, so it was sent to a warehouse in Waldorf, Maryland, pending further instructions.

Galvin then began tearing down the walls, quite literally. He wanted to open up the newspaper's lobby and turn it into a sidewalk café. That seemed to me, at first blush, a completely ridiculous idea, but he was insistent. "Let's invite the world in!" he admonished me. "It's time for our people to stop hiding behind their desks and live a little." So the contractors blew a hole in the glass-and-steel facade big enough to create a new open-air atrium, three stories high. Out front, Galvin decreed there would be a huge awning, as colorful as a circus tent, beckoning the public to come join us. He had the construction crew working day and night and spent much of the time with them, badgering and kibitzing.

When the heavy construction was finally done, Galvin gave the workers a giant banner and told them to drape it across the new atrium. The banner had been a secret project—he hadn't even told me about it. It proclaimed in huge letters the *Sun*'s new slogan: GET REAL! That was the message. He would snarl it to editors who brought him stories that were too long or too boring. He would use it to push the production department to print more papers with the late baseball scores. He loved his slogan and repeated it continually. He even ordered fifty thousand buttons bearing the new credo. He wore one everywhere he went and was disappointed, though not surprised, when the staff failed to wear them too.

I SAW THEM TALKING in the cafeteria. They were sitting over by the window, in a corner. Maybe Galvin thought nobody would notice them there. They were eating salads off plastic trays. He was in his shirtsleeves; his upper body looked huge, and I thought to myself that he must have those shirts made specially for him, so they didn't pull. Candace caught my eye and motioned for me to come to their table. I think she realized that everyone was watching them. She had a guilty look on her face, as if she'd been caught shoplifting.

"What's happening?" I asked.

"Candace wants more money for foreign news," he answered peevishly. "She's being a pain in the ass. I told her we won't sell a single extra paper in Falls Church because of our coverage of the Indonesian debt crisis, but she won't let it go."

"What are you going to do?" I asked him. She was sitting there pertly, mouthing the word *money* over and over.

"Give it to her," answered Galvin with genial resignation. He liked having his pocket picked, at least by her.

"Do you understand him?" I asked when he had left the table.

"I think so. He has a short attention span. He's easily influenced by the last person he talks to, so I try to make sure it's me."

"He's in love with you," I said.

"No, he isn't. What makes you think so?" That was her one blind spot, I thought at the time. She didn't understand the effect she had on men. It was a common failing of beautiful women. They were so conscious of themselves, they found it difficult to see how the world appeared to someone else.

"It's the way he looks at you. You're his prize. I sometimes think you're the reason he bought the paper."

She looked at me like I was the biggest idiot in town. "You're nuts," she said. "Nobody makes Sandy do anything."

SANDY GALVIN HELD HIS first meeting with the newsroom staff a few weeks after he took over. He was uncharacteristically nervous beforehand—asking me what he should wear and whether he should tell an opening joke. I told him to look serious and *be* serious—this was the staff's first real chance to see their new publisher and hear what he really wanted. They were scared. Newspaper people liked to pretend they were open-minded, but when it came to their own affairs, they were intensely conservative. They hated change. So the fewer gimmicks, the better.

The staff gathered in the new atrium. It was a cool October morning; the wind was gusty, and fallen leaves occasionally swirled up from the billowy piles along the sidewalk and into the lobby. Galvin had decreed that, just this once, the lobby would be closed to outsiders so that we could hold our family meeting in private. Folding chairs had been arranged in a great semicircle around the podium, but as usually happens at such events, there was a crush of people sitting at the back, while the first few rows were empty. Galvin grabbed the microphone and announced that he would personally pay fifty dollars to the first person who sat in the front row. There was an immediate surge of people to the front, and

Galvin handed the winner a crisp new bill. That took care of the seating problem.

A little after ten-thirty, Galvin began his speech. He was dressed in a simple blue suit, immaculately tailored, as always, but not flashy. He looked a little anxious, I thought, but that was probably good—it made him seem more "real." I was standing behind the podium with the other assistant managing editors—my new colleagues! Candace Ridgway was next to me. "He looks like he's auditioning for the part," I whispered. She nodded, and I could see that she was worried too. He had never run a newspaper. These were her people; she wanted to protect him from their oceanic ill will, but she couldn't.

"Good morning," said Galvin. A few dozen voices reflexively answered back, "Good morning!"—as if it were a mass reeducation camp. He looked out at the stone wall of faces. "Are we having fun yet?" he asked teasingly. Nobody answered, until finally someone in the back shouted out, "No!"

"Well, lighten up, for God's sake!" He looked back in my direction and winked. He'd promised, weeks before, to deliver that line at his first staff meeting, but I'd assumed he was joking. He turned back to his wary staff. "This business should be fun. Otherwise, what's the point? We don't pay most of you enough to put up with being miserable." I looked out at the audience. The few people who had any visible reaction were rolling their eyes. They instinctively mistrusted him. Galvin didn't care; he suspected already that most journalists were fools.

"You don't know me," Galvin continued, "and I'm sure many of you are worried that I'm going to rock the boat. So as we begin our life together, I want to reassure you on that score: You're absolutely right! I *am* going to rock the boat. Because I'm convinced that without a little rocking, the boat is going to sink."

"Welcome aboard the *Titanic*!" croaked a wiseass in the back.

"Whoever said that, gets a raise," said Galvin, beaming. "Because this *is* the *Titanic*! That's my message to you: We're in *trouble*. Forget about business as usual. The newspaper you love—which pays your salaries and provides medical care for your kids—is mortally wounded, and without help it may die. How do I know that? That's what you're thinking, isn't it? This man isn't a journalist. What does *he* know? And you're right, I'm just a businessman. This newspaper's distinguished past has absolutely no relevance for me—all I care about is the future."

"How's he doing?" I asked Candace. She knew the crowd.

"If he wants to scare them, he's doing a good job," she whispered. "They look terrified."

"All I can do is look at the numbers," Galvin went on, "and here's what I see: The *Sun*'s circulation has fallen every year for the past eight years. The declines haven't been huge—a few thousand fewer people reading the paper each year—but they add up. What's really scary is when you compare our losses in circulation with the growth of this region. Total population in the Washington area has increased fifty-eight percent in the past ten years. Yet over those same ten years, the *Sun*'s circulation has actually *declined* by about twelve percent. Did everybody get that? Population up fifty-eight percent; circulation down twelve percent.

"Now, what would you say about a business like that—that was selling fewer of its products each year, even though the market was growing by leaps and bounds?" There was silence in the great atrium. The loudest sound was the GET REAL! banner snapping in the breeze. "Come on, all you smart journalists. What would you say about a business like that? I want an answer."

"It's in trouble," said the man in the first row who had won the fifty dollars. He must have felt he owed Galvin something.

"It's *dying!*" shouted the new publisher. "Not a quick death, but a slow one—which is a horrible way to go. And I promise you, if the *Sun* continues on its current path, in ten years it *will* be dead. People will get their news other ways—from television, from the Internet, from radio, there are lots of possibilities. But they won't keep buying a newspaper that is so stuck in its ways that it doesn't even realize it's bleeding to death. No, sir. They won't buy a newspaper that bores them, just because it's *distinguished*. Sorry, but life's too short."

"Jesus!" whispered Candace. "Where's this headed? Mass suicide?" But I knew that Galvin was playing with them.

"How long do you think advertisers will put up with this situation?" he queried the group. "I've been talking to a lot of them the past few weeks, so I know the answer. Not very goddamn long! They will continue to advertise in the *Sun* as long as we are the best way to reach people who buy groceries and automobiles and furniture. The magic number is fifty percent. They will continue to advertise in the *Sun* as long as we reach at least half the households in this area.

"But do you know what our actual circulation penetration was last quarter? Do any of you museum-keepers want to hazard a guess? It was forty-seven percent, and falling. We are *dying,* I'm telling you. The advertisers all liked the Hazens and the Crosbys, and they'll like me too. They think we publish a fine newspaper. But as a way to sell things, it's a dinosaur. It's heading for extinction."

Galvin paused and surveyed the room. The audience looked shell-shocked. Harold Hazen had never made a speech like this in his life. He didn't believe in talking about business in front of the editorial staff; it was undignified. Galvin reveled in it. Business was life—the raw human energy that made the serious, abstract stuff bearable. But he could see that they were dazed, nearing the point where they would stop listening.

"Have you heard enough bad news yet?" he asked. This time there were cries from the multitude. "Stop!" "Enough, already!" Even Candace and the other AMEs were shouting.

He took a step back from the podium. That sly half smile was on his face for the first time that morning. *Let us conspire together,* it said. Most of his new colleagues had never seen it before, but I knew what was coming. The gravitational force field of his charm had been deployed; he was going to draw them all in.

"So, what's the *good* news?" He paused as if he was waiting for someone, anyone who liked, to answer the question and offer an alternative vision of where the paper should go. But there was only silence.

"The good news is that we can change. And we are *going* to change. We're going to move from being losers to winners, and we're going to do it in a way the world can measure—by gaining back the circulation we've been losing these past ten years. We are going to defy the conventional wisdom of the newspaper industry, and *grow*.

"I am so confident we can succeed that I am making a bet. It's a pretty damn big bet too—I just invested a billion dollars in this newspaper. And the bet is that the *Sun* will increase its circulation by two hundred thousand over the next two years. That would put us over a million daily—and back over fifty-percent penetration. Gains like that are unheard of in the newspaper industry—they would make us the most successful paper in America. But I think the *Sun* can do it. Now, is anybody prepared to join me?"

The room was quiet. They were stunned, I think, by the boldness of what he was proposing. Noble failure had become part of the culture of the newspaper business. The idea of flamboyant success was foreign to most of these people. Galvin looked around and shook his head. How were they going to climb the mountain if they sat on their hands?

"Okay," he said. "To make it easier for you, I'm going to sweeten the bet. I am prepared to set aside a portion of my stock to share with all of you—the newspaper's employees. That stock is now trading at fifty-two dollars a share. If we can achieve my goal, the value of that stock will double or triple. As co-owners, we'll all make money. If our bet fails, we all lose. What do you think of that?"

There was some applause, finally. The prospect of making money will do that, even for a roomful of journalists. I couldn't help smiling. It was like being conned by an expert.

He took questions after that. An older man who identified himself as the Newspaper Guild shop steward jumped up immediately. He didn't have a question so much as a rebuttal: Galvin's stock-ownership plan was just a cover to allow him to cut wages and benefits. The Guild would fight to protect employees from the machinations of the new boss. Galvin had a disarming answer. He'd love to cut labor costs, he said—they were too high, in his opinion—but he couldn't. They were covered by long-term collective bargaining agreements. As for the stock, any employee who didn't want it was free to say no. Another questioner wanted details. How would Galvin raise circulation by 200,000? What could possibly lure so many new readers to the paper?

"Fun!" answered Galvin. "Surprise. Passion. And a bingo game!" That was the first public hint of Galvin's love affair with contests. It turned out he'd had his consultants do a study of circulation gains by the major British papers in the 1990s, and a big factor had turned out to be contests—lotto, bingo, poker, football and basketball pools, crossword puzzles—all paying cash prizes to the winners. People loved them, and the *Sun* would have the best in the world.

Finally, one of the older reporters asked what I took to be the essential question. "This is all very interesting," he said. "But what if we don't want to do it your way? What if we don't trust you, and we think you're going to wreck the newspaper? What should we do then?"

There was no politic way to answer that one, and Galvin didn't try. "You should look for another job," he said.

AFTERWARD GALVIN WANTED TO know how he'd done. It was endearing, this new self-consciousness. I told him he'd done fine, but that he had set himself an impossible goal. He could not possibly add 200,000 new subscribers to the paper in two years. There might be 200,000 extra households out there, but they were all busy watching television; he was setting himself up to fail. He seemed surprisingly unfazed. Two years was a lifetime away to him. If his bet was a loser, he would figure something out later. The issue was now.

"What did Candace think of my speech?" he asked.

"How should I know? Why don't you ask her yourself?" I was tired of being an intermediary. If they could dance together, they could talk to each other too.

"She won't answer. She says I'm her boss now, and it's not appropriate. What kind of nonsense is that? If the publisher can't talk to the foreign editor, what's the point of owning a newspaper?"

I told him not to worry. "Nobody wants you to succeed more than Candace does. If she's being careful, that's why. She'll relax. We'll all relax. Even you."

I SAT AT MY desk in my new office and watched the people scurry past my door. There were so many of them. News aides, copy aides, reporters, secretaries, assignment editors, copy editors, art designers—and they all worked for me! It was absurd, on its face, that they were under the nominal supervision of a reclusive creature of anxiety—a man who did not open worrisome letters, did not return problematic phone calls. I stared at the shiny brown finish of my desk—it was like staring at a muddy river on a hot day. It was teak, polished each night by invisible workers who emptied the trash and stacked my magazines and newspapers in neat piles.

I took the letter opener that had thoughtfully been provided for me, and began to carve my initials into the soft
wood of the desk. The stain was so rich and deep that it took
some effort, but eventually it was visible: DC. My secretary
came in while I was finishing the C. She was a nice woman in
her mid-thirties; a working mother, two children at home.
"Need anything from the cafeteria?" she asked, ignoring my
act of vandalism. Her attitude seemed to be that the boss was
always right, even a bizarre boss like me. I could have lit a fire
in the trash can and she wouldn't have said a word.

I decided after a few days that I had to decorate the office;
mere desecration wasn't enough. I got a poster from a movie
store of *The Little Mermaid*, which in my view is one of the
two or three greatest movies ever made—definitely ahead of
Citizen Kane, but probably behind *Gone With the Wind*. That
was cheering, to be able to look up whenever I liked at Ariel's
sweet smile and cascading red hair, which never seemed to
get wet, even though she lived underwater. Other secret fans
of *The Little Mermaid* presented themselves—they were men,
mostly; the women around here disapproved of well-coiffed
mermaids who fell in love with princes.

And I held a morning staff meeting. It had become obvious the first week that holding a morning meeting was the
essential—and perhaps the only—requirement for being a
good manager. So I gathered my half-dozen various editors at
eleven o'clock each day and asked them to suggest ideas
that might actually make the next morning's paper worth
reading. In the beginning, they answered by reading lists—
what movies were opening the next weekend, what celebri-
ties were being thrust at us by the publicists, what awards,

banquets and other nuggets of social news were in the queue. No wonder the *Sun* was so dreadful, if this was how they did things. *Reveal,* even at its most ridiculous, had been more interesting than this.

The first few days, I just said no. No, no, no, no—until they began to bring me better ideas. I astounded my staff when I approved a story proposal on the five best and worst places to go parking with your date. (Best all-around spot: Potomac Overlook off the George Washington Parkway in Virginia; worst all-around spot: Westmoreland Park in Montgomery County—the cops shine their lights in the car and make you get out, even if you're naked.)

It was fun being a wiseass and saying whatever came into my head, and having the various subeditors laugh at my jokes. But after several weeks, I began to wonder if I had really found the right *niche* for someone with my sort of interests. Sandy Galvin's razzmatazz about circulation wars and billion-dollar bets was all fine, and I hoped it motivated everyone to produce a less boring newspaper, but it was irrelevant to me. I didn't care about money, and I certainly didn't care about being a news bureaucrat. That wasn't why I had signed on with Galvin.

My purposes were complex; make no mistake about that. But at the core, intellectually, was a desire to make people uncomfortable. Galvin had me exactly right. I was a born troublemaker, but it wasn't simple mischief that motivated me. Much as I might pretend otherwise, my antics were not simply those of a court jester. What motivated me was a *need*— as powerful as another person's need to paint or sing or seduce twenty-three-year-old interns.

My need was to tell the truth, especially when it made people squirm. I'd done it with my father, for as long as he was alive—needling him, pouncing on his mistakes, even publishing a homemade newspaper called *The Dirt on Dad.* In college, I had written a series of articles attacking the dean of the medical school for his consulting relationship with one of the drug companies. (He responded, reasonably enough, that he was helping them make better drugs, but so what?) Before I got fired from my first job at a newspaper in North Carolina, I had written an exposé of the owner of a local furniture store, a sometime Baptist preacher who ensnared customers with a trick he called "rent-to-buy."

There's an old saw about how journalists should afflict the comfortable and comfort the afflicted. Well, I don't know about the latter part—the afflicted should probably look elsewhere, but I definitely understood the first part. I simply could not resist the opportunity to fire off a spitball at my betters—especially in a target-rich environment like Washington, D.C., where pious nonsense is practically mandatory.

Religious fanatics are always telling us that we were put on this planet for a purpose. I doubt it, other than to be fertilizer for other less-complex life forms, but let's assume for the moment that it is so. In that case, I knew very well that my larger purpose was not to be Sandy Galvin's bag carrier, much less to be his assistant managing editor in charge of the Lifestyle section. Those were just means to an end, and the end was—forgive the sentimentality—*to tell the truth.* To be a permanent truth-telling affliction; to say the terrible, true things that most people never dared to speak. That was my vocation, and now, thanks to the man who was at once my patron and rival, it was within my reach.

I WROTE GALVIN A memo. That is what News Bureaucrats did; we wrote memos to other NBs outlining our plans, so that we could ask them at meetings, "Did you get my memo?" and they could answer, "Yes, and I've sent one to you, outlining my thoughts on yours." My memo to Galvin read as follows:

> Dear Publisher Sir:
>
> I would like to write a column for your newspaper. I have given it some thought and I would like this to be a weekly column, appearing in the Lifestyle section, which I will continue to edit in my haphazard but invigorating fashion. I have a name for my column. I want to call it "The Savant." The name has a certain insouciance, does it not? And it was copyrighted several years ago, by me, in anticipation of the day when it would finally appear. This column will be about whatever I like. My only promise is that it will make people squirm. You told the staff recently that you want the *Sun* to be surprising and fun. Well, here's your first chance to deliver.
>
> Your news slave,
> David Cantor

Galvin received my memo two days later through the interoffice mail, which seemed to be even slower than the U.S. Postal Service. He called me immediately. "What if I say no?" he asked.

"Then, good publisher sir, I will quit. I will follow the sensible advice you gave recently to employees—that those who cannot accommodate themselves to the big picture should take a walk. Which I will do."

"You can't leave," he said. But of course I could. That was the advantage of having no discernable real-world ambition. It made such threats credible. I had him, and he knew it. He promised I could start as soon as I liked—and he even increased my salary, which was already at the ridiculous level of $112,000, to the even more ridiculous level of $135,000. There was a lesson in that—obvious, but worth remembering. When they know they can't own you, they're willing to pay considerably more in rent. I told him the first column would appear in several weeks, when I had found something worth being really snide about.

GALVIN CONTINUED TO DISPATCH workmen to the new lobby. They hung more banners and pennants, and big posters of Mark Trail and Dogbert and other characters from the *Sun's* comic pages. The place looked increasingly like a set for a Chinese opera. But none of us realized, until Galvin installed the cameras, that it actually *was* the set for a new television show.

He had made a deal with one of the cable giants to distribute a daily news feed, which he planned to call *The Anti-News*. He had always loved the way the *Today* show opened its set onto the streets of New York—drawing the life and energy of the city into its broadcasts. Now he wanted to do the same thing with the nation's capital. Washington was a carnival—especially now, in the era of permanent scandal.

Why pretend any longer? Galvin wanted to have jugglers and fortune-tellers wandering the lobby, rubbing shoulders with the deputy secretary of state and the chairman of the Federal Reserve and whoever else was visiting the paper that day. He wanted to ban the stuffy boardroom lunches that had been a feature of the *Sun* for generations and replace them with free-form discussion in the open-air café—with reporters, editors and the Aunt Minnies who had wandered in off the street all joining in questioning the newsmakers of the day. It was all part of his strange but well-considered strategy. He wanted to create instruments that would subvert the old newspaper that must die and help create the new one that could survive.

The cameras went up in the lobby with dizzying speed, and Galvin soon decreed that it was time to launch *The Anti-News*. No scripts, no rehearsals, precious little planning. His concept for *The Anti-News* was *Cops* meets Dan Rather. It was all going to be raw, live, unrehearsed. People were going to run onto the set screaming when they had a scoop, just the way they did in the newsroom. The reporters were going to wear their actual rumpled Dockers and sweat-stained shirts, and we were going to watch them do their jobs—squeeze sources, ferret out wrongdoing, rejoice in life's small daily triumphs of good over evil.

The whole point, Galvin said, was that we were going to let people see how the news business really worked. People hated the journalists they usually saw on television—asking obnoxious questions, pouting at press conferences, puffing themselves up to look more important than the people they were interviewing. But real reporters weren't like that, at least not all the time, and Galvin was convinced that if people saw the real thing, they would like it.

To anchor the show, Galvin chose a beautiful business reporter in her twenties who had caught his eye in the cafeteria. Her name was Angelica, and everyone in the building instantly assumed that Galvin must be banging her, but it wasn't that. She had *spark;* she didn't want to be a worthy bore, she wanted to be noticed. Her colleagues, especially the women, frowned at her short skirts and tight blouses and hair that always looked as if she had just tumbled out of bed. They thought she was unserious, but they had it backward. What could possibly be more serious than raw sexual energy?

The first morning, Galvin sat with Angelica in the booth and acted as cohost. I think he wanted to establish the mood himself, because he didn't trust anyone else (other than the beautiful, wide-eyed Angelica) to get it right. He was wearing a cashmere blazer and an open-neck Armani shirt—all in all, a pretty cool newspaper publisher. He *was* the show, in a sense. He had already decided that he would make his own personality part of the pitch—sort of a hip version of Frank Perdue, the tough man who makes a tender chicken, or that razor guy who liked the shaver so much, he bought the company.

"Folks, what does a newspaper *do?*" he asked in the opening segment. "I just bought this one, and over the next weeks and months, you and I are going to find out." It was disarming. You had the sense, watching him, that he was inviting viewers to observe something real happening, in real time. Ordinary people would be able to watch him grapple with a great journalistic institution and the oversize egos who passed through its doors—and see how he did. He was publisher, pot washer and pitchman. He even did some of the ads himself—holding up the logo for Koons Ford and saying he could vouch for them because he'd bought his own car there. I knew it was a lie—he'd leased a big Lexus from somewhere else—but it was still good television, at once supermodern and old-fashioned kitsch.

Galvin joined in the interviews too—over the inevitable protest of his editor, Howard Bacon, who thought it was inappropriate for the publisher to blur the lines of pitchman and journalist (showing how little Bacon understood, since that blurring was the whole *point,* as far as Galvin was concerned). The first interview of the morning was with the President's lawyer, who also happened to be a social friend of Galvin's. Instead of the usual cat-and-mouse about the President's legal problems, Galvin opened by telling the lawyer that he looked tired, which was certainly true, and asking if he was getting enough sleep. "What do you want out of life?" Galvin asked him at one point, and it produced a few moments of sublime television, in which the lawyer—who probably hadn't been asked that question in years—tried to answer honestly.

I had meant to watch only a few minutes, but I frankly couldn't stop. Galvin and Angelica were mesmerizing. Another of the guests was a rock star who was visiting town for a concert. Instead of the usual crap about the tour and his latest album, Angelica demanded that he sing her favorite song—right there, a cappella—and she was such a babe that he agreed, whereupon *she* stood up and started boogying on the set—I thought for a minute she was going to take her clothes off. It had that feeling. It was live, real, out of control. Galvin walked off the set at the end, shaking his head, amazed at himself. He was rolling now, and the real pleasure of it for him, I now suspect, was that even he didn't know for sure where he was heading.

THIRTEEN

SUMMER SEEMED TO LAST FOREVER THAT YEAR. THE DAYS were long and dry, and the only painful result was that the city was overrun with bees—the tough little ones with yellow stripes on their backs. And they were *angry*, presumably because they didn't have enough to eat. I paid a personal price on my way to work one morning. I was walking innocently enough, carrying my breakfast in one hand—a can of Coca-Cola—and shooing away the bees. I stopped to take a drink and felt something crunchy and fuzzy go down with that delicious elixir of Coca-Cola and—*gak!*—it was a bee. He stung the inside of my lip, which swelled up to blubber-lip size by the time I got to work.

Howard Bacon came by my office that morning, soon after I arrived. He had just left Galvin's meeting of the vice presidents, and he was visibly upset. He was a light-skinned man, with the fine blond hair that newborn babies have, and blond eyebrows that were barely visible on his forehead. And when he was angry, as now, his cheeks turned a bright, blotchy pink. I had my own throbbing facial problem at that moment, and I didn't really want to talk, but Bacon was insistent.

"Your friend Galvin is driving me crazy," he said. "I don't understand most of his ideas, and the rest are just flat-out wrong." He looked at me curiously. "What's wrong with your lip?"

"Bee 'ting," I said. My lower lip was so swollen I wasn't speaking very well. Bacon went on, oblivious.

"Galvin kept asking this morning where the good news was. How am I supposed to answer that? Is it my fault the President's in trouble, or the stock market is in a slump, or a plane crashed in Canada? What does he want—for us to *make up* good news?"

"Pwobabwy not. You can't wule that out, but I doubt he wants us to fabwicate the news. Not yet, anyway."

"Seriously, Cantor, you know him. What is he doing? Does he want me to quit? Okay, fine. He can ask for my resignation, and I'll be gone the next day. I have better things to do than stick around here and ruin my reputation."

I shook my head. "He just wants the newspapew to be mo' intewesting. He tink it turn off weader. He want more wivewy 'towie."

"Animal stories," Bacon muttered. "Last week we had three animal stories on the front page. The runaway zebra at the zoo. The horse in Manassas that can count to ten. And that one about all the dead fish—that wasn't an animal story, really, but Jesus Christ! I didn't get into the business to do this. What does he *want* from me?"

He was ranting. People from the Lifestyle section were

looking through the glass partition to see what all the ruckus was about. I could imagine all the electronic messages that were zapping through computer terminals around the newsroom. "Bacon is losing it. He's in Cantor's office, screaming, *right now!*"

"Take a wacation," I said. "Shumpwace wainy, wiffout so many bee." I meant it. He looked so stressed out, I was afraid he was going to pop, right there in my office.

"You know the latest? He wants to run editorials on the front page—so readers can see that the paper has a heart. He just told us in the staff meeting. 'The newspaper with a heart'! What horseshit! He wants to turn the *Sun* into a fucking tabloid."

The swelling was going down. I could feel my lip again and, with effort, I could avoid sounding like Elmer Fudd. "Tabloids are gaining readers," I said, "and we're losing. That's what Galvin sees. It's not personal. He's a businessman. He just looks at numbers."

Bacon wasn't listening. "The staff isn't going to put up with it! They're in revolt already. They don't want to work for a paper that runs TV ads touting its weather map. That isn't what they got into the business for."

"Weather is important," I said. I was getting tired of his rant. He was my boss, but my lip still hurt and I wanted him out of my office. "People care about the weather."

"Of *course* they care about the weather. I know that. I was the one who spent the money to get a decent weather map in the first place. But that's all fluff. This is a great newspaper. It has fourteen bureaus around the world. It has distinguished columnists and critics. People should love us for *that*. Not for all this shit that Galvin is pumping in. 'The newspaper with a heart.' Jesus fucking Christ!"

A crowd was gathering outside. I told Bacon he should probably talk more quietly, or leave. He rose to go.

"Does he listen to you?" he asked.

"No, not really. Not about important things. He knows what he wants. He doesn't care what most people think."

"Does he listen to anybody?"

"You. I think he would listen to one person, and that's Candace Ridgway. They went out in college—you probably know the story. But she won't talk to him."

"Why not?" asked Bacon.

"I'm not sure. It's a strange relationship. He's the boss, and she's uncomfortable about that, but it's more complicated. I think she's afraid to get too close."

"Well, maybe she should start talking to him. Now. Somebody needs to communicate with him, or this place is going to explode."

I told him I'd see what I could do, but if he really wanted to pass a message to Candace, he should just tell her himself. She worked for him, after all, and I was an unreliable messenger boy.

CANDACE RIDGWAY WAS TALKING on the telephone when I wandered by. Her office was cozier than mine. She always had fresh flowers that arrived on her desk from somewhere— I had once assumed they were sent by the aging wonder boy, Mr. Assistant Secretary, but lately I had begun to suspect otherwise. Propped on her couch was a stuffed animal—a lumpy teddy bear with half its ear missing, which Candace had kept with her ever since she was a girl. She'd boasted once that she had taken it into war zones, to presidential summits and now here it was, sitting in silent reproach as she played nanny to the foreign staff.

I had come to invite Candace to lunch. If I was going to be an errand boy, at least I would get a good meal out of it.

She was still on the phone, haranguing the White House press secretary about why the *Sun* was being charged for a hotel room in Paris during a presidential trip there the previous week, when our correspondent had stayed with his uncle. Those were the sort of issues that editors had to worry about. She kept making silly gestures as she talked, sticking her finger down her throat and holding her nose.

As she talked, I took a seat on the couch. Unlike my office, this one belonged to a real newspaper person. On one wall was a certificate from Columbia University announcing that she had won the Pulitzer Prize for foreign reporting, for a series of stories a few years back about foreign bribery. On a far wall was a collection of the press passes she had received from the various lunatic militias she had covered in Lebanon during the early 1980s—little slips of paper covered with Arabic scribble, each graced with her picture. She looked remarkably beautiful in these simple photos—her windblown hair tacked down with barrettes, her eyes shining back fearlessly at the camera; her face cool and serene in whatever bunker or basement cavern had served as a makeshift studio. Candace had a look of pure indifference, a certainty that nothing could diminish her beauty, a look that she had used to intimidate a thousand would-be suitors. It had been captured by these Lebanese thugs and stapled crudely to their laissez-passer.

The one incongruity in the room was the picture in the silver frame on her desk. It was of her father, Dwight Ridgway. The photograph had been taken just a few weeks before he gave up the last pretense of coping. It was a composed, patrician face—that was what made the hints of disorder so striking. The tie was knotted precisely against the button of his white shirt; the steel-gray hair was combed in that easy, automatic way of WASP men—perfectly in place. But there was a wild look in his eyes, the look of a man who had been to the abyss—seen the absolute worst about himself—and returned, inwardly disfigured. There were other marks of stress on that face too—the severe creases on either side of the mouth, the sharp lines drawn across the forehead, the deep circles under the eyes—signs of a sleeplessness so profound that no drug could trick him into unconsciousness. It was a face that made you wonder: What had gone so wrong with his patrician life that he was left like this, staring out hollow-eyed at his daughter?

When Candace finally put down the phone, she saw me studying the picture. I was lost in my own imagining of who he had been, what road he had traveled to get to that place. She looked pleased that I had noticed the portrait and been reminded of the vortex that had shaped her life. But she was uncomfortable too. This was a newspaper office; our vocation was the little truth, not the big truth.

"What brings you over here?" she asked. "You're supposed to be in Lifestyle, with the creative people. This is an idea-free zone."

"Bacon just went bonkers in my office. He thinks Galvin is wrecking the newspaper. He wants you to go talk with Sandy, get him to back off on some of his new ideas. Bacon thinks it will help."

"I *hate* this!" she said. "What should I do?" She found Bacon's assumption that she had special leverage over Galvin insulting, even if it was true.

"Have lunch with me. The rest is too complicated. We'll go to a fancy restaurant. I'll buy."

"Ouch!" she said. "I can't today. I promised my mother I would stop by to see her. But I'd *love* to run up your expense account another time."

"I'll come with you to your mother's house," I said rashly. "I've never seen what it looks like. Never met your mother. It would be part of my education. The Savant needs to know everything about Washington."

She was pleased that I wanted to visit her mom, just as she had been pleased to see me looking at the photograph of her father. But she wagged a cautionary finger. "It won't be very interesting. My mother is seventy-eight years old. She's not much of a conversationalist, especially with people she doesn't know." I said I didn't mind. Anything was better than talking to my new colleagues about the fall TV schedule.

BETTY RIDGWAY LIVED IN an old stone mansion in Georgetown, just west of Wisconsin Avenue and a few blocks from Candace's own house. The cobblestone street looked to be a hundred years old; the ancient streetcar tracks were still embedded amid the stones, making driving treacherous. The house itself was gray and forbidding, but as with so many of these Georgetown houses, it concealed a vast, bright garden that had been lovingly tended. Mrs. Ridgway was in her sitting room; a small fire had been laid by her maid. (Somehow, she had kept enough money through her widowhood to afford a maid, but that was the true secret of the WASP elite, wasn't it?—the preservation of capital.) She had her feet up on a stool and was reading an Agatha Christie novel. It was a scene that might have occurred just this way at any time over the last fifty years. That was another thing I envied about the WASP elite: their utter imperviousness to time and fashion.

Mrs. Ridgway reluctantly said hello to me. She had been looking forward to chatting with her daughter and had prepared a little cold plate for lunch—tiny lettuces and bits of meat that wouldn't be enough for a bunny.

"My goodness," she said. "You're certainly tall."

I lied and said I'd already had lunch, but she wouldn't hear of it. She sent the maid into the larder to come up with something manly to eat, which turned out to be a cold, half-devoured joint of roast beef that was graying at the edges and looked to be a week old. The maid served it up just like that, on a big plate, with a knife and fork and some ketchup.

We all picked at our food. Candace tried to stoke up a little conversation by explaining to her mother that before joining the *Sun*, I had been editor of *Reveal* magazine and one of Washington's social arbiters. Mrs. Ridgeway took a look at me and nodded severely. The notion that the stringy young man across from her had anything to do with society confirmed her worst fears. "Who *are* all these people I read about in *Reveal*?" she asked. "The Bernsteins and the Rubins and the Greens? Who are they?"

"They're Jews," I said. There was a long pause—very long—and I thought that I had blown it forever. But I saw Candace trying to suppress a chuckle, unsuccessfully, and suddenly she was laughing and so, incongruously, were Mrs. Ridgway and I. Hard to be sure who was the real anti-Semite in the group, but it didn't matter. It broke the ice.

We talked for a few minutes about parties and charity balls. Candace mentioned a survey we had done once called "Bang for the Buck"—about how much it cost to put on each of the big charity events, and how little was left over for the underlying good causes. Mrs. Ridgway remembered it—had loved it, in fact, for it had confirmed her conviction that the balls were a fraud conceived by nouveaux-riches social climbers to get their pictures in *Reveal* magazine. I admired her frankness. If I had still been at *Reveal,* I might have tried to hire her as social editor.

After a few more minutes of this, and a dessert of thin, tasteless cookies, Mrs. Ridgway excused herself and retired upstairs. Candace seemed to think I had been a great hit. Old ladies like to be teased. You get so much piety at that age, it must begin to feel suffocating. You're going to die soon anyway; why rush it?

I asked Candace to show me around the house. I wanted to understand how she had blossomed forth so full of life and color from this dry soil. She consented. I had breached the walls of the family fortress. The secrets of this prominent

Washington family, as celebrated in its time as any in Georgetown, were open to my examination.

She led me to the room in the back of the house that had
been her father's study. It was lined on three sides with dark
shelves of books, but the pallor was relieved by a large window that looked out onto the garden. The rays of sunlight
seemed to catch the particles of dust and suspend them mo-
tionless in the air. "Daddy's books are all still here," she said.
"We never touched them. Look around if you like."

I walked to the shelves. It was the rationalist's emporium;
a road map to the explainable world. The faith of a generation was lined up in neat rows. On the top shelf were the
philosophers of history—the Durants, Toynbee, Gibbon,
even Spengler—who told the story as a parable to instruct the
present. To a man like Mr. Ridgway, the message surely was
that the civilized world was like a trust fund; it could be
squandered by imprudent heirs. Below that shelf were the
memoirs of twentieth-century presidents and generals and
secretaries of state. So many lessons there; so much to live up
to. The collection seemed to stop at about 1965—he must
have stopped reading history then, exhausted by the effort of
making it.

Nearby, Mr. Ridgway had placed a more subversive explanation for the mess of modern life—the works of Sigmund
Freud. I took his copy of *The Interpretation of Dreams* down off
the shelf. The book was yellowed, but you could see that
it had been carefully read—with pages turned down and
notes in the margins. Farther along were popular works of
sociology, which then as now ratified what people already

suspected about life—*The Organization Man, The Lonely Crowd, The End of Ideology.* Snapshots of American self-awareness at mid-century.

The American cultural rebellion was chronicled on his shelves too—the earthquake that produced Candace and me and our whole generation of pill-popping, free-loving miscreants. He had collected the literary harbingers of the great unzipping: *Lady Chatterley's Lover, Ulysses, Lolita, Tropic of Cancer*—in their risqué, banned-in-Boston first editions. Back then, Norman Mailer hadn't even been able to say *fuck* in a novel about soldiers, so he'd had to write *fug* and *fuggin* over and over; and yet just a few years later, in the blink of an eye, he could write *fuck* and *cunt* and *shit* on every page. What had happened to sever the moorings so quickly? Mailer would be appalled at the thought, but the true liberators were probably the feminist writers shelved nearby—Simone de Beauvoir, Mary McCarthy, Betty Friedan—who had opened the door on the humid hurricane.

Mr. Ridgway had left behind shelves of records too, collected near an old LP turntable. His favorites, to judge by the worn jackets, were the musical comedies of Rodgers and Hammerstein: *Carousel, Oklahoma!, South Pacific*—the music that taught his generation how to love and marry and grow old. He was a jazz fan as well, with some old recordings of Billie Holiday before she became a junkie, some early tracks by Miles Davis, a whole shelf of Dave Brubeck. I pulled one battered album down; it showed Brubeck and his band on tour out West, dressed in tweed jackets and baggy wool pants. I wondered if Mr. Ridgway had ever smoked marijuana—

probably he had; probably he'd brought a joint up to the family house in Maine one summer and gotten high as a kite with the missus, and then had a delicious screw on the beach.

I was beginning to like this man. He had surrounded himself with the things that mattered, the guidebooks and testaments of the twentieth century. What had happened, to blow him so far off course?

Candace was sitting in an easy chair by the window, watching me watch what was left of her dead father. She never interrupted my exploration; quite the opposite, she observed carefully as I prowled the shelves and fetched the books. She could see that I was trying to solve the same puzzle she had been turning over in her head for the better part of thirty years.

"What happened to him?" I asked. I wanted to understand, now that I had seen his books.

"Vietnam," she answered. That was a one-word shorthand, but there was more she wanted to say.

THE WAR DESTROYED DWIGHT Ridgway, and all of his friends. Candace had watched it happen, but she hadn't understood it until many years later. They were like boys in a fancy convertible, driving as fast as they could—if they hadn't been so sure of themselves, they wouldn't have been going so fast. They hit a wall at a hundred miles an hour, and there was nothing left of most of them. Even the ones who walked away, like Mr. Ridgway, were destroyed inside. They never stopped bleeding. Those were the Vietnam casualties it was hardest to feel sorry for—the men who made the war. But their suffering was as real as that of the soldiers who never came home.

These were men who had never known failure; they couldn't live with ambiguity or doubt or any hint of weakness. That was why their mistakes were so devastating—because they had believed they were invincible. They were the generation that had *won* the big war—how could they lose this little one? Mr. Ridgway thought he could outwork the problem. He would come home from the Pentagon each night, exhausted by his struggle to make it all work. He had a black limousine with a little flag on the front, which identified him as deputy secretary of defense. The chauffeur would carry his briefcase up the steps; Mrs. Ridgway and Candace would be waiting at the door. He would give his daughter a hug—so wearily, he barely touched her. Then he would walk straight back to his study and mix a cocktail. And he would drink for the next hour or so, until he didn't feel so tired.

Candace wasn't allowed in the room—Mother's orders—so she would stand just beyond the door, peering in, trying to make her father smile. Sometimes he would be in a good mood and tell a funny story. But mostly it was black, black, black. You had to see it from the inside, to understand how much these men were hurting. The public saw steely bureaucrats with slicked-back hair and imperious manners. You had to see them at home, enveloped in the depression that was gathering around them, to understand that they were putting up a desperate front.

Mr. Ridgway traveled to Vietnam every few months, to talk to the generals and see how the war was going. He would usually stop off in Hawaii on the way back, and bring his daughter a necklace of flowers, or a muumuu. When he first got back, he was always upbeat—the generals would do such an incredible snow job. All they needed was a few hundred thousand more troops or a little more bombing or a new offensive—just a little more and the enemy would collapse. Mr. Ridgway wanted to believe it would work. They all did, fervently—they'd staked their careers on it. But after he'd be home awhile, and watch the casualty numbers add up week after week, he would begin to wonder. Doubt wasn't permitted; they were all trying to act tough for each other. Mr. Ridgway would go to the funerals, as many as he could. That was part of his code, but it added to the pain.

And then, sometime in 1967, Mr. Ridgway and some of the others began to realize that it was a mistake. It wasn't working. It was possible—likely—that they had sent all those boys off to die for nothing. It was that seed of doubt that began to make him crazy. Perhaps all of us have mental illness lying dormant within us, waiting for an extreme moment of stress that will set the poison free—to multiply like a mental cancer until it has destroyed our good sense. That was what began to happen to Mr. Ridgway. The tragedy of Vietnam tapped something deep and dark that must have been in him all along, and gradually the darkness enveloped him.

You had to have known him when he was well, to understand the devastation. Mr. Ridgway was one of those men who could do anything. He was a superb athlete who had lettered in three sports in high school, a scholar who delivered the Latin oration at his Harvard commencement, a man of

natural grace and refinement who understood why a particular painting or piece of music was beautiful—and could explain it to his daughter. It was too much to say that Candace
worshiped him, for she had an irreverent streak even then.
But she had believed he could do anything. She didn't truly
understand how weak he was until he killed himself.

And yet there had been signs. That was what made it so
painful for Candace, the sense that if she hadn't been so
caught up in her own world, she could have helped him survive. He had been drinking more. She would hear him, after
she went to bed, bumping downstairs to get another scotch.
He couldn't sleep. Candace couldn't know what his night-
mares were like, but she would hear him cry out sometimes
in the middle of the night. Mrs. Ridgway couldn't take it. She
moved out and made her own bedroom down the hall. She
was embarrassed—that was the worst of it. She had lost faith
in him, and he knew it. He would stay up even later, drinking
and reading, and then get up the next morning and go back to
work and pretend everything was fine.

After he left government in 1969, he joined a foundation
and tried to write a book. But he was a mess. His doctor sent
him to the hospital, and it was only many years later that Candace realized he had been given shock treatment there. It was
still a primitive form of therapy back then, not much beyond
applying leeches to cure a fever. That was why he'd come back
from the hospital so sad-eyed, barely able to recognize his own
daughter. They had blown electricity through his head.

His collapse happened in slow motion. He took a mistress—a divorced woman who had an apartment in one of
the big buildings on Connecticut Avenue. Like Mr. Ridgway,

she had played tennis in college. People watched them playing together at the Chevy Chase Club and wondered what was going on. But even as a girl, Candace had thought she understood it. Her mother was getting older; she had taken a separate bedroom. Her father—in his up phases, at least—was still a youthful, handsome man. That was the official version. But really, he was going crazy.

CANDACE SHOWED ME THE room where he killed himself. We climbed the broad stairway to the second floor, and then a narrower staircase to the third floor. It was bright and airy up there; the sun beamed in through a skylight. A child's room was in the front of the house, still filled with posters and dolls and glass figurines. It was Candace's room. In the back was a smaller room—a sewing room, it appeared. The door was locked, but Candace opened it. Inside was a couch, a big easy chair and a window that looked out over the treetops. He liked to come up there in the afternoon, after he had stopped working. He would sit and read. He said it made him feel better.

It happened one day in the fall of 1971, when Candace was away at college. Mr. Ridgway walked up to that sunny room and hanged himself. He didn't leave a note, but he left a Bible on his reading table, open to the passage in the Song of Solomon that talks about how love is stronger than death. He had scratched out the words. Mrs. Ridgway found him. She reached Candace at Radcliffe and told her that her father was dead. She didn't say that he had committed suicide; she was ashamed. Candace learned the truth later that afternoon, from a stranger.

I TOOK HER IN my arms. She was crying. Most of the time, she contained the horror within her perfect shell, but now she was turned inside out. I had rarely felt so close to anyone as I did to Candace that day. And in spite of everything that happened afterward, I still count myself lucky to have walked together with her, backward in time, into that room.

Before we left the house, she spent some time with her mother, and then some time alone, putting herself back together. We drove back to the paper, mostly in silence. Her face was a little puffy—a good cry will do that—but otherwise she looked fine. She was a resilient person—you would have to be to have lived her life, but it wasn't simply adaptation to difficult circumstances. She had an elasticity to her; she was the tree that would bend in the wind but not break. That was the paradoxical gift her father had given her. She knew what pain was, and how to survive it. And I wanted to believe she had learned compassion, too.

As we were nearing the paper, I asked her if she had ever talked about her father like that with anyone else. I wanted to be special to her, at least in that way. "Just one other person," she answered, and I knew the rest. She had told Galvin. I think she wanted me to feel flattered, that I was the other member of that club, but it was another wound. I could not escape him. At every turn, his face popped up like a shooting-range target.

FOURTEEN

THE SAVANT PUT A LARGE SIGN ON HIS OFFICE DOOR THAT read IF YOU CAN'T SAY ANYTHING NICE ABOUT SOMEONE . . . THEN YOU'VE COME TO THE RIGHT PLACE. It was intended to invite what are known in the intelligence trade as "walk-ins"—the spontaneous defectors who divulge secrets because they hate their wives or they're angry they didn't get promoted or whatever other flimsy reason might lead someone to betray his deepest secrets. The Savant was trolling for information off the dark side of the bridge; he did not scruple about his sources.

Writing a column was not the typing exercise I had imagined. I wasn't afraid of offending my friends (for I didn't really have any), but I hadn't reckoned with the realities of writing for a Serious Newspaper. Certainly I could write: "Newt Gingrich is a fatuous man who lectures other people about morality even though he dumped his first wife when she was in the hospital with cancer." But the *Sun* had libel lawyers, who would warn that such a statement might be "actionable."

And the *Sun* had editors, who would ask whether that reference to Newt dumping his wife was, perhaps, gratuitous, and
take it out. I could throw a tantrum—that was what real writers did, wasn't it, when editors fiddled with their copy?—but
that wasn't really an answer. Inescapably, to be a newspaper
columnist, I would have to choose my targets wisely.

I once heard a story about a British journalist named
Claude Cockburn. He was an aristocrat, an ex-Communist, a
cad with women and in other respects an endearingly repre-
hensible fellow. It was said that when he was searching for a
good subject to attack in one of his own columns, he once
asked a friend, "Who's the most admired man in the world?"
The friend pondered for a while, weighing various luminaries
from the realms of science, music, letters, and finally declared that the most admired man in the world was the kindly
Alsatian doctor who had devoted his life to helping the poor
and needy in Africa, Dr. Albert Schweitzer. "Well, then,"
Cockburn replied, "let's have a go at old Schweitzer."

It was this state of mind The Savant hoped to emulate.
He wanted to know, as he sat that morning at his lustrous
teak desk, who was the most admired person in Washington. Was it perhaps Ralph Nader, the sainted consumer
advocate—the man who, by forcing automakers to build
safer cars, had probably saved more lives than had been lost
at Hiroshima and Nagasaki? Nader had led a blameless, abstemious life. Rightee-o! Let's have a go at old Ralph! Perhaps
an inquiry into his sex life—CONSUMER GURU'S LOVE SECRETS.
But on reflection, Nader was yesterday's saint. He'd done his
work. Nobody would care anymore if he slept with a dog.

What about Justice Sandra Day O'Connor? The woman

had practically been canonized! She had created the moderate center on the Supreme Court, saved *Roe* v. *Wade,* kept the right-wingers from putting the Constitution through the Veg-O-Matic. There was something infuriatingly admirable about the woman. Let's have a go at old Sandra! Surely she was a closet cigarette smoker, or had cheated at line calls in tennis. But the *Sun's* lawyers would want evidence; that was the problem with going after a sitting Supreme Court justice. The lawyers always stuck together. They were worse than the Gambino family.

I skittered along in this way, looking for suitable subjects and then thinking of reasons why they were not so suitable, when into my lap fell the name-dropping exterminator. Actually, it was a suggestion from Candace. She mentioned during one of my increasingly frantic visits in search of ideas that her mother had an exterminator who was always gossiping about the bug problems of famous Washingtonians. He was a sign of what the city was coming to, she said—even the exterminators would soon be writing their memoirs. I got his number from Candace and called him at home. His name was Sanjay, and he was a garrulous Indian man in his late thirties. He knew my name from *Reveal,* he said. Exterminating was just a temporary job; he wanted to be a writer, too.

After a little coaxing, the bug stories came crawling out. There was a certain prominent Washington lobbyist, reputed to be the President's best friend, as a matter of fact. A fine fellow, no doubt, and very clean personally, but he had bugs *everywhere.* Big ones!—even the c-bugs (he couldn't bring himself to say *cockroaches*), and mice too! The secretary of transportation also had bug problems, he was sorry to report.

A lovely lady—salt of the earth—and the President's difficulties certainly weren't *her* fault. But still. . . . The secretary had been giving a dinner party one night when across the table crawled a large spider—dangerously close to the butter dish. It was a near disaster. The woman called the exterminators the next day and cursed them out! As if it were their fault.

And the TV people, those news reporters. Some of them just left food right out on the counter, where the bugs practically *had* to eat it. And then they wondered what was wrong? He mentioned a particularly prominent television reporter who'd had an infestation of moths in her cereal boxes, and he had tried to tell her, *Close the damn boxes!* But she hadn't listened, and the moths were still there—and she wondered why.

It was a metaphor, the way he saw it, for the *inner rot*. You can't lie to bugs, he confided. They can teach you a lot, if you pay attention. Bugs *see* things. The man was obsessed. I just let him talk. The *Sun*'s lawyers wouldn't let me use real names—they seemed to think it was defamatory to say that people had big, fat, ugly bugs crawling all over their houses—so I took the real names out. But The Savant had his first column.

GALVIN LOVED THE NAME-DROPPING exterminator. He arranged for me and Sanjay to go on *The Anti-News* the next day. Sanjay was a natural on TV. He looked just enough like an Asian version of the Maytag repairman to be believable, and he couldn't stop talking. It turned out he had a whole lot more stories about the infestations of famous people's houses. After the show, he asked me if I could help him get a literary agent, and everything seemed to be going great. But then the secretary of transportation sent a letter to the exterminating company, protesting the invasion of her privacy— ("Has this country sunk so low that even the kitchen cupboards of public officials are open to prying eyes?")—and the exterminators promptly fired Sanjay.

I felt mildly guilty and called Galvin, hoping we could help Sanjay find other work. But the publisher was ecstatic. This was a perfect story for the new *Sun*. A heartless bureaucrat had destroyed the livelihood of a working man. He proposed a Save Sanjay campaign. "We'll demand that the secretary of transportation apologize for ruining this guy's life," he enthused, "and we'll force the exterminators to hire him back. We're the newspaper that fights for the little guy. The newspaper that won't be intimidated! The newspaper with a heart!"

He wasn't kidding. He ordered up a front-page story the next day, over the strenuous protest of Howard Bacon. The story recounted the sad tale of the intrepid, truth-telling exterminator—omitting the fact that he was even at that moment shopping his memoirs and looking for a movie deal. It ran under the headline EXTERMINATOR BUGS PRESIDENT'S PAL, and it made great reading. A box next to the story supplied the telephone number and e-mail address of the secretary of transportation, so that readers could tell her what they thought. Needless to say, an abject letter of apology was forthcoming within twenty-four hours, and Sanjay was offered his old job back—which he turned down; he was already working on a screenplay. All in all, it was a big win for the *Sun*.

GALVIN STOPPED BY MY office one afternoon. He was jingling some coins in his pocket. He looked happy. "I love that movie," he said, pointing to my *Little Mermaid* poster. "It always makes me cry." Despite his genial mood, I assumed he must want something. Galvin was meddling in every department lately, and Bacon wasn't the only person he was driving crazy. He had a kind of manic determination to remake everything in sight, as if he were rushing against a secret deadline. But he didn't have any advice for me this time, it turned out. It was a social call. He wanted me to come have dinner with him, two nights hence. He said it would be a celebration, for a small group of friends.

I NEEDED A SECOND column. The name-dropping exterminator had been such a hit that it raised the ante. I wanted something piquant for the next installment. Someone once observed that writing a column was like being married to a nymphomaniac—as soon as you were finished, it was time to start again. Much as it was against my nature, I sensed the need to do a little *reporting*.

Topping my list of usual suspects was Hugo Bell, the shadowy prince of real estate. I was awed by his ability to mine the most obscure records and bring back nuggets of gold: Who was buying a fancy new house because of a fat book contract? Who was having to sell his fancy house because of an impending divorce? Who was getting sued by a neighbor for letting his dog run wild? Bell knew it all. I hadn't seen him lately, and I wasn't sure whether he owed me a favor, or vice versa, but he was worth a try.

"Hey, buddy," I crooned into the phone. "This is The Savant calling. Tell me something *hot!*"

Hugo was deep into a crossword puzzle when I called—that was another of his quirks, the notion that it was an act of rebellion for a black man to do the *New York Times* crossword puzzle—and he wasn't happy about being disturbed. But he had a few tidbits. Ted Koppel was thinking of selling his country place on the Maryland shore. Larry King was remodeling the bathrooms in his penthouse apartment. King Hussein's comely former housekeeper was trying to sell her memoirs, inaptly titled *The King and Me.* None of it seemed quite right for The Savant. I asked if he had anything else.

"How about bankruptcies?" he asked. "Lot of those on the way. Something spooky is happening in the real estate market. The last time I saw it was at the end of the eighties, before the commercial market crashed."

"What's so spooky?" I asked. This didn't sound like a column, but you never knew.

"Well, in the last two weeks, you can't find any buyers for the high-end properties—only sellers. That's scary. And some of the deals that were pending last week have cratered. Money is tight all of a sudden. Lenders are nervous."

"Why? What's the problem?" I was a fool when it came to business. I couldn't see what was in front of my nose.

"The economy is going soft, my friend. These rich folks are the canaries in the coal mine. Everything's bopping along and then—*wham!*—they can't get financing. Lenders are holding back. The squeeze is starting. The hand is on the throat. I can feel it. I've been here before."

"Who's getting squeezed? Help me out. I need to write a column."

"Well, now . . ." He always saved his best stuff for last. "I might have some information for you about a certain local investment tycoon, a certain owner of two *choice* local properties, a certain financier whose finances are of mysterious origin. Would you be interested in that?"

He had my full attention now. "Cut the crap. Have you got something on Galvin?"

"Um-hmm." He was purring. "Looks to me like your boss has a teeny-weeny money problem."

"I doubt that very much. The man is richer than God. Your friend Jack gave me all the details. He's a billionaire."

"Maybe so. But Jack said he had a lot of debts too. And remember how I told you that he was using an *unusual* source of funds to buy those houses—in that the mortgage money was coming from an offshore bank in the Netherlands Antilles—where nice people do *not* go for mortgage money? You remember that?"

"Of course I do. So what? A mortgage is a mortgage."

"Well, now. Were you aware that Mr. Galvin has put that choice property in Georgetown on the market for two-point-six million?"

"Yes, I knew he had decided to sell the Georgetown place—he told me—but I didn't know the price."

"That price will not remain the price, my friend, because the property is not selling. There is a glut of fine residences at the moment, as I told you, and *no* buyers. That is particularly bad news for Mr. Galvin, because he has an additional problem—or so I am reliably informed. Which is that the mortgage on his Georgetown home was purchased recently by another financial concern—which *also* just happens to have an offshore address in the Caribbean. And the new owners are foreclosing on the property, due to nonpayment of interest."

"Ridiculous. Nobody would foreclose on a billionaire." I was trying to remember if Galvin had ever mentioned any business cronies who might have a piece of him. It was hard to imagine. Galvin didn't seem like the sort of person who would let anyone do him favors. "Who bought the mortgage?"

"Hard to know, from what I've seen. It's just a box number in Willemstad. Could be anybody. But not anybody *you'd* like to know."

"How much does he owe?"

"The principal is two-point-five million. The interest payments are in excess of twenty thousand a month."

"Does anyone else know this, Hugo?"

"No. I believe I am the only local possessor of this information. And I sincerely doubt anyone else will follow me into the archives. So it's all yours."

I am not secretive by nature, but I wanted to lock this one in a dark closet. Hugo duly promised that his lips would remain sealed, pending further word from me. It wasn't that I wanted to protect Galvin or do him a favor. It was more that, at this stage, I didn't understand what I had been told. I didn't know what doors the information might unlock, or what might lie behind them. I did not, in truth, know whether I was grieved that my mentor had money problems, or pleased. That was the luxury afforded the journalist. It was possible—nay, desirable—to refrain from declaring allegiance and simply to watch.

THE SAVANT EVENTUALLY FOUND something else to write about that week. I had gotten to know a Nigerian taxi driver a few years before who was running a liberation movement from the basement of my apartment building. (www.freenigerianow.com—"All Nigeria, all the time!") His name was Kano, and he was a cultivated fellow. He collected Ibo poetry and folk tales, when he wasn't driving the cab or posting political manifestos on his Web site. I didn't know much about Nigeria, but I figured that if Kano didn't like the crew that was running things in Lagos, there must be something wrong with them.

Kano was becoming Washington's favorite Nigeria expert—even though his political group, as far as I could tell, had no actual members. He was quoted regularly in newspapers, interviewed on NPR, called to testify before Congress. It seemed to me that he embodied one of Washington's essential secrets, which is that in order to be powerful, it's enough to be seen as powerful.

One October night I came home from the *Sun* to find Kano sitting outside, surrounded by baggage and sticks of furniture. He had been evicted—for no reason whatsoever, he insisted, though I assumed it was for nonpayment of his rent. Here was another cause for the new *Sun*. I wrote up an account of his plight—PROMINENT AFRICAN DISSIDENT HUMBLED BY LANDLORD. Our photographer took a poignant pic-

ture of him, camped in front of my building with his motley
belongings. He went on *The Anti-News,* too. Within a week,
he was living rent-free in an apartment in my building, on
one of the upper floors, overlooking the city. It was the apartment I had once coveted, actually, but I didn't care. I was
making so much money now, I could move into the Water-
gate if I liked. And it was another triumph for the newspaper
with a heart.

WAS IT POSSIBLE THAT people envied me, now that I was a
columnist? That was a disorienting thought, as I began to re-
ceive notes on fancy stationery from my former Harvard
classmates—people who had managed to get by quite ade-
quately without corresponding all these years, but now just
had to tell me how much they liked that last column in the
Sun! I gobbled down the false praise, and then wanted to
vomit it all back up so that I could return to my ordinary state
of aggrieved isolation. I had a *success disorder*—that was my
problem. Indeed, it was not inconceivable that, with a little
work, I could land a guest spot on *Jerry Springer.*

It was becoming more obvious with each passing year
that we were hothouse flowers, we Harvard journalists. Poi-
sonous daffodils of ambition. We had been watered and fer-
tilized from birth to be special—but unlike our simple,
sensible classmates who went off to law or business school
and got rich, we inflicted our *selves* on the world. We were
crazy; that was our secret—crazy with talent and insecurity.
The ones who lacked in either category fell by the wayside,
but the survivors thrived like intellectual kudzu.

It was becoming more obvious with each passing year
One member of the brethren made clear, after his first

theater review for the *Crimson,* that someday he would be the drama critic of *The New York Times,* and a few years later he actually was. It wasn't even surprising; the shock would have been if he had failed. An aspiring film critic got so upset when a classmate criticized his review of a Sam Peckinpah film that he punched him in the nose, literally; he now reviewed films for *The New Yorker* and *Salon.* A third vastly talented man had edited three of America's leading magazines by the time he was forty. He was famous, in our set, for the aphorism "No matter where you go, there you are." A long-haired radical who liked to write essays about Trotsky had become one of the nation's leading business editors and a courtier to the wealthy and powerful. What a gallery!

But I had hidden away, wrapped myself up into a tight and inconsequential ball of failure and been quite happy with it all these years. Nobody had ever written the editor of *Reveal* to say what an interesting cover story we had on Washington's hottest Zip Codes (20016, 20007 and 20854, if you missed that issue). Failure had been my security blanket; it had given me an excuse for the paucity of the rest of my life.

But I had an unpleasant feeling that success had been lying dormant within me too, all these years—like a virus. It was multiplying and taking root. Next it would demand that I make friends, form relationships, have a real life.

I was stronger than that, I told myself. I could fight off the pox a bit longer. To stay healthy, I would stop opening those flattering letters from my classmates.

FIFTEEN

THE LONG INDIAN SUMMER FINALLY ENDED IN LATE October. The bees disappeared to wherever bees go, and a wintry mist hung in the air. The leaves were falling in wet clumps. Driving up the parkway to Galvin's house, I could see the river and the cityscape beyond, through the bare branches of the trees. It was a cold, unflattering vista. Washington imagines itself in green, living in a perpetual summer; if you fly over the city in mid-July, its neighborhoods seem to disappear under a leafy canopy. But the city loses that camouflage with the coming of fall. The potholes, the peeling paint, the untidy public spaces all become visible. That is the essence of Washington's self-delusion—that the shabbiness of winter always comes as a surprise.

I made my way down Galvin's driveway. I was curious about this celebration. What had our titan prepared for us? He was moving so fast these days, but the rest of the world was slowing down. He was out of phase. I wondered if he knew it. At the bottom of the drive, his oversize house came into view; I could see late-flowering pansies blooming in neatly laid flower beds. That should be his motto, I thought: Always in bloom.

From somewhere to the left of the house came the *thwack! thwack!* of tennis balls. I followed the sound until I came to a rustic stone wall draped with ivy and clematis. This stone amphitheater had been constructed a few months before, in place of the usual chain-link fence, to enclose the tennis court. The court itself was Har-Tru, swept and rolled each day by one of the gardeners, with lights for night play as bright as those at the ballpark.

Galvin was rallying with Candace. She seemed to be the only other close friend who had been invited to the celebration. Otherwise, except for the servants, the place was empty. She was dressed in loose-fitting cotton shorts and a baggy sweatshirt, so that all you saw were legs and arms and hair. She was a surprisingly good player: Her strokes whispered lessons at the club and Sunday afternoon games with her father. She hit a two-handed backhand, with as clean and powerful a motion as a woodsman felling a tree. Galvin chased back and forth after her shots. He was dressed in a black T-shirt and blue gym shorts—the outfit he probably wore when he lifted weights before work. It was a mismatch. She was a far better player than he; all his strength was a useless encumbrance. He stumbled once, going after a crosscourt forehand. He got up slowly, and there was a look of surprise and sudden fatigue on his face—how could this be? But when Candace ran toward him, he laughed it off.

I sat down in the pavilion that overlooked the court.

Galvin called out for me to grab a racket and come take his place, but I begged off. I didn't play tennis, and even if I did, I would have said no. I had the feeling that I was watching a sublimated act of sex. The more points he lost, the giddier he became—screaming at her that she was cheating, that it was all just luck. They came off the court eventually, flushed and sweating, and flopped into two chairs. Candace drank a glass of Gatorade and made jokes about how bad Galvin was, and then excused herself to go take a shower.

"Why did you invite me?" I asked Galvin when we were alone. It was obvious that I was redundant.

"She wouldn't come without you, old boy. You're my excuse."

"Well, I'm leaving. You don't need an excuse anymore. This is embarrassing."

"Stay!" he implored. "We have a lot to talk about. And there's the celebration."

He went off to shower. I stayed a few minutes more by the court. A big yellow Labrador retriever lumbered over with a tennis ball in his mouth and dropped it at my feet. I threw it as far as I could, and he loyally brought it back, dropping it at my feet again. This time I got up and walked away. He followed with the ball, and we walked back toward the house, the dog and I, ambling along the stone path toward the swimming pool. The dog's pace quickened as we neared the pool, which shimmered before us, milky white, under a halo cast by the underwater lights.

The dog dropped the ball again. I threw it into the pool, and he leaped in after it—making a big splash as his golden

fur hit the illuminated water. He swam with amazing dex-
terity toward the yellow ball, clenched it in his teeth and pad-
dled back toward me, dropping it by the edge of the pool. He
wanted me to throw it again, but I thought it should be my
turn—he should throw it to me this time—but that wasn't
going to happen. The dog emerged from the pool and shook
off several gallons of water in my direction as we shambled
off together toward the house. I couldn't complain; he was
my date.

GALVIN HAD LIT A fire in the study. He and Candace seemed
relieved when the dog and I arrived. I was the beard, the easy
way for Candace to reassure herself that this wasn't a private
encounter. She had changed into a pair of black jeans and a
loose top, with a sweater thrown over her shoulders; her hair
was up, but wisps of it were falling out of place. Nobody was
talking. There was a silky, sparky feeling of sexual tension in
the room—as if all the circuits had been wired through our
adrenal glands. Even the fire was popping in the hearth—
little explosions of light and color as pieces of bark caught
flame.

"What shall we have to drink, eh?" asked Galvin. He was
nervous. I could hear it in his voice. "Should we open a bottle
of wine?"

Candace said that would be fine. I didn't answer because
I wasn't sure my view really counted. But Galvin turned to
me solicitously. "Come downstairs with us to the cellar, and
we'll pick it out together." He still needed me as a foil, to pre-
serve the illusion that this was a group endeavor.

We followed him down the hall, past a large metal safe, to a doorway that led down to a room with glass doors and elaborate temperature controls. Galvin deactivated an alarm and unlocked the door. Inside, it was as cool as a refrigerator. He flipped a light switch, illuminating the wine bottles that were racked floor to ceiling along three walls. It was like a little art gallery: Each bottle had a white plastic tag, identifying the name of the wine and its vintage—and below that the year when it would be ready to drink. I didn't know much about wines, but I couldn't help recognizing the famous names along Galvin's wall: Léoville-Las-Cases, Le Corton, Montrachet, Romanée-Conti; row after row, vintage after vintage.

"It's so perfect," said Candace. She seemed surprised. This was the clearest physical evidence she had seen of Galvin's wealth. What appeared to fascinate her, though, was less the opulence than the sheer order and precision of it, like a collection of stamps or butterflies.

"This is an interesting one," said Galvin, taking an old bottle off the shelf and blowing away the dust so we could see the label. It was a 1945 Mouton-Rothschild—the first vintage after the war, with a little *V* for victory at the top of the label. He handed it to Candace. She held the 1945 Bordeaux in her hand, and then a 1900 bottle of Madeira, then a 1926 magnum of champagne. She hefted each one, held it up to the light to assay the color and study the label.

"Where did you get them?" she asked.

"I have a man in New York. When he finds interesting things coming on the market, he buys them for me. I started buying wine in Hong Kong. Japanese clients liked the fancy names. They would throw business my way for a glass of Nuits-St.-Georges."

"How much did all this cost?" I asked. That was the crass question, so inevitably I had to pose it.

"I don't know. I've bought it in little bits over a long period. I suppose there must be close to a million dollars' worth of wine in this room. Hard to say; you'd have to auction it off, to be sure what it's worth."

"Will you ever sell it?" That wasn't simply another of my vulgar questions. I was curious. Would a man hold on to his wines, even if he was in danger of losing one of his houses?

He looked at me with disappointment. How could I imagine such a thing? This was an investment in good living.

"I intend to drink every bottle, with help from my friends." He smiled at both of us, but his eyes lingered on Candace. She was still scanning the racks of bottles. He moved toward her.

"I'm happy you're here," he said. "I've wanted to show this to you for years. I wanted to know what you'd say when you saw it."

She took his hand and gave it a little squeeze. "That's sweet." She kissed him on the cheek. She obviously didn't know what to do. The evening was already slipping across the mental boundary she had established in her mind.

"So what shall we drink?" Galvin surveyed the shelves that contained his prize Burgundies and selected a 1990 Batard-Montrachet and a 1985 La Tâche. He held the bottles so that Candace could examine the labels.

"Just right," she said. Like all good ex–foreign correspondents, she knew her wines.

Galvin seated us in what he called the "small dining room," which I had never seen before. It was a circular room, painted a deep red, with a handsome round table in the middle. Candace sat between me and our host. On the walls were three Matisse etchings: a nude lying on a rug; another woman clothed, gazing at a fishbowl; a third woman lying facedown, her eyes peering out provocatively above her folded arms. They were simple drawings, a few nimble lines capturing the freshness and sensuality of the artist's model. They all looked like Candace, it suddenly occurred to me.

Our host was ebullient, glowing with the wine and his inner spark, and I kept wondering whether something specific had happened, or if it was just his pleasure at having Candace with him. The food arrived—a cold seafood salad, followed by lamb chops—served by a pretty French girl who was married to Galvin's chef. "The staff," he liked to call them—all these people underfoot, fed by a hidden river of cash that quite obviously continued to flow, whatever troubles might lie over the horizon.

We finished the white Burgundy and were rolling through the red. Galvin and Candace were talking animatedly, remembering something from their golden youth. It was a train trip, I gathered, taken across the western United States in the summer of 1971, the summer after they met. They had run out of money in Wyoming—no! It was Salt Lake City!—and they had decided to hop a ride on a freight train. Galvin had read an article about how to do it. It was a canned-goods car, remember? They were finishing each other's sentences, racing to the next part of the story, the way a couple will do.

Candace turned to me, her eyes as bright as they must have been that day rumbling out of Salt Lake City. They sat with their feet dangling over the edge of the boxcar, she remembered. The sun had been setting over the Great Salt Lake, shimmering orange and gold in the desert heat. The hobos on the boxcar began to drink and sing train songs. One of them got so drunk he fell off in Elko, Nevada.

Galvin stirred at the memory. " *'They call me Hoppy,'* " he said in a quavering, sad-sack voice. " *'They all know me in Winnemucca. You just tell them Hoppy sent you, when you get to Winnemucca.'* "

"And crossing the Sierra mountains," she continued. "Tell him what happened in the Sierras when the train stopped."

Galvin gave her a playful push on the shoulder. "No, you tell it. It's your story."

She closed her eyes, fixing her mind on that rocking, bumping boxcar. "We'd been traveling for about twenty-four hours," she said, "and I was so tired and dirty. No bath, no toilet, nothing to wash with. The train was winding through the Sierras, snow on the mountains, and we came to this high pass and for some reason the train just *stopped,* and we sat there waiting—five minutes, ten minutes. Just below us, maybe twenty yards from the tracks, there was a little mountain pond—clear water, icy cold, surrounded by wildflowers. It was the most beautiful thing I'd ever seen, and I kept staring at it, thinking how nice it would be to jump in the water.

"Sandy dared me to run down and take a swim. I felt so filthy, and the train hadn't moved in a long time, and it seemed like we could be there for hours, so I decided, why not? I ran across the meadow to the pond, stripped down to my underwear and dived in the water—and it felt so *good*! I was floating on my back looking up at the blue sky when I heard a whistle and the lurch of the wheels.

"My God! I was so scared. I scrambled up the bank with my clothes in my hand. I thought I was going to be left behind. The train was moving faster. Sandy held out his hand and screamed at me, 'Run faster!' and finally hauled me up into the boxcar. I was dripping wet, practically naked, and he was *laughing* at me. Here I had almost been stranded in the Sierras, and he was laughing like it was the funniest thing he'd ever seen.

"You *bastard*." She looked at him so tenderly as she said that. She made *bastard* sound like the sweetest word in the dictionary.

"WHAT ARE WE CELEBRATING tonight?" I asked. I didn't want to disturb their reminiscence, but I was beginning to wonder whether Galvin had devised any nominal excuse to stage this reunion.

"Right! I almost forgot. But if we're going to celebrate, we need another bottle of wine." We had killed the La Tâche by then, so Galvin led us back downstairs, the three of us lurching into the wine cellar. "The wines we've already had were so *good*," he said, "that we have to find something *even better*. Otherwise, what's the point? It has to be red Burgundy, doesn't it? Can't drink a Bordeaux now. Can't drink white."

He pulled a 1978 Romanée-Conti from the rack. "This is my favorite wine in the house. A thousand dollars a bottle. I've been saving it for a special occasion, and this is it. No question about it."

Galvin lifted his glass ceremoniously when we were back upstairs. Even when he was tipsy, he was a gentleman. "I ask you both to join me in a toast to the *new Washington Sun and Tribune*! That's what I asked you here to celebrate tonight. Because it's working. Despite all the crap from Bacon and his flunkies, we're making progress. We are climbing that mountain."

"What do you mean?" I asked. "What's working?"

He had a coy half smile on his face, like the first time I met him on the lawn behind his house. "I just got preliminary circulation numbers through October fifteenth. We're up more than ten thousand in newsstand sales. That may not sound like much, but the *Sun* hasn't had a month-to-month circulation gain in more than three years. Most of that is probably the bingo game, but so what? It's working. We're going to make it! We just have to keep up the pressure. Push, push, push—get people to stop all their negative bullshit and get with the plan, because we're *rolling*. They better get on board, or they'll be left behind."

"Push, push, push!" said Candace, imitating his cheerleading voice. She put her arms around his neck and gave him a big kiss. She was drunk, but still . . .

"Congratulations, boss," I said. He was hard to resist when he was in this mood. It was the secret of carnival barkers and army generals and religious prophets too—that ability to get listeners to suspend their own judgment and ac-

cept the other person's. It was working! All his goofy ideas—
The Anti-News, the contests, even the front-page editorials—
were finding an audience. He was declaring war on the
newspaper now; I hoped he understood that. But listening to
him, crazy as his ideas were, it was hard not to think he might
be right.

GALVIN WANTED TO SMOKE a cigar, so we went back outside, to his patio overlooking the pool. Candace lay down on
the couch beside him and rested her head in his lap. The wine
and the free fall in time had left her pleasantly disoriented.
She was humming show tunes and making occasional wise-
cracks to Galvin. My date reappeared, wagging his tail and
carrying that tennis ball in his mouth. I lobbed it into the pool
and he dived in after it—creating a golden wake, like phos-
phorescence, in the floodlit water.

Candace was barely listening. It seemed like a good time
to ask the question that had been on my mind all evening. I
wondered how to approach it. He was such a good actor, it
would be hard to know whether he was telling the truth.

"What's happening in the market?" I asked. "I don't
know anything about the financial world, but people tell me
things are getting soft. Anything to that?"

"Your friends are right," he said. "The squeeze is on, and
it's going to get unpleasant for people who don't know what
they're doing."

"What does that mean? Remember, I'm a financial
illiterate."

"Do you know what liquidity is? No, of course you
don't—but it's basically just a fancy word for money. And

there isn't any. Starting about a month ago, money began to get tight. The junk-bond market basically vanished. In practical terms, that means you can't issue any debt now that's rated below A. Lenders will charge you more in interest than you're going to make back on the project. The IPO market is dead too. Two months ago, people would invest in any fool thing, but now everybody's risk-averse. It's a funny market. Not for amateurs."

"But you don't have to worry? Personally, I mean. You don't have money problems?"

"Me?" He laughed, and it seemed a genuine, involuntary eruption of mirth. "No, of course not. What made you think that?"

"People talk. You know me, I'm a gossip, and people tell me things."

Galvin was still smiling. "What do they say, these people who talk?"

"They say you're being forced to sell your house in Georgetown, because some front company in the Caribbean is foreclosing on your mortgage."

He laughed again and shook his head. "Where do they get this stuff? I told you weeks ago that I was going to sell the Georgetown place. In fact, I told you that the first time I met you. The buyer is using an offshore account, I think, but so what?"

"They're not foreclosing?"

"Come on. Do I look like a man who's being foreclosed? No! I'm settling a debt with some people I've done business with. They're acquiring the Georgetown property in settlement of the debt. It's easier to do it that way, for tax reasons, than pay them cash. It's good business. Otherwise, I wouldn't do it."

It all sounded reasonable, and I certainly didn't know enough to question him about specifics. And there was the look of the man—the house, the clothes, the wines. We had just poured over a thousand dollars down our throats. That was liquidity! How could he be hurting for money, even in a market that was getting soft?

GALVIN KISSED CANDACE ON the forehead. "Wake up, my love," he said. She awakened in that drowsy mental twilight where we think and say exactly what we really feel.

"Hello, darling," she said. She reached up her arms toward him and pulled him down, and kissed him on the lips. She was obviously unaware of my presence—unaware of anyone but him. "Let's go upstairs," she said.

Galvin cradled her in his arms, resting his head gently against hers.

I was already on my feet and tiptoeing away. I would have made it without anyone realizing I had left, if the dog hadn't started barking. Maybe he wanted a kiss too.

"Good night," I called out. But there was no answer. They had waited a long time for this moment, and I don't think anyone else mattered to either of them.

SIXTEEN

IT'S HARD TO REMEMBER JUST WHEN TED AMARA FIRST showed up at the *Sun*, but it wasn't long after that intimate "celebration" at Galvin's house. Amara arrived with the unassuming title of special assistant to the publisher. He was a lawyer who had lived until recently in Paris, but he lacked the sort of credentials that make people in Washington pay attention. Yet it soon became clear to everyone that he was a powerful man.

Galvin insisted that he attend all the important meetings—that was part of it. But it was also the way Amara carried himself. He was short and dark, with the sharply drawn features of the Mediterranean, and he dressed in double-breasted suits that seemed at once too tight and too baggy. He had a nervous habit of biting on wooden toothpicks, which he cached in that ill-fitting suit jacket. Probably he was just trying to quit smoking, but the effect was menacing—you couldn't help thinking, as you watched him chewing away on that toothpick, that he'd much rather be chewing on you.

We hadn't seen too many people like Amara around the newspaper, and it would have been easy to dismiss him as a thug, except for one thing: He proved to be very smart. The few things he said in meetings were precisely on point. And when Galvin sent him out to do a job, like talk with union representatives about contract issues, it would be done crisply and cleanly. He had an aura of toughness, an ability to signal others subtly that he meant what he said—which made it easy to get things done. It was enough, just to look into his dark, unyielding eyes, to know that he was serious.

I was curious about him, naturally. I saw him one morning sitting alone in the cafeteria, reading a newspaper, so I joined his table. He seemed pleased to have company—I think people had been avoiding him for fear he might shoot them if they said the wrong thing—and he was surprisingly forthcoming. It turned out he had gone to Columbia Law School in the late 1960s and worked during the summers on various liberal causes—working in Allard Lowenstein's campaign and directing a summer youth program in the South Bronx. He was a do-gooder, under that double-breasted suit! Or at least he had been, until he wandered into the world of international business in the early 1970s and discovered his true calling in life. Which, as near as I could tell, was to be a fixer—the guy who gets the deal done, subtly and quietly—please don't ask how.

"What does Ted Amara do?" I asked Galvin one day. "He seems like a very competent fellow, but what's his job?"

"He does whatever I ask him to do. Sort of like you—except he's shorter."

"Where did you find him?"

"Ted has worked for me, off and on, for nearly twenty years. In the commodities business, you find many untrustworthy people. I needed someone like Ted, who could help me find out what was real and what wasn't. That's still his job. The newspaper business turns out to be a lot like the commodities business."

MY FIRST OPPORTUNITY TO watch Ted Amara in action came a few weeks after he arrived. Galvin was just beginning his effort to help the D.C. government, a project that would become an obsession for him. God knows why he directed his philanthropy in this direction—the District had the sorriest, most corrupt collection of local politicians you could find this side of Chicago. But Galvin had decided that the newspaper with a heart had a responsibility to its hometown. "Let's *do* something for this city!" he kept telling people in the newsroom. He had convinced himself that the real cause of the city's problems was racism—and that folks were down on the local politicians just because they were black.

So Galvin decided to befriend the mayor, a black man named Alistair P. Marquand who had shown an uncanny ability over the years to upset and intimidate white people. Galvin took that as a challenge. He sent Amara to visit the mayor and invite him to the *Sun* for lunch, and the mayor, amazingly enough, accepted. It was to be a small gathering—for "healing," Galvin said. Bacon wasn't invited, nor were any reporters from the city staff. But for some reason, the publisher wanted me to attend. "Maybe you can find something good to write about," he said. "Help counter all the negativism."

The mayor was dark-skinned with a well-trimmed salt-and-pepper beard. He looked like a jazz musician. He wasted the first half of the lunch with a long diatribe about the "racist *Sun*," and how the newspaper had investigated him up and down, harassed his friends, blocked his political initiatives. Even his precious daughter couldn't give a piano recital, he said, without some *Sun* reporter barging in the door, and he was sick of it! Galvin listened intently for a while, nodding his head—he'd said a lot of the same things himself—but as the harangue wore on, he began to tune out. Ted Amara had been watching his boss carefully, and at a certain point he interrupted the mayor—just broke in, in mid-sentence.

"We didn't invite you here to talk about all that," he said. "We want to talk about something else."

Mayor Marquand looked at him cross-eyed and muttered something like, "Fuck you." But he stopped and listened. Amara had that effect. He was not a man to trifle with, and the mayor—who understood power instinctively—grasped that.

"Mr. Galvin wants to talk about scholarships," said Amara. Then he went silent again, and turned the floor over to his boss.

"Fine," said the mayor. "Let's talk." You had the sense that it took an effort of will on his part not to end each sentence with the word "motherfucker."

Galvin spread his big arms wide on the table in supplication. "Mr. Mayor, I want to do something good for this city. That's why I asked for this meeting."

The mayor gave him a toothy smile that said *Sure you do, white boy.*

"So I have a proposal for you. I am prepared to offer a thousand-dollar scholarship to every senior who graduates from the D.C. public schools next spring. They can use it at any college, junior college or trade school they like. For any graduating senior who maintains a B average for the first two years in college, I will provide an additional five-thousand-dollar scholarship."

"Well, now," said the mayor, his voice a bottomless pool of suspicion. "That's mighty generous of you."

"Yes, it is," said Galvin. "As a matter of fact, I can tell you precisely how much it will cost. Mr. Amara has prepared an estimate." He reached into his pocket for a sheet of paper. "In the first year, assuming that all of the roughly four thousand seniors graduate, it will cost me four million dollars, and that's likely to be an average annual cost. Assuming that two in ten graduating seniors keeps a B average after two years, that will be an additional eight million. So, over the next four years, I expect to provide nearly twenty-five million dollars in scholarship aid for District students, out of my own pocket."

The mayor shook his head and turned to his aide. "This man is crazy!"

"I'm not finished. I also want you to help me distribute the money, Mayor Marquand. It will be a joint effort, by your office and the *Sun*. It is my plan to name these scholarships after you."

By now, the mayor was truly vexed. He didn't understand the angle. Galvin didn't look like the usual guilty white liberal, and Ted Amara certainly didn't. "What's in it for you?" he asked.

"Healing," answered Galvin.

"Right. Well, healing's a nice idea—amen to that!—but it's not a twenty-five-million-dollar idea."

"I have a selfish goal too. I want to increase the *Sun's* circulation. And it's obvious to me I can't do that without being generous to the people of this city. Because the simple fact is, we cannot have a healthy newspaper in a city that's full of hate. It's good business: The more black Washington prospers, the more newspapers I'll sell."

It was hard for anybody to disagree with that—even our dyspeptic, race-baiting mayor. He shook hands with Galvin, although there was a look in his eye that said, *I still don't get this. What's the scam?* As the mayor's party headed for the elevator, I saw Ted Amara slide alongside the mayor and lead him down the corridor for a brief, private conversation—which ended with both of them nodding their heads.

HOWARD BACON KNEW ABOUT the visit moments after Hizzoner arrived in the building. You can't keep secrets in a newspaper. When you have a whole enterprise devoted to gathering dirt and picking at scabs, some of that creative energy inevitably will be directed inward. Bacon also knew that I had been present for the mayor's lunch, and he was furious—regarding that as disloyalty to the newsroom. What he required from me, as penance, was that I spill the beans.

"What's Galvin plotting with Marquand?" he demanded.

He had summoned me to his office a scant fifteen minutes after the man's departure. There was something feverish in Bacon's demeanor these days. His washed-out face was bearing the blotchy red hue of permanent anxiety.

I gave Bacon an account of the meeting, including the particulars of Galvin's $25 million pledge of scholarships to be awarded jointly by the mayor and the newspaper. I described the mayor's tirade, and the publisher's appeal for the city and the newspaper to work together.

"He can't do that," said Bacon. "It's unethical. The mayor is a crack-head and a convicted felon, but even if he were a saint, it would still be wrong. Newspapers don't get in bed with city governments. Doesn't he understand anything?"

"He understands the rules," I said. "He just thinks they're wrong."

"Jesus Christ!" Bacon was shouting; you could tell from the sound of his voice that he was losing his grip. "What am I going to do? This man is crazy. He's running through every red light. Someone from *The New York Times* called me this week, to ask about Galvin's campaign contributions. He's giving thousands of dollars to candidates in the November elections—did you know that? Members of the House and Senate, local candidates, for God's sake. He can't do that! It's totally unethical. He's destroying the newspaper."

"I don't know, Howard. Maybe not. I mean, circulation is up—I heard newsstand sales jumped another five thousand copies last week. And the stock price is up more than twenty dollars from when he bought the paper. People like the newspaper now. I hate to say it, but it has more energy. Maybe Galvin knows what he's doing."

"Bullshit! He's a menace. And I forbid you to put any good-news nonsense about these ridiculous scholarships in the Lifestyle section. We will not turn the newspaper into a propaganda organ for the publisher's pet causes. If he wants people to know about them, he can run a house ad. Do you hear me? That's an order."

I DIDN'T TELL GALVIN about Bacon's outburst. It would only have hastened the inevitable final battle. Bacon holed up in his office the next few days, reading *The New York Review of Books* and talking on the phone with his editor pals in New York. Who needs this job, anyway? That was the attitude he tried to convey, but he wasn't really the carefree type. A sign of the stress he was under was that he was losing weight. His trousers were hanging loose, and he had stopped shining his shoes—always a bad sign. He knew he was failing, but he didn't understand why; the termite of middle age was burrowing into his soul, hollowing him out.

CANDACE WAS WORKING LATE. She was trying to finish editing a long feature story about the insolvency of the Japanese banks. It was a classic Candace project. She had conceived the idea several months ago—deciding that the only way to make readers understand the severity of the financial crisis in Japan was to focus on one faltering bank and take apart its balance sheet. She had worked with our Tokyo reporter to find the right bank—one whose records had been pried open through a lawsuit. And inside this one institution, they had found uncollectable loans totaling more than five billion dollars. The story made you understand the make-believe world at the core of Japan Incorporated. It was a potential prize-winner, and Candace wanted it to be just right.

I was working late that night too, trying to finish The Savant's next column. This one was about a Salvadoran immigrant boy from a nice, hardworking family who'd gone to the hospital complaining of severe stomach pains, and the doctor had sent him home—too many hot tamales, he figured. It turned out the boy's appendix had ruptured, and he nearly died. Now he'd hired a fancy K Street lawyer and was suing the hospital for $10 million. The American dream, updated.

I was hoping to cadge a ride from Candace, since she was working late too. I was on my way to her office when I saw her entering the elevator. I ran down the stairs after her, still hoping to grab a ride. I was about to call out when I saw her dart across the street and embrace Galvin, who was standing in the shadows. He'd been waiting for her. They were going home together, obviously. He had his arm around her, and her head was nestled against his chest. They must have thought nobody saw them. I watched them walk away, their voices lost in the noise of the traffic.

"I WANT TO SHOW you something!" called out Galvin's jaunty voice through the telephone a few days later. "Meet me downstairs in five minutes." It was midmorning, the normal time for my meeting with the assignment editors to plan the day's agenda of puffery and character assassination. But they could manage that admirably without me.

The publisher was waiting in the atrium, passing time with a group of schoolchildren who had come down from

Gaithersburg to watch *The Anti-News*. They were crowding around for autographs—he was already a local star, thanks to the TV show—and he was scribbling his name as fast as he could, writing on notebooks and T-shirts and baseball caps. He was in one of his up phases this morning; I could see it in his eyes the moment I saw him in the lobby.

"Let's take a walk!" he said, grabbing me by the arm.

We set out a brisk pace toward Dupont Circle. He talked with animation about the new business deals he was cooking up. It was the relentlessly upbeat tone of an infomercial. He was negotiating a partnership with one of the big phone companies to create a nationwide Internet lottery—based on the success of the *Sun's* bingo game. He was talking to Paramount about producing a nightly *Get Real* TV show—which would talk about what people really cared about, as opposed to what they were supposed to care about. The concept seemed to be *Entertainment Tonight* meets *Wall Street Week*. He was even talking to some investors about creating a national edition of the *Sun*, keyed to *The Anti-News*. So many deals. Rat-tat-tat. The look in his eyes was that of a teenage boy who has been playing video games too long and is firing the joystick at anything that moves.

We had passed Dupont Circle now, and were nearing Florida Avenue. The complexion of the city was changing—from white to cocoa brown, as we entered the Hispanic and African American neighborhoods that bordered the northern edge of downtown. Galvin continued to rattle along with his plans and projects.

"Are you all right?" I asked during a momentary lull.

"Why? Of course I am. Why wouldn't I be all right?"

"You just seem a little intense today, that's all. I was wondering if anything was bothering you."

"Not in the slightest. My only problem is that I have too many good ideas. It's like what Churchill said when someone asked him if he planned to drink a whole roomful of booze: 'So much to do, so little time in which to do it.' "

We were crossing Fourteenth Street. For decades, this had been the crossroads of black Washington. The Lincoln Theatre, which had hosted the great Negro entertainers of the 1940s and 1950s, was a few blocks away. A jazz club called the Bohemian Caverns was a little farther along, still vibrating with the ghosts of John Coltrane and Miles Davis. Near the corner was the city's premier all-night rendezvous, a tiny hole-in-the-wall called Ben's Chili Bowl.

"Where are we going?" I asked. Frankly, I wondered if he really knew where he was. White folks seldom ventured east of Fourteenth Street. It was unwise. The assumption hereabouts was that a white man on the streets was either stupid, or a cop.

"Don't be scared," he said. "Big Daddy will take care of you." And it was true, he didn't look scared in the least. When we got to Seventh Street—lots of folks staring at us now—Galvin took my elbow and steered me another block south. We stopped in front of a dilapidated yellowing hulk of a building at Seventh and T.

"This is it!" he said. "The home of the greatest rhythm-and-blues music in America. Once upon a time, this was ground zero. Not the Apollo in Harlem, but right here. The Howard Theatre."

I looked at the wreckage of the building. It was hard to

imagine it as a shrine to anything except America's racial disorder. It had been trashed during the riots in 1968 that followed the death of Martin Luther King, Jr., and left for dead, a ruined shell. All that remained of its glory was a vertical marquee, spelling out the theater's name.

"It looks like shit," I said.

"Maybe now. But it's going to see glory again, thanks to the *Sun*. Because we're going to rebuild it."

It was just past noon. A big black Town Car was pulling up on Seventh Street, with a D.C. police escort, fore and aft. The door opened, and out stepped the unmistakable figure of our mayor, followed a moment later by Ted Amara. The mayor, I noticed, was putting an envelope in his jacket.

"Well, well, well," said Marquand. "How's my favorite newspaper publisher?" Galvin had his hand outstretched, but the mayor clasped him in a bear hug; he wasn't one to do things halfway. Galvin was still keyed up; he was rocking on the balls of his feet, almost like a dance. He pointed toward the ruins of the Howard.

"Mr. Mayor, you may not realize it, but this is a holy place for me. When I was a teenager, I used to drive all day from Pittsburgh to see James Brown, the Temptations, folks like that."

The mayor was squinting, trying to imagine it; even after the bear hug, he was dubious about Sandy Galvin's adventures as a soul brother.

"Why'd you come all the way down here?" asked the mayor. "That's a four-hour trip."

"Because this was the *place*. The Howard was so small, and the acoustics were so good that, when the band began to play, the whole place would just shake with the energy. It wasn't possible to be a white man or a black man in there—all the electrons just got jumbled together."

Galvin took the mayor's arm and led him toward the charred building. "Listen to this, Mr. Mayor. You want to know how crazy I was? Nearly every Saturday I would plead with the manager to let me go backstage and interview the singers for my high school paper. After they got to know me, they'd let me watch the show through the curtain and then go down to the dressing rooms. I interviewed the Manhattans that way, and the Contours, and Junior Walker."

"*Shotgu-un!*" sang out the mayor obligingly. He was a Junior Walker fan, evidently. Marquand was the same age as Galvin and had listened to the same music, but he was a more practical man. He had not only graduated from college, but had gone on to law school.

"Listen to this," said Galvin conspiratorially. "One Saturday night, I actually interviewed the bass man of the Temptations. His name was Melvin, I think"—the mayor nodded, that was indeed the bass man's name—"and he said we could do the interview on the way back to his hotel, because he had to meet some people there. So I sat in his limo all the way to Fourteenth Street, asking ridiculous questions about whether his roots were in gospel music, and he's just nodding and saying 'um-hmm,' and 'that's right' in that deep bass voice until we got back to his hotel. He took me up to his room and there were these *fine* women standing around, and people getting high in the corner, and I pleaded with him to let me stay. But Melvin decided it was time to say good-bye."

"You did all that?" asked the mayor. He was beginning to

suspect that there was something unusual about Sandy Galvin.

"Yes, sir. I did. I have been up there on that mountaintop, where black folks and white folks held hands and sang together. And do you know what? *I want to go back!* I don't care about O.J. and Farrakhan and any of the rest of it. I'm tired of living in a city of hate. Sick to death of it. So I have another proposal for you. We are going to do something great here, you and me. We are going to rebuild this holy place—a black man and a white man—so that our children can come together and listen to the music we loved. What do you think about that? Can we do that?"

"Well, now," said the mayor, looking at Galvin and then at Ted Amara. "I've been on that mountaintop too, and it's a mighty long way back. But nothing's wrong with giving it a try."

THEY HELD A CEREMONY at Seventh and T a week later to mark the beginning of reconstruction of the Howard. Galvin pledged $15 million toward rebuilding the theater. Aretha Franklin cut the ribbon and sang "Respect." Tens of thousands of people sang along with her. There were a lot of R & B fans left in D.C., it turned out—police said it was one of the largest multiracial gatherings in the city in decades. The *Sun* bannered the story on the front page. Galvin played it like the Second Coming: Black and white together, we shall not be moved! Bacon had given up trying to impose his usual standards. It was slipping out of his control. We would all follow Melvin the bass man into the promised land.

A week after that, Galvin declared Racial Healing Day.

He ran a front-page editorial about it, and organized a con-
vocation in front of the *Sun*'s headquarters. The mayor
pulled out all the stops for this one. Black folks came from
every neighborhood in the city, from Anacostia to Shaw, and
stood in orderly lines. I could only guess at how much money
Ted Amara had put out on the streets, but it had done the
trick. White people came in from the suburbs too, in roughly
equal numbers. For once, people weren't scared.

Galvin gave a speech about love and racial tolerance. He
seemed to be looking much of the time at Candace, who
was standing in the front row, beaming. When he was
done, Galvin embraced Marquand, the members of the city
council—anyone he could find. The mayor grabbed the microphone and shouted, "Now give your neighbors a hug!"
and the audience joined in, black and white, hugging anyone
they could find. Galvin's cameras from *The Anti-News* broadcast the whole glorious, gooey mess to the country.

People began to talk after that. They couldn't help it. One
of America's most prominent newspapers was gushing about
racial healing; blacks and whites were hugging in the streets
of a city that had been addicted to race baiting. This couldn't
be Washington. Most of all, people talked about the charis-
matic publisher and his newspaper with a heart. He seemed
to have that most inexplicable and essential human gift—the
ability to make people forget about their problems. For a city
that had been suffering under a perpetual cloud of righteous
misery, it was as if the sun was finally breaking through.

SEVENTEEN

GALVIN BEGAN MEETING REGULARLY WITH THE PRESI-
dent that fall. They were drawn together partly by the *Sun's*
Racial Healing campaign, which intrigued the President and
emboldened the publisher. But it was inevitable that those
two would connect; they had emerged from the same majes-
tic swamp of ambition and aspiration. They were roughly the
same age and had achieved success through a similar mix of
charm and intellect. Most of all, they shared the same mysterious life force—conveyed through the eyes, the handshake,
the physical presence—that gave them power over others, if
not always over themselves.

Any relationship in Washington begins with a core of
mutual opportunism, and that was doubtless true in this
case. But they also seemed to like each other. The first meeting took place at the White House, but soon Galvin began
inviting the President to his house in Virginia to drink fine
wine, smoke cigars and talk about their troubles (or the President's troubles, at least; Galvin wasn't supposed to have any).

I think both of them intended for the meetings to be secret, and the President traveled without his usual press escort. But discretion was not a viable long-term option in Washington.

I discovered the meetings by accident. I had driven out to the Virginia house one day to pick up Galvin's theater tickets for the Kennedy Center that night, which he had offered to give me. At the bottom of the driveway were two bulky Ford Crown Victorias, the model beloved by law enforcement agencies. When I asked the housekeeper who was visiting, she pointed to the living room, where a half-dozen Secret Service agents were busily inspecting the house in preparation for a presidential visit. They demanded to know who I was, in the imperious way of the Secret Service; it took a phone call to Galvin to straighten things out.

I had to promise not to tell anyone, and in fact, I told just one person—Candace. But of course she already knew. Galvin had told her days ago.

I would have liked to witness the first of their meetings, to see these two aging baby boomers size each other up—fix each other with the same nimble, searching gaze; approach with the same winsome smile; extend hands as they looked with the greatest sincerity and interest into the other's eyes. Who would win the Charisma Bowl? I had my money on Galvin.

There are people who can establish intimacy easily, by talking about themselves and their dreams and encouraging the other person to do the same. Galvin and the President both had that quality, and from what I could pick up, their conversations had that flavor of instant intimacy. They discussed what they wanted out of life; they talked about what

they would do next (for there is always a "next"); they tried
out ideas. Each had been validated—Galvin by his wealth,
the President by his political success—as a member of
the meritocratic elite. It was a group of tormented over-
achievers, with the same paradoxical combination of self-
confidence and insecurity as the early capitalists who gave the
world the Protestant ethic. That yearning for validation—
let's be modern and call it status anxiety—was the moving
force of history, no matter what the historians might say.

According to Candace, two topics dominated their
conversations—the President's legal problems (naturally)
and the perilous state of the world economy. Galvin regarded
the President's troubles as a symptom of the sickness that afflicted Washington. He counseled the President to stay in the
arena. The public hated all the carping and criticism; they
saw the President's critics for the dwarves they were. Since
this was precisely what the President wanted to hear, they
found much to agree about. I was able to glean less about
their discussions of the world economy. Galvin apparently
spent a lot of time explaining to the President how global
markets worked, and why they had been so volatile. It
sounded like a seminar. If he offered the President specific advice, he didn't share it with me or Candace.

The President asked Galvin's views on the foreign policy
worries of the day: whether to bomb Serbia; how to over-
throw the ruler of Iraq; how to foster democracy in Cuba.
They plotted covert action together. Politicians hadn't discussed such topics with newspaper publishers since the days
of Lyndon Johnson and Phil Graham. But with these two,
everything was on the table. I liked to imagine the pair of

them, drinking fine old brandy and smoking cigars on
Galvin's heated porch—surveying the far banks of the Potomac as they discussed where to target a cruise missile.

THESE CONVERSATIONS WOULD HAVE been of historical interest only—grist for someone's memoir—if Galvin hadn't
chosen to ignore the normal rules once again. He decided
after his first meeting with the President that he liked the
man. And it followed that if he liked someone, he should do
everything in his power to help that person. Galvin didn't
understand arguments for caution. Caution smacked of com-
promise and cowardice—and he wanted none of it.

So he ordered up a front-page editorial. This wasn't a
safe, gee-whiz bromide about the need for racial tolerance. It
was a screamer, boxed in three columns at the top left corner
of the front page, under the headline: GET OFF HIS BACK! The
editorial, which Galvin wrote and signed himself, said it was
time to stop tearing the President apart and get back to business. The editorial expressed what a lot of people were feeling at that time, if you believed the polls, and the President's
friends certainly liked it. But within the insular culture of
Washington, it exploded like a stink bomb.

Galvin was making himself some real enemies now. The
Speaker of the House called a news conference to denounce
"unprecedented meddling" by a newspaper owner in the affairs of government. *The New York Times* ran an exposé about
Galvin's secret meetings with the President. They had a lot of
detail—God knows where they got it—and they made it all
sound like a conspiracy. Galvin loved the attention. He was
on *The Anti-News* every morning, fulminating against what

he called the capital's culture of misery. He even did a live interview with the President from the White House, which was carried in prime time by one of the networks. I thought it was great television, worthy of *Jerry Springer*. A sort of "Super-Zack: The 220-pound Baby." Galvin asked the President at one point whether he was a happy man—and rather than the usual pap, he got a real answer. No, the President was not happy. He wasn't even sure what that meant anymore. It was the baby boomer's lament: We had it all, and we blew it.

Galvin's biggest problem was the newsroom. It wasn't just Howard Bacon and his dweeb friends grumbling anymore. Throughout the building, people felt that the publisher had crossed the line in his advocacy of the President. Reporters and editors came to visit me, still thinking that I had some influence with the man. They were embarrassed. Their colleagues at other newspapers and magazines were chiding them—how could they continue to work for a paper like that?—and some of the experienced reporters were wondering if they should quit.

The publisher's only defense was that the public agreed with him. Circulation was continuing to climb—it was up nearly eighty thousand daily from what it had been when he bought the paper. And the stock price had nearly doubled, to ninety dollars a share, making the employee shareholders considerably more prosperous. Perhaps it was hypocritical—the employees who were criticizing Galvin's actions were also benefiting from them. But there's something to be said for hypocrisy. The world would be a worse place, surely, if everyone always acted on their convictions. It's a sign of maturity and mental health to be able to carry contradictory ideas in your mind, without discomfort.

CANDACE DID HER BEST to hide her relationship with Galvin from the newsroom. I knew about it, so I tended to assume that others did too. But I think most people were actually unaware. They knew Candace and the publisher had been lovers once, and they knew they were still friendly. But Candace continued to be seen in public with Mark Pavel, the peripatetic assistant secretary. And her assignations with Galvin were well disguised. As far as the world knew, she never stayed overnight with him. The foreign desk would call her little house in Georgetown in the middle of the night when a plane crashed in France or when the Serbs shelled Kosovo, and she always answered the phone. Perhaps she just had it switched, so that it rang at Galvin's place. It was impossible, really, to be sure of anything about that relationship.

"Be careful, Candace," I said to her one morning, after I had again seen them leaving the building together.

"I'm always careful," she answered. "That's one thing you have to understand about me, David. I never get caught."

GALVIN SEEMED TO AGE slightly as the winter set in. It probably wasn't visible to most people, but I could see that he was thinner, his hair was graying, his face was losing the creaseless look of perpetual youth. It was a surprise, I must say—Galvin was one of those people who seemed to exist out of time. He got sick in late November, for the first time I could remember. He was congested and red-nosed and baggy-eyed, and he seemed to move around the building in slow motion. He was cranky, too. Some people bear illness with grace and good humor—or have the sense to stay at home until they get better—but he was not one of them. I told him to take a vacation, but he was too wound up with his many projects to consider the possibility of leaving. This was his moment. He didn't want to waste a second of it lying on a beach somewhere.

CURIOSITY ABOUT OUR MERCURIAL publisher had reached the point that I began getting calls from journalists who were writing profiles about him. Evidently they had been tipped by newsroom gossips that I was Galvin's friend and factotum, and might know the sort of idiotic "color" that I myself had once tried to worm out of people for articles in *Reveal*. My subsequent rise in the world hadn't made me any more generous, so most of the calls went unanswered. But I received one call from a reporter I genuinely admired, named Michelle Hagel, a woman who had made her way by writing exactly what she thought—the more people she offended in the process, the better. She had succeeded none the less and was now a regular contributor to *The New Yorker*, but I couldn't really blame her for that—talent will out.

So I agreed to meet her for drinks, with the forewarning that I didn't really think I'd be able to offer much help (a line I'd often heard from prospective sources back at *Reveal*, which nearly always preceded a hemorrhage of information). She was an attractive woman, it turned out. Not a stunner like Candace—she was a bit heavier, and frumpier—but still a handsome woman. And she was Jewish; that was nice. She might have been my sister.

"What's Galvin *really* like, once you get past the charm?" she wanted to know. That's what people always ask about someone interesting—as if what they see with their own eyes couldn't possibly be the real story. I told her it was a silly question, and threw back a nugget from Oscar Wilde: "It is only shallow people who do not judge by appearances. The mystery of the world is the visible, not the invisible." It was fun to show off for such a clever woman, but she cut me off—insisting that I had misunderstood.

The point about Galvin, she said, was that his actions couldn't possibly be explained by the known facts. His affairs made no sense: He was nominally in the commodities business, but most of his assets had vanished; he was friendly with the President, but had no clear political interest or agenda; he had bought a newspaper, but rumors were circulating in New York that he intended to sell it. He was a series of puzzles. Hagel asked whether I could help her sort it out.

"He wants something," I said, "but he doesn't know how to get it. That upsets him."

She leaned toward me, her hand resting on her frizzy black hair. In the dark light of the bar, she looked softer, less like my sister. She asked what it was that Galvin wanted. She was giving me the treatment, but I liked it.

"He wants love," I said. She nodded sympathetically. I said there was a particular woman I couldn't name, whom he adored. But it wasn't just that. He wanted everyone to love him. That was the truth. It would have been easier to make something up, but I wanted to be honest.

"Why do you like him so much?" she asked. To her,

Galvin seemed like the sort of person who had tricked and cheated people his whole career. He was like the other tycoons—larger than life, but also smaller. She didn't understand why someone like me would take him seriously. That was flattering, of course. And it made me wonder. Why was I drawn to him? The only answer I could think of was one that sounded ridiculous.

"Galvin makes me feel good," I said. "He does that to people. He's like a good officer in the army. He makes you want to follow him." Was that it? Was it that simple? I wasn't sure. Michelle was waiting, wanting to hear more. "He's always interesting," I offered. "I'm never sure what he's going to do, and I doubt he really knows either. He's inventing himself as he goes along. That's part of his appeal—you want to know how the story will turn out."

"He sounds like Gatsby," she said, giving me a wink.

Come on, I thought. Why did every tycoon have to remind people of Gatsby? It was like calling every blond woman a real Marilyn Monroe. But she was waiting for an answer. It had been years since I'd read the book, and I tried to remember what Fitzgerald's character had been all about.

"I don't think so," I said eventually. "Gatsby wanted respectability more than love. He wanted Daisy the same way he wanted a big house in East Egg, across the bay. Galvin doesn't really care about that stuff. It's different with him. He wants love."

Hagel asked if we could talk again, if she came up with something damaging. Rumors were flying, she said. Would I help her track the information down? I thought about what that would be like, if something devastating surfaced about Galvin. He wasn't used to failure. He wouldn't know how to deal with it.

Yes, I answered, of course I would talk to her. I wanted to know. My investment in Galvin was as deep as any banker's. But she never called me back. *The New Yorker* must have decided to drop the story, or maybe Ted Amara had paid someone a visit, you could never be sure. What I remember, though, is that I had the weirdest feeling after Michelle Hagel left the bar that night. I wished she were still there; you could almost say I missed her.

HUGO BELL ASKED ME to meet him for coffee. He had something hot, he said. That worried me. Hugo was a human version of the letter you want to leave on the table unopened for a while until it cools off. But he was useful; inside, there was always a valuable piece of information. We met in Georgetown, at a little place on M Street with plastic chairs and tables out front—one of the few tacky places left in the neighborhood. The rest of the street looked like a movie set: The old brick facades, which just a decade ago had survived in splendid decay, now served as fronts for megastores selling books and basketball shoes and designer clothing. M Street had been transformed from a place into a destination.

Hugo looked more prosperous than I remembered. He was wearing an Italian suit and carrying a shiny chrome briefcase. He had developed a new sideline that fall—doing opposition research for political candidates. It was amazing how much dirt you could find on people in public records, he said.

And information was color-blind. It was all dirt, whether it stuck to a black man or a white man.

I asked Hugo what he had for me that was so hot.

"It's *official*," he said with relish. "Your boss has money problems."

"That's old news, and I'm not even sure it's true."

"Oh, it's true all right. Your friend Mr. Galvin is liquidating assets—not just his own, but the *Sun's*, too. It's a fire sale. He's going to have to report it in his next quarterly filing with the SEC, unless he's a bigger crook than I think."

"What's he selling?" I was still dubious.

"The Georgetown house is history, for starters. The moving van has come and gone. The place is empty."

"I know that. What else?"

"He's selling land the *Sun* owns in Montgomery County—a big tract north of Rockville that the Hazens and the Crosbys bought in the fifties when it was just farmland. It's worth north of thirty million dollars. He's also selling timberland in Canada, and a paper mill up there. That could fetch a hundred million, maybe more. And I hear he may sell the old *Sun* plant in Northeast too, if he can find anyone to buy it. I'm telling you, he's hurting."

"I haven't heard a word about it at the paper. Who's handling the sale?"

"Not the same people the *Sun* used before. A new guy. The real estate people are upset. Someone named Amara."

That's when I knew it must be true. "His name is Ted Amara," I said. "He's Galvin's personal lawyer."

"Well, he's a hard-nosed SOB, from what I hear. He's

demanding sealed bids and all cash at settlement. People are wondering what's up."

I WAS CURIOUS MYSELF, so I decided to ask the great man. I went up to his office, blew his secretary a kiss and walked into the room. He was sitting at his desk, studying the Bloomberg terminal he had installed a few weeks before. Most of the Asian markets were still spilling blood that week, and he had a gloomy, preoccupied look on his face.

"How can smart people be so stupid?" he muttered to the Bloomberg terminal. "This market doesn't make any sense. It's having a nervous breakdown. If you bought things that were cheap two months ago, you're worse off today than if you had bought things that were expensive. That doesn't make sense, does it?"

He wasn't really expecting an answer. He was upset; you could see that in his eyes, and in the nervous way he was playing with Scotch tape—peeling pieces off the dispenser and rolling them into little tubes between his thumb and forefinger.

Something on the screen caught his eye. It was a summary of trading in foreign currency markets. "Excuse me a minute," he said. He looked almost embarrassed to be conducting business when a colleague from the newspaper was around. He picked up the phone and called someone—a broker, I assumed, but it might have been Ted Amara. "We're getting killed in Hong Kong," he said into the telephone. A brief discussion ensued about whether to unload the position Galvin was holding, followed by a long pause and then Galvin's order to hold fast.

"What did you just do?" I asked.

"I made a bet a few weeks ago that the Hong Kong dollar would fall, along with everything else in Asia. So far I've been wrong. The Hong Kong market's up sharply again today. But it will turn around."

There was a tautness to his face, with the skin pulled tight against his jaw. "What if it doesn't turn around?" I asked.

"Then I'll lose that bet. But I've got lots of others. Italian bonds. Brazilian coffee. Nigerian oil. American stocks. Some go up, some go down. They balance out."

He said it with such certainty, it didn't sound like betting at all. But there was that tight cast to his face, and the tension in his voice on the telephone a few moments before.

"Are you in money trouble?" I asked him.

He thought a moment. "Not really," he replied. It wasn't a reflexive answer, like the one he had given when I asked a similar question some weeks before. "I have what is technically called a 'short-term liquidity problem.' So does everyone who's in this market. But so what? I'm dealing with it. I'm working my way out. Why do you ask? Are people talking again?"

I nodded. "The word is that you've got Ted Amara out hustling the *Sun*'s real estate."

He smiled sheepishly, like someone who had been caught playing a little trick. "Well, that's true. I'm trying to clean up the balance sheet. The Hazens and the Crosbys bought all sorts of things they didn't need. They lumped them all together and forgot about them. That's silly. Why should the *Sun* own timberland and newsprint mills? Let someone else make paper, and we'll buy it from them. Why should we be in commercial real estate? Let someone else develop our properties. What's wrong with that?"

The business case sounded so reasonable, it was hard to disagree with him. And he never acted like a man who had anything to conceal. If you asked him a question, he always gave you an answer. And yet I knew that something was wrong.

"I have no business giving you advice," I said, "but I'm going to do it anyway. You need to be careful. You've upset the applecart more than you realize. You've done things that make people angry. If you have any weaknesses, people are going to take advantage of them."

"Of course I have weaknesses," he answered. "I'm human."

"But Washington isn't human. It doesn't forgive. You only get one strike here and you're out. So you have to be careful."

"I know, I know. But I *like* it here." He smiled, as jaunty as FDR in the dark days of 1934. "I'm doing what I've always wanted. Everything will be fine. Don't become a worrier, David. It doesn't fit your personality."

I looked out his big window. There was a low winter sun coming at the buildings almost sideways and casting shadows that seemed to stretch for blocks. It was disorienting. We're used to seeing our world illuminated from above. We don't recognize things when the sun traces a different trajectory, low and flat in the sky at midday.

CANDACE WENT INTO HER own kind of hibernation. She stopped coming by my office to gossip on her way down to the cafeteria. And she seemed less playful, less resilient to my teasing. Perhaps she had become so careful about her relationship with Galvin that it had rubbed off on other parts of her personality. I don't know. But her reticence only increased my curiosity. I wanted to understand the bond between her and Galvin. It remained a mystery, frankly. As well as I knew each of them separately, I didn't comprehend what had united them long ago, blown them apart, and then bound them together again.

My curiosity about Candace's relationship was given an unlikely prod by her old friend, Ariane Hazen. She continued to hang around the paper, as head of the *Sun*'s charitable foundation. Galvin had been faithful to his pledge to keep her engaged, and she had more than once repaid him, by passing along information about problems in the community, or among advertisers. She even liked some of the changes he had made, especially the shower of money for the city that had accompanied the Racial Healing campaign.

I encountered Ariane one afternoon standing in line at the ATM machine across from the *Sun*. She seemed to have forgotten my absurd visit to her house in Cleveland Park the previous summer, when Galvin was first stalking the *Sun*. Now we were colleagues. I asked whether she'd seen much of our mutual friend and she said no, alas—Candace was spending all her time with the publisher. I gave her a wink. We were among the few who really knew what was going on.

"I don't understand that relationship," I ventured. "I don't see why they got back together any better than I see why they broke up in college."

Ariane said I would have to buy her a cup of coffee if I

wanted an answer. She wasn't going to tell me anything standing up. I took her to a Brazilian bar near the office that was always filled with fabulous-looking men and women putting the make on each other. They wisely gave us a table in the back, where the Brazilians wouldn't have to look at us. Ariane ordered a piña colada, which instantly made me like her.

"Candace broke his heart," she confided after several sips. "He wanted to get married after her father died, and she refused. And that was the end of it."

"How do you know?" I asked. She didn't, really. She was inferring, and guessing. But she knew what Candace had been like in the weeks before everything fell apart, because they had been together, here in Washington.

IT TURNED OUT THAT the two school chums had met at a party late in the summer of 1971, just before Candace went back to start her sophomore year. She looked terrible, Ariane had thought. She was thin, wary, with a sadness in her eyes that hadn't been there before. Candace had confided that she was seeing someone at Harvard—a man who was mad about her—but she never mentioned his name. It was only recently that Ariane had figured out she must have been referring to Galvin.

Her friend's emotional frailty had surprised Ariane. Candace had always been the golden girl at school—the girl who won the academic prizes without ever seeming to study; who took the penalty shots for her team in field hockey because she had steady nerves. Ariane hadn't seen her since she went off to college, and it was obvious that freshman year had taken a toll. She looked like the oldest nineteen-year-old in the world. The unnamed boyfriend was part of it, but there was more.

Candace said that her father had gone back into the hospital that summer. It was all quite mysterious, but Ariane understood that this wasn't an ordinary hospital, where they took your appendix out and sewed you back together, but a mental hospital. There were other rumors about Mr. Ridgway, too—that he was having an affair with a divorced woman, that his drinking was out of control. His wife was embarrassed—trying to pretend that it wasn't happening and telling lies to her friends. But Candace seemed to understand that her father was experiencing a kind of pain he couldn't express, even to his daughter.

Ariane had sensed that her friend was coping by dividing her life into compartments; when one got too full to manage, she closed it and put it away. She had that ability to pretend that everything was all right, even when it wasn't. But Candace's boyfriend—whoever he was—was making that hard. His kind of love was a cataclysm—a vacuum that sucked you in so totally that you couldn't breathe without your lover feeding you the oxygen.

And it had begun to frighten Candace. That's what Ariane had seen. She was like a flower pressed between the pages of a book. Beautiful, perfect to look at—but flat and lifeless. And rather than surrender to that perfect nonexistence, she was on the verge of rebelling that September. She did that a few weeks later, when she exercised her only

remaining power—which was to say no. And when she refused to marry her boyfriend, she broke his heart. That was
what Ariane believed, at least.

I CALLED CANDACE THAT night, after I talked with Ariane. I
suppose I was frightened for her. Galvin was still a typhoon of
a man—still capable of sucking the air out of a person's
lungs. And he was more dangerous now. He wasn't a charis-
matic undergraduate. He had built himself a pyramid that included a newspaper, a president, a city. But it was an unstable
platform, and if Candace was with him when it all collapsed,
she would get hurt. Or so I thought.

She answered the phone. I don't know whether it was
ringing at her house or Galvin's, but it didn't matter.

"I was worrying about you," I said.

"That's sweet. Why were you worrying?"

I explained that I had been talking that day with her old
pal, Ariane. And I'd sensed how painful the breakup of her relationship with Galvin must have been. "I'm your friend," I
said. "I don't want that to happen again. He's moving so fast
now, I'm afraid he's going to crash. I don't want you to be
hurt."

She didn't answer, and I thought it might be because
Galvin was lying next to her in bed, listening to what she said.
But it probably wasn't that. She was wondering how to an-
swer me.

"I'll be fine," she said evenly. "Some things are just complicated."

"Is he in some kind of trouble? He hasn't been looking
well, and he seems to be under a lot of stress."

"I don't know. There's a lot he doesn't tell me. He may be worried about money, but I'm not sure. Sandy keeps a lot to himself."

"Be careful. The newspaper could get hurt."

That was a strange thing for me to say—I'd never given a damn about the *Sun*. But newspapers do that to you. They're like old pets. You begin to love them, even though they drool and bark and generally make a nuisance of themselves.

"I'll never hurt the newspaper." Her voice had a tone of resignation and duty, more than passion. "I'm not just the publisher's girlfriend," she said. "I know where the lines are."

IT WAS LATE—ELEVEN o'clock, the news hour. Once upon a time, the local rerun channel had taken pity on the news-saturated and broadcast old *Baywatch* episodes at that hour, so you could watch David Hasselhoff and Pamela Anderson in bathing suits instead of the newsreaders. But now there was no escape except to turn off the TV. And even then, the morning newspaper was lying on the floor reproachfully next to my bed. I wasn't ready to go to sleep; talking to Candace had depressed me.

I picked up the *Sun* and began leafing through the Local News section. I never read the paper carefully, now that I worked there. That was the worst thing about newspaper work; it made life seem less interesting. It was all cut up into stories—you couldn't find the real people anymore.

I came to the obituary page, something I rarely looked at, and found myself glancing at the "In Memoriam" notices. There were pictures of people who had passed away, in some cases long ago, accompanied by brief, heartsick messages. A wife and four daughters remembered a man who had died thirty-four years before: "Your memory is constant in our minds," it said. "The hole in our hearts will never be filled." Another had a picture of a young man, smartly dressed in his high school cap and gown, who had died eight years before at the age of thirty-one. His family had written a prayer—"A letter we cannot send you, your body we cannot touch. But, God, please take these words to the one we love so much."

How strange people were; they thought God read the newspaper.

I leafed a few more pages to the Personals. Occasionally I scanned these for the colorful ways people chose to describe themselves. "Affectionate, voluptuous, likes travel, fit." They never said "lonely." On this evening, my eye wandered to a category I'd never noticed, called "I Saw You." They were little notes, posted by people after chance encounters with someone who had caught their eye and made them think later, when they were alone, maybe that was the *one*. "Starbucks, Dupont Circle, 10/28, You: brunette, red coat. Me: sandy hair, leather jacket. You smiled." "National Gallery, 10/30, 1 p.m. by the Rembrandt painting. You said hi. I was too shy." "St. Mark's Church, 10/25, you sat next to me. Are you single?"

They were the saddest things I had ever read, those notes. Each expressed in a few lines the pain of realizing, too late, that love might have been right next to you, and you had let it slip away. I tried to imagine the failures of nerve that lay behind each of the plaintive messages—the embarrassment that had come over someone's face, the sentence that wasn't finished, the pounding heart. They were afraid to speak. *He'll think I sound stupid. . . . She'll think I'm too forward.* And then the moment had passed, the person was gone—and instantly, they began to regret it, and wanted it back. So they bought these advertisements, in the hope they could rewind the tape and try again.

IF I HAD BEEN a real human being, I would have resolved that night to do something about my own loneliness and isolation. But I was a journalist, so I decided to commission a story. At my morning meeting the next day, I told my Lifestyle colleagues that we were going to do a piece looking for the people who were looking for love. We would investigate those notices on the "I Saw You" page and see if we could find the people—the brunette in Starbucks who smiled, the man in the pew at St. Mark's Church—and bring them together. Love was the last frontier in our fragmented, bewildering country, I told my colleagues. Where did we find it? How did some people escape the inevitability of unhappiness? Was it luck, or an act of will?

Everybody thought it was a good idea. But I could tell by the looks in their eyes that they were wondering whether something was wrong with me.

EIGHTEEN

HOWARD BACON'S FINAL BATTLE WITH GALVIN WAS TRIG-
gered by something so ordinary that nobody saw it coming—
least of all Bacon. I saw him at a story conference the day
before the flap began, and he was his usual self—those long
silences punctuated by niggling questions about stories. I'm
not sure he had focused on the story that ultimately got him
in trouble. When the Local editor pitched it at the three
o'clock meeting, the only question he asked was whether it
had been lawyered.

The story concerned the pastor of New Calvary Full-
Gospel Temple, a church in Northeast where the mayor
sometimes worshiped. The pastor's name was Elwood R.
Carnes, and the story alleged that Mayor Marquand had been
steering city contracts to him—to administer antidrug programs and senior-citizen housing. In return, the story said,
Pastor Carnes had been a loyal lieutenant in Marquand's political machine, delivering voters by the thousands on elec-

tion day and contributing handsomely to his campaigns. It was an ordinary, garden-variety local corruption story—the kind the *Sun* ran every few months to absolutely no effect, other than infuriating black readers and convincing the mayor that the paper was out to get him. There was nothing libelous in the story; one of our lawyers had indeed vetted it prior to publication. But there was a tone, an implicit sneer at black Washington and its political and religious institutions— which had been intertwined for years, whether the *Sun* liked it or not.

Galvin arrived at his usual seven-thirty the next morning to read the paper and take phone calls. He'd started publishing a special phone number so people could call him between eight and nine and tell him what they thought about the newspaper with a heart. This morning, the phone had been ringing since dawn. The first to reach him was Pastor Carnes himself. He was in tears, Galvin told me later. He couldn't understand why, among the dozens of local ministers who were on the mayor's payroll, the *Sun* had landed on *him*.

Soon after that, Mayor Marquand called.

"So I see we're back to the old racist bullshit," said the mayor. "But now, you don't just send your dogs after *me*, you go after my pastor! Racial Healing, my ass!" He was angry. He had stuck his neck out in the black community for Galvin, and now it had been chopped off.

"I didn't know the Carnes story was coming," answered Galvin. "Honestly, I'm as upset about this as you are."

"Bullshit," said the mayor succinctly. "You know how I

found out about this? My wife, Edna, called me at six-thirty from the *health club*. Jesus!"

"Heads will roll, when I find out how this happened. I promise you that."

"Bullshit," the mayor repeated. "I don't believe you. You're the boss over there. Nothing runs in that newspaper without your say-so. Don't lie to me! But at least now I know where I stand with you. I *know* how to deal with your racist newspaper—been doin' it for years—and so does this community."

"I am genuinely, deeply sorry," said Galvin. And you couldn't doubt it, listening to him tell the story. All that racial baggage he'd tried to clear away had been dumped back in the hallway, for him and everybody else to trip over.

BACON DIDN'T ARRIVE UNTIL nine forty-five—which made matters considerably worse, because it gave Galvin more time to listen to nasty calls, and more time to get angry. It also gave him time to summon me to his office. He wanted someone to watch, like a witness at an execution. When Bacon entered the building, the guard in the lobby told him to go up to the publisher's office immediately.

"How could this have happened?" Galvin screamed at his editor, pointing to the Carnes story. Bacon was flummoxed. He hadn't realized he was walking into a combat zone.

"This story is a piece of *shit!*" Galvin raged on. "It illustrates everything I hate about journalism. It's a cheap shot. It pisses off the community to no purpose, and it's racist to boot. It ignores the essential fact about this minister, which is that he's done a lot of good for people. How the *fuck* could this have gotten into the newspaper?"

"The lawyers looked at it," answered Bacon. "They didn't find anything wrong with it. Neither did I."

"Well, then, you are a sorrier editor than I ever imagined. Why didn't you tell me it was coming? I am the publisher of this newspaper. I have been working with the mayor to try to help our city. This story concerns me, surely. Didn't it occur to you to give me some advance warning?"

"Mr. Hazen never asked to read anything in advance. He thought that was inappropriate."

The reference to the previous publisher pushed Galvin's fury to a higher level. He was usually careful not to show his anger or to curse. But he had lost control. "You chickenshit!" he muttered, and as he spoke, he impulsively grabbed a Plexiglas tombstone off his desk and hurled it against the wall— missing Bacon's head by a few feet, but close enough that the editor ducked.

"You're pathetic." The publisher shook his head in disgust. "I want a correction in the paper tomorrow. That's the least we can do to repair the damage this article has caused. I want the correction on the front page, in the same place where the article ran."

Galvin was a big man, and he was in a towering rage. But the editor stood his ground. "We don't have anything to correct," he said. "There were no mistakes in that article."

"The whole article was a mistake! It attacked the religious life of the mayor of this city and a majority of its population. Jesus! You don't get it, do you? This is why America hates journalists. You people think it's okay to take a shit on someone, and when they get upset, you tell them it's unethical! What's the matter with you? Do you *like* to piss people off for no good reason? Is that it?"

"I stand by the article." Bacon was trembling now with his own indignation. "And I must say that just because this newspaper is in bed with the mayor—as a result of the publisher's poor judgment—that doesn't mean we should stop investigating local corruption, or apologize when we find something wrong. Your friend the mayor is wasting the taxpayer's money to support his cronies. Taxpayers are readers too. Don't they matter?"

"Publish the correction," said Galvin.

"I refuse. It would violate journalistic ethics to correct a story that has no mistakes, simply because it embarrasses the publisher."

"You cocksucker! Don't you talk that way to me. This is why America hates you. Because you're arrogant. You don't know how to apologize when you're wrong. I'm telling you for the last time: Publish the correction in tomorrow's newspaper."

"I refuse." Bacon's voice was small but firm.

"Then you're fired." Galvin rose from his chair and walked over to where Bacon was sitting. He looked enormous, looming over the pink-faced editor. He took Bacon's arm and pulled him to his feet. "I want you out of this building by twelve o'clock." Galvin grasped his editor by the shoulders and pushed him out the door.

BACON CALLED A MEETING of the newsroom at eleven o'clock. He stood atop a desk so that everyone could see him, and told the staff that he had just been fired. He explained the publisher's demand for a correction of the Carnes story, and the reasons for his refusal, and made a flowery speech about journalistic ethics that had a lot of people crying. Bacon knew his audience. Journalists are sentimentalists. They're always ready to sing the "Marseillaise."

When Bacon walked out of the building at noon, the whole staff stood and applauded. People were in tears again—praising the editor and cursing the publisher. And then something curious happened. A few reporters who had worked for years with Bacon walked out after him in protest, and then a few dozen more—and suddenly the whole newsroom was marching out of the building and down into the street. It was a mob scene. There must have been five hundred people raising their fists in the air and screaming up at Galvin's office. I joined the walkout too, partly because I was afraid to look like Galvin's stoolie. As I surveyed the angry crowd, I thought, This is how revolutions begin. They were chanting and hollering—calling for a strike to shut down the paper until Galvin resigned.

It would have gotten ugly, I'm sure, if Bacon hadn't stepped in. He grabbed a bullhorn and called out to the crowd. He told them he appreciated their support, but the best way they could honor him was to go back upstairs and publish a great paper the next day. This wasn't a strike issue, he said. The community might misinterpret their protest, and that would damage the *Sun*. "Please go back to work," he urged them. "The battle for good journalism is one you're going to have to fight with this publisher every day."

A class act, you'd have to say. I still didn't like Bacon, but I must concede that he played the last hand pretty well. It landed him a fat teaching job at Berkeley too, which illustrated another rule about Washington. If you leave it the right way, you're in fat city forever.

GALVIN THEN COMMITTED WHAT people thought at the time was an act of desperation and folly. At one o'clock, he posted a notice on the board downstairs that he had accepted Bacon's resignation. As Bacon's successor, the notice said, he was naming the *Sun*'s Pulitzer Prize–winning foreign editor, Candace Ridgway.

Candace raced up to his office when she heard the news. So did I. The announcement scared me. It was too quick, too open to misinterpretation. The newsroom was completely crazy by that point, and people were shouting to Candace as she headed upstairs that she should refuse the job. I met her in the lobby outside Galvin's door. She was dressed elegantly in a blue suit, with a short skirt and a fitted jacket—too stylish for an editor.

"He's gone nuts!" she said when she saw me. "What am I going to do?"

The door opened and out walked Sandy Galvin. He was beaming. As far as he was concerned, something wonderful had just happened. He'd found an excuse to get rid of an editor he regarded as incompetent and untrustworthy, and install someone talented and pliant.

"You can't go through with this!" said Candace when we were inside his office. "This is a mistake."

Galvin shook his head. Journalists were crazy. They didn't understand management. That was the only explanation, in his mind, for Candace's reluctance. "It's not a mistake. You're the best editor at the paper, with the credentials to prove it. The fact that you're also my friend is irrelevant. You're the best. I'd pick you even if I didn't like you. Isn't that right, David?"

I didn't answer. This was one argument I didn't want to be in the middle of.

"You should have told me, at least, before you announced it," she said.

"But that would have given you a chance to say no. This way, you can't back out."

"Yes, I can. I can issue my own press statement declining the job. Things are so screwed up around here already, it wouldn't surprise anyone."

"Don't do that, my dear," he said tenderly. "Accept this promotion. You've earned it. I'm offering you a chance to run one of the greatest newspapers in the world. It's my gift to you. It makes me happier than anything I've ever done. Take it, and do great things with it. That's all I want."

She folded her arms across her chest and looked him in the eye. "You may regret it," she said.

"Impossible. How could I conceivably regret it?"

"If I take this job, I'm going to do it the right way. I'm a journalist, and I believe in our code of ethics, even if you think it's stupid. Right now, the credibility of the newspaper is at stake. If people think I'm your lackey, it will destroy the *Sun*."

Galvin's smile widened. "I agree with everything you just said. That's why I'm naming you editor. Because I trust you to do what's right for the paper." He reached out to shake her hand, but she wasn't finished.

"I won't run that correction," she said. "Bacon was right. The Carnes article may have been a cheap shot, but it wasn't factually incorrect."

Galvin stiffened; the smile vanished. "Give me this one, Candace. The mayor expects a correction. He deserves one. I've worked hard to get this city on a new footing, and I don't want to backslide. A correction will say to the community that we're sorry we offended them. What's wrong with that?"

"What's wrong is that it's *wrong*. It's the principle. Sometimes a great newspaper offends people. It's inevitable. We don't apologize for that; it's our job. But people will forgive us in time, if we show we care about them."

"I want that correction on the front page tomorrow, Candace. It's important to me. I don't want to have to back down on this. It would send the wrong signal."

They stood a few feet apart—the highborn journalist and the lowborn tycoon who wanted to be a publisher. This was their moment; they had traveled such a long way to get here. I couldn't see how either could back down; they would have to undo their life histories. But I didn't understand then where the fulcrum really lay in that relationship.

Candace turned to me. "We need some time alone to work this out, David. Would you excuse us?"

I left the room and waited at the end of the corridor in one of the leather chairs set out for visitors. After five minutes, Candace emerged from Galvin's office. She shook his hand; he kissed her cheek. She walked toward me, her eyes glowing, ready to step right out of the frame of that picture and into another.

"What happened?" I asked.

"We compromised," she said. "I agreed to become editor, and he agreed not to publish a correction of the Carnes story."

"You won," I said, with genuine astonishment. But she had already headed down the hall to the elevator, to greet her new staff.

CANDACE HELD A STAFF meeting that afternoon at four. She didn't stand on the desk the way Bacon had, but she bellowed out her remarks. There was a huge crowd, bigger even than for Bacon's teary departure. A lot of people in the newsroom didn't know Candace—she'd spent so many years overseas. And she was the first woman ever to hold the top editing job, so there was curiosity. People wanted to believe that she would be a good leader, but Bacon's pals were already circulating the rumor that Galvin was sleeping with her.

Someone asked me whether it was true they were having an affair. I thought a moment. "Could be," I said. I wasn't going to lie to protect them. She was going to have to deal with it eventually.

People crowded around the new editor as she emerged from her office in Foreign. She had been to the beauty parlor since I saw her outside Galvin's office. The wispy look I loved—the windblown hair falling across her face—was gone. It was all neat, clipped, hair-sprayed in place. She looked so regal, people pressed toward her to get a closer look. It was as if they needed to touch her to make sure that she was real—that she had ballast, and wouldn't just float away. And they did need her now. Publishing a serious newspaper requires an act of will. It's so much easier to tell lies, bend to pressure, tell people what they want to hear. That was the part Galvin didn't understand, in all his righteous indignation. There is a difference between newspapers that tell the truth, and those that don't.

"This has been a roller-coaster day," Candace began, "but I hope it will have a happy ending." People clapped, even at that; they were so eager for something to hold on to.

"Mr. Galvin asked me to become editor today, as you know. What you probably don't know is that I refused his offer, until he promised that I would be independent of the business side of the newspaper—including the publisher." At this, there was a spontaneous burst of applause. Candace called out for quiet. I could see the determination on her face: She was going to lead this institution; it was her destiny.

"Mr. Galvin also asked me to publish a front-page correction of this morning's story about Pastor Carnes, just as he had asked Howard Bacon to do this morning. Like Howard, I refused. I told Mr. Galvin I would not take the job unless he withdrew this demand. After some discussion, he agreed, and there will be no correction." There were more shouts now, of real jubilation. She had forced him to back down. She had defied the publisher and won.

"I proposed, instead, to meet with Pastor Carnes tomorrow and hear his complaints about the article. That's some-

thing a good newspaper is always ready to do." There was silence as the crowd pondered whether this amounted to a
cave-in, and then applause as they concluded that it didn't.

"I told the publisher, finally, that I agree with him that we
need to rethink many of the things we do in journalism. The
Sun can be more exciting and readable—and many of the
changes Mr. Galvin has made have been good for us. But I
also told him that I want the *Sun* to remain a great newspaper—not just a fun paper, but a great one—and that can
only be done by the professional journalists in this room."

A roar went up when she was done—a sigh of relief as
much as a cheer. People wouldn't stop clapping. She had
saved the paper, saved their jobs too—for many of them had
been on the verge of quitting. She was a wonder-worker. Despite her patrician upbringing, she was one of them—a real
journalist who had won a Pulitzer Prize. And they loved her.

I stopped by Candace's office later to congratulate her. I
had to wait a few minutes, there was such a crush of well-
wishers. People couldn't wait to start sucking up to the new
boss. I closed the door so that the adoring masses couldn't
eavesdrop.

"Was that for real?" I asked her. "I mean, it was a great
speech, and the staff ate it up. But did Galvin really agree to
all that?"

"Of course he did. I wouldn't lie about it. He wanted me
to be the editor, and he was willing to make concessions to
get me to say yes."

"But you're his *girlfriend*. Isn't that going to cause problems?"

"Why should it? People understand these things. I'll do my job, and he'll do his. What happens outside the office is our business."

She looked so tough and taut. My vision of her had been fulfilled, but not in the ways I had imagined. All the softness had gone hard.

"How can a journalist love a liar?" I asked. She was silent, but I knew the answer. Everyone loves a liar.

CANDACE WAS A CELEBRITY, instantly. All the newspapers had stories the next day—about how she had faced down the publisher on an issue of principle. The stories were full of details that could only have come from her. The *Times* mentioned that she and Galvin had been involved romantically in college, but was strangely silent on the current state of their relationship. She went on two of the morning talk shows too, and they didn't ask about her personal life either. The media elite were taking a dive. Candace was part of the club, and they would protect her as long as they could.

I had never resented Candace's success before. She had always been exempt from my malediction on those who survived and prospered in the media fun house. But I confess that I felt angry now, and that a part of me wished her ill.

NINETEEN

THE ASSAULT ON GALVIN BEGAN IN EARNEST IN DECEM-
ber. I'd never doubted that it would come. Every action
creates a counteraction, and that's especially true in a zero-
gravity place like Washington. Galvin had broken too many
rules. You can get away with that sort of iconoclasm as long
as you appear to be powerful. But the minute you seem vulnerable, your enemies gather for the feast. This is what Washington has in common with Lagos or Beirut. At the end of
the day, when the legalisms are stripped away, politics is about
the ability to inflict pain.

The opening salvo appeared on the front page of *The
Wall Street Journal*. The story was a detailed account of how
the Commodities Futures Trading Commission and the Treasury Department had quietly come to Galvin's aid the previous month—by encouraging some big banks to provide an
$800-million bridge loan to his investment firm. According to
the *Journal* story, Galvin had lost hundreds of millions of dollars betting the wrong way on interest rates and had gotten

squeezed by his creditors. I assumed that was the "liquidity problem" he had mentioned to me in his pleasantly off-handed way around that time.

What made the *Journal* story interesting was the allegation that Galvin had discussed his financial problems with the President during one of their wine and cigar evenings, and that the President had personally asked the CFTC and Treasury to see what they could do to help Galvin. It was a damaging leak, and it testified that Galvin had made powerful enemies.

Candace looked unhappy that morning as we rode up together in the elevator. She had the *Journal* under her arm. She had underlined passages from the Galvin article in yellow highlighter. She'd had the good times—she'd gotten to give her Gipper speech and save the newsroom—but now she would have to do some serious shoveling.

"What are we going to do about that little item?" I asked, pointing to the *Journal*.

"Cover the story," she said. "We have no choice." She had already called our best financial reporter at home, and told him to come in and interview Galvin. The reporter was upstairs now, she said. Galvin had been so angry about the story, his first instinct had been to catch a plane for Europe. But she'd convinced him to stay and face the music.

We published the interview the next day. The publisher gave cagey answers that confirmed most of what the *Journal* had—he couldn't very well deny it; they had names and dates and direct quotes from meetings—but didn't add much new information. Candace put the story on the front page. I'm sure Galvin hated that, but it was the right call. He wanted to write a first-person editorial explaining himself—and describing how treacherous the financial markets had become—but Candace told him to forget it. This was no time for him to be delivering lectures.

The *Journal* story created an opening for Galvin's enemies, especially for congressional Republicans, who hated both him and the President and were delighted to have an opportunity to attack them both simultaneously. The chairman of the House Commerce Committee announced that he would hold hearings on Galvin's business affairs in January, when the new Congress was seated. The committee staff would begin gathering information immediately. I could only imagine what the reaction must be among Galvin's business associates: They would say it was his own fault, for moving his business operations to a lunatic asylum like Washington. They would charge him more to borrow money, too—making it that much harder to pay it back. That was what happened when you got caught in the squeeze.

The White House issued a careful statement in response to the *Journal* story. It denied any impropriety in the President's contacts with Galvin but promised full cooperation with the House inquiry. They were going to roll over on him; they had to—the President had too many other problems just then to worry about Galvin, no matter how many bottles of fancy wine they'd put away together. It was a funny time. There's a phrase for it in most languages: *sauve qui peut; sal si puedes.* I suppose the current English vernacular would be *Cover your ass.*

I received a letter from the House committee, requesting my voluntary cooperation with their inquiry and setting a date in December when they wanted me to come in for an informal chat. That posed a dilemma—not a moral one, exactly, but a practical one.

I called an old friend from college who was now an overpaid Washington lawyer and a man I normally treated with cordial contempt. I told him about the letter and asked which was likely to cause more trouble for me personally— testifying or not testifying. That was hard to answer, he said. I could refuse to talk to them, on the grounds that I was a journalist—but that could cause a flap. Or I could agree to an informal interview, but insist that it be off the record. In that case, he advised me to tell the truth—and to say I knew nothing of Galvin's misdeeds. I liked that; it had an attractive symmetry. He urged me, especially, not to talk to anyone about my summons.

I MADE AN APPOINTMENT to see Candace. You had to do that now, she was so busy. She had moved into Bacon's office and installed a plucky brunette named Eileen as her secretary, whose job was to keep the well-wishers and ass-kissers at bay. Candace didn't wander around the newsroom anymore on her way to the ladies' room; she had her own toilet now.

She had already redecorated the office. Bacon's worthy books about politics and foreign policy were gone, replaced by shelves full of novels. Jane Austen in place of Zbigniew Brzezinski—who wouldn't make that trade? She'd done other things to make the office feel homey—put in a couple of easy chairs in place of Bacon's leather couch, and replaced the fluorescent lighting with several nice table lamps. The picture of her father was there too, newly framed. Atop her coffee table rested a lavish spray of cut flowers, courtesy of the publisher. The teddy bear was gone, though—just when she needed him most.

"You'd better do something about Galvin," I said. "The vultures are circling."

"I know. The House committee sent me a letter yesterday. I told our lawyer I wouldn't go. They have no business even asking me—I'm the editor of the paper, not to mention his close friend. The lawyer thinks they'll drop it. It's a fishing expedition."

"That's good." I didn't mention my own letter from the committee; I hadn't decided what to do about it yet.

"Besides," she said, "I don't know anything about Sandy's finances. We never talk about money. Although I must say, that's starting to bother me. I worry that there's all this *stuff* out there involving him, which nobody at the paper knows anything about—except that creepy Ted Amara. And I didn't like having to chase someone else's story about our own publisher this week. That was embarrassing."

"What are you going to do? You don't have a lot of time. The House investigation is rolling."

She moved uncomfortably in her chair, as if a weight were pressing against her. Her eyes turned toward the flowers on the table—a hundred dollars' worth of irises and orchids and roses thrown her way, like an extravagant kiss. She didn't want to look at me. She was trying to be an editor, and it was lonely.

"I've been thinking that we need our own investigation,"

she said. "To protect Sandy and the *Sun* from any accusation that we're covering things up. We could look into things quietly, on our own. That way we won't get blindsided. I'm sure there's nothing terrible out there. Sandy isn't dishonest. We'd form a little team, and keep it very quiet, and then publish a story. That's what a serious newspaper should do in a situation like this, I think. Does that make sense to you?"

"I guess so," I said. "This isn't going to go away. You have to do something. Are you going to tell Galvin that you're investigating him?"

"I don't think so. Not in the beginning, at least. I'll have to ask him for comment when we're done—the way we would with any story. But this needs to look independent. That's what Sandy would want. He didn't buy the *Sun* to make it a propaganda sheet, whatever people may think. He wants to publish a great newspaper."

I offered my help. I said I knew some people who might have information about Galvin's business, and she seemed pleased to have someone to share the burden. I should meet with the reporting team, she said. She had selected two trustworthy reporters—an investigative reporter and our Wall Street reporter in New York. That would make four of us who knew. She stressed the need to keep it all confidential. The Savant would have to steer clear of his usual gossip channels, and I was happy to agree. I understood that she was doing the right thing—journalistically speaking.

CHARACTERISTICALLY, GALVIN HIMSELF SEEMED largely oblivious of the storm clouds gathering over his head. Circulation was continuing to rise, regardless of his financial problems. The paper was up more than a hundred thousand now—and the trade publications were writing articles about the "miracle turnaround" at the *Sun*. He was looking for ways to keep the momentum going. That was the thing about Galvin's kind of business; it was unstable—if it ever stopped growing, it was in danger of imploding.

Galvin's current obsession was buying the local MLS men's soccer team. He had decided that soccer would be the next big thing in the United States, and he wanted the *Sun* to profit from it. He stopped by my office one day to ask why we weren't writing more about the team in the Lifestyle section. They were in the playoffs, but the paper was ignoring them. Did we dislike Spanish speakers? Was that it? he wondered aloud. What was the point of buying the soccer team at all, if the paper wouldn't cover it?

"These players are great stories," he said. "Colorful guys, far from home."

"A little too colorful. I think a couple of them were accused of molesting a young woman last year."

"Negative, negative. Those two were never convicted of anything. I had Ted Amara look into it. The fans don't care about that stuff anyway. Soccer players are the new superstars. Babetto, Zidane, Baggio. They're gods. In Brazil, they name children after soccer players. It's going to be that way in America soon. And we're going to be ready."

Galvin planned to rename the team the Suns. "The team with a heart, brought to you by the newspaper with a heart." He'd talked to the local cable people, and they were willing to carry every away game—if the *Sun* agreed to do cross-promotion for it in the paper. He was even thinking about sponsoring a *Sun* youth league, with coaching tips in the paper, and the players giving free clinics.

He was in one of his remake-the-world phases again, the way he'd been with racial healing. The energy was all there, but the package was shopworn. There was a thinness in his voice too, as if there were something caught way down in his throat. That was the Sun King's only weakness, that I could see. He could defy the financial markets and House investigative committees, but he couldn't permanently defy time. His universe was beginning to bend back upon itself.

GALVIN DISPATCHED TED AMARA to talk with the owners of the soccer team. They were a group of local real estate developers who had made their money in the seventies and early eighties building the malls and office buildings that now ringed the capital. Amara met them at the Tower Club in Tysons Corner—a giant office block that rose out of the old farmland by the Beltway. This was the gathering spot for northern Virginia's newly rich, the suburban entrepreneurs who'd made fortunes in clean, bloodless businesses like telecommunications and computer services. From the club's picture window, Washington and its problems looked small and far away.

Amara arrived with his briefcase and bad suit. In this citadel of bland success, he was the odd man out. But he had a way of establishing common ground, even here. Galvin was vague about precisely what Amara had offered. The *Sun* proposed to pay a small premium over what the owners had originally spent for the team, plus a share of its profits in the future. They weren't really thinking about selling until Amara's visit, Galvin said. But by the time he left, he had a preliminary agreement.

"How does Amara do that?" I asked. He had an uncanny ability to get people to do what he wanted. "Is he a gangster?"

"Quite the contrary," answered Galvin. "Ted is the most honest person I know. He just helps people understand what's in their best interest." In this case, Galvin explained, Amara had understood he was talking to real estate people. They had a lot of money at risk in a market that was going soft. Amara happened to know that some of their deals were in trouble—a big shopping-mall project in Leesburg, for example, that couldn't close the previous week because the financing dried up. So Amara had helped them find money to complete that deal. He had told the group about some other things that were over the horizon, which they might not have known about, and they were grateful. Businesspeople weren't stupid, regardless of what journalists might think, Galvin said. They understood where their interests lay.

I shook my head; I didn't get it. Where did Galvin have the money to be bailing out other investors?

"Shouldn't you be more careful?" I said. "You're in the same boat as these real estate people. You have money problems, no matter how high the *Sun*'s stock price is. Some of your deals are going soft. This isn't the time for you to be a sugar daddy."

Galvin laughed. He thought that was funny, that I was giving him financial advice. "Don't be such a worrier. Everything will turn out all right." He pointed to the *Little Mermaid* poster on my wall. "Don't forget how the story turns out. The prince marries the mermaid and they live happily ever after."

WHEN THE SPORTS EDITOR learned that Galvin was about to buy the local soccer team and rename it "The Suns—The Team with a Heart," he made a broken-field run to Candace's office. "He's killing me!" he said. "You gotta make him stop!"

Like most journalists at the *Sun,* the sports editor saw himself as a professional. He'd been supervising sports coverage for more than a decade—and during that time he had faced ceaseless pressure from owners and managers who wanted favorable stories about their teams. They'd all made the same pitch: We're the home team! We're the good guys! We should get positive coverage in the hometown newspaper! To which the sports editor had always replied, "Go to hell! The *Sun* doesn't root for anyone." Now the publisher was threatening to destroy that precious credibility.

"I'll try to turn him around," Candace said. "But what will you do if he won't back down?"

This was not an easy question. The sports editor was fifty-two years old and had three children—one in college and two more in high school, and it was unlikely that he could earn anything approaching his current salary if he left.

"I'll have to quit," he said. "There's no point in working for people who don't understand the rules."

Discretion was not the sports editor's strong suit, and the

newsroom quickly learned about his ultimatum to the new editor. Poor Candace. She didn't need this fight right now. She didn't give a hoot about soccer, or about sports coverage in general, and she had so many other problems to worry about. But the sports editor was popular with the staff, and she knew that on principle, he was right: The *Sun* had no business owning a local sports team.

SHE ASKED GALVIN TO take a walk by the river. She told me about it when she got back; I think she was surprised at how it had turned out. It was a sunny December day, cold and clear, with the sky a perfect crystalline blue as if the color had been frozen in the upper atmosphere. They left the *Sun* building and walked down Virginia Avenue to the waterfront. The sculls were out on the river, struggling to make their way upstream against the current and the wind.

"You can't buy the team," she said. "The sports editor will quit if you do."

"Let him go. He may be a good editor, but he's a pain in the ass."

"He says it's bad ethics—a newspaper owning a sports team. We'd be tempted to write puff pieces, just because we owned the team. Then all the other team owners would demand that same break. He feels strongly about it."

"Screw ethics! I'm sick of ethics. These people should all become priests if they care about ethics so much. All I know is that buying a sports team is good business. It's a good fit for a communications company. That's why Turner bought the Atlanta Braves. He wanted product for his TV stations. That's why Murdoch bought the Dodgers, and Disney bought the

Angels. It makes business sense. And besides, this town wants a winner! I don't know if you've noticed, but Washington's other teams are pathetic. That's bad for circulation."

Candace put her arm through his; she didn't say anything for a while. They walked arm in arm along the grassy path that bordered the riverbank. The wind was forming small whitecaps on the dark water, like swirls of frosting atop a cake. Across the river was the still, dense forest of Roosevelt Island—a bit of wilderness that had survived amid the builders and wreckers. She let them walk on like this. She wanted him to feel the December sun on his face.

"You have to decide," she said after a while, "what kind of a newspaper publisher you want to be. We can't keep having these fights every few weeks. It's no fun. The sports editor is right. We shouldn't buy the team. It may be good business, but it's bad journalism. When those two conflict, journalism should always win."

She didn't threaten to resign, although she told me she was prepared to do it, if it had come to that. But she didn't have to. The problem just went away. Galvin didn't even answer her directly. He kissed her on the cheek and held her tight.

"I love you," he said.

THEY SAT DOWN ON a bench by the river. It was battered, missing half of its wooden slats, so they had to sit close together. Galvin gathered her in his arm; she snuggled tight against his side, as if she were burrowing into the warmth and bulk of him. They sat there for a long while, so long that they lost track of time. He whispered little jokes and memories from long ago. She sang to him in a sweet, thin soprano voice—something she was usually too self-conscious to do. They were folks songs and show tunes, the same ones she had sung to him in the months when they were first dating. Her lips were next to his ear; no one could hear her but him.

The airplanes roared overhead; the joggers glided past; the pigeons wheeled along the riverbank. But they were alone. He looked to be the happiest man on earth on his rickety bench, surrounded by noise and people but with all his attention focused on the lovely woman next to him. And she felt a sense of peace and joy that day too, she said. It was one of the last times they were alone together. The safety catch was off, and she was letting herself be in the moment with him—although from time to time, a neuron would fire somewhere and she would look over her shoulder to see if anyone was watching.

TWENTY

I MADE MY WAY DOWN A LONG CORRIDOR OF THE RAY-
burn House Office Building. The marble floors had been
waxed to such a high gloss, it was impossible not to imagine
that I had walked onto a movie set. That was the problem
with Congress—it was an extreme cinematic version of itself.
Every detail was so right: the ornate buildings glistening in
the sun as if the studio water truck had just hosed them
down to get the right sheen; the vacant-looking congressional aides promenading in the halls like extras—some even
with speaking parts ("Congressman Jones! You're needed on
the floor!"); the B-list actors who played the members of
Congress, speaking lines written for them by B-list screen-
writers. No wonder people didn't vote on Election Day; they
were waiting for it to come out on video.

My heels clicked on the marble floor like John Travolta's
as I made my way to see the deputy chief counsel of the
House Commerce Committee. This was an "informal" visit

to prepare for the January hearings, he had stressed, not a sworn deposition—which meant that I didn't have to answer questions. Even as I approached his office, I wasn't sure why I had agreed to come. I certainly knew I was doing something naughty as far as the paper was concerned. It wasn't necessarily a desire to harm Galvin; in some ways, I imagined I might be protecting him—by gathering intelligence about his tormentors. My strongest motivation was probably simple curiosity. I had never visited the Rayburn building on official business, never been interrogated by a congressional aide, never had even a *bit* part in this movie. The Savant wanted to know what it felt like.

The deputy chief counsel was named Ewan Buzby. He was a semi-intelligent young man—probably too smart to run for Congress himself, but not quite smart enough to get a real job with a law firm. Congress had hundreds of these people—the well-scrubbed, protectively dumb. They were drawn to Washington as irresistibly as young stage actors are to New York. Ask yourself: What kind of young person today would dream of making a career in government?

Ewan Buzby insisted on taking me into a private office where nobody could see us, which made me uncomfortable— he acted like I was his star witness. He had a long list of questions written on a yellow legal pad. "You don't mind if I tape-record this?" he asked as we were about to start, and I said yes, I certainly *did* mind—how could it be informal and off the record if it was all on tape? So he turned his recorder off, but I wondered if there was another machine somewhere, spooling away.

"I'm going to ask you some questions about Carl Galvin," he said. "Although you're not under oath, I expect you to tell me the truth."

"No problem," I answered. "I'll let you know if I decide to lie."

He didn't smile. Humorlessness was another essential feature of Capitol Hill culture. "How long have you known Mr. Galvin?" he began.

"Not long. About nine months."

"Who introduced you?" He had the slick, taut face of someone who spent too much time at the gym. A disagreeable wholesomeness.

"Nobody. I called Galvin up and asked him if he wanted to be profiled in my magazine. *Reveal.* Quite well known in its day, but it's dead now."

"Did he pay you for the profile?"

"No! Of course not." I laughed, but then wondered if perhaps Galvin had done just that. "Not directly, at least. He did give me a job later."

"Were you aware when you met Mr. Galvin that he was in financial difficulty?"

"No. I'm not aware of that now, really. Except for what I read in *The Wall Street Journal,* and a few things that people have said. Is it true?"

Mr. Ewan Buzby didn't answer. I wasn't supposed to ask questions, clearly. He fiddled with his tie. It had little elephants on it—very loyal of him; they were probably printed on his boxer shorts too.

"In the course of interviewing Mr. Galvin for your magazine, I assume you talked to him about his past."

"I tried to. He didn't tell me much." That probably sounded damning. "He did tell me a few things later, after I got to know him better."

"Did he ever tell you that he worked for the CIA in Asia?"

"No. But I've always been curious. Was he really a spook?"

"Sorry. I can't answer that."

I assumed that meant he had indeed worked for the agency. Son of a gun! You had to admire that, in a perverse sort of way—a young Harvard dropout in the early 1970s going to work for the Big Boys. That explained how he'd gotten such a fast start as a commodities trader.

"Did Mr. Galvin ever tell you about his business dealings as an oil trader?"

"A little. I gather he was good at making relationships with people. Someone told me he operated at the margins— that he would go into dicey places and do whatever it took to get the deal done. He told me once that the commodities business was tricky, because it involved inherently untrustworthy people."

Young Mr. Buzby fixed me with his semi-intelligent eyes. That last bit was probably beyond him. "Did anyone ever tell you that Mr. Galvin has paid bribes to obtain business?"

Now this was getting interesting. I'd never heard anything about bribes before. "That's a hard question to answer, in such general terms," I said. "Which countries are you talking about?"

"Angola, for a start. Do you know anything about bribes he might have paid to the rebels there, to obtain contracts to sell oil?"

"Nope. I heard he was active there after the Portuguese left, but that's it."

"How about Nigeria?"

"Nope. Nothing about Nigeria. Why? Did he pay bribes there too?"

"Did he ever talk about selling oil to South Africa?"

"Now, let me think." I rubbed my forehead. This was fun. "I know I heard about that somewhere, but I can't remember if Galvin told me or someone else. Refresh my memory about that one."

"The question is whether Galvin smuggled Russian oil into South Africa during the eighties, in violation of sanctions. He supposedly made a commission of ten dollars a barrel. That ring any bells?"

"Faintly. Sorry, but my memory is so bad."

"What about Iran? Do you know anything about his lifting oil from Bandar Abbas, despite sanctions?"

"Yes. I heard about that. Definitely. But I can't tell you any more than that."

"Heard about it from Galvin?"

"No. From someone else. But that person sounded pretty confident."

Ewan Buzby was frowning. He was beginning to wonder if his leg was being pulled, but he was too serious and trusting a person to believe that anyone could really take an interview with a congressional committee so lightly. He pressed on.

"What about Iraq? Did Galvin ever say anything about buying Iraqi oil, in violation of sanctions?"

"Not in so many words. But I heard about that from the

other people too. That he went into Iraq and did that business when nobody else wanted to, and made a lot of money."

"What did they tell you, these other people?"

"Just that he did it. They didn't have a lot of other information. It sounds like you already know what they told me."

"Who are these other people you keep mentioning?"

"It's actually just one person. He's a broker in town. He gave me his card, but I lost it."

"You're not being very helpful. We can subpoena you, you know."

"Fine. Do that. Then I won't tell you anything at all."

He sat back peevishly. He looked upset, like a kid whose playmate won't share the toys. He wanted to get through the list of questions on his yellow pad.

"How about Russia? Did anyone tell you about Galvin's activities there?"

"Which activities are you referring to in Russia? Maybe I can help you on that." It was worth another try, to see if I could bluff a bit more out of him. Perhaps I had been wrong about Mr. Buzby. Possibly he *was* stupid enough to run for Congress.

The interrogator's eyes clicked into focus again. "Specifically, did you hear anything about Galvin buying oil and other commodities from former Soviet officials who were privatizing natural resources and converting them to private use? We're also interested in any information you might have about whether Galvin helped these Russians set up private banking relationships in Switzerland."

"Nope. Sorry. That's new to me. I guess I don't know much about Russia. I was mistaken."

He was pissed now. He thought I was making fun of him. His tone grew testier.

"Do you know someone named Ted Amara?"

"Yes. He works at the *Sun*. He's a lawyer. A tough guy, acts like a gangster. I've seen him around the building."

"Are you aware that he has been making cash payments to the mayor of Washington?"

"No. I've seen him with the mayor, and I assumed something was going on between them. I mean, the mayor doesn't play ball with white newspaper owners for free. And everybody knows Galvin was pumping a lot of money into the city for his scholarships and the Howard Theatre restoration. But I don't really know anything."

"Are you aware of any other places where Mr. Amara has acted as Mr. Galvin's intermediary?"

"I know he used to live in France. But you'll have to be more specific if you want my help."

"We're curious about Mr. Amara's activities in Russia, Switzerland and Iraq. Any information about those places?"

"No. I'm sorry. I know he went to Tysons Corner to talk about buying a soccer team. And I know he travels a lot for Galvin. But I don't think I have what you're looking for."

Buzby shook his head. I was a disappointment. He flipped a page in his yellow pad and started on what appeared to be a new list of questions. "Now, Mr. Cantor," he said firmly, "I want to talk to you about your role in the purchase of *The Washington Sun and Tribune*." He made a point of using the paper's full name, as if that made it more sinister.

His tone made me nervous. He wasn't just fishing now;

he had something. "I didn't have any role," I answered, "except to carry Galvin's bag."

"That's not my understanding, Mr. Cantor. I'm told that you played an important part in the takeover. Is it true, for example, that you informed the Hazen family that a holding company called PalmTrust was secretly buying shares of the *Sun*?"

Oh shit, I thought to myself.

He was smiling, watching my discomfort.

"Galvin brought me along to a meeting with Ariane Hazen. He made it seem like I was the person who dug up the information on PalmTrust, but I wasn't. It was one of his games. That's all."

"And I believe you accompanied Mr. Galvin when he made his presentation to the Hazen and Crosby families, as well."

"I was his sidekick. That probably sounds strange, but I came along for the ride, as an observer. This is Washington. People do that here. This is a city of voyeurs."

He ignored my cultural commentary. "Were you aware at the time that Mr. Galvin had extensive business dealings with Melvin Wolfe, the owner of PalmTrust?"

"No. I didn't know that."

"Did you know that Mr. Wolfe had extended more than two hundred million dollars in credit to Mr. Galvin? And that Mr. Wolfe and Mr. Galvin were secretly collaborating on the supposedly competing bids for the *Sun*?"

"No, I didn't know any of that. I had suspicions, I guess. But I didn't know anything." I could feel the color draining from my face, and the beads of perspiration beginning to form on my forehead. This seemed like a good moment to call my lawyer, or eat the pages of my address book, or do whatever guilty suspects do. "I wonder, Mr. Buzby, if I could take a bathroom break."

He smiled. "I'll be done in a minute, if you can hold on. I have just one more question, actually. Did you ever ask Mr. Galvin during the last few months whether he was in financial trouble?"

Was that a trick question? I couldn't tell anymore.

"Yes. I asked him several times whether he had money problems. I was getting concerned about what might happen to him. Regardless of what you may think, I didn't know anything about his finances—I don't know anything now, in fact. But I was worried."

"And what did he say, when you asked him?"

"He told me that everything was okay. He said to stop worrying. It was all just short-term. Everything would turn out fine in the end."

"And you believed him?"

He asked it in such a callow way, I couldn't very well say that of course I had believed him—that I had trouble doubting Galvin even now, after what I'd just heard. That was the problem when the rules of ordinary life intersected with the mercurial and ephemeral. It was so hard to explain to the enforcers why the rules had been suspended. It was like trying to explain "special" to "ordinary."

IT WAS OBVIOUS TO me, as I left Mr. Ewan Buzby's office, that I was in a potentially awkward position. That view was confirmed when I replayed the conversation for my lawyer friend. He wanted to know more of the details himself—especially about my knowledge of Galvin's collusion with Melvin Wolfe. But I put him off. There would be enough time later to attend to the petty business of escaping legal jeopardy. My immediate problem was emotional jeopardy.

I returned to the office to write my column, which I was supposed to have delivered the night before. The Savant was never late, but unfortunately The Savant that week was experiencing an intellectual capital shortage. I scanned the folder of ideas that I kept for the proverbial rainy day, but they all seemed too heavy or too light. I wondered: Could I get away with a column arguing that the baby boom generation's most important contribution to American life was the popularization of oral sex? Before roughly 1965, nice girls wouldn't do it; after that, well . . . you know the story. But no, that column probably wasn't a good idea.

Finally, in desperation, I decided to update an old Russell Baker column (*steal* would be a better word, actually) about presidential character, pets and children. I observed that presidents who had dogs and daughters tended to make serious errors of judgment—Baker had pointed to Nixon, a dog and daughter man all the way, but the same could be said of the current incumbent—because of all the uncritical affection they received. The Savant, by comparison, was affection starved; that was what gave him his edge.

I HAD AN APPOINTMENT to meet with Candace's investigative team that evening at a bar near my apartment. It was a bitterly cold night. Snow and freezing rain were forecast for the next day, and it was altogether an evening to stay home and curl up with some strong spirits and an affectionate, un-critical dog, if one could be located. I wondered whether to cancel the meeting with the two reporters and decided that it might look odd—I was becoming concerned with appear-ances, a dangerous sign—so I went ahead with the ren-dezvous.

We met in a smoky basement bar—their choice; they wanted to be in that same old movie about journalism. The two reporters were both in their mid-thirties and hungry for the chase. Their names were Taub and Loden—not quite right for the book jacket. They ordered beers and barely touched them; I ordered a martini, and then another. I looked around the bar. It was an odd place; nobody was try-ing to pick anyone up. It must have been unhappy hour. I wasn't sure, at first, whether to share with my *Sun* colleagues the information I had picked up from the eponymous Mr. Buzby that morning. But it occurred to me that *this* might be my escape. As long as I was part of the newspaper's team exposing Galvin's misdeeds, it would be harder for someone to accuse me of taking part in them. So without mentioning the fact that I had just talked with the House committee, I ran through the laundry list of what Buzby seemed to be chasing—Angola, Nigeria, South Africa, Iran, Iraq, Russia. I also mentioned my suspicions about Galvin's collusion with PalmTrust many months ago, when he had acquired the paper. It was all truthful—that was the sneaky part.

The two reporters listened intently, and took pages of notes. They kept nodding when I brought up a subject, and finishing sentences for me. It became obvious, after a half hour or so, that they already knew most of what I was telling them. "What are you going to do with all this?" I asked when they were done, and one of them answered solemnly that Candace Ridgway would decide.

TWENTY-ONE

THE FOLLOWING DAY WAS A SATURDAY, AND I WOULD have stayed at home reading Trollope or searching for perverse Web sites on the Internet, but Galvin called that morning and asked me to come visit. He was feeling poorly, he said; Candace had begged off and he was quite alone in his big house and could use some company. He sounded surprisingly frail, and there was a sad undertone in his voice, which, in anyone else, I would have taken for melancholy.

Outside was a deadly fairyland. The temperature had continued to drop, chilling the city down to blue ice and then relenting hideously for a few hours before plummeting again. The precipitation came in that interlude of relative warmth—not as a dusting of snow but as an assault of freezing rain that made the roads as slick as a hockey rink. The trees sparkled in their frigid armor—every branch and twig encased in a thin, hard shell. The power lines sagged overhead with the weight of the ice; up Connecticut Avenue, I could hear one that was already down, crackling against the icy pavement. I walked two blocks to the parking lot on Florida Avenue where I kept my car. It was hard just keeping my footing on the sidewalk, and the Pakistani gentleman who managed the parking lot suggested that I was out of my mind, sir, to consider driving anywhere in these conditions.

I pointed to my battered gray Honda. "Perfect car for a day like this," I said. "And it's fate, you see. I'll either crash, or I won't." That disturbed him even more—the possibility that the ruinous fatalism of the East, which he had fled in search of a better and more rational life, was now infecting Washington.

Out on the street everything was fine, until you had to stop. That was all but impossible, especially on hills. The application of the brakes did not produce the usual effect of halting the car's forward motion. Instead the car skated along the slick surface until its forward momentum dissipated, or it hit something. I plotted as flat a course as possible to Galvin's house, but I hadn't reckoned on the steep pitch of his driveway. I tried to tiptoe down it, going just a few feet before applying the brake. But as the drive grew steeper this strategy failed, and I drifted off the road twice—once hitting a tree and adding another nice dent to my Honda. When I finally arrived at the bottom of the drive and rang the bell, I felt I had achieved something, just in being there.

Galvin answered the door himself, in a black satin smoking jacket and red velvet slippers embroidered with his initials. At first glance, he still had the look of an old-time movie star, an Errol Flynn, perhaps, or a Clark Gable. But there were dark circles under his eyes and his skin had lost the luminous summertime glow. It was dryer now, almost translucent, with the pale surface admitting the imperfections of age. He looked weary.

"Thank you for coming," he said. "I appreciate it very much." Poor man. He really did seem touched that I had made the trip through the ice and bitter cold.

"Where are the servants?" I asked. He had never answered the door himself that I could remember. Even the dog, that beautiful yellow Lab, was gone.

"I let the servants go. All except the housekeeper. Things may get ragged around here, and I didn't want them to get caught up in it. This way, I could pay their year-end bonuses and kiss them all good-bye."

He led me into the small study where we'd sat that magical night with Candace—magical for the two of them, at least. He had a fire blazing away, and a big mug of tea on the side table. The place wasn't quite so tidy now, with the servants gone. That made it more attractive—it seemed like a place where a real person lived. A crocheted blanket lay on the couch; Galvin folded it and put it aside. He asked if I wanted some coffee or tea, but I poured myself a glass of whiskey instead.

"You don't look well," I said.

"It's this damned cold," he answered. "I haven't been able to shake it. It's hard to sleep at night, with all the coughing and blowing my nose. But I'm all right. Better in no time."

I nodded. Whatever he wanted to say was fine with me.

"These must be tough times for you," I said. "I'm sorry

you're under the weather, in addition to everything else." It was hard to find the right words. He was a man who gave encouragement and affection so easily to others but found them hard to accept himself.

"Not at all," he answered. "In most respects, this is the happiest time of my life. I've achieved the things I wanted." His smile was gentle and unfeigned, and for all the fatigue that showed on his face, he radiated his own kind of serenity. He meant it, obviously. Yet I felt a need to warn him, even if I couldn't protect him from what lay ahead.

"They're coming after you," I said. "The House committee is gathering a lot of material. They're looking at every deal you've ever done, every commission you've ever paid. If you or Ted Amara ever bribed anyone, anywhere, they're going to find out about it."

"I know, I know." He sounded bored, more than pained. "Let them collect all the garbage they want. There's nothing I can do about it. I haven't done anything illegal—nothing that matters, at least. I have a clean heart. So let them take their shot. We still have our newspaper. I don't care about the rest."

A chill came over him; he bundled himself tighter in the smoking jacket and laid the blanket over his lap. He looked so gentle and forgiving sitting there, it gave me a bad feeling—not about him, but about myself. I didn't like confessions, but I owed him one.

"I have to tell you something," I said. "I talked a few days ago to an investigator from the House committee. They invited me to come in for an interview, and I agreed. They asked me a lot of questions, and I didn't really tell them any-thing. But it bothers me, and I thought I should tell you." I blurted it out, and then stared at the floor in embarrassment.

"I know you went to see them," said Galvin.

"You do?" I was astonished. Why had he been so civil if he knew I'd been meeting with his enemies?

"A committee staff guy called me afterward, claiming you were cooperating with them. I didn't believe it. They're just trying to squeeze me. This is what they do when they decide to make you a target. But I don't care. I haven't done anything wrong."

"They wanted to know how you bought the *Sun*. They think you were colluding with Wolfe. They made it sound like fraud, and they seemed to think I was part of it."

"Don't worry." He patted my hand. "They don't have anything on you. If it comes to it, I'll swear I never told you a thing. But it won't."

It wasn't even possible to betray this man. His serenity was so enveloping, it left you defenseless. But all the calm in the world wouldn't pay his bills.

"How will you survive financially? They made it sound like you're in real trouble. How can you hold on to the news-paper when people are squeezing you for money?"

"I *do* have money trouble," he said. "I'll admit it—to you, at least. My commodities business owes more than a billion dollars, and I've run out of people who'll lend me more money. It will go bankrupt in a few days or weeks, de-pending on when people decide to take it down. But so what? It's finished, and I'm not sorry. The people I owe money to have too much of it already, and most of them are idiots.

I won't miss them. All I care about now is protecting the newspaper."

"How can you save the *Sun* if all your other businesses are in the toilet?"

"I've taken steps, set some things up. What do you think Ted Amara has been working on? But don't ask for details. It's too complicated."

He called to the housekeeper to make him some more tea, and then shuffled off to the bathroom in his velvet slippers. He took little steps now, like an old man, instead of those thirty-league strides I remembered from our first encounter. But in most respects, he hadn't really changed. I thought of all the people who had stood on his back lawn at those early parties, drinking his liquor and basking in his reflection. I was certain that not one of them would come to his aid now that he had been brought to ground.

GALVIN WANTED TO SIT in the sunroom. It was a glassed-in porch that overlooked the back gardens and the rocky hillside that led down to the river. He'd cranked the heat up so that it felt toasty, despite the chill outside. The ice-coated trees glinted in the low winter sun, their bare and spindly branches bound in the shimmering wrappers. It was like a primeval forest that had been frozen dead in time by some catastrophic event—the eruption of a volcano, or the crash of a meteor. I could see where the tent had stood the night of his triumphal party—and see in my mind's eye the figure of Candace, spinning in his arms on the dance floor.

Our conversation turned to her, inevitably. She was the maypole around which we had been dancing for all these months, though I doubt that Galvin even then realized the depth or complexity of my feelings for her. I still found their relationship puzzling. I saw the effects, but not the cause. And the more I'd tried to explore it, the more confused I had become.

He brought Candace up. That was the odd thing. I had assumed that I would never get him to open up about her—he was so private about the things that really mattered to him. But he wanted to talk. Maybe I was the only person who knew them both well enough to be a good listener.

"The thing you have to understand about Candace is that she's frightened," he said during a lull in the conversation. We had been talking about the newspaper, and how Candace was doing in her first weeks as editor.

"Frightened of what?" I asked. That wasn't the first word that would have come to mind to describe her.

"Commitment. Failure. All the things people are usually afraid of, plus what her father's death added to the pile. She was different after that."

He was inviting the question, so I asked it. What had happened to Candace in the weeks surrounding her father's death? Why had she left Galvin, if she had loved him so much? If I could understand that, maybe the rest would be clear.

"You want to hear the story?" he mused. "How it ended?" Of course I did, he could see that, and he was a man who liked to give other people what they wanted.

THEY WERE DRUNK WITH love, as Galvin remembered it, but they both knew it was time to sober up and settle in. He was twenty-one; she was nineteen. They had returned from that palmy trip across the country, riding freight trains and sleeping on the beach, but the Kerouac days were over. It was the fall of 1971: The circus was leaving town, and people were cleaning up the debris.

Candace had gone home first to Washington, to see her parents before school started. She came back to Harvard looking frazzled. Her father's problems were getting worse. She wouldn't talk about it, but it was obvious that he was unwell. Her mother, in her anxiety, was nagging at Candace. She didn't approve of her relationship with Galvin, and had tried to stop her from traveling across the country—relenting only when Mr. Ridgway told her to relax, a little rebelliousness was a good thing. Inwardly, she blamed Candace for making her father's illness worse. There had been a terrible scene before Candace left, with her mother screaming and Candace in tears.

All this discontent burdened Candace when she arrived back at school. Galvin wanted to lighten her load, but he wasn't sure how. She was spending more time by herself in the dorm; she said she needed to study more sophomore year, but Galvin knew it wasn't that. She was pulling away. Her family and its tight-lipped craziness were reclaiming her, he thought. One bright Sunday in October, Galvin made a picnic and took her to Walden Pond. They came back to his room that night and made love. But she was gone at first light, and he was too sleepy to say good-bye.

As things turned out, that was the day her father killed himself. Galvin heard about it as he was leaving a seminar in William James Hall, from a friend who'd heard the news on the radio. By the time he called Candace, she had already left for Washington.

Galvin followed her. He was there for the funeral, but he felt like an outsider. This wasn't his tribe, and all his latent insecurities about his girlfriend's elite background returned. Candace submerged her grief in the work of planning the funeral. This was a public event, and the family's friends and retainers crowded around. Her mother was overwhelmed, and much of the planning fell to Candace. Galvin knew that the most generous gift he could offer was to stay out of the way.

The funeral service was held in Washington Cathedral, with many hundreds of people crowding the nave. The Establishment understood that Dwight Ridgway was a casualty of war. They had watched him come apart, layer by layer; he was a symbol of the ruination of their world. Candace was dry-eyed through the service—making it easier for the others, trying to be her father's daughter. She read the passage from the Song of Solomon that had been open on her father's reading table the morning he died. The way she read it, she made you believe that love *was* stronger than death, that many waters truly couldn't quench it nor floods drown it. That had been her idea. It was as close as they had to a suicide note. The organ surged at the end of the service, and even the immense pillars at the crossing seemed to resonate with the sound. At the reception later, a long line of people waited to kiss Candace and tell her how proud her father would have been of her.

When the public events of the funeral were over, she was overwhelmed with grief. She couldn't eat, couldn't sleep, could barely talk. It was like watching someone waste away.

Galvin didn't know what to do. He had never seen anyone grieve like that. He returned to Cambridge, and she followed a few days later. He waited for her to get better, calling several times a day and bringing her flowers or food. Sometimes they would take long walks together, but she would go for twenty or thirty minutes without talking. She had to return home twice that month to Washington, to take care of her mother, who was in even worse shape. By November, Galvin began to worry seriously about Candace. The family was taking its revenge; they would swallow her alive.

Galvin knew that he loved her. And he believed that, in time, he could heal the pain she was feeling. He felt a responsibility. She was so alone now; he was her real family. One clear, crisp Saturday in mid-November he invited her to have dinner with him. A graduate-student friend was away for the weekend, and Galvin borrowed his apartment along the Charles. It was in a high-rise building; through the big picture window you could see the dark ribbon of water bending back and forth all the way up to Fresh Pond. They arrived in the late afternoon, as the sun was setting. The low clouds were tufted with a rosy pink, almost a lobster red at the western edge, and then suddenly they went dark as the sun set.

Galvin lit a candle and opened a bottle of champagne. The bed was turned down, for later. He sat Candace down on the couch, looking out at the panorama of the city, and took her hand in his. He wanted everything to be just right, so that they would always remember how perfect it was. "Will you marry me?" he asked. He had said the words before, as another way of saying that he loved her, but this time he meant it. Now was the time. She was falling apart. He could give her happiness, if she would let him. He opened the box and took out the engagement ring.

She looked at him distractedly, as if she hadn't heard, and then began crying. For a brief moment, he thought they were tears of joy. He repeated his proposal, and this time she said it out loud: "No." She didn't want to marry him.

When he pressed for a reason, she got angry. She said she couldn't breathe. Galvin was smothering her. She had too many responsibilities, plans, things to do. She loved him, but she had a duty to herself and her family. That was the problem, Galvin told her sharply. That was what had killed her father. He pleaded with her to come away—to save herself and start a new life. But she refused. "Stop trying to hustle me!" she screamed. She grabbed her coat and ran to the elevator—leaving Galvin alone with his candle and bottle of champagne and engagement ring, and her words ringing in his ears.

It was the worst moment of his life, he said. Even now, nearly thirty years later, he could feel the intense pain of that rejection. She had finally said it; he was a hustler. He wasn't good enough for her, after all. He might be handsome and charming, but he wasn't marriage material.

And then Galvin decided to go away. He felt rejected—not just by her, but by the world she represented. The Ridgways were gods at Harvard. Her father had gone there; her cousins went there. It was a family industry. Galvin couldn't bear to remain. He tried to study, go to the gym, date other girls—but it was all dust in his mouth. The game was over. He was a young guy from Pittsburgh with a screwball socialist for a dad, and he didn't have two nickels to rub together.

But his instinct for self-preservation was intact. He had an overwhelming desire to leave that place and get *started*.

So he left. It was early December of his senior year. He told the deans he would return the next fall to get his degree, but needed some time away. They understood; the Harvard deans lived to say yes. He wanted to go to Asia. After some phone calls, he found work in Bangkok, and he never looked back. Harvard kept sending him letters for a few years, asking when he would return, but they stopped eventually. And then one year, Galvin began sending *them* letters, containing large contributions. That was his answer, or at least part of it.

"DID YOU REALLY WORK for the CIA in Bangkok?" I asked when he ended his tale. That particular detail intrigued me. It was like eating forbidden fruit—a sign of how totally Galvin had broken with the world of Harvard.

"Yeah. A little. Why not? It was fun, and I learned a lot. It was better than the Foreign Legion. I kept doing things for them when I moved to Hong Kong, and for years after that. The truth is, if one of their people walked into this room right now and asked me to help with something, I'd say yes— and ask what it was later."

"And you never saw Candace again, after you went away to Asia—until you came to Washington?"

He looked at me curiously. "No. I saw a lot of her over the years. Who told you that?"

"She did."

He shook his head and laughed. "That's my girl! No, we stayed in touch. I was a regular source for her when she was overseas. I helped her win that Pulitzer Prize, if you want to know. It was a series about foreign bribery, right? Well, where do you think she got her information about foreign bribery? From a reliable source. We kept in touch, all right. That's the reason I moved back to Washington. She was sending signals that the time might be right, after all these years, to try again."

He stopped talking. The wind was playing on those ghostly trees, and you could hear a brittle little noise, like the sound of wind chimes, as the ice-covered branches blew against one another. I was angry at Candace for lying to me. I had known that she was a controlling person who used her beauty and intelligence to order the world as she wanted it. But I hadn't thought of her as a liar until then. That knowledge was a kind of poison. It went to the heart.

"She's investigating you," I said.

Galvin looked up in surprise, not comprehending what I was talking about. "Sorry. I didn't catch that," he said.

"She's investigating you," I repeated. "She has a team of reporters, from the *Sun,* looking into your finances and your bribes and dirty deals. She's going to publish the results."

"Impossible!" he said with a dismissive gesture of his hand. "You must have misunderstood. She'd never do that. Not in my newspaper, without telling me."

"It's true," I said softly.

"You'll never get me to believe that," he said. "Candace may have her problems, but she'd never publish an attack on me in my own newspaper. You're just mad at her because she won't sleep with you."

He gave me a wink, and a punch on the shoulder, and that was the end of it. We chatted for a little longer, but we were both talked out. We never really had a private conversation again, after that morning. I will never forget the sight of him wrapped in his blanket in the sunroom, smiling and staring out at his trees and the riverfront—the ruins of his empire. He was a happy man. Whatever he had done for others, he had found a way to give that gift to himself, too.

TWENTY-TWO

CANDACE GATHERED THE INVESTIGATIVE TEAM AT HER house in Georgetown for a final report. She felt it was too sensitive a topic for us to meet at the newspaper. She'd kept the lid on so far, but if people saw this unlikely group together, word might leak out that the *Sun* was investigating its publisher. The lobbying would begin, for and against publication. Candace wanted a free hand; she claimed she hadn't decided yet what to do. She was still hoping that, in the end, the charges against Galvin would prove to be baseless—and that the whole sorry business would blow away. I suspected she didn't really believe that, but it was part of her survival kit—the ability to pretend she had other options on the eve of a stark yes-or-no decision. It allowed her to keep up appearances.

Christmas was just a week away, and Georgetown was crowded with shoppers as I drove toward Candace's town house. I have always taken special pleasure in Christmas. How wonderful it is, that the good Christian folk are putting on this show for me—smiling at me for no reason in the street; giving me a hearty handshake; wishing me "Happy Holiday" and being polite enough not to add: "Jewboy!" Hard to beat Christmas for omnidirectional good cheer. And so cunningly staged at the time of the year when the days are darkest and the true prevailing sentiment is soulless misery. Jerry Springer once had a show called "We're in Holiday Hell!" where he staged a mock Christmas dinner, and all the guests started screaming at each other and throwing things. Something real there; the authentic American spirit that lurks just below the "Howdy, neighbor!" smile.

Candace had put up a Christmas tree in her living room. It was beautifully decorated with handmade ornaments she had collected as a child—glass baubles; wooden elves and reindeer; cherubs made of gauze and foil. Atop the tree was an angel dressed in a purple robe with golden wings. Her perfect waxen face and blond hair were the image of Candace's.

We three unwise men trooped awkwardly past the tree into the dining room, where Candace had laid out coffee and juice and a stack of legal pads—just like a breakfast meeting at a hotel. She seated us around her table and thanked us for coming. It was odd to see her so stiff and formal at home. She was wearing a pinstriped business suit: not the zippy designs she used to wear, with the short skirts that showed off her legs, but something plain. She wanted to hear what the reporters had discovered. Then she would decide what to do. Whatever happened, she said, we needed to maintain absolute secrecy until she talked to Galvin. If we failed in that, we would do him a terrible injustice. She said it with absolute sincerity and conviction—and no sense of irony.

I'd already met the two reporters—Mark Taub and
Henry Loden, back at that smoky bar. Taub was our Wall
Street reporter; he had worked for *The Bond Buyer* before joining the paper, and he understood how financial markets
worked. Loden was the investigative reporter; he was a more
taciturn fellow, with a face pitted by acne scars and hollow,
unforgiving eyes. His main job had been to investigate
Galvin's purchase of the *Sun*.

Candace turned to the Wall Street reporter and asked
him to summarize what their inquiry had yielded. Taub
wanted to impress the boss. He'd brought along lists and
charts to help him explain the complicated structure of
Galvin's business empire and how it had evolved over time.
He drew a picture that, for me, was already familiar.

Carl Galvin Corporation, known to the world by the initials CGC, had established itself as one of the world's leading
commodities brokers. Galvin had made his early fortune by
betting that oil prices would rise. And he'd made many other
smart bets since then, as other commodities grew scarce.
Tin, copper, manganese, nickel, bauxite. As the world
economy grew in the late seventies and early eighties, each
had its momentary spike in price, as demand surged but supply remained constrained. In a few cases, Taub said, Galvin
had helped create these market imbalances—by buying up
available supplies of nickel, say, to create a spot-market shortage that drove up prices and made his holdings more valuable. But everyone did that in the commodities business, if
they had the brains and the market power.

Candace kept nodding as Taub recounted his findings.
She seemed to know, or suspect, most of it already. Taub re-

peated the stories I'd heard about Galvin's derring-do in Africa and the Middle East. He'd probably busted sanctions in South Africa, Iran, Iraq and other places too, Taub said. But it was likely he'd done so with the connivance of his friends at the CIA, and he would never be prosecuted for any of that.

"His business is managing risk," Taub observed. Galvin had learned over the years to balance exposure in one commodity or region of the world against another. If he was long on dollar-denominated oil contracts to Japan, he would short the dollar against the yen in the currency market so that he was protected either way in case of any sudden change. And he bet on longer-term trends too. He had been quick to see that fiber-optic cable would replace copper wire, and he had made millions shorting copper contracts. As his company grew, he inevitably became a market maker—which meant that he sometimes had to be on both sides of a deal. That was fine, so long as the markets were robust.

The only real danger for Galvin's business was the possibility that all of the world's major commodities might decline in price at the same time—oil, metals, chemicals, paper. But in an era of rapid economic growth, such a general decline had seemed impossible. Yet that was just what had happened in the 1990s. Against all odds, commodity prices had fallen through much of the decade. By the late nineties, when the Asian crash hit, the basic industrial commodities—oil, metals, chemicals and paper—were all plummeting toward catastrophic low prices. Some were selling as cheaply, on an inflation-adjusted basis, as they had in half a century. This was the one bet that Galvin hadn't anticipated, and it had proved disastrous.

"But he's still a wealthy man, isn't he?" Candace asked. It was hard for her to understand the notion that Galvin could have made fundamental errors of judgment as a commodities trader. She had anticipated allegations of fraud and bribery, but not business mistakes.

"He's broke," said Taub. He had the flat, affectless voice of a midwesterner. "As near as we can tell, he's been broke since the mid-nineties. When oil and the other commodities markets tanked, he went down with them. He never recovered."

"Don't let him fool you!" she exclaimed. "He must be hiding money, to keep it from his creditors. He's probably still a billionaire; he's just playing a shell game."

Taub shook his head. "He may owe a billion dollars to other people, but he doesn't have it himself." He and Loden had talked to dozens of people—all of them looking for Galvin's hidden loot, and they had concluded that there wasn't any. "He kept stringing things along to maintain appearances, bringing in just enough money to roll over his debts. But he was in trouble long before he came to Washington."

Candace arched her brows, still skeptical. "That can't be. What about the two houses, and the parties, and scholarships and charitable contributions? That was real money."

"Borrowed money," said Taub. "His whole time in Washington was basically an act—a piece of theater. It's easy to appear rich if people believe you are rich—because they keep lending you money. Khashoggi got away with it for years, before anybody realized he was broke. When Galvin's creditors began to sense he was in real trouble, they tightened the screws, but there was nothing left to squeeze."

This was a strange moment of truth for Candace. She'd gone searching in the forest of Galvin's business affairs, suspecting that she would turn up some dreadful abuses of financial power. But she had encountered a far bigger surprise: Galvin's wealth was an illusion.

"How did he buy the *Sun*?" she asked. She had watched that process unfold, every step of the way, and she had thought she understood it. "Where did the money come from?"

The answer came from Loden, the laconic investigative reporter. "He worked with his partner, Melvin Wolfe. They rigged the deal so that Wolfe's stock would go up, no matter what."

"I know that," she snapped. Galvin's fraud was a given, but not his poverty. "But whose money did they use?"

"Wolfe put up the collateral," said Loden. "Then Galvin borrowed against it. Galvin didn't have a dime of his own to put into the paper."

"So who controls Galvin's interest in the *Sun*? Him or his creditors?"

"Hard to tell," said Loden. He explained that Galvin had been consulting the last few weeks with Ted Amara and his other lawyers. Their discussions were hidden from view, protected by private banking relationships and attorney-client privilege. But the rumor making the rounds at several law firms was that Galvin was tinkering with the ownership structure of the newspaper—creating new trusts to control the voting shares. Candace nodded. That didn't seem to bother her—the notion that Galvin and Amara were taking precautions. It wasn't part of her investigation.

The Hardy Boys continued their briefing for another hour or so. Neither of them had actually met Galvin, as far as I knew. That accounted for the bloodless tone of their narrative. They were like biographers who tell you every single fact they have gathered about the subject, but who somehow miss the essence of who he is. But we all knew what the story was now, even if we couldn't put flesh and blood on it. Our magnificent publisher was bankrupt. He had acquired our newspaper by fraud. We were living in a journalistic house of cards, which was about to come down around us.

CANDACE LOOKED EXHAUSTED. WHEN she finally called a halt to the briefing just after noon, the reporters were getting their second wind; they looked as if they could go on for the rest of the day. But she didn't need any more facts; she had to decide what to do with them. She thanked the reporters. They'd done the hardest thing any newspaper ever has to do, she said—which was to investigate itself. It was a badge of glory. As they were about to go, she told them to leave behind all copies of their notes, please, while she deliberated.

I was walking out the door with them, but Candace asked me to stay. She needed to talk. What she really needed was a drink. I poured her a glass of wine and made some tuna fish sandwiches for lunch, while she stared out the window at her garden. It had the barren emptiness of winter. She excused herself while I was toasting the bread, and went upstairs to change out of that awful pinstriped suit. She came back downstairs in chinos and an old cashmere sweater.

"What did you make of all that?" she asked.

I had been thinking about that same question, wondering how to put it all together. I understood how the little pieces fit—the money troubles and the fraud and the collapse of his business. But there was a larger design embedded in the picture that I had been struggling to see, and it was becoming clearer. The puzzle wasn't really that complicated.

"He did it for you," I said. "All of it. This whole crazy play was staged for you, because he loves you."

She looked me in the eye coldly. She hadn't intended for me to answer the question that way. "Maybe so," she said. "But that's irrelevant right now."

"No, it isn't," I said firmly. "This is about you. You can't pretend you aren't involved. Galvin needs you. He's in trouble. You should go see him. It bothers him that you're staying away."

"Not now," she said. That same surprising coldness was in her voice. "I'm his editor. I can't be his friend while all this is going on. I have to protect the newspaper. When it's over, we can be together again."

"That's a Washington answer. It's inhuman."

She shook her head and bit her lip. She stared out again at the lifeless garden. "Don't make this harder," she said.

I looked at her, leaning against the window, hard as iron under her soft sweater. And I began to understand what it must have been like for Galvin, so many years ago, when he wanted to reach her but couldn't break through. "This is what you do, isn't it?" I mused aloud. "You're so beautiful, people forget what a hard person you are. When they really need you, you go cold. You did this same thing to Sandy a long time ago."

"That's a terrible thing to say, David. Especially now." She rose from her window seat and walked toward me. I had made her angry; that was good. "If you don't want to help me, you should go," she said. "This is too painful."

I ignored her. I didn't really care what she wanted. "Why wouldn't you marry him back in college? I keep trying to figure that out. I asked Galvin, but I don't think he really knows. That's why he came back. He thought he could get it right."

"I want you to leave. Right now. You're making me angry."

I stood there, as thin and useless as an old stick but intent on blocking her escape. I wanted to hear her confess her rigidity and faithlessness, admit it just once. "Answer my question," I said. "Then I'll go, and you can do whatever you want to Galvin."

She slapped me. That was all she had left. I could feel a red tingle on my cheek, and then a prickly feeling as the skin came back to life. "Fuck you, David!" she said.

"Tell me," I repeated. Her defenses were gone. I knew she would answer. She needed to explain herself to someone.

THE NIGHT GALVIN HAD proposed survived in her memory like a photographic negative. The brightest color was the black of the night into which she escaped. She was a grief-stricken young woman of nineteen, still trying to say good-bye to her father—taking tranquilizers so that she wouldn't cry all day. Her boyfriend had carried her off to a Hugh Hefner bachelor pad with a big picture window and a mirror over the bed, popped open a bottle of champagne and tried to give her a diamond ring. What was he thinking? That was a measure of his vanity, that he thought it was the right time to propose marriage.

Saying no had been the hardest thing she'd ever done. When she got outside the apartment building and was standing alone on Memorial Drive, she vomited. She went to the student health center, and they gave her sleeping pills to make all the circuits go dead, which was what she wanted. But that just masked the pain; she couldn't escape it—she had to embrace it. She went into a place she called the white room. It wasn't a real place, but somewhere in her mind—silent, warm, with walls that seemed to breathe in time with her. She had gone there once before, when her father died. When she was inside it, she knew that she would be safe.

Suffering had made Candace stronger—that was what Galvin hadn't understood. He thought she was weak and needed his help, but she had been changed. The morning her father died, she had been called from class and brought to the office of the dean of students. Nobody told her what it was about, but she knew that someone must have died, and she remembered hoping that it was her mother. The dean of students handed her a telephone, and her mother was on the line. Mrs. Ridgway was sobbing, but Candace heard the words, "Your father is dead." She didn't say how it had happened. At first, Candace blamed her bitterly for that omission, but she relented. The poor woman had only found the body an hour before; the police were in the house, asking questions. Of course she had wanted to suppress the truth. So Candace heard it on the radio, in the taxi on the way to Logan Airport. The driver stopped the car and put his arm around her. He said he had a daughter too.

She sat in the back of the plane, wrapped in a blanket. On that plane ride, she had found her way to the white room. When she entered it, she didn't know if she could survive in the frigid vacuum of her loss. She pulled the blanket around her head so that nobody could see her, and thought about her father. He would never come back. She was alone in the world. Yet inside the white chamber of her heart, she was alive. When she closed her eyes, she could see rays of light. She aged ten years on that flight; a different person got off the plane than the one who had boarded.

Sandy had wanted to understand what she was going through—just as he wanted to understand and possess every-thing around him. He didn't see that she was temporarily out of reach. Candace had always loved his vanity and self-absorption; they were part of what made him seem larger than life. But now she needed solitude. That was the way for her to get better, but he couldn't see it. When he tried to put that ring on her finger, she felt a physical sense of disgust. It was so wrong, such an intrusion. He had misread the signals so totally. She wondered whether he really loved her if he could do something so selfish. So she had run away—back to the shelter of her white room.

And then Sandy Galvin went away. He never told her he was leaving Harvard, he was so angry. She only found out when she called his number, one day in January, to see if he was all right. She hadn't been sure what she would say to him; perhaps they would just take a walk. But the telephone had been disconnected. It was a shock, to know that he was gone. She felt numb again—the way she had the night he proposed—and then she ached. She thought it would go away, but it didn't—all that winter and into the spring. She kept waiting for him to return, or at least call her to say that he was alive, in some distant place. But he didn't.

She had dated other men in college, and many since then. But the ache of longing didn't go away. Galvin was like a tattoo; he was indelible. First love is sometimes that way—so pure and potent that it creates a place in your heart that didn't exist before, and leaves behind a permanent emptiness. What she concluded, in those weeks and months—and finally, years—was the sad, simple truth that some things in life don't work out. Some people aren't fated to be happy in love. They miss their chance, for whatever reason, and don't get it back. They can't have what they want. That was a concept Galvin could not possibly have understood, but it had become part of her identity.

CANDACE WAS CRADLING HER head in her hands. I walked to the refrigerator and poured us another glass of wine. It was getting dark outside. A fat winter cloud had settled over what was left of the sun. I put my hand on her shoulder to comfort her; she let it rest there, but that was all. She looked up at me. I'd come this far. What else did I want to know?

"You stayed in touch with Galvin after that," I said. "That's what he told me. He said he helped you win your Pulitzer Prize."

"It's true. Nobody's supposed to know that, but he helped me a lot over the years. After he got rich, he sent me gifts and gave me information. He still wanted me, and I couldn't say no. Then he wanted to move to Washington, and I let him. It was more than that—I wanted him to come. I thought perhaps now, this time, it could be different. I'm sorry that I lied to you about that, but there was so much to hide. This story was really so complicated, you see."

What a long time they'd spent living in suspended animation. I thought again of that Graham Greene passage Candace had read to me many years ago, about how a cold heart was more precious than diamonds. Was her heart finally warm? Would it melt through the chains of obligation and responsibility that surrounded her? I honestly didn't know.

"Do you love him?" That was the question I had asked her once before in this house, after the night of Galvin's party. She had equivocated then, but not now.

"Yes, of course I do. I always have. As much as I can love anyone, I love Sandy."

It's a terrible thing to say, but even after that intense and overpowering conversation, I wasn't sure that she was telling me the truth.

TWENTY-THREE

A MOVING VAN WAS PARKED IN FRONT OF GALVIN'S HOUSE. It was a huge double-length trailer—so big I wondered how they had gotten it down Galvin's narrow driveway. The cab was parked in a flower bed to the left of the house, and the big trailer tires had torn up a swath of the lawn. On the front grille of the cab, I noticed, was a Christmas wreath. Large men with arms the size of hams were marching in and out of the house, toting the objects Galvin had collected over the years and stowing them in the cavernous truck. The movers had been hired by the committee of creditors that now controlled Galvin's fate. They had rushed to seize Galvin's property after debt-repayment negotiations collapsed the day before. It wasn't public yet—he still had a few days of grace before the formal bankruptcy papers were filed in court. But his treasures were already being hauled away, to be auctioned off to some other bold entrepreneur.

Candace and I had driven out that morning to see him. She had decided to publish the investigative article, and she asked me to accompany her. That seemed hideously inappropriate; surely she owed him a last private moment. But she insisted that I come—this was about the survival of the newspaper, she said. It had to be done right, with a witness. And I had acceded, selfishly, on the condition that I would be a passive onlooker only. For in truth, I wanted to be there. My role in this drama, at every point, had been to observe and chronicle it. That was my power and, you might say, my vengeance. I will leave to the reader the Heisenberg question—the problem of whether, in the act of observing, I changed the phenomena I am now describing.

The house was nearly empty. The movers had done their job with ruthless efficiency by the time we arrived. The rooms were bare; the fine carpets had been rolled up and stowed in that vast truck; the paintings pulled down from the wall and packed in wooden crates. Galvin asked us to come sit in the sunroom. It was the only room that seemed to have any furniture left. The locusts had stripped him of everything else in the space of a few hours. He sat on a wicker couch with bright yellow cushions. Candace took the chair next to him, while I sat some distance away, as close to disappearing as I could manage.

Galvin's health had deteriorated further. There was a pallor to his skin, and a puffiness around the eyes, as if he had been taking drugs. He gathered the blanket across his lap as we talked. From the strain on his face he looked to be in some pain, though it was hard to tell, he was so good at concealment. On the coffee table in front of him were the Matisse etchings that had been hanging on the wall of his small dining room—the ones of the tauntingly beautiful model who looked so much like Candace. He was keeping them close now, like a bag of gold coins. They were all he had left.

"This is one hell of a situation!" he said in the most blustery voice he could summon. "Carting away a man's furniture in the middle of the night. I promise you, they'll regret it. When I'm back on my feet, I'll make them eat every stick they've taken out of here." He sat back gingerly on the couch after his brief burst of bravado.

Candace mumbled apologies for disturbing him on such a difficult day. She was having trouble looking at him; she was feeling the embarrassment of a healthy person visiting a sick one, when there are no right words to say, only wrong ones. It was a shock to her, obviously. It had been several weeks since she had been with him, and she wasn't prepared to see him so visibly changed.

He took her hand. It was still twice the size of hers, however papery and thin it had become. "Hey, sweetie," he said. "Cheer up. Everything's fine. I'll buy more furniture."

Candace laughed nervously. It was obvious she hadn't told him yet why she was there. For all he knew, it was just a social call.

"To what do I owe the pleasure?" he asked. "I've been looking forward to seeing you, Candace, although I must say, you could have chosen a better day."

"This is hard," she said awkwardly. "You aren't going to like it."

"I don't like anything that's happening to me right now, except the fact that you're here with me." He took her hand again and gave her the sick man's version of his bedroom smile.

"It's about the newspaper." She looked at the floor, not at him, and kept talking. "You're in financial and legal trouble. That puts the *Sun* in a difficult position. We have to publish something about you before everyone else does. If we don't, it will look like we're covering things up—just because you're the publisher. So a few weeks ago I asked two reporters to do an independent investigation of your finances. I thought it was a way of protecting you, and the newspaper."

"Right. Sure." He studied her face. Who was she, really? What was she made of? He would finally know. "So what did they discover?"

"Painful things. The reporters found that you're in default on a billion dollars in loans. They found that you've been in financial trouble for more than two years, and that you've been living on borrowed money ever since you arrived in Washington. They found that the SEC and the Justice Department are investigating you, and will probably bring charges soon. They found evidence that you acquired the *Sun* by fraud." As she went through the list, she sounded like a newspaper reporter.

He looked at her dumbly, unable to speak for a moment. It was as if she had given him a kick in the solar plexus and knocked the wind out of him. This was the answer to his question: She was in league with the misery makers. "What do you want from me?" he said, barely above a whisper.

"We need your comment. Then we're going to run the story. I'm sorry."

"You're kidding me." He was shaking his head; the blood was rising in his pale cheeks. He hadn't let himself believe it before, when I tried to tell him. He loved her too much to think that she would deliberately hurt him. "You want to run this crap in *my* newspaper? And you want me to *comment?*"

"Yes. I apologize, but that's standard procedure. It would be wrong to run a story about anyone without letting them comment. Those are the rules."

"Okay, here's my comment. What you said is total bullshit, and I'll sue anybody who runs such a story. How would that be? I'll sue myself, and win!"

"Don't make this harder than it has to be, Sandy. Please. For my sake."

"For your sake?" He took her forearm and pulled her toward him, hard enough that she cried out. "Don't do this, Candace. Don't play by these rules. You don't have to."

"Yes, I do." He was still holding her arm tightly. He hadn't entirely lost his boxer's strength. She was trembling, her face a few inches from his, and it was obvious that she was frightened. When Galvin saw that, he relaxed his grip.

"You're crazy," he said. "Completely crazy."

"No, I'm not. You made me the editor of your newspaper. I told you then that I would do it the right way. I never imagined we would have a problem like this. But I have to protect the integrity of the paper. That's the most important thing right now."

"No, it's not, Candace. Duty to others is *not* the most important thing. Neither are rules or appearances. If you love me, you can't possibly do this. It's wrong. You'll regret it the rest of your life."

"I'm a journalist. I have a responsibility to my colleagues. They're depending on me to do what's right."

"What an excuse! I guess I'm supposed to roll over and

say 'of course, darling,' then do the 'right thing.' But it won't work with me. We've had this argument before. That time, you didn't bother to ask me for comment before you stuck a dagger in me."

She fell back in her chair; his words had wounded her as if he had struck with his own dagger. The look on her face now was one of pain and resignation. He would never understand. It was pointless to argue.

"I should leave," she said. "I have to get back to the office. I'll send you a copy of the story for you to read, and if you have anything you want to say, you can call me."

She rose again and stood a few feet from him, her arms folded implacably across her chest. He looked up at her, whispering a cry of sadness to himself, and his eyes suddenly filled with tears. How could it have come to this? How could love be so powerless? She was frozen as if in an iceberg, drifting away from him forever, and he couldn't pry her loose.

"Sit down," he said weakly. She sat, in deference to his tears if nothing else. He was such a big man; it was hard to see him humbled. He blew his nose in a handkerchief and dried his eyes with his sleeve.

He took her hand one last time. "Come away with me," he said. "Forget all these rules and obligations. They've never made you happy. Come away with me now. We'll leave tonight for Switzerland. I still have a house there, and we can sit by the lake and be together for a little while, at least."

"I can't. I have to edit the paper."

"Come away," he repeated. "Let yourself be happy."

"It's impossible. I would have to resign my job. The paper would collapse. It would be a scandal."

"Come away with me," he repeated a final time. "I'm very sick. That must be obvious to you. I need to rest. I don't know how much time I have, but however much it is, I want to spend it with you. I love you, Candace. The only mistake I truly regret in my life is that I made it too hard for you to accept my love. But there's still time. You can still break the rules."

"No, I can't." She spoke the words quietly but firmly.

She rose from the chair a last time and walked out the door. I followed her. We left him alone in that big, empty house, wrapped in his blanket, clutching the drawings of the woman he loved so perfectly in his heart but could not capture in life. As we drove away, I could see him standing at the window of his sunroom, looking down at the Potomac far below. Ice had formed at the banks of the river, but at the center there was still a powerful rush of water onward that flowed to the city—and past it, to the ocean.

In an odd sense, Galvin had gotten what he wanted from Washington. His world had come tumbling down around him, but he had done what he'd come here for—he had lived for love. He had done everything in his power to bring his beloved along with him; and if she had refused, he could not blame himself. It didn't diminish his love, that she wouldn't accept it.

TWENTY-FOUR

GALVIN CAUGHT A FLIGHT THAT NIGHT FOR GENEVA WITH
Ted Amara, so he never saw the story that appeared the next
morning in his newspaper. It was a masterful piece of journalism, by the usual standards of the profession. It explained
in clear language Galvin's astounding rise to financial power
and his spectacular collapse. The lead of the story, inevitably,
was the fact that the Justice Department was conducting a
criminal investigation of the publisher of *The Washington Sun
and Tribune,* focusing on his fraudulent misrepresentations in
acquiring the paper. The reporters had ably gathered the
facts. They had quotes from Harold Hazen, his daughter Ariane, and even Galvin's putative partner in the scheme, Melvin
Wolfe. Galvin's refusal to comment was high in the story. My
modest role in assisting Galvin went unmentioned.

Candace Ridgway wrote a signed commentary piece on
the editorial page, which explained why the newspaper had
taken the unusual step of investigating its own publisher. It
was an eloquent statement of the values that animate good

journalism, and in its own way, it was compelling. She also disclosed in the article that for many years she had maintained a close personal relationship with Galvin. That was a wise addition. It rendered the information valueless to others, and blocked any criticism of her.

Candace was lionized by the rest of the media. *The New York Times* ran a front-page profile of her, and published an editorial commending her courageous stand. The fact that she'd chosen to investigate the publisher, even though he'd been her close friend, was seen as further evidence of her probity and incorruptibility. She was lauded as a model of everything that journalism stood for, and that was true enough. Commentators were already predicting that the paper's courageous self-examination would win the Pulitzer Prize for Public Service the next April—the profession's highest award.

THERE WAS A GREAT commotion over what would happen to the newspaper. Galvin's creditors moved immediately to seize it, to repay his debts. But they hadn't anticipated the publisher's legal wizardry. It turned out he no longer owned any interest in the *Sun*. With Ted Amara's help, he had months ago placed his shares in a trust for the benefit of the newspaper's employees. They now owned the newspaper. As administrator of the trust, Galvin had designated the paper's editor, Candace Ridgway. She was now, in effect, the chief executive officer of the company.

Galvin's creditors were furious, needless to say, about this legal chicanery, and several of them tried to challenge Galvin's transfer of ownership to the employees. But the paper had become so popular, thanks to Candace, that there was a political uproar at the notion that greedy Wall Street bankers might grab it to repay Galvin's debts. Members of Congress even talked of introducing legislation to prevent seizure of the paper's assets, but that proved unnecessary. The creditors backed off.

CANDACE SUMMONED ME TO her office in January, a few weeks after Galvin's departure. She asked for my resignation, and made clear that she would fire me outright if I refused to go quietly. The reason, she said, was that I had been in league with Galvin in his fraudulent takeover of the paper. I had escaped prosecution or public exposure, but what I had done was unconscionable. The newspaper couldn't tolerate it. I didn't really argue with her, but I suspected that wasn't the real reason I had to go.

My problem, I felt certain, was that I had glimpsed the truth about Candace. Not about her relationship with Galvin, or the eternal torment of her father's suicide. Those were private truths that nobody else could possibly understand. No, my curse was that I had finally come to understand her. She needed to be in control, and she had been. This had been *her* piece of theater all along, not Galvin's. She had lured him to Washington, and used him to achieve her ambition. He had followed her direction, sometimes wittingly, other times not. Or so I imagined.

"Now you have what you want," I told her the day she fired me. "Congratulations."

The color drained from her face—the opposite of what I expected. I had assumed that she would behave like a captain of industry now, throwing me overboard and sailing on to new ports. But rather than her confident smile and keen eyes, which in recent months had come almost to resemble Galvin's, I saw a face of infinite sadness.

"Do you think I won?" she asked. There was a sound of doom in her voice, as if she had actually survived a shipwreck.

"Of course. You got what you wanted. You always wanted to run a newspaper. And now you don't have Galvin in the way, messing things up."

She looked at me and shook her head. She was speechless. How could I have heard the story and not understood it? She closed her eyes. This was her fate, to be misunderstood. People always wanted love to *speak,* to turn somersaults and fire rockets in the air, but sometimes it was silent. Sometimes it was hidden away, unable to connect or comfort, but it was still love. Couldn't I see that?

"I am destroyed, David," she said. "Do you think any success in the world could make up for what I have lost?"

For once, I realized the limits of cynicism as a tool of understanding. It had been coming on slowly, this sense that sneering wasn't an adequate response to the world. But seeing Candace that last day—as dry as a bone, surrounded by the empty tokens of status and power—made me want to tinker with my own life plan just a bit. I did not want to arrive at middle age with the look I saw on her face—bereft, loveless, having traveled so far, only to say: Is this all? I did not want to post a mental notice at the end of my days to the people I might have loved, if only I'd found the words.

AT THE END OF every *Jerry Springer Show,* Jerry offers what he calls "A Final Thought." It's the only part of the show I really hate. Here we've just spent an hour watching lesbian lovers slug it out with their ex-boyfriends, and new brides plead for divorce after seeing videos of their husbands' debauched bachelor parties—and then Jerry closes by saying something pious like: Folks, whatever flavor they come in, relationships are a priceless gift. Or, Folks, remember, if you want a do-right woman, you've got to be a do-right man. Yeah, right, Jer, I always think. Forget the sermon. Bring back the lesbians.

But in this case, I probably do need to say a final word, about myself and about Candace.

Over the months I watched this story unfold, I began to escape from a kind of malign self-delusion. Maybe that's the trick of anyone who observes other people carefully, that he will eventually learn something from their experience. In my case, I had been living in an acid bath for so long that it had begun to feel normal. But now it hurt, and I realized that I wanted to live like ordinary people. That's a strange aspiration for a Harvard man, I'll grant, but it's genuine (a word that has always made me squirm, but never mind, I'm trying to reform).

Certainly I learned what I did not want to be anymore— which was a newspaperman. I would have quit the *Sun,* actually, if Candace hadn't fired me. For me, a newspaper had been an emblem of solitude and isolation. Reading the sports page was what I did, obsessively, as a boy, rather than playing sports. In the middle of my life, reading about politics and world events became a substitute for living them. Rather than marrying, I read the marriage notices in *The New York Times* compulsively every Sunday, studying them like a lesson in social archaeology. Rich people tended to marry beautiful people—I'd noticed that over the years. And the very richest women, if they were lucky, tended to marry men like Galvin, men who—wherever they were from—had the contained heat of the life force blazing in their eyes. In my old age, I was sure, I would dutifully read the obituary notices to study how to die, wondering what words the newspaper would use about me. I had been trapped in two dimensions for so many years, captured by these flat pages.

But enough! Loneliness, like newspaper reading, was a habit, and it was one I intended to break. I wanted to take the dare, to step across the ice floe toward what I sensed might be on the other side. It was coldness I had loved in Candace, as pure and perfect as a snowflake, but that had made my affection for her unreal. And I wondered now: What would someone real and imperfect be like—someone like that journalist I had admired, Michelle Hagel, with the comfy body and frizzy hair. What would it be like if, instead of making a wisecrack, I had reached out in that bar and touched her hand? Would she have recoiled? Or would she have smiled and pulled me toward her? I wanted to know.

My final thought about Candace is that she was a woman of her time. In that sense, it was beyond her control. She was one of those dazzling creatures that inhabit the American landscape at the end of our century, who appear to have everything—beauty, brilliance, success in their careers—but have missed finding the treasure. It was there; these women knew it—but they could not find their way to it. They didn't know how to cut corners and seize it. That was what they could have learned from men like Galvin, but it wasn't their way. They were the people who had it all, and yet knew the absolute emptiness of not having the one thing they wanted.

GALVIN HAD BEEN MUCH sicker than anyone had realized, other than himself. He had liver cancer, and though he was treated aggressively in Switzerland, he was dead by the end of January. I suspect he had known for many months that he was dying. Perhaps that was why he had come to Washington—he wanted to write the last chapter. But none of us is really allowed to do that. There was a brief effort to extradite him so that he could face charges in the United States, and the chairman of the House Commerce Committee was greatly disappointed that the star witness would not appear for his ritual flaying. But when it became known how desperately ill Galvin was, the hunters lost interest. There was no sport in pursuing a quarry that was nearly dead.

Candace wanted to see him at the end. She flew to Switzerland and went to the hospital. By then the cancer had spread so far that he was delirious much of the time, falling in and out of consciousness. The doctor said it might be better to leave him alone—he was so far gone, it was better to remember him the way he had been. But Candace insisted on going into that room. She sat by his bed, day and night, holding his hand, unsure whether he knew it was her. She never had to explain anything; he was past that. She was with him when he died, holding that now-frail hand in her own. When the doctor told her it was time to leave, she kissed his lips and said good-bye.

There was a brief funeral in Geneva, and the body was cremated, at Galvin's request. He was just shy of fifty. It seemed a terrible way to die, for a man who had given such abundant life to others. But I could not imagine Galvin being unhappy, even at the end. He had nothing to regret. That was what made him so different from other men of his generation. They struggled against the inevitability of decline because they had never come of age in the first place. They lived their middle years with a growing sense of regret at what they had failed to achieve—and worse, what they had failed to attempt. Galvin's luck was that he had avoided middle age entirely; his light had been extinguished in an instant, with the afterglow still pulsing in my eyes even after he was gone. I could see that lovely smile of his that said, *What a life! What a gift! What a lucky man I have been.*

Acknowledgments

I owe special thanks to my editor, Jon Karp, who encouraged me to write this time about people, rather than spies. I'm also grateful to the friends who read the manuscript and offered comments, including my wife, Dr. Eve Ignatius; my agent, Raphael Sagalyn; Garrett Epps; Lincoln Caplan; Susan Shreve; Graham Wisner; and Craig Stoltz. Above all, I'm indebted to Don Graham and the late Meg Greenfield, who gave me time and encouragement at a moment when I needed both.

About the Author

DAVID IGNATIUS is the author of four acclaimed novels, the most recent of which is *A Firing Offense*. Currently an op-ed columnist at *The Washington Post*, he has also been a reporter and war correspondent for *The Wall Street Journal*. He is a graduate of Harvard University and Cambridge University and lives in Washington, D.C.

About the Type

This book was set in Monotype Dante, a typeface designed by Giovanni Mardersteig (1892–1977). Conceived as a private type for the Officina Bodoni in Verona, Italy, Dante was originally cut only for hand composition by Charles Malin, the famous Parisian punch cutter, between 1946 and 1952. Its first use was in an edition of Boccaccio's *Trattatello in laude di Dante* that appeared in 1954. The Monotype Corporation's version of Dante followed in 1957. Though modeled on the Aldine type used for Pietro Cardinal Bembo's treatise *De Aetna* in 1495, Dante is a thoroughly modern interpretation of that venerable face.

the NEW

Fat Flush Cookbook

Also by Ann Louise Gittleman, PhD, CNS

The New Complete Fat Flush Program

The New Fat Flush Cookbook

The New Fat Flush Foods

The New Fat Flush Journal and Shopping Guide

The New Fat Flush Fitness Plan

The New Fat Flush Plan

Fat Flush for Life

Zapped

The Gut Flush Plan

The Fast Track Detox Diet

Hot Times

Ann Louise Gittleman's Guide to the 40/30/30 Phenomenon

Eat Fat, Lose Weight Cookbook

The Living Beauty Detox Program

Why Am I Always So Tired?

Super Nutrition for Men

How to Stay Young and Healthy in a Toxic World

Eat Fat, Lose Weight

Overcoming Parasites

Super Nutrition for Menopause

Beyond Probiotics

The 40/30/30 Phenomenon

Before the Change

Your Body Knows Best

Get the Salt Out

Get the Sugar Out

Guess What Came to Dinner? Parasites and Your Health

Super Nutrition for Women

Beyond Pritikin

Eat Fat, Lose Weight for Kindle

the
NEW
Fat Flush
Cookbook

ANN LOUISE GITTLEMAN,
PhD, C.N.S.

New York Chicago San Francisco Athens
London Madrid Mexico City Milan New Delhi
Singapore Sydney Toronto

Copyright © 2017, 2003 by Ann Louise Gittleman. All rights reserved. Printed in the United States of America. Except as permitted under the United States Copyright Act of 1976, no part of this publication may be reproduced or distributed in any form or by any means, or stored in a database or retrieval system, without the prior written permission of the publisher.

2 3 4 5 6 7 8 9   LCR   22 21 20 19

ISBN   978-1-260-01204-0
MHID   1-260-01204-2

e-ISBN   978-1-260-01205-7
e-MHID   1-260-01205-0

McGraw-Hill Education books are available at special quantity discounts to use as premiums and sales promotions or for use in corporate training programs. To contact a representative, please visit the Contact Us pages at www.mhprofessional.com.

Contents

Acknowledgments

I will be eternally grateful to my extraordinary band of Fat Flush angels who made this cookbook come together. First and foremost, a huge thank you to my "significant brother" Stuart Gittleman who helped manage the project in record time with my very capable assistant and brand manager who can multi-task like no other—Ally Mortensen.

Teresa Pfaff headed up our Fat Flush Taste Kitchen and tweaked many a tried and true favorites with even more deliciousness and flavor. She followed in the footsteps of Linda Shapiro, Kari Wheaton, Jackie Scott, and Rose Grandy.

Thanks to the entire McGraw-Hill staff, including Christopher Brown, Cheryl Ringer, Donya Dickerson, Ann Pryor, Chelsea Van Der Gaag, and Courtney Fischer. Thank you as well to Jillian Sanders for all of her hard work getting the Fat Flush name on the front lines. I also have tremendous appreciation for Patty Wallenburg, who is simply wonderful to work with.

My deepest appreciation goes out to all of our Fat Flush moderators— past and present—for making our Fat Flush Nation such a positive, supportive community. They include Kathleen Sullivan, Linda Leekley, Linda Mitchell, Linda Shapiro, Charli Sorenson, Nina Moreau, Janine Forbes, Terri White, Carol Ackerman, Sue Durand, Michelle O'Reardon, Cathy Gorbenko, Elisa Bieg, Linda Pankhurst, Kathy Jensen, Lisa Nectoux, Jackie Scott, Mary Dodge, Barbara Anderson, Chris Patterson, and Priscilla Underwood.

I must acknowledge the staff at *First for Women* magazine, who have always championed my insights and Fat Flush brand for decades. These special souls include Editor in Chief Carol Brooks, Deputy Editor in Chief Maggie Jaqua, as well as their wonderful staff: Melissa Gotthardt, Melissa Sorrells, Rebecca Haynes, Lisa Maxbauer, Julie Relevant, Brenda Kearns, and Jennifer Joseph. I must also acknowledge my fabulous poster girl Casey Thomaston, who looked incredible representing Fat Flush success in *Woman's World*. I'm also grateful for continuing coverage and support from *MindBodyGreen*, the *Huffington Post*, and *Woman's Day*.

And most of all, thanks to you, dear readers and Fat Flush fans for embracing my program with so much love and grace.

1 Fat Flush Rebooted

As millions of satisfied Fat Flushers already know, the Fat Flush concepts represent a paradigm shift in weight loss and lasting weight control by uniquely focusing on the liver and bile as key weight loss factors. In fact, believe it or not, nothing you do to control your weight is as important as keeping your liver healthy in this era of toxic overload.

This is truly the biggest weight loss breakthrough in over a decade.

And that's why I believe that *The Fat Flush Plan* became a *New York Times* and *USA Today* bestseller within the first two months of publication in 2002. It's also the reason that shortly thereafter Fat Flush swept onto the bestseller lists of *Publisher's Weekly*, the *Wall Street Journal*, the *Dallas Morning News*, and the *San Francisco Chronicle*. The book was featured in nearly every women's magazine in the country in the ensuing years. I appeared on *The View* television show for an amazing six segments in which a Fat Flush candidate—Julie Gough—consistently lost more weight than any other competing dieter on the show.

So, since the publication of *The New Fat Flush Plan*, I wanted to further assist you in your Fat Flush lifestyle so you could integrate all the new smart fats, sweeteners, and other superfoods the "flagship" book now includes.

I have now updated this companion cookbook with whole food recipes that are ever-more supercharged to reset metabolism, flush out bloat, and speed up or maintain fat loss while providing a daily detox boost.

The *new* Fat Flush principles and ingredients incorporated in these recipes are life-changing on many levels. The added bonus of internal cleansing, liver detoxification, and body purification will provide you with unexpected mental and emotional benefits such as mental alertness, increased energy, appetite control, satiety without food cravings, and a noticeable decrease in depression, irritability, and anxiety.

There are more than 200 brand-new Fat Flush recipes and snacks—many of them ready in less than 20 minutes—which are easily identified for each of the three weight loss phases of the plan. For example, the phase 1 Two-Week Fat Flush recipes are designed for accelerated weight loss; the phase 2 Ongoing Fat Flush recipes are designed for transitional weight loss wherein more food choices are provided; while the phase 3 Lifestyle Eating recipes are designed for a lifetime plan to help you stay fit permanently without having to give up your favorite foods.

Keep in mind that the entrées, soups, salads, dressings, condiments, beverages, and even sweet indulgences contain the world's best fat-flushing ingredients (such as cranberries, coconut oil, flaxseed oil, apple cider vinegar, turmeric, and lemons) plus cleansing and metabolism-boosting herbs and spices (such as ginger, cayenne, cumin, mustard, cinnamon, cloves, bay leaves, and fennel), which are far more than just flavor enhancers.

Everyday science reveals not only that some of the original *Fat Flush* staples and spices, such as cranberries, apple cider vinegar, ginger, and cilantro, are good for weight loss but that they provide spectacular health benefits as well. Just before the original Fat Flush Plan was published, a highly publicized study appeared in the *Journal of Agricultural and Food Chemistry*, which ranked cranberries as one of the most healthful foods to consume. Scientists at the University of Scranton proclaimed that cranberries, when compared with 19 other fruits commonly eaten in the United States, have extraordinarily high amounts of a certain antioxidant called phenols, which protects against heart disease, cancer, and stroke.

Apple cider vinegar—long heralded in folk medicine for its cleansing and therapeutic effects on obesity and arthritis because of its high concentration of potassium, trace minerals, and enzymes—has been the subject of university studies and has been found to live up to its legend. A recent Arizona State University trial found that participants who consumed as little as 1½ tablespoons of the vinegar ate 200 fewer calories at the following meal.

Ginger, a primary fat-flushing herb that boosts metabolism and reduces fatty buildup, has recently been found by Danish scientists to head off migraines and ease arthritic aches and pains.

Another Fat Flush favorite, cilantro, also known as Mexican or Chinese parsley, is more than just a frequent flavor enhancer in the recipes. It has been found to help with the removal of heavy metals from the system, primarily mercury, which can negatively affect the central nervous system.

The Fat Flush recipes have been specifically created with many of these superstar health foods and spices as well as lots of colorful veggies, fruits, lean proteins, and satisfying oils to zap *all* the 10 hidden weight gain stumbling blocks, which underlie the excess poundage currently plaguing over 114 million Americans.

My research, online counseling, and hands-on experience with nearly 10 million dieters over the past 20 years have revealed that the real culprits behind weight gain are not simply a lack of willpower, overeating, or underexercising as you have been told. They are far more insidious and alarming.

Here's a thumbnail sketch of the *10 hidden weight gain factors* that provide the scientific foundation behind the Fat Flush philosophy. While these factors are crucial issues to consider for stubborn weight loss concerns, they also play a part in many inflammatory and autoimmune disorders. So now you have a powerful toolbox in safeguarding your family and loved ones from every health condition in our increasingly toxic world.

1. **Your tired, toxic liver.** The number one weight loss stumbling block is a liver overloaded with pollutants and toxins. A toxic liver cannot efficiently burn body fat, and thus it will sabotage your weight loss and detox efforts. The recipes eliminate all liver-damaging elements. They omit caffeine, sugar, trans fats (hydrogenated and partially hydrogenated vegetable fats and oils) from fried foods, margarine, vegetable shortenings and commercial vegetable oils, and yeast-based foods (soy sauce and most vinegars). And they feature liver-loving ingredients like cruciferous vegetables (broccoli, brussels sprouts, and kale), eggs (high in amino acids that are needed for the liver to break down fats), and liver-supporting herbs and spices such as garlic, onion, and ginger root.

2. **False fat.** Waterlogged tissues rank as the number two stumbling block to weight loss. Waterlogged tissues result when you consume too little water and protein, and they can result from food sensitivities, hormonal fluctuations, and certain medications. You'll find that pure water is a major component in all the diet phase protocols because of its purifying properties and ability to remove wastes from the body. Powerful (yet so simple and easy to make) protein-based recipes are provided with beef, chicken, fish, eggs, tofu, and whey. A classic Fat Flush staple and lymph-mover—ruby red cranberries—are found in several recipes such as Sunny Day Muffins and Quick Cran-Raspberry Sauce. In addition, the majority of the recipes eliminate two of the food groups that can trigger immune disorders and inflammation resulting in water retention—gluten-rich grains and dairy products. The flaxseed oil featured in the salad dressings acts as a natural hormone balancer and as replacement therapy. Parsley, cilantro, fennel, and anise are sprinkled throughout the recipes because of their diuretic qualities.

3. **Fear of eating fat.** The number three weight loss stumbling block—lack of fat-burning fats—flies in the face of everything you may have been brainwashed about for the past 20 years. The truth is that certain fats [like flaxseed oil, coconut oil, medium chain triglyceride oil (MCT oil), gamma linoleic acid (GLA) from evening primrose oil, borage or black currant seed oil, and conjugated linoleic acid (CLA)] can accelerate fat burning, trigger fat loss, and provide long-term satiety while maintaining lean muscle mass. While the GLA and CLA fats are taken as dietary supplements, nutty ground-up flax seeds (in addition to the flaxseed oil that serves as a basis for delightfully light dressings and vinaigrettes) are contained in many of the breakfast smoothie recipes and their variations. Coconut oil and MCT oil are great add-ins for smoothies and that one cup of coffee or dandelion root tea. I also encourage you to select meats from grass-fed cattle whenever possible. This is the best natural food source of CLA.

4. **Insulin resistance and inflammation.** The number four weight loss stumbling block—elevated insulin—is a premier fat-promoting hor-

mone created by foods high in carbohydrates. The Fat Flush program combats excess insulin and excess inflammation by providing a diet equation of at least 40 percent total calories from anti-inflammatory essential (and blood sugar–stabilizing) fats, with the rest of the calories divided between powerful protein dishes (which produce the hormone glucagon that counteracts insulin) and low glycemic (or slow-acting) carbs from rainbow-colored veggies and fruits, Mother Nature's anti-inflammatory foods. The Fat Flush dietary approach increases insulin efficiency and transforms the body into a fat-burning, not fat-building, mode.

5. **Stress as a fat maker.** Stress—the number five weight loss stumbling block—functions as a fat maker because the stress hormone cortisol, like insulin, is a major fat-promoting hormone. Cortisol, however, has a propensity for stimulating central fat or tummy fat. Fat Flush recipes feature lightning-fast meals and quick-and-easy snacks that can correct the stress fat cycle by reducing cortisol levels through proper meal timing. The key here is to eat something about every three hours *before* you are hungry. The meals-in-minutes techniques help to balance blood sugar throughout the day, thereby avoiding cravings and fat storage.

6. **Messy microbiome.** The number six weight loss stumbling block—a messy microbiome—is a doozy, as it plays a major role in every one of the first five stumbling blocks above. The word *microbiome* refers to the trillions of bacteria that live in your body, mostly in your gut. Numerous studies have intimately linked a messy, unbalanced microbiome to weight gain and obesity. In fact, its influential role in our metabolism gives our bacterial ecosystem substantial control over our weight. A damaged microbiome cannot properly perform its role in metabolizing blood sugar or regulating hormones (including hunger hormones) and may turn on genes that encourage obesity. Interestingly, scientists have started to attribute some of the weight loss associated with bypass surgery to healthier gut bacteria that occur as a result of the procedure and an accompanying change in the diet.

7. **Backed-up bile.** The number seven weight loss stumbling block is backed-up bile. No conversation about weight is complete without discussing this yellowish-green liquid that the liver produces about a quart of every day. Bile is stored in the gallbladder, where it waits until it is transported to the intestines during digestion. Made from lecithin, cholesterol, and bilirubin, your bile has two jobs. First, it emulsifies and digests fat, breaking it down into small particles so that your intestines can absorb them. Second, it helps escort toxins that your liver has removed out of the body. Healthy bile is brilliant, but backed-up bile leads to hypothyroidism, weight gain, and nutritional deficiency.

8. **Tuckered-out thyroid.** The number eight weight loss stumbling block is your tuckered-out thyroid. Because the thyroid has a decisive role in hor-

mone regulation, its ability to function has consequences for every aspect of your health. This mighty gland regulates body temperature, as well as supports the immune system, the nervous system, and the intestines. It impacts the brain, muscles, heart, gallbladder, and liver. Thyroid hormones help strengthen hair, nails, and skin, and they support normal bone growth. The thyroid's hormonal control makes it a significant part of metabolism. Rehabilitating your tuckered-out thyroid can be the key to finally inciting your metabolic burn.

9. **Hidden hitchhikers—parasites.** The number nine weight loss stumbling block is hidden hitchhikers—parasites. These pesky critters can make you fat! I know this may sound like the strangest stumbling block of all, but it's true. Just like every other stressful, pathogenic, disruptive substance or organism I have discussed, parasites can sabotage any weight loss effort or attempt to create a healthier body. Parasites place a major burden on the immune system and are especially toxic to the liver. By eliminating parasites first and foremost, your body can then reduce its toxic load, and your system can more efficiently clear pathogenic bacteria, heavy metals, fungus, and mold. Best of all, you may just lose weight once and for all.

10. **Missing magnesium.** Last but by no means least, the tenth weight loss stumbling block is missing magnesium. As far as the nutritional world is concerned, magnesium is to minerals as vitamin D is to vitamins: a superstar. Magnesium plays a starring role in Fat Flush as a critical mineral that helps turn food into fuel. Without enough of this vital catalyst, you lack a major nutritional component that triggers efficient fat burning. This mighty mineral also contributes to hormonal regulation. It prevents excess cortisol, increases insulin sensitivity, and aids in the production of thyroid hormone. Through only this one facet of its function, magnesium improves almost all the hidden weight gain factors. A lack of magnesium does not just spell trouble for weight loss. Magnesium has been linked to a litany of other conditions that also plague Fat Flushers. If high blood pressure, leg cramps, migraines, anxiety, irritability, depression, heart disease, unstable blood sugar, or insomnia is challenging your well-being, then it's time to get on the magnesium bandwagon.

COUNT DOWN TO FAT FLUSH

You're getting closer and closer to the next level of the Fat Flush experience. The next chapter includes comprehensive food options for each level of the plan, with recommended portions to help you make the program more convenient and more practical than ever. Then I'll help you set up your Fat Flush kitchen with some suggestions on the best time-saving utensils and equipment to have on hand to maximize your results. And before you know it, you'll be ready to start on that fast and fabulous food. Just make sure you also make some time for shopping—clothes shopping, that is, because you'll soon be ready for a fabulous new wardrobe!

2 The Fat Flush Evolution

Over the years Fat Flush has not been just a revolution in health. More than a diet, it is an eating evolution for total well-being! It's not just for weight loss anymore. The Fat Flush principles are all about ridding your body of inflammation and boosting immunity for all-around good health!

As many of you already know, a foundational and comprehensive list of acceptable foods, beverages, spices, and brand names for each of the three phases of the program is provided in *The New Fat Flush Plan*. Also provided are sample menu plans and culinary ideas for each phase. As new research has surfaced, additional herbs, spices, fats, gluten-free options, sweeteners, and brand names have been added to your evolving Fat Flush repertoire to keep things fresh and current.

And so what else is new?

BEFORE YOU BEGIN OR IF YOU HAVE FALLEN OFF THE FAT FLUSH WAGON

Before you begin the Three-Day Fat Flush Tune-Up, there are many practical ways to prepare your body for the Fat Flush experience. As I explain in *The New Fat Flush Plan*, tapering off alcohol, coffee, tea, colas, and other soft drinks (which are major liver stressors) and substituting herbal coffees is probably the single most important thing you can do to prepare your system for cleansing. This step will also help to forestall the withdrawal symptoms of fatigue, headaches, irritability, and increased hunger once you are on the full-fledged program.

Besides getting caffeine out of your life, I have learned that the next two biggest Fat Flush challenges are getting rid of sugar and getting the excess salt out. So let's take out the sugar first!

In *The New Fat Flush Plan*, in Chapter 2, "Top 10 Hidden Weight Gain Factors #1 Through #5," you learned that white sugar (and white flour and white rice, which are metabolized like sugar) adversely affects your blood sugar and insulin levels as well as triggers yeast overgrowth. While high blood sugar, excess insulin, and excess yeast can lead to a slew of health challenges like adult-onset diabetes, cardiovascular disease, and impaired immunity, they can also sabotage your weight loss efforts.

Whether you are trying to lose weight or improve your overall health, here's what you need to do to get started so your transition to the phase 1 Two-Week Fat Flush will be as painless as possible.

PRE–FAT FLUSH: 12 TRANSITIONAL TIPS TO GET THE SUGAR OUT

If you are hooked on sugar, these tips are absolutely essential for your Fat Flush success:

1. *Right now*, stop adding sugar to foods such as cereal and fruits and to any of your drinks—even those herbal coffee substitutes or herbal teas you are now using. All forms of sugar, sugar alcohols, and artificial sweeteners are out for this transitional phase. The noncaloric sugar alcohols (such as mannitol, sorbitol, and xylitol) found in sugar-free chewing gums are often the cause of cramps, diarrhea, and bloating. Artificial sweeteners like aspartame (also known as Equal or NutraSweet) can increase both sugar and carbohydrate cravings by blocking production of serotonin. Insufficient serotonin creates more sugar and carbohydrate cravings, which can then increase the likelihood of binging. Watch out for all the fancy names for any of the above, like dehydrated cane crystals, cane juice crystals, cane sugar, caramel, corn syrup, corn syrup solids, dextrose, diastase, fructose, fruit juice and fruit juice concentrates, invert sugar, lactose, malt syrup, maltodextrin, maltose, sorghum syrup, regular sugar, raw sugar, turbinado sugar, and brown sugar. (Ideally, these should not be consumed at all, unless they are listed right near the end of the ingredients—way after the first five ingredients.)

2. Get rid of processed carbohydrates from your kitchen starting today. As I mentioned previously but this is well worth repeating, refined carbohydrates in the form of white rice, white bread, and white pasta (the "wicked whites") are rapidly converted to sugars in the body and upset the body's blood sugar and fat-controlling systems. Keeping these products out of the house is a very simple yet most effective way to maintain a well-balanced blood sugar level for long-term energy and the avoidance of hunger (and temptations).

3. Foodwise, just remember to go with unrefined and unprocessed as much as possible. This is the *only* way to ensure that you are really reducing your sugar intake, especially the hidden sugars in sauces, cereals, dressings, and such. Most vegetables and fruits as well as chicken, meat, fish, tofu, and eggs are as sugar free as you can get. The naturally occurring sugars present in legumes, grains, vegetables, fruits, nuts, and seeds are combined with fiber and other nutrients that help to balance your blood

sugar by slowing down the body's absorption and assimilation of the natural sugars present.

4. Fructose is the new fat! Did you know that fruits can make you fat? Years ago we used to think fructose, the fruit-based sweetener, was the sweetener of choice because it did not raise insulin like so many other sugars. What we have since learned, however, is that fructose is absorbed more slowly into the bloodstream. It creates a more level blood sugar than plain glucose from simple sugars. Fructose has a delayed response. While it doesn't raise insulin, it goes right to the liver, the only organ that can metabolize it, which then turns it into triglycerides (a form of fat) that can ultimately end up around your tummy and in "love handles." High triglyceride levels are associated with heart disease, especially in women. So fruits, which all contain some degree of fructose—but especially high-fructose ones like raisins, figs, dates, prunes, peaches, grapes, apricots, apples, and pears—need to be kept to a bare minimum or eliminated from your diet completely. Furthermore, today's fruits are hybridized sugar bombs. Yesteryear's apples, for instance, only contained somewhere around two grams of fructose. Today, thanks to modern agricultural practices and genetic engineering, these "Frankenfruits" now contain up to 30 times as much fructose as fruits in the past. That's why an apple *today* may no longer keep the doctor away. The takeaway here is that regardless of whether you are overweight or underweight, your insulin balance can easily become out of whack. That's why it is so important to consume smart fats *and* protein, because both of these macronutrients act as blood sugar–stabilizing agents, keeping blood sugar at an even keel.

5. Dilute even the natural sweeteners or naturally sweetened foods whenever you can. If you are a health nut already and are using healthful sweeteners like barley malt or brown rice syrup, for example, then dilute these concentrated sweeteners with water.

6. Avoid any food with the label "fat free," the marketing trick that makes you think such foods may help you lose weight but have actually contributed to our increasing weight and health problems. (Remember that section in Chapter 2 of *The New Fat Flush Plan* that discusses the consequences of the fear of eating fat—even the right fat-burning fats?) When "fat free" is on the label, you can be sure to find lots of sugar in various disguises ending with "-ose" like sucrose, glucose, dextrose, and laevulose to improve the taste factor. Excess amounts of sugar that are not balanced with protein and fat cause the pancreas to release insulin, the body's main fat storage hormone.

7. The more natural, the better the food for you. So load up on fresh veggies, and when you do eat fruits, fresh and organic is best whenever possible. The more processed a food may be (think potato chips and even orange juice), the more it will tend to raise your blood sugar because the fiber and nutrients are missing.

8. Make a vow to ingest foods *only* with 0 to 4 grams of sugars per serving. Become a sugar sleuth. To cut the sugar out, you have to know where it is hiding first. There's no way around it. If you are still buying packaged foods, you have to pay attention to what's in them. Three-quarters of the sugars Americans ingest are "hidden" in processed foods, so you have to become a health detective. Learn to read those labels and search for the various names for sugar itemized in tip 1 above.

9. Now that we are on the topic of labels, note that the label "sugar free" means that the food contains fewer than 0.5 gram of sugar. The labels "no added sugar," "without added sugar," and "no sugar added" mean that no sugar or ingredients containing sugars were added during the processing or packing of the products and that the product has no ingredients that were made with added sugars, such as jams, jellies, or concentrated fruit juices. The term "reduced sugar" means that the product contains at least 25 percent less sugar than the original product.

10. Start eating for taste and good health. The human body requires only about 2 teaspoons of sugar in the bloodstream at any one time. You can easily meet this requirement with fresh fruits and veggies, protein, and fat.

11. Listen to your body. Think about what happens when you eat that decadently chocolaty dessert. You may feel an initial high, but an hour later the irritability, depression, and lethargy set in; what is your body telling you? Try to choose foods that make you feel good for the long term— mentally, emotionally, and physically.

12. Start to eat regular, balanced meals and mini-snacks. Think protein (eggs, poultry, beef, fish, lamb, tofu), veggies (the more vibrant the color, the better), and quality fats (flaxseed and olive oil) at every meal. Concentrate on fresh fruits twice a day between meals.

PRE–FAT FLUSH: 11 TRANSITIONAL TIPS TO GET THE RIGHT SALT IN AND THE BAD SALT OUT

Sugar is on its way out of your diet once again. Now if you are still addicted to excess salt, listen up. As you already know, excess salt—especially commercial refined salt—is a primary dietary culprit for waterlogged tissues, one of the ten hidden weight gain factors discussed earlier. Excessive consumption of salt is also linked to strokes, hypertension, and a variety of cardiovascular problems. However, our bodies absolutely need the right amount of the right salt in order to function.

The truth is that sodium—found in the form of sodium chloride, or salt—plays countless critical roles in the human body that no other macromineral can come close to matching! Without the right kind of salt, our bodies would become like statues. Sodium has a surprisingly pivotal effect on all our muscles (especially the heart), a calming effect on stress, and a catalytic role in digestion.

Sodium permeates the fluid between cells (often called the extracellular fluid), while its balancing mineral, potassium, exists mainly on the inside of the cells, or the intracellular fluid. These minerals need to be in constant dynamic balance so nutrient and waste exchange can take place across cell membranes with sufficient water intake.

At least 1,000–2,000 milligrams of daily salt is vital for the blood and the lymphatic fluid. But most surprisingly of all is the understanding that sodium (along with zinc and iodine) is necessary for the production of hydrochloric acid—the digestive fluid secreted by the stomach in order to break down protein and keep calcium, magnesium, and iron properly metabolized. Nearly 70 percent of Americans over 40 years old are HCL deficient, so a lack of this important mineral may be the key to understanding why so many of us take prescription and over-the-counter digestive aids.

Along with its sister minerals potassium and magnesium, sodium is required for the proper functioning of our nerves and the contraction of our muscles—including the heart. It's said that our Paleolithic bodies developed a "taste" for salt to ensure adequate sodium intake. At that time, we thrived on minimal amounts of sodium and much more potassium, which we estimate to be a 1 to 4 ratio in favor of potassium. On an average day, our hunter-gatherer forefathers consumed about 700 milligrams of sodium—the equivalent of about ⅓ teaspoon of salt.

Today, however, we are faced with a growing number of environmental, emotional, and physiological stresses that actually require more sodium than our Paleolithic ancestors consumed. Sodium plays a key role in mitigating the stress response and supporting the adrenal glands—which are under constant assault in our 24/7 lifestyles.

So you see, salt is really important. In fact, it's so important, that—back in the day—it used to be worth its weight in gold and was used as a form of currency. Unfortunately, most of what is typically consumed in America today is *not* the right kind of salt our bodies need. Not only is commercial refined salt stripped of all minerals except sodium and chloride, but it is also heated to such high temperatures that the chemical structure actually changes. Additionally, refined salt is also chemically cleaned, bleached, and treated with anticaking agents, which prevent salt from mixing with water in the salt shaker. Unfortunately, the anticaking agents perform the same function in the human body, so refined salt does not dissolve and combine with the water to assimilate in our bodily fluids. Instead, it builds up in the body and leaves deposits in organs and tissues.

Two of the most common anticaking agents used in the mass production of salt are sodium aluminosilicate and aluminum calcium silicate. These are both a source of aluminum, which is notoriously drying to the body, interferes with pepsin in the stomach, and neutralizes the beneficial effects of magnesium. So in order to keep our body healthy, we need to ingest the right salt on a daily basis. This means that we need to consume sodium in its most natural form. And in nature, the highest amount of sodium is found in sea-water along with synergistic and complementary trace minerals. As an iso-tonic solution, the highest concentration of the elements in an unrefined sea salt includes magnesium, potassium, chloride, sodium, and calcium—similar to the mineral profile of our very own bodies.

The following 11 transitional tips suggest simple ways to shake the bad salt out so that once you begin your Fat Flush journey, you can sprinkle the good salt in.

1. Use natural sea salt for all your salt needs.

2. During the week before you begin Fat Flush, reduce the amount of refined commercial salt you use in cooking. The salt added in cooking accounts for more than 40 percent of the sodium we consume. Try to reduce the salt called for in recipes by at least one-quarter to one-half.

3. Add sea salt to foods *after* cooking for heightened flavor. Did you know that salt added before or during cooking doesn't taste as salty as salt that is added after cooking? Why? The salty flavor rapidly dissipates in the cooking process.

4. There are 2,000 milligrams of sodium in a teaspoon of salt. This amount is more than sufficient for the majority of Americans in a single day.

5. Become a salt sleuth. Like sugar, the overwhelming majority of the refined commercial salt we consume is cleverly "hidden" in processed and refined foods. Salt can be disguised in lots of ways: sodium alginate, sodium aluminum sulfate, sodium ascorbate, sodium benzoate, sodium bisulfite, sodium carboxymethyl cellulose, sodium caseinate, sodium nitrite, sodium propionate, sodium saccharin, baking powder, baking soda, disodium phosphate, and monosodium glutamate (MSG).

6. Focus on buying foods that carry the label "sodium free" or "low sodium." The sodium-free foods contain 35 or fewer milligrams of sodium per serving. The low-sodium foods contain 140 milligrams per serving.

7. According to Asian medicine, salt cravings can signal your body's attempt to balance excessive sugar or alcohol in the diet. Since you will be eliminating both sugar and alcohol in this pre–Fat Flush transitional phase, your salt cravings should disappear gradually.

8. If you still find yourself craving salt even though you have cut out both sugar and alcohol, then this may be a sign of burned-out adrenal glands (your stress glands). You can strengthen these glands by eating frequent mini-meals and learning relaxation techniques, and for those of you who

have been diagnosed with low blood pressure, a pinch of sea salt can be helpful.

9. Get used to garlic, cayenne, ginger, mustard, cinnamon, cloves, and dill as tasty replacements for regular table salt. These healthful herbs and spices can heighten food flavors naturally as well as aid your weight loss efforts by revving up metabolism and helping to balance blood sugar.

10. Focus on the K factor. The symbol "K" stands for potassium, the mineral that counteracts excess sodium in the diet. Potassium is found in all Fat Flush veggies and fruits—especially tomatoes, squash, and citrus fruits.

11. Kick the salt habit by *overstimulating* other tastes. Use cider vinegar and the juices of lemons and limes liberally on your salads, in your veggies, and in marinades.

Now that you know the secrets of how to get both sugar and refined salt out of your diet for the pre–Fat Flush phase, there's even better news about what you can look forward to on the New Fat Flush Plan.

As the past 10 years have flown by since my first mini-update of the plan in 2006, I have heard from people across the globe, and they have requested "more." Specifically, they asked for more healthy fats, more food options, more snacks, more recipes, more vegan substitutes, and more exercise variations.

What distinguishes this book from the earlier version is that this edition presents a whole array of breakthroughs. Among them: an accelerated Three-Day Ultra Fat Flush Tune-Up as a jump-start to the phase 1 two-week program. There is a brand-new Fat Flush bone broth that is a supercharged side and snack and can be tweaked for specific health concerns. Popular slimming fats are introduced much earlier in the program, such as metabolism-revving coconut oil, appetite-taming avocado, and chia and hemp seeds, which are now a "legal" exchange for phytohormone-rich flax seed. There is a new vegan protein powder made from GMO-free pea and rice as well as expanded natural sweetening options beyond stevia, such as a monk fruit–erythritol blend and chicory root syrup. A large, updated recipe section includes more family-friendly meals, and there's a shopping list that mentions brand names.

As alluded to earlier, a key innovative concept that this version showcases is how bile—the body's ignored but key method of breaking down fats and eliminating toxins—can be linked to stubborn fat deposits and a host of seemingly unrelated symptoms. While the original Fat Flush introduced the importance of the liver as an unrecognized fat-burning organ, the updated program takes this many steps further by explaining the importance of bile, especially for those without a gallbladder—and those with a gallbladder still intact!

THE FAT FLUSH FATTY ACID FACTOR—FEMALES

Flax seeds are the richest source of a naturally occurring substance known as *lignans*, which are natural plant-based hormones that have the ability to modulate estrogen levels. Lignans are concentrated 800 times more in whole flax seeds than in other plants. For those in perimenopause and menopause, the lignans in flax seeds can have a positive effect on eradicating symptoms like hot flashes and night sweats as well as reducing ovarian dysfunction, balancing menstrual cycle changes, and helping to reduce the risk of osteoporosis by increasing bone density. Some researchers have even observed that the beneficial effects of lignans match those of tamoxifen, the anticancer drug used for breast cancer.

THE FAT FLUSH FLAX FACTOR—KIDS

Perhaps the best news about flax as well as its sister seeds, chia and hemp, is their positive effect on children.

Essential fatty acids contained in flaxseed oil and flax seeds, chia, and hemp have a dramatic impact on health and vitality throughout our lives, beginning with the development of the infant brain. Over half the brain (60 percent, to be exact) is composed of fat. Brain chemicals known as neurotransmitters are regulated by tissue-like hormones called prostaglandins, which are produced by essential fatty acids. The brain—and the entire nervous system, for that matter—needs the right kind of fats for nourishment and protection.

I strongly suspect that the previous three generations of American kids have not been eating the right kinds of fats for the development of the brain. Could this be a reason why we have so many kids diagnosed with attention deficit hyperactivity disorder (ADHD)?

Our kids are being diagnosed right and left with ADHD and are being prescribed the drug Ritalin. Do you really think our kids are suffering from an epidemic Ritalin deficiency? A growing body of research shows that these children are really suffering from an essential fatty acid deficiency, because the clinical signs of such a deficiency match those of ADHD, such as the inability to focus, a short attention span, restlessness, irritability, mood swings, and even panic attacks. Numerous studies over the past two decades have confirmed that kids with ADHD have lower omega-3 levels in their blood than do normal children. When children diagnosed with ADHD start eating the right kinds of fats, many parents notice that their children become calmer and more focused.

THE NEW FAT FLUSH PLAN PROTOCOLS

Here are the New Fat Flush Plan protocols.

Phase 1: The Two-Week Fat Flush

Fats and Oils

DAILY INTAKE: Flaxseed, coconut, or MCT (medium-chain triglyceride) oil at 1 tablespoon twice daily, and ½ avocado daily plus avocado spray for cooking.

PURPOSE: Flaxseed oil is essential for its high–omega-3 fat-fighting and insulin-regulating potential. (If intolerant, then opt for omega-3–rich fish oil that is subtly flavored with lemon or orange.) Coconut oil, a rich source of medium-chain fatty acids, boosts metabolism by 50 percent and speeds up the thyroid. Avocado triggers adiponectin, the appetite hormone, for satiety and is also rich in glutathione to help with liver cleansing. MCT oil is a concentrated form of both coconut and palm oil that provides an even more potent source of energy for easy digestion, fat burning, and the brain.

Fiber-Rich Seeds

DAILY INTAKE: 1 tablespoon twice daily of chia seeds, ground flax seeds, or hemp seeds.

PURPOSE: All three seed types provide soluble and insoluble fiber to help maintain regularity and provide satiety to meals and snacks. Their high omega-3 content controls cortisol production, and in the case of flax seeds, the high lignan content (800 times more than in any other food) controls haywire hormones. Hemp seeds offer up skin-beautifying and -strengthening omega-6.

Lean Protein

DAILY INTAKE: 1 serving of whey or brown rice and pea protein powder, up to 2 eggs (optional), and a minimum of 8 ounces of cooked lean protein.

CHOOSE FROM: All varieties of fresh or frozen fish (with the exception of high-mercury swordfish and farm-raised tilapia) as well as canned fish (like Wild Planet Albacore and Skipjack Tuna, Vital Choice canned seafood, and Oregon Choice canned seafood), fresh or frozen seafood, lean beef, lamb, and skinless turkey or chicken; also tofu and tempeh, which may be consumed no more than twice per week. Use meat that is organic and comes from grass-fed animals whenever possible. Choose hormone-free, unheated, undenatured, lactose-free, high-protein whey powders (like Fat Flush Vanilla and Chocolate Whey) with about 20 grams of protein per serving and negligible carbohydrates from nonmutated A2 milk. Choose non-GMO vegan protein powders (like Fat Flush Body Protein) with low carbohydrates and verification of low heavy-metal content (especially arsenic and lead).

PURPOSE: Protein raises metabolism by 25 percent and activates the liver's detoxifying enzymes.

Eggs (Optional)

DAILY INTAKE: Up to 2 per day.

PURPOSE: For those without allergies or gallbladder issues, the omega-3–enriched eggs are not only delicious but also brimming with antioxidants (e.g., lutein and zeaxanthin) for the eyes and brain, cholesterol-protective phosphatidylcholine, and sulfur to support your liver's cleansing process.

Vegetables

DAILY INTAKE: Unlimited (unless otherwise noted), raw or steamed. Put special emphasis on the bitter veggies (like arugula, watercress, escarole, and radishes) to help support liver and gallbladder health for greater cleansing power.

CHOOSE FROM: Arugula, endive, asparagus, green beans, broccoli, broccolini, broccoli rabe, brussels sprouts, cabbage, cauliflower, celery, Chinese cabbage, carrots (1), cucumbers, daikon, globe artichoke, Jerusalem artichoke, artichoke heart, fennel, eggplant, spinach, escarole, collard greens, rhubarb (1 cup), burdock, hearts of palm, kale, mustard greens, romaine lettuce, radicchio, endive, parsley, onions, watercress, chives, leeks, Swiss chard, bell peppers (yellow, orange, green, and red), jicama, mushrooms, olives (3), radishes, horseradish, okra, tomatoes, red or green loose-leaf lettuce, snow peas, zucchini, yellow squash, water chestnuts, bamboo shoots, garlic, spaghetti squash, and sprouts (alfalfa, broccoli, radish, and mung bean).

SEA VEGGIES: Agar-agar, hijiki, kombu, nori, wakame, or a sea veggie–based seasoning (like Eden Seaweed Gomasio, kelp granules, or dulse flakes from Maine).

PURPOSE: These fibrous and colorful phytonutrient-rich vegetables will help speed your liver's cleansing and provide valuable carotenoids. Broccoli sprouts are especially high in sulforaphane—a very powerful antioxidant that targets cellular health. Two ounces per day would be ideal. The sea veggies and seasonings provide iodine and trace minerals to help nourish the thyroid and counteract environmental pollutants.

Fruits

DAILY INTAKE: Up to 2 whole portions daily.

CHOOSE FROM: 1 small apple, ½ grapefruit, 1 small orange, 2 medium plums, 6 large strawberries, 10 large cherries, 1 nectarine, 1 pomegranate, 1 peach, 1 pear, and 1 cup berries (blueberries, blackberries, or raspberries).

PURPOSE: Nature's cleansers are high in enzymes and minerals (e.g., potassium) and lowest in fructose—a sneaky fat promoter.

Fat Flush Cran-Water

DAILY INTAKE: 8 eight-ounce glasses per day.

PURPOSE: The cranberry juice–water mixture eliminates water retention, cleanses accumulated wastes from the lymphatic system, and also helps to reduce the appearance of cellulite.

HOW TO: To prepare cranberry water, purchase Knudsen's, Trader Joe's, or Mountain Sun's Unsweetened Cranberry Juice. Then get two empty 32-ounce bottles. Fill each 32-ounce water bottle with 4 ounces of unsweetened cranberry juice and 28 ounces of water. Or purchase Knudsen's or Tree of Life Cranberry Concentrate and add 1½ tablespoons to each 32 ounces of water.

Fat Flushing Herbs and Spices

DAILY INTAKE: To taste.

CHOOSE FROM: Cayenne pepper, cumin, dried mustard, cinnamon, ginger, dill, garlic, anise, fennel, cloves, bay leaves, coriander, parsley, cilantro, apple cider vinegar, coconut vinegar, and cumin.

PURPOSE: Metabolism boosters.

Legal Cheat

1 cup of organic coffee in the morning.

Fat Flush Sweeteners

DAILY INTAKE: Organic SweetLeaf Stevia, Lakanto Monkfruit Sweetener, or Uni Key Flora-Key.

WHAT MAKES THEM LEGAL: Both SweetLeaf Stevia and Lakanto are sugar-free and low-glycemic sweeteners. The plant-based stevia is 30 times sweeter than sugar, so a little goes a long way, and it is great for baking. According to the manufacturers, Lakanto can be used in a 1 to 1 ratio to replace sugar because it tastes, bakes, and looks like the white stuff. But I find that easily one-half that amount is a sweet-enough substitution.

You might also want to consider reducing the amount of Lakanto due to the presence of erythritol, which causes some folks to experience loose stools and digestive upsets. That's why I also recommend the prebiotic and probiotic sweetener Flora-Key as another alternative. This immune-boosting probiotic formula contains various strains of acidophilus, bifidus, and a special prebiotic, rather sweet-tasting substance known as inulin to stimulate the growth of the beneficial bacteria. This product helps to ward off toxins and aids in the synthesis of key vitamins and minerals while helping to support the good bacteria in the gut. It can be used in your morning smoothie, and it is an optional ingredient in several of the recipes for the New Fat Flush Plan. Flora-Key should only be used in nonheat recipes, as heating will destroy the beneficial bacteria, whereas both stevia and Lakanto can be used in recipes that require heat.

Phase 2: The Metabolic Reset

Fats and Oils

DAILY INTAKE: Flaxseed, coconut, or MCT (medium-chain triglyceride) oil at 1 tablespoon twice daily, and ½ avocado daily plus avocado spray for cooking.

PURPOSE: Flaxseed oil is essential for its high–omega-3 fat-fighting and insulin-regulating potential. (If intolerant, then opt for omega-3–rich fish oil that is subtly flavored with lemon or orange.) Coconut oil, a rich source of medium-chain fatty acids, boosts metabolism by 50 percent and speeds the thyroid. Avocado triggers adiponectin, the appetite hormone, for satiety. Also rich in glutathione to help with liver cleansing, MCT oil is a concentrated form of both coconut and palm oil and provides an even more concentrated source of energy for easy digestion, fat burning, and the brain.

Fiber-Rich Seeds

DAILY INTAKE: 1 tablespoon twice daily of chia seeds, ground flax seeds, or hemp seeds.

PURPOSE: All three seed types provide soluble and insoluble fiber to help maintain regularity and provide satiety to meals and snacks. Their high omega-3 content controls cortisol production, and in the case of flax seeds, the high lignan content (800 times more than in any other food) controls haywire hormones. Hemp seeds offer up skin-beautifying and -strengthening omega-6.

Lean Protein

DAILY INTAKE: 1 whey or rice and pea protein serving, up to 2 eggs (optional), and a minimum of 8 ounces of cooked lean protein.

CHOOSE FROM: All varieties of fresh or frozen fish (with the exception of high-mercury swordfish and farm-raised tilapia) as well as canned fish (like Wild Planet Albacore and Skipjack Tuna, Vital Choice canned seafood, and Oregon Choice canned seafood), fresh or frozen seafood, lean beef, lamb, and skinless turkey or chicken; also tofu and tempeh, which may be consumed no more than twice per week. Use meat that is organic and comes from grass-fed animals whenever possible. Choose hormone-free, unheated, undenatured, lactose-free, high-protein whey powders (like Fat Flush Vanilla and Chocolate Whey) with about 20 grams of protein per serving and negligible carbohydrates from nonmutated A2 milk. Choose non-GMO vegan protein powders (like Fat Flush Body Protein) with low carbohydrates and verification of low heavy-metal content (especially arsenic and lead).

PURPOSE: Protein raises metabolism by 25 percent and activates the liver's detoxifying enzymes.

Eggs (Optional)

DAILY INTAKE: Up to 2 per day.

PURPOSE: For those without allergies or gallbladder issues, the omega-3-enriched eggs not only are delicious but also are brimming with antioxidants (e.g., lutein and zeaxanthin) for the eyes and brain, cholesterol-protective phosphatidylcholine, and sulfur to support your liver's cleansing process.

Vegetables

DAILY INTAKE: Unlimited (unless otherwise noted), raw or steamed. Put special emphasis on the bitter veggies (like arugula, watercress, escarole, and radishes) to help support liver and gallbladder health for greater cleansing power.

CHOOSE FROM: Arugula, asparagus, green beans, broccoli, broccolini, broccoli rabe, brussels sprouts, cabbage, cauliflower, celery, Chinese cabbage, carrots (1), cucumbers, daikon, globe artichoke, Jerusalem artichoke, artichoke heart, fennel, eggplant, spinach, escarole, collard greens, kale, mustard greens, romaine lettuce, rhubarb (1 cup), burdock, hearts of palm, radicchio, endive, parsley, onions, watercress, chives, leeks, Swiss chard, bell peppers (yellow, orange, green, and red), jicama, mushrooms, olives (3), radishes, horseradish, okra, tomatoes, red or green loose-leaf lettuce, snow peas, zucchini, yellow squash, water chestnuts, bamboo shoots, garlic, spaghetti squash, and sprouts (alfalfa, broccoli, radish, and mung bean).

SEA VEGGIES: Agar-agar, hijiki, kombu, nori, wakame, or a sea veggie–based seasoning (like Eden Seaweed Gomasio, kelp granules, or dulse flakes from Maine).

PURPOSE: These fibrous and colorful phytonutrient-rich vegetables will help speed your liver's cleansing and provide valuable carotenoids. Broccoli sprouts are especially high in sulforaphane—a very potent antioxidant that targets cellular health. Two ounces per day would be ideal. The sea veggies and seasonings provide iodine and trace minerals to help nourish the thyroid and counteract environmental pollutants.

Friendly Carbohydrates

DAILY INTAKE: Start with small increments (even half a serving), and work your way up gradually to the following portions, especially with the starchy vegetables:

Week 1, Phase 2: 1 serving per day.

Week 2, Phase 2: 2 servings per day.

CHOOSE FROM: 1 small sweet potato, ½ cup green peas, ½ cup cooked carrots, ½ cup butternut or acorn squash, ½ cup beets, ½ cup oatmeal, and ½ cup quinoa.

Fruits

DAILY INTAKE: Up to 2 whole portions daily.

CHOOSE FROM: 1 small apple, ½ grapefruit, 1 small orange, 2 medium plums, 6 large strawberries, 10 large cherries, 1 nectarine, 1 peach, 1 pear, 1 cup berries (blueberries, blackberries, or raspberries), 1 pomegranate, ½ or 1 small banana, and ½ cup pineapple.

PURPOSE: Nature's cleansers are high in enzymes and minerals (e.g., potassium) and low on the glycemic load.

Fat Flush Cran-Water

DAILY INTAKE: 8 eight-ounce glasses per day.

PURPOSE: The cranberry juice–water mixture eliminates water retention, cleanses accumulated wastes from the lymphatic system, and also helps to reduce the appearance of cellulite.

Fat-Flushing Herbs and Spices

DAILY INTAKE: To taste.

CHOOSE FROM: Cayenne pepper, dried mustard, cinnamon, ginger, dill, garlic, anise, fennel, cloves, bay leaves, coriander, parsley, cilantro, turmeric, apple cider vinegar, coconut vinegar, and cumin.

PURPOSE: Metabolism boosters.

Legal Cheat

1 cup of organic coffee at breakfast.

Fat Flush Sweeteners

DAILY INTAKE: Organic SweetLeaf Stevia, Lakanto Monkfruit Sweetener, or Uni Key's Flora-Key.

WHAT MAKES THEM LEGAL: Both SweetLeaf Stevia and Lakanto are sugar-free and low-glycemic sweeteners. The plant-based stevia is 30 times sweeter than sugar, so a little goes a long way, and it is great for baking. According to the manufacturer, Lakanto can be used in a 1 to 1 ratio to replace sugar because it tastes, bakes, and looks like the white stuff. But I find that easily one-half that amount is a sweet-enough substitution. You might also want to consider reducing the amount of Lakanto due to the presence of erythritol, which causes some folks to experience loose stools and digestive upsets. That's why I also recommend the prebiotic and probiotic sweetener Flora-Key as another alternative. This immune-boosting probiotic formula contains various strains of acidophilus, bifidus, and a special prebiotic, rather sweet-tasting substance known as inulin to stimulate the growth of the beneficial bacteria. This product helps to ward off toxins and aids in the synthesis of key vitamins and minerals while helping to support the good bacteria in the gut. It can be used in morning smoothies and is an optional ingredient in several of the recipes for the New Fat Flush Plan. Flora-Key should only be used in nonheat recipes, as heating will destroy the beneficial bacteria, whereas both stevia and Lakanto can be used in recipes that require heat.

Phase 3: The Lifestyle Eating Plan

Fats and Oils

DAILY INTAKE: Up to 3 tablespoons of oil daily; ½ avocado daily plus avocado spray for cooking.

CHOOSE FROM: Flaxseed oil, coconut oil, olive oil, MCT (medium-chain triglyceride) oil, sesame oil, avocado oil, or macadamia nut oil.

PURPOSE: Flaxseed oil is essential for its high–omega-3 fat-fighting and insulin-regulating potential. (If intolerant, then opt for omega-3–rich fish oil that is subtly flavored with lemon or orange.) Coconut oil, a rich source of medium-chain fatty acids, boosts metabolism by 50 percent and speeds the thyroid. Avocado triggers adiponectin, the appetite hormone, for satiety and is also rich in filling omega-9 and glutathione, which helps with liver cleansing. MCT oil is a concentrated form of coconut oil and palm oil that provides an even more potent source of energy for easy digestion, fat burning, and the brain. Sesame seed oil can help heart health by regulating insulin and preventing atherosclerotic lesions with the antioxidant and anti-inflammatory compound known as sesamol. Sesame seeds contain anticancer compounds including phytic acid, magnesium, and phytosterols. Macadamia nut oil is high in monounsaturated fatty acids, including oleic acid (omega-9), as well as collagen-boosting omega-7—all of which are very moisturizing, regenerating, and softening to the skin. All these fatty acids also have anti-inflammatory properties, which dial down hunger hormones.

BONUS FOODS: To replace a tablespoon of oil, you can choose from a handful of nuts (almonds, walnuts, or macadamias), a couple of tablespoons of seeds (e.g., pumpkin, sunflower, or tahini or sesame), a tablespoon of nut butter, 2 tablespoons of shredded coconut, 1 tablespoon of ghee (clarified butter), or 3 ounces of full-fat coconut milk. A pat of butter, a smear of cream cheese, and a dollop of sour cream (or coconut cream) are all tasty add-ons, and when enjoyed in the specified amounts, they are "free" add-ons. Unsweetened organic almond milk, organic almond flour, organic coconut flour, and organic shredded coconut are fine once a day.

Fiber-Rich Seeds

DAILY INTAKE: 1 tablespoon twice daily of chia seeds, ground flax seeds, or hemp seeds.

PURPOSE: All three seed types provide soluble and insoluble fiber to help maintain regularity and provide satiety to meals and snacks. Their high–omega-3 content controls cortisol production, and in the case of flax seeds, the high lignan content (800 times more than in any other food) controls haywire hormones. Hemp seeds offer up skin-beautifying and -strengthening omega-6.

Lean Protein

DAILY INTAKE: 1 whey or rice and pea protein powder serving, up to 2 eggs (optional), and a minimum of 8 ounces of cooked lean protein. You can add nitrate-free turkey bacon once or twice a week for added flavor. Since it contains a minimal amount of protein grams (6 grams in one strip), turkey bacon does not have to be included in daily totals.

CHOOSE FROM: All varieties of fresh or frozen fish (with the exception of high-mercury swordfish and farm-raised tilapia) as well as canned fish (like Wild Planet Albacore and Skipjack Tuna, Vital Choice canned seafood, and Oregon Choice canned seafood), fresh or frozen seafood, lean beef, lamb, and skinless turkey or chicken; also tofu and tempeh, which may be consumed no more than twice per week. Use meat that is organic and comes from grass-fed animals whenever possible. Choose hormone-free, unheated, undenatured, lactose-free, high-protein whey powders (like Fat Flush Vanilla and Chocolate Whey) with about 20 grams of protein per serving and negligible carbohydrates from nonmutated A2 milk. Choose non-GMO vegan protein powders (like Fat Flush Body Protein) with low carbohydrates and verification of low heavy-metal content (especially arsenic and lead).

PURPOSE: Protein raises metabolism by 25 percent and activates the liver's detoxifying enzymes.

Eggs (Optional)

DAILY INTAKE: Up to 2 per day.

PURPOSE: The omega-3–enriched eggs not only are delicious but also are brimming with antioxidants (e.g., lutein and zeaxanthin) for the eyes and brain, cholesterol-protective phosphatidylcholine, and sulfur to support your liver's cleansing process.

Vegetables

DAILY INTAKE: Unlimited (unless otherwise noted), raw or steamed. Put special emphasis on the bitter veggies (like arugula, watercress, escarole, and radishes) to help support liver and gallbladder health for greater cleansing power.

CHOOSE FROM: Arugula, asparagus, green beans, broccoli, broccolini, broccoli rabe, brussels sprouts, cabbage, cauliflower, celery, Chinese cabbage, carrots (1), cucumbers, daikon, globe artichoke, Jerusalem artichoke, artichoke heart, fennel, eggplant, spinach, escarole, collard greens, kale, mustard greens, romaine lettuce, radicchio, endive, rhubarb (1 cup), burdock, hearts of palm, parsley, onions, watercress, chives, leeks, Swiss chard, bell peppers (yellow, orange, green, and red), jicama, mushrooms, olives (3), radishes, horseradish, okra, tomatoes, red or green loose-leaf lettuce, snow peas, zucchini, yellow squash, water chestnuts, bamboo shoots, garlic, spaghetti squash, and sprouts (alfalfa, broccoli, radish, and mung bean).

SEA VEGGIES: Agar-agar, hijiki, kombu, nori, wakame, or a sea veggie–based seasoning (like Eden Seaweed Gomasio, kelp granules, or dulse flakes from Maine).

PURPOSE: These fibrous and colorful phytonutrient-rich vegetables will help speed your liver's cleansing and provide valuable carotenoids. Broccoli sprouts are especially high in sulforaphane—a very potent antioxidant that targets cellular health. Two ounces per day would be ideal. The sea veggies and seasonings provide iodine and trace minerals to help nourish the thyroid and counteract environmental pollutants.

Fruits

DAILY INTAKE: Up to 2 portions daily.

CHOOSE FROM: 1 small apple, ½ grapefruit, 1 small orange, 2 medium plums, 1 cup berries (e.g., strawberries, blueberries, blackberries, or raspberries), 10 large cherries, 12 large grapes, 1 nectarine, 1 peach, 1 small kiwi, 1 pear, 1 pomegranate, ½ banana, ½ cup mango, ½ cup papaya, ½ cup melon (e.g., cantaloupe, honeydew, or watermelon), and ½ cup pineapple.

SPECIAL OCCASION: Dried fruits (1 large fig, 2 dates, 2 tablespoons raisins or currants, 2 dried plums or prunes, 3 dried apricot halves), 2 tablespoons unsweetened fruit preserves, and ½ cup unsweetened juice.

PURPOSE: Nature's cleansers are high in enzymes and minerals (e.g., potassium) and low in fructose.

Dairy (Optional)

DAILY INTAKE: Up to 2 servings per day.

CHOOSE FROM: 1 ounce hard cheese, ½ cup full-fat cottage or ricotta cheese, 4 tablespoons Romano cheese, 4 tablespoons Parmesan cheese, ½ cup buttermilk, and 1 cup plain full-fat or Greek yogurt.

PURPOSE: Dairy foods provide calcium, protein, and saturated fats for energy.

Friendly Carbohydrates

DAILY INTAKE: Work up to 4 servings per day or as many servings as you can tolerate.

Week 1, Phase 3: Substitute a new friendly carb for one of those from phase 2, adding no new servings, to gauge the body's response.

Week 2, Phase 3: Add 1 serving, making 3 servings total per day, noting the body's response.

Week 3, Phase 3: Add 1 serving, making 4 servings total per day, noting the body's response.

CHOOSE FROM: A handful of tigernuts (small root vegetables); 4 large chestnuts; 1 Ezekiel 4:9 Sprouted Tortilla; 1 non-GMO corn tortilla; ½ cup peas; ½ cup cooked carrots; 1 small sweet potato; ½ cup acorn or butternut squash; ½ cup beets; ½ cup cooked turnips, rutabaga, parsnips, or pumpkin; 1 small corn on the cob; 1 small baked potato or ½ cup red potato; ½ cup chickpeas, pinto beans, adzuki, black beans, or kidney beans; ½ cup brown rice, oatmeal, quinoa, buckwheat groats, millet, or amaranth; or 3 cups popcorn. If dairy sensitive, choose coconut alternatives when possible.

> **TIP**
>
> **Tigernut flour is a gluten-free, nut-free, and dairy-free flour substitute. It is an exceptionally rich source of resistant starch, which is a prebiotic fiber that is not digested but instead functions as food for probiotics in your gut.**

Fat Flush Cran-Water

DAILY INTAKE: 8 eight-ounce glasses per day.

PURPOSE: The cranberry juice–water mixture eliminates water retention, cleanses accumulated wastes from the lymphatic system, and also helps to reduce the appearance of cellulite.

Beverages

Drink spiced teas (ginger, fennel, and peppermint), dandelion root tea, or red tea (rooibos tea).

Fat-Flushing Herbs and Spices

DAILY INTAKE: To taste.

CHOOSE FROM: Cayenne pepper, dried mustard, cinnamon, ginger, dill, garlic, anise, fennel, cloves, bay leaves, coriander, parsley, cilantro, turmeric, apple cider vinegar, coconut vinegar, cumin, basil, oregano, rosemary, and thyme. You also may add other flavorful spices (like curry in small amounts) and any other herb as you wish, but keep these as your main focus.

PURPOSE: Metabolism boosting.

Legal Cheat

1 cup of organic coffee at breakfast.

Salt

DAILY INTAKE: 350–400 milligrams per meal from Selina's Celtic Sea Salt. Due to environmental, political, and ecological concerns, I prefer Selina brand salt products rather than Himalayan salt. If on a low-sodium diet, then check out the Selina Makai Sea Salt, which is lower in sodium and higher in potassium than any other type of sea salt on the market.

SPECIAL OCCASION: ½ tablespoon of low-sodium tamari and capers, rinsed and drained.

Fat Flush Sweeteners

DAILY INTAKE: Organic SweetLeaf Stevia, Lakanto Monkfruit Sweetener, Uni Key Flora-Key, and yacon syrup.

WHAT MAKES THEM LEGAL: Both SweetLeaf Stevia and Lakanto are sugar-free and low-glycemic sweeteners. The plant-based stevia is 30 times sweeter than sugar, so a little goes a long way and is great for baking. According to the manufacturer, Lakanto can be used in a 1 to 1 ratio to replace sugar because it tastes, bakes, and looks like the white stuff. But I find that easily one-half that amount is a sweet-enough substitution. You might also want to consider reducing the amount of Lakanto due to the presence of erythritol, which causes some folks to experience loose stools and digestive upsets. That's why I also recommend the prebiotic and probiotic sweetener Flora-Key as another alternative. This immune-boosting probiotic formula contains various strains of acidophilus, bifidus, and a special prebiotic, rather sweet-tasting substance known as inulin to stimulate the growth of the beneficial bacteria. This product helps to ward off toxins and aids in the synthesis of key vitamins and minerals while helping to support the good bacteria in the gut. It can be used in morning smoothies and is an optional ingredient in several of the recipes for the New Fat Flush Plan. Flora-Key should only be used in nonheat recipes, as heating will destroy the beneficial bacteria, whereas both stevia and Lakanto can be used in recipes that require heat. Yacon syrup is made from chicory root and can be used as a honey substitute in recipes in equal measure. It is considered a prebiotic and will feed the skinny gut bacteria.

SPECIAL OCCASION: 1 tablespoon raw honey, maple syrup, date sugar, or blackstrap molasses. (This replaces one fruit each.)

Alcohol

WEEKLY INTAKE: Should you choose to indulge, you may have 1 drink per week and on special occasions, of course.

CHOOSE FROM: Organic wine or grain-free hard liquor.

3 The Fat Flush Kitchen

Cooking the Fat Flush way is easy when you are well equipped with the tools of the trade. In addition to a selection of herbs and spices for revving up your metabolism, powering up your health, and tickling your taste buds, there are some basic Fat Flush–friendly cooking utensils that merit your consideration. Utensils like waterless cookware and high-quality knives are a lifetime investment in health and well-being. Following is a list of very basic equipment for your Fat Flush kitchen.

ESSENTIAL UTENSILS

I personally prefer heavy-duty, stainless-steel, waterless cookware, which cooks in a vacuum seal. When food cooks in its own juices, high flavor, tenderness, and high nutritional value are guaranteed. In fact, studies have shown that cooking in vacuum-sealed cookware rather than nonsealed cookware retains more vitamins and minerals and produces less fat. At the same time, less salt and less of every seasoning is required for high-quality taste. I personally use Le Creuset cookware for all my cooking. Although it is a heavier line of cookware, I feel secure that it is enamel-covered iron and safe.
Enamel, Corning Ware, glass, and Pyrex are also acceptable. For those of you who are anemic, you might consider cooking with iron-based utensils because the extra iron picked up from cooking can actually be therapeutic. When a high acid-based food like spaghetti sauce, for example, is cooked in iron pots, it contains six times more iron than when it is made in ceramic cookware.
Choose heavy-duty tin or black steel for your baking needs.

STAY AWAY FROM ALUMINUM

As a quick reminder, do aluminum-proof the kitchen as much as possible. Aluminum inhibits the body's utilization of key minerals like magnesium, calcium, and phosphorus. Scary, right? On top of that, some researchers believe that it can neutralize pepsin, an important digestive enzyme in the stomach. Replace all aluminum steamers, measuring cups, spoons, bread pans, and cookie sheets with stainless steel or Pyrex.

You should avoid aluminum foil also. When cooking, opt for parchment paper (like Beyond Gourmet unbleached parchment paper), which the French have used for years in their "en papillote" dishes to seal in juices. This can be used for roasting veggies as well. For storing and freezing, you can first cover with wax paper then foil, which prevents the aluminum from leaching into foods.

Can't tell whether your utensils are fused with aluminum that could leach into your food? Simple: test with a magnet. A magnet will not cling to aluminum but will to tin or nickel—which is often used with stainless steel.

CURB THE COPPER

You would also be wise to replace all copper-lined cookware. This metal can upset the sensitive zinc-copper balance in your system. Excess copper has been linked to depression, insomnia, anorexia nervosa, compulsive behavior, anxiety, hyperactivity, various skin disorders, and hair loss. Need I say more?

CONSIDER A WATER FILTER FOR YOUR HOME

With pure, clean water becoming extinct and with bottled water not always being reliable, a home water filter is no longer a luxury but a necessity. I recommend the CWR Crown Ultra-Ceramic Water Filter, the most effective water filtration system available. The filter is made of ultrafine ceramic with pores so small that they trap bacteria, parasites, and particles down to 0.8 micron in size. The filtering system provides a comprehensive, three-stage process.

In the first stage the tiny pores in the ceramic remove bacteria, parasites, rust, and dirt. The second filter state is composed of high-density matrix carbon that removes chlorine, pesticides, and other chemicals like chloramines and trihalomethanes. In the third stage, a heavy-metal–removing compound eliminates lead and copper.

KNIVES

I would be remiss if I did not remind you how important the right knives are for chopping, paring, slicing, and carving—everything from fruits and veggies to roasts and turkeys. At the very least, you will need one high-quality utility knife and one 4-inch paring knife for the majority of your cutting needs in the smart kitchen. If you are planning to purchase a new knife set and you want something durable, then I highly recommend MAC Japanese knives, which are acclaimed by chefs all over the world as the world's finest knives. The MAC knives are what I personally use because they have a razor-sharp edge, stay sharp a long time, and have thin blades for easy slicing. They are easily available online

THERMOS

A wide-mouthed thermos is helpful for taking soups, stews, and leftovers to work with you.

THE FLAXSEED GRINDER

Since ground flax seeds are such a potent source of metabolism-boosting omega-3s and fiber-rich lignans—which function as natural hormone balancers—a specially designed flaxseed grinder is a valuable smart kitchen item. The Krups F203 Electric Spice and Coffee Grinder with stainless-steel blades is an efficient, easy-to-use grinder. You can find it and similar products online.

MORTAR AND PESTLE

Many of the recipes call for crushed dried herbs. To crush my herbs, I like to use a mortar and pestle, which is best for extracting the essence of the dried herbs and spices used in the recipes. The mortar and pestle crushes the herbs, which in turn release the volatile oils that contain the herbs' health and aromatic qualities. The aromas of the ground, dried herbs or spices are nearly four times as strong as the aromas from the same herbs and spices before they are ground.

SEED GRINDER

For grinding and crushing seeds (like anise, fennel, or coriander), a small hand-turned mill is very useful.

THE THRILL OF THE GRILL: GAS VERSUS CHARCOAL

Grilling is here to stay. And nothing says outdoor fun more than a cookout. Many Fat Flush recipes from the delicious main course lamb and fish kebabs to snacks featuring various seasonal fruit kebabs make use of a grill. Healthwise, the oxidative reaction of charcoal grilling (a combination of browning and charring) may be somewhat toxic. Food can soak up added chemicals from the charcoal briquettes, too. So if you are a charcoal fan, then please be sure to cut off any charred, burned, or blackened portions of food.

Gas grilling is another way to go, especially if there is no sensitivity to hydrocarbons that are the by-products of gas combustion. Healthier or not, gas grills seem to be preferred by most grill owners because the grills are easier to light. To compensate for the smoky flavor that charcoal imparts, many gas grill owners use natural wood chips from hickory, mesquite, or oak.

The safest way to protect your food from harmful substances formed during the grilling process is to marinate, marinate, marinate. Some research shows that marinades can cut down on carcinogen production by nearly 99 percent.

> **MARINADE TIP**
>
> In the phase 3 lifestyle program, you can make some easy grilling marinades by combining about 1 cup of olive oil, 1/2 cup of fresh lime or lemon juice, and cup of cider vinegar seasoned with some of your favorite herbs. For special occasions, this basic marinade can be jazzed up with a tablespoon of date sugar or honey.

OTHER HELPFUL FAT FLUSH KITCHEN EQUIPMENT

- Food processor or blender for whipping up smoothies and pâtés
- Toaster oven

HELPFUL FAT FLUSH COOKWARE

- Nonstick skillets and saucepans (various sizes)
- Stainless-steel steamer
- Dutch oven, 3½-quart or 6-quart slow cooker or Crock-Pot
- Air fryer (like GoWise USA)

HELPFUL FAT FLUSH BAKEWARE

- Ramekins
- Nonstick baking sheets
- Ovenproof baking dishes
- Casseroles

HELPFUL FAT FLUSH COOKING TOOLS AND CUTLERY

- Wooden spoons
- Measuring spoons
- Measuring cups
- Slotted spoon
- 2 chopping boards (1 for meats, 1 for veggies)
- Rubber spatulas
- Mixing bowls (various sizes)
- Lemon juicer
- Tongs
- Pastry brush for basting
- Garlic press
- Grater
- Can opener
- Utility knife
- 4-inch paring knife
- Scissors
- Ceramic sharpening rod
- Masher
- Whisk
- Popsicle molds
- Freezer-safe, airtight containers
- Grilling accessories (broad-headed jumbo tongs and turner tongs with one-sided spatula)
- Vegetable spiralizer for zucchini "zoodles"
- Food processor or blender for whipping up smoothies and pâtés. (I like Vitamix, NutriBullet, and immersion blenders for these purposes. Blending retains more fiber and nutrients than juicing.)

FAT FLUSH INGREDIENT EQUIVALENTS

WHEN YOU DON'T HAVE:	YOU CAN USE:
Garlic, 1 clove, fresh	1/8 teaspoon garlic powder
Gingerroot, 1 teaspoon, grated, fresh	1/4 teaspoon ground ginger
Herb, 1 tablespoon, fresh	1/2 to 1 teaspoon dried herb, crushed
Herb, 1 teaspoon, fresh	1/2 teaspoon dried herb, ground
Onion, 1 small (1/3 cup)	1 teaspoon onion powder or 1 tablespoon dried minced onion
Tomato sauce, 2 cups	3/4 cup tomato paste plus 1 cup water

FAT FLUSH RECIPE MAKEOVERS FOR EVERY DAY AND SPECIAL OCCASIONS

WHEN THE RECIPE CALLS FOR:	YOU CAN USE INSTEAD (IF APPROPRIATE TO YOUR PHASE):
1 tablespoon brown sugar	1 tablespoon date sugar. (If used in baking, this is best added toward the end to prevent burning. Adding water to the date sugar to make a syrup consistency will also work.)
1 tablespoon sugar	1 teaspoon Flora-Key, 1½ packets stevia (SweetLeaf Stevia), 1 tablespoon Lakanto or ½ tablespoon honey, molasses, or pure maple syrup
1 cup sugar for baking	½ cup honey. (If you are using as much as 3/4 cup honey, then decrease other liquids by 1/4 cup for each 3/4 cup honey. If there is no liquid in recipe, then add 1/4 cup flaxseed meal for each 3/4 cup honey. Also lower the baking temperature to a maximum of 250°F; both honey and molasses tend to caramelize at higher temperatures.)
1 ounce or 1 square baking chocolate	3 tablespoons carob powder plus 1 tablespoon water plus 1 tablespoon sesame or rice bran oil
Breading	Toasted Nuts (Chapter 10) or ground flax seeds. (Keep in mind that cooking with ground flax seeds above 300°F can damage the seeds' oil and convert it into the unhealthy trans form, but the lignans will not be damaged at high heat.)
Sauce and soup thickeners	Arrowroot, tapioca, kudzu, and tigernut—for sauces, soups, and gravies

1 tablespoon margarine or cooking oil	1 tablespoon butter or ghee or 3 tablespoons ground flax seed. (Either shorten baking time or lower oven temperature by 25°F because baked goods will brown more quickly with flax seed.)

FAT FLUSH EQUIVALENTS CHART FOR DRY MEASUREMENTS

- Multiply ounces by 28 to convert into grams.
- Multiply pounds by 0.45 to convert into kilograms.
- Multiply grams by 0.035 to convert into ounces.
- Multiply kilograms by 2.2 to convert into pounds.

FAT FLUSH EQUIVALENTS FOR LIQUID MEASUREMENTS

- Multiply ounces by 30 to convert into milliliters
- Multiply pints by 0.47 to convert into liters
- Multiply quarts by 0.95 to convert into liters
- Multiply gallons by 3.8 to convert into liters
- Multiply milliliters by 0.34 to convert into ounces

FAT FLUSH EQUIVALENTS CHART

U.S.	METRIC
1/8 teaspoon	0.5 milliliter
1/4 teaspoon	1 milliliter
1/2 teaspoon	2 milliliters
1 teaspoon	5 milliliters
1 tablespoon	15 milliliters
1/4 cup or 2 fluid ounces	60 milliliters
1/3 cup or 3 fluid ounces	80 milliliters
1/2 cup or 4 fluid ounces	120 milliliters
2/3 cup or 5 fluid ounces	160 milliliters
3/4 cup or 6 fluid ounces	180 milliliters
1 cup or 8 fluid ounces	240 milliliters
1 1/2 cups	355 milliliters
2 cups	473 milliliters
1 quart	1.2 liters

½ inch   1.27 centimeter
1 inch   2.54 centimeter

HANDY INFORMATION EQUIVALENTS

8 drops = a dash
⅛ teaspoon = a pinch
3 teaspoons = 1 tablespoon
2 tablespoons (liquid) = 1 ounce
4 tablespoons = ¼ cup
5⅓ tablespoons = ⅓ cup
8 tablespoons = ½ cup
10⅔ tablespoons = ⅔ cup
16 tablespoons = 1 cup
⅛ cup = 2 tablespoons
⅓ cup = 5 tablespoons plus 1 teaspoon
⅔ cup = 10 tablespoons plus 2 teaspoons
8 fluid ounces = 1 cup
16 fluid ounces = 2 cups = 1 pint
2 pints = 1 quart
4 cups = 1 quart
4 quarts = 1 gallon

FAT FLUSH BAKING PAN SIZES

U.S.	METRIC
8-inch by 1½-inch pan	20-centimeter by 4-centimeter cake or sandwich tin
9-inch by 1½-inch pan	23-centimeter by 4-centimeter cake or sandwich tin
11-inch by 7-inch pan	28-centimeter by 18-centimeter baking tin
13-inch by 9-inch pan	33-centimeter by 23-centimeter baking tin
15-inch by 10-inch pan	38-centimeter by 25.5-centimeter baking tin
1½-quart casserole	1.5-liter casserole
2-quart casserole	2-liter casserole
2-quart rectangular baking dish	30-centimeter by 20-centimeter by 3-centimeter baking tin
9-inch pie plate	22-centimeter by 4-centimeter or 23-centimeter by 4-centimeter pie plate

7- or 8-inch springform pan

18-centimeter or 20-centimeter springform or loose bottom cake tin

9-inch by 5-inch loaf pan or 2-pound narrow loaf tin

23-centimeter by 13-centimeter

OVEN TEMPERATURE CONVERSIONS

FAHRENHEIT	CELSIUS	GAS SETTING
300 degrees F	150 degrees C	2
325 degrees F	160 degrees C	3
350 degrees F	180 degrees C	4
375 degrees F	190 degrees C	5
400 degrees F	200 degrees C	6
425 degrees F	220 degrees C	7
450 degrees F	230 degrees C	8
Broil		Grill

4 The Fat Flush Herbs and Spices for Weight Loss and Health

As you may recall from reading *The New Fat Flush Plan*, the recommended herbs and spices are much more than simply flavor enhancers. Certain seasonings are utilized in the initial two phases because they are helpful in boosting metabolism (cayenne, ginger, and mustard), keeping blood sugar levels stable (cinnamon, cloves, and bay leaves), removing fluid from the system (parsley, cilantro, and coriander), nourishing the liver (garlic and turmeric), and aiding digestion (anise, fennel, cumin, and dill). Later in phase 3, the addition of basil and oregano is helpful for combating germs and viruses. Rosemary, also a new phase 3 seasoning, acts as a potent antioxidant, helping to protect breast health. Others, like phase 3 add-ons cardamom, nutmeg, saffron, and marjoram, are rich in minerals like potassium, manganese, and iron and also assist in digestive function.

While fresh herbs are generally preferable to dried ones (with the exception of oregano), it is not always possible to find fresh. But if you do have fresh herbs easily available, they are generally better than the dried for salads and sauces. The dried go best with the longer-cooking dishes like stews, soups, and casseroles. The rule of thumb is that 1 teaspoon of dried equals 1 tablespoon of fresh.

Do keep in mind that fresh herbs can be frozen. So whether you buy your herbs in the produce section of your supermarket or grow them yourself (some do quite well right on your windowsill), there is no reason to let them go bad in the fridge or just wilt away. Freeze 'em!

Put the leaves, whether whole or chopped, in small bags and freeze them for future use. And the best part of all is that when you do decide to use your fresh frozen herbs for culinary purposes, you can add them frozen to your cooked dishes. There is no need to defrost them beforehand.

Dried herbs and spices have a shelf life of about six months. After this amount of time, many of them lose their flavor and become flat. So store your herbs and spices in small, airtight jars in a cool, dry, dark place away from the kitchen stove where heat can affect them. A cool environment protects the volatile oils from warmth and moisture, which can change zesty, aromatic, and pungent flavors.

If you are buying your herbs and spices in stores, try to find nonirradiated herbs and spices such as Frontier Herbs and The Spice Hunter. When you open a jar of dried herbs, there should be a fresh, strong, and distinctive aroma. If there is not—and they also taste like dried grass rather than lovely herbs (this is the truly best way to explain this)—then you won't be deriving the weight loss and health benefits from these herbal helpers. Their full flavor potential will be lost, and it is high time to replace your supply.

Here is a rundown of the main Fat Flush herbs used in this cookbook so you can see at a glance how they have traditionally been used in culinary applications as well as how they can enhance your health at the same time.

Anise
MILDLY AROMATIC

Culinary. Found in whole-seed form. Licorice-like taste is similar to fennel and great for seasoning cabbage, cauliflower, turnips, beef, shellfish, cakes, and cookies. Chewing on a few seeds has a natural breath mint–like effect. Provides a nice touch to teas.

Therapeutic. Helpful for liver, kidneys, and stomach. Enhances lactation. Once considered an aphrodisiac.

Basil
AROMATICALLY ROBUST

A native of India, folklore says it blesses those it touches.

Culinary. Found in fresh, dried-leaf, or flaked form. Leaves are wonderful with any type of tomato dish. Mini-strips of fresh basil are great with tomato dishes from sauces to soups. Goes well with sauces, stews, soups, stuffings, and dips. A pesto staple. Frequently found in Mediterranean-style dishes from Italy and Greece. Chopped basil is a special treat with fresh corn on the cob.

Therapeutic. Helps nervous exhaustion, anxiety, colds, depression, substance abuse, and drug withdrawal. Appetite stimulant.

Bay Leaf
SEMIMILD TASTE AND AROMA

Keeps bugs out of the cupboard!

Culinary. Found in dried-leaf form. Stronger if the leaves are torn for cooking. Used in soups, chowders, stews, roasts, gravies, and marinades. Remember to remove before eating.

Therapeutic. Known to relieve bronchitis, arthritis, and atherosclerosis. Tones and strengthens digestive tract.

Cardamom
STRONGLY AROMATIC WITH AN AFTERTASTE REMINISCENT OF LEMONS

Culinary. Found in whole or ground form. Highlighted in Indian foods. Goes well with curries, rice, and breads. Especially nice in teas and herbal coffees.

Therapeutic. Helps treat indigestion, asthma, bronchitis, celiac disease, bad breath, spastic colon, and vomiting. Considered an aphrodisiac in the Middle East. Potent digestive aid for grains.

Cayenne
HOT AND SPICY

Culinary. A member of the chili family, found most frequently in ground form. Good with sauces, vegetables, beans, and dips and tangy in fish and meat dishes. A prime ingredient in Tex-Mex cuisine and Asian types of foods.

Therapeutic. Soothing to irritated tissues. Stimulates circulation, relieves migraines, assists digestion, breaks up congestion, and stimulates the production of adrenal hormones that speed up the breakdown of fat by 25 percent. Cayenne's heat comes from capsicum, which increases the body's metabolic rate and cleans fat out of the arteries. Cayenne does so much more than create a tongue-tingling meal. It is loaded with vitamins C, B, A, and E and also contains calcium, phosphorus, and iron. It is high in immune-boosting beta-carotene and is used as a painkiller, an antiseptic, and a digestive aid. It adds a real kick to all your veggies, sauces, dips, and soups. I even like a pinch of this hot stuff in my smoothie.

Cilantro
MILDLY SPICY

Culinary. Also known as Mexican or Chinese parsley, cilantro is a fresh herb with a more pungent taste than parsley. It is good with salads, soups, and tomato-based dishes and as a garnish. Frequently found in Mexican food and in Asian cuisine.

Therapeutic. A heavy-metal eliminator, cilantro helps relieve bloating, diarrhea, and GI tract disorders.

Cinnamon
SUBTLE, SWEET-SPICY

Cinnamon's scent has been found by the Smell and Taste Research Institute to enhance arousal in males.

Culinary. Very versatile and typically found in stick or ground form. Can be used in lamb, beef, and chicken dishes as well as with fruits, breads, onions, squash, tomatoes, sweet potatoes, and cereal grains. Good seasoning for teas.

Therapeutic. Helpful for diabetics by making cells more insulin-sensitive; can boost body's ability to balance blood sugar about 20-fold. Good for cramps, bloating, and flatulence. I only recommend Ceylon cinnamon because most commercial cinnamons contain the liver-damaging ingredient coumarin that can be harmful to health when taken in excess. Cinnamon in general, however, is most helpful in controlling blood sugar levels so that insulin spikes are kept in check, and it can even reduce the glycemic impact of a meal by nearly 30 percent. As a delicious metabolism booster, cinnamon can rock desserts, lamb, coffee, tea, and smoothies

Cloves
HIGHLY AROMATIC AND SWEET

Culinary. Whole or in ground form, cloves are good for adding spice to stewed fruit and character to roasts, sweet potatoes, and wild game. Lovely for seasoning teas.

Therapeutic. Acts as a parasite fighter; also aids in relieving diarrhea, sore throats, toothaches, and stomach cramps.

Coriander
MODERATELY SPICY WITH A HINT OF ORANGE PEEL

Coriander actually comes from the seeds of the cilantro plant. I have a perfume called Coriandre from Paris that I absolutely adore and that has become my signature scent.

Culinary. Found in seed or ground form, coriander is a favorite in Latin American and Indian curry-based dishes. Excellent seasoning for carrots, fish, chicken, eggs, beans, and rice.

Therapeutic. Treats bloating, cramps, and GI disorders.

Cumin
DISTINCTIVELY SPICY WITH EARTHY, MEATY FLAVOR

Culinary. Found in seed or ground form in Middle Eastern, East Indian, African, and Mexican cuisine. Good with beans, dips, stews, lamb, beef, and sauces.

Therapeutic. Improves liver function and relieves gas, colic, and digestive-connected headaches. This peppery biblical spice is a wonderful taste enhancer and catalyst for weight loss. The latest research out of the Middle East, where cumin is popularly consumed, shows that one teaspoon of this spice boosts weight loss by 50 percent, most likely due to its ability to raise body temperature, thereby heating up metabolism. This is one great spice for hummus, beans, chili, and any variation of a Mexican food dish.

Dill
MILDLY AROMATIC

Culinary. Found in fresh, seed, or dried form. Featured in Northern and Eastern European cooking. Enhances fish dishes, cucumbers, beans, salads, cabbage, soup, salad dressings, cottage cheese, egg dishes, and tofu dips.

Therapeutic. Helpful for indigestion, colic, bad breath, and insomnia.

Fennel
MILD TASTE AND AROMA

Culinary. Found in fresh, dried-leaf, or seed form. The distinctive licorice-like taste goes well with fish, turkey, cabbage, onions, tomato sauces, and stews. Provides a nice touch for cookies and cakes (healthy ones, of course).

Therapeutic. Helpful as a natural digestive aid and as a phytoestrogen. Good for bad breath, diabetes, kidney stones, and nausea.

Garlic, the King of Herbs
PUNGENT

Culinary. Found in fresh, powdered, or minced form. Garlic is featured in worldwide cuisines especially for fish, poultry, game, vegetables, soups, beans, salsas, salad dressings, casseroles, and marinades.

Therapeutic. Most potent healthwise when garlic is mashed, smashed, or minced raw. Helps to protect against heart disease, asthma, diabetes, flu, and stomach cancer. Garlic is the best antiparasitic, antifungal, and antiyeast herb.

Ginger

HOT, PUNGENT, AND WARMING

Culinary. Found in fresh, whole-root, or ground form. Highlighted in Chinese and Indian spice mixtures. Perks up meats, marinades, root vegetables, fruits, cookies, and cakes.

Therapeutic. Good for motion sickness, muscle soreness, arthritis, headaches, poor circulation, flatulence, and menstrual cramps. Serves as a natural blood thinner and anti-inflammatory. According to an Australian study, ginger can cause a metabolic boost of as much as 20 percent. It both energizes and cleanses while providing warmth. Ginger revs circulation and promotes healthy sweating, encouraging detoxification of the body. It supports liver function, clears up clogged arteries, and lowers serum cholesterol levels. It is effective for motion sickness and nausea. Ginger lends itself well to cookies (I just love ginger snaps), as well as puddings and custards, and it is quite tasty on salmon. Ginger tea settles the stomach.

Horseradish

PUNGENT

Culinary. Fresh root or dried in powdered form. Great addition to dips, meatloaf, egg dishes, and sauces.

Therapeutic. Helpful for relieving sinus congestion and clearing excess mucus and phlegm.

Marjoram

FRAGRANT AND FLAVORFUL

Sweet marjoram is a milder relative of oregano. Also used in perfumes!

Culinary. Found in fresh or dried-leaf form. Featured in Greek, French, and Italian cooking, sweet marjoram is a nice addition to sauces, soups, stews, stuffings, and salads.

Therapeutic. Relieves menstrual cramps and bronchitis, calms nerves, and is helpful for insomnia.

Mint

MILDLY AROMATIC

Culinary. Found in fresh or dried-leaf form. Perfect for lamb, peas, salads, lentils, and beverages.

Therapeutic. Helps relieve flatulence, fatigue, gallbladder problems, morning sickness, and nausea. Acts as a parasite fighter, an antimicrobial, and a digestive aid.

Mustard
MODERATELY SPICY

Culinary. Found in whole-seed or ground form. Used with egg dishes like deviled eggs. Also used with meat, sauces, dips, condiments, salad dressings, marinades, and shellfish.

Therapeutic. Increases body's fat-burning ability, raises body temperature, acts as a diuretic, and increases circulation. Mustard is a must in my kitchen. In the dried, powdered state or as a prepared mustard spread, it not only gives a burst of tangy spiciness, but helps flush fat by kicking metabolism into high gear. Study data from Oxford Polytechnic Institute shows that mustard spikes metabolic rates by 25 percent. By adding mustard to a meal, participants burned at least 45 extra calories during the next three hours. Try just a pinch of dried mustard in your homemade salad dressings, mayo, and pickles. I really love it on my deviled eggs.

Nutmeg
WARMING, POWERFUL, AND SWEET

Culinary. Found in whole or ground form. Most pungent when grated fresh at the end of cooking. Used to infuse soups, sauces, cheese dishes, and shellfish dishes. Goes well with spinach and cauliflower.

Therapeutic. A natural digestive aid, nutmeg relieves flatulence and coughs and reduces pain.

Oregano
PUNGENT AND MILDLY SPICY

Oregano contains the highest amount of antioxidants in the herb kingdom.

Culinary. Found in fresh or dried-leaf form. Best when added toward the end of cooking, or it can become bitter. A staple of Italian and Mediterranean cooking, oregano seasons tomatoes, vegetables, salad dressings, and sauces.

Therapeutic. A well-respected antibacterial, antiviral, anti-inflammatory, and antioxidant, oregano relieves candida, nausea, colic, bronchitis, and motion sickness.

Parsley
MILD TASTE AND AROMA

Culinary. Found in fresh or dried-leaf form. This is one herb in which the dried form is not at all flavorful. Most flavorful when fresh parsley is added near the end of cooking. Complements all cuisine, especially salads, soups, tofu dishes, soufflés, dips, and pâtés.

Therapeutic. Great natural diuretic and helps to treat problems with kidneys, gout, anemia, jaundice, and arthritis.

Rosemary
PUNGENTLY SPICY

Culinary. Found in fresh or dried-leaf form. Great with Italian dishes, lamb, chicken, marinades, and casseroles and as flavoring for bread.

Therapeutic. Is a potent antioxidant and energy booster, relieves upset stomach, and is good for the memory and hair.

Sage
SHARP, SPICY, AND HIGHLY AROMATIC

The American Indians used sage to smudge away evil spirits.

Culinary. Found in fresh or dried-leaf form. Goes well with stuffing, poultry, onions, peas, cottage cheese, casseroles, sauces, and omelets.

Therapeutic. A natural phytoestrogen, sage is helpful as a menopause remedy and also helps to stimulate and regulate the flow of bile so it is good with fatty foods. It is a decongestant, gargle, and astringent (natural deodorants use sage), and it treats fevers, colds, and flu.

Tarragon
MILD AND AROMATIC

Culinary. Found in fresh or dried-leaf form. A favorite of French cooks, tarragon's delicate flavor enhances chicken, fish, and seafood. Good for salad dressings and with apple cider vinegar.

Therapeutic. Helps to eliminate parasites in children, acts like a natural diuretic, and supports digestive function.

Thyme
DELICATE AND AROMATIC

Culinary. Found in fresh or dried-leaf form. Goes well with stuffing, soups, sauces, stews, peas, and lentils.

Therapeutic. A natural antibiotic, good for asthma, colds, colic, hangovers, hay fever, headaches, and cough. Helps with digestion of fatty foods.

Turmeric
MILDLY SPICY

Culinary. This yellowish relative of ginger is a fat digestant. Most commonly used with curries, beans, and fish dishes and in scrambled tofu. Turmeric can be added to curries, beans, meat stews, fish dinners, omelets, and soups. It is the best spice for a barbecue because turmeric added to meats before they are grilled reduces toxic compounds up to 40 percent.

Therapeutic. Packed with anticancer antioxidants, turmeric contains curcumin, which helps the body detoxify harmful chemicals. Treats arthritis and stops food poisoning, especially salmonella. Turmeric is widely known for its high antioxidant content, thanks to its curcumin content. It is the superstar of the popular curry spice blend. But this natural anti-inflammatory really stands out because it can help thin and decongest bile so your body can metabolize fat more efficiently.

FAT FLUSH BONUS TIPS

- Learn the art of herbal infusions! Herbed vinegars are Fat Flush friendly for all phases, depending upon the herbs you choose. For example, in phase 1, you could fill up a clean jar or glass bottle with about 1 cup of fresh herbs such as dill or parsley and add 1 quart of cider vinegar. In phase 2, you might choose dill or cilantro, and in phase 3, tarragon or thyme. Cover the bottle. Let this stand in your pantry or some other cool, dark place, and if you wish, after a few days, add even more vinegar. Let stand for another three to four weeks, and you have a ready-made salad dressing accompaniment or a steamed veggie pick-me-up.

- In phase 3, you can make an olive, grape seed, or sesame seed infusion by filling up a glass jar with 3 tablespoons of fresh herbs (make sure you pound them slightly to help release the volatile oils and flavor). Then add ½ cup of lightly warmed oil of your choice. Let the oil cool, seal the jar, and place it in the fridge for a couple of weeks before you are ready to serve. What a treat on steamed veggies, salads, or brown rice!

5 Breakfast

For most of us, it's simply no contest: breakfast is the most critical meal of the day. Your body has been without food for approximately 12 hours and needs to be nourished. Eating the right breakfast high in protein and slimming smart fats will help rev up your mind, get your energy back in gear, and even out blood sugar levels. Moreover, it fills and satisfies, so you're less likely to hunt out the false energy highs of lots of coffee and sugar-filled breakfast pastries.

In less than two minutes, you can whip up a variety of refreshing and filling smoothies like our Friendly Fennel Orange Smoothie or even our Ginger Pear Smoothie to start your day. And while you have that flaxseed oil out for your smoothie, it's the perfect time to blend some of that oil with softened butter for the kids. Melt some of this "better butter" on their gluten-free toast or in their hot cereal so they get an omega triple-header: support for their immune, cardiovascular, and central nervous systems. More and more studies reveal the incredible ability of omega-3 oils to improve concentration, enhance feelings of well-being, and reduce aggression. There's no better way to send yourself to the office or the kids to school than with an omega-rich breakfast.

Hearty breakfast eaters will enjoy our tempting Simple Sweet Potato Hash. And for your hubby, please don't shy away from eggs—the organic, free-range ones of course. Contrary to what you may think, eggs are the good guys for your guy. A complete source of protein, eggs are packed with vital nutrients, such as vitamins, minerals, amino acids, and antioxidants—especially a whopping 215 micrograms of lutein and zeaxanthin for the eyes. And they're just about the best source of choline, a crucial component of the neurotransmitter phosphatidylcholine, which can ward off Alzheimer's. Eggs have cholesterol-lowering properties! In fact, studies conducted by the Harvard School of Public Health reveal that eating an egg daily doesn't elevate the risk of heart disease. Plus, eggs satisfy your hunger, and they can be made in just a few minutes.

Eggs, however, for some of you may be a different story. As you may remember from the New Fat Flush Plan, eggs are the number one allergy food for gallbladder issues. So if you have gallbladder discomfort or gallstones, it's best to omit eggs for the time being and substitute one of the following choices.

RECIPES IN THIS CHAPTER	PAGE

SMOOTHIES

Within minutes, you can create one of our lip-smacking breakfast smoothies. They're powered up with flax or coconut oil to help you start your day with nourishing fats.

EGGS 'N' SUCH

RECIPES IN THIS CHAPTER

CEREAL

SMOOTHIES

Here's the basic recipe you may remember from the New Fat Flush Plan. The great thing about smoothies is that they are not just for breakfast anymore. They make great snacks and even desserts.

Fat Flush Smoothie

8   ounces water or Fat Flush Cran-Water (Chapter 12)
1   scoop protein powder
1   fruit serving of your choosing
    Small handful of romaine lettuce, kale, or spinach or scoop of green powder
1   tablespoon flaxseed oil or coconut oil
1   tablespoon ground flax seeds, chia seeds, or hemp seeds
1   scoop powdered probiotic
1   tablespoon non-GMO soy or sunflower lecithin
    Ice cubes (optional)

In a blender, blend the water, protein powder, fruit, and leafy vegetables or green powder until smooth.

Add the other ingredients.

If using flaxseed oil, stream it in while the blender is running.

TIPS

Make 2 smoothies at a time—put the extra in the refrigerator to enjoy later.

To burn more fat, support the thyroid, slow down carb absorption, heal leaky gut, or lower insulin, try adding a dash of turmeric, Ceylon cinnamon, cream of tartar, or collagen powder or 1 tablespoon of apple cider vinegar.

ALL PHASES; MAKES 1 SERVING.

Ginger Pear Smoothie

This is a smoothie combo I learned from my good friend Jonny Bowden, and it has become one of my personal all-time faves.

8	ounces water or Fat Flush Cran-Water (Chapter 12)
1	scoop protein powder
1	pear
2	celery stalks with leaves
1	tablespoon coconut oil
1	tablespoon chia seeds
1	scoop powdered probiotic
1	tablespoon non-GMO soy or sunflower lecithin
	1-inch piece gingerroot
	Ice cubes (optional)

In a blender, blend the water, protein powder, pear, and celery until smooth.
Add the other ingredients.
Stream in the oil while the blender is running.

TIP
Freeze a portion of this smoothie for a yummy snack.

ALL PHASES; MAKES 1 SERVING.

Awesome Apple Smoothie

This apple a day will definitely help keep the doctor away—with blood sugar–balancing cinnamon and antioxidant-rich Fat Flush Cran-Water.

8   ounces water or Fat Flush Cran-Water (Chapter 12)
1   scoop protein powder
1   medium apple, peeled, cored, cut into chunks, and frozen
    Small handful of romaine lettuce
1   tablespoon flaxseed oil
1   tablespoon ground flax seeds
1   scoop powdered probiotic
1   teaspoon non-GMO soy or sunflower lecithin
¼   teaspoon Ceylon cinnamon or to taste
2   teaspoons fresh lemon juice (can use up to 1 tablespoon)
    Ice cubes (optional)

In a blender, blend the water, protein powder, apple, and lettuce until smooth.

Add the other ingredients.

Stream in the oil while the blender is running.

> **TIP**
> **Freeze the apple chunks the night before for fast-and-easy smoothie making in the morning. Freezing the apple also makes it crisper.**

ALL PHASES; MAKES 1 SERVING.

Berry Cherry Smoothie

Just ½ cup of strawberries is almost equivalent to a whole day's worth of vitamin C. Combine them with cherries, and you've got a surprisingly rich and tasty antioxidant-filled treat for your a.m. meal.

8 ounces water or Fat Flush Cran-Water (Chapter 12)
1 scoop vanilla protein powder
5 frozen cherries, pitted
½ cup frozen strawberries
   Small handful of spinach
1 tablespoon coconut oil
1 tablespoon hemp seeds
1 scoop powdered probiotic
1 tablespoon non-GMO soy or sunflower lecithin
   Ice cubes (optional)

In a blender, blend the water, protein powder, fruit, and spinach until smooth.

Add the other ingredients.

Stream in the oil while the blender is running.

ALL PHASES; MAKES 1 SERVING.

Spicy Tomato Veggie Smoothie

When you're ready for something savory versus sweet, try this zesty smoothie just brimming with vitamin- and mineral-rich veggies and seeds.

8	ounces water
1	scoop vanilla protein powder
	Small handful of mixed greens
1	scallion, chopped
¼	cup cucumber, seeded and chopped
1	medium tomato, chopped
1	tablespoon flaxseed oil
1	tablespoon chia seeds
⅛	teaspoon celery seed
1	scoop powdered probiotic
1	tablespoon non-GMO soy or sunflower lecithin

In a blender, blend the water, protein powder, and vegetables until smooth.
Add the other ingredients.
Stream in the oil while the blender is running.

ALL PHASES; MAKES 1 SERVING.

Friendly Fennel Orange Smoothie

Bloat-banishing fennel is your GI tract's newest BFF. Among its many other claims to fame, this licorice-tasting, aromatic herb is a phytoestrogenic, diuretic, and heart-healthy wonder. The ancients even believed fennel could favor one with long life, courage, and strength. In this recipe, the fennel tea replaces the cup of water or cran-water from the basic smoothie recipe.

1   cup brewed organic fennel tea
1   scoop vanilla protein powder
    Small handful of kale
1   orange, cut and quartered
1   tablespoon coconut oil
1   tablespoon ground flax seeds
1   scoop powdered probiotic
1   tablespoon non-GMO soy or sunflower lecithin
    Zest of 1 orange
    Ice cubes (optional)

In a blender, blend the water, protein powder, kale, and orange until smooth.
Add the other ingredients.
Stream in the oil while the blender is running.

Variations

- If you'd like a little more licorice taste, use two tea bags when brewing.
- Or you can make your own fennel tea from scratch. Take 1 teaspoon of organic fennel seeds, lightly bruise them with the edge of a kitchen knife to release the volatile oils, place in a cup, and pour very hot (not boiling) water over. Cover and steep for 10 minutes.

ALL PHASES; MAKES 1 SERVING.

Chocolate Peppermint Smoothie

So good it feels like you're cheating!

1   cup organic peppermint tea
1   scoop chocolate protein powder
1   tablespoon flaxseed oil
1   tablespoon ground flax seeds
1   scoop powdered probiotic
1   tablespoon non-GMO soy or sunflower lecithin
½   cup crushed ice
    Mint leaves

In a blender, blend the tea and protein powder until smooth.
Add the other ingredients.
Stream in the oil while the blender is running.

ALL PHASES; MAKES 1 SERVING.

Purple Passion Smoothie

This smoothie is a royal treat! The zesty arugula replaces the romaine lettuce, kale, or spinach in the basic Fat Flush Smoothie.

8	ounces Fat Flush Cran-Water (Chapter 12)
1	scoop vanilla protein powder
	Small handful of arugula
1	plum
½	cup frozen blueberries
1	tablespoon flaxseed oil
1	tablespoon ground flax seeds
1	scoop powdered probiotic
1	tablespoon non-GMO soy or sunflower lecithin
	Ice cubes (optional)

In a blender, blend the water, protein powder, arugula, and fruit until smooth.
Add the other ingredients.
Stream in the oil while the blender is running.

ALL PHASES; MAKES 1 SERVING.

Rockin' Red Smoothie

This gorgeous red smoothie rocks the antioxidant, vitamin, and mineral content for an energetic meal or snack. The red leaf lettuce replaces the other leafy greens in the basic smoothie recipe.

8   ounces Fat Flush Cran-Water (Chapter 12)
1   scoop vanilla protein powder
     Small handful of red leaf lettuce
3   frozen strawberries
5   frozen cherries
⅓   cup raspberries, fresh or frozen
1   tablespoon coconut oil
1   tablespoon chia seeds
1   scoop powdered probiotic
1   tablespoon non-GMO soy or sunflower lecithin
     Dash of cloves
     Ice cubes (optional)

In a blender, blend the water, protein powder, lettuce, and fruit until smooth.
Add the other ingredients.
Stream in the oil while the blender is running.

ALL PHASES; MAKES 1 SERVING.

Mocha Cafe Kick Smoothie

With tasty thermogenic spices and organic coffee, this smoothie is just the thing to kick your morning into gear.

1   cup chilled regular organic coffee
1   scoop chocolate protein powder
    Small handful of romaine lettuce
1   tablespoon coconut oil
1   tablespoon chia seeds
1   scoop powdered probiotic
1   tablespoon non-GMO soy or sunflower lecithin
½   teaspoon Ceylon cinnamon
¼   teaspoon cayenne or to taste
    Ice cubes (optional)

In a blender, blend the coffee, protein powder, and lettuce until smooth.
Add the other ingredients.
Stream in the oil while the blender is running.

Variation
• When you're on phase 3, try ½ teaspoon of organic cardamom in place of the cinnamon.

ALL PHASES; MAKES 1 SERVING.

Pumpkin Pie Smoothie

Canned pumpkin is most likely canned squash these days, wouldn't you know? Its high beta-carotene content will beautify your skin, hair, and nails while you flush the fat away.

8   ounces Fat Flush Cran-Water (Chapter 12)
1   scoop protein powder
      Small handful of spinach
½   unsweetened canned pumpkin
1   tablespoon flaxseed oil
1   tablespoon ground flax seeds
1   scoop powdered probiotic
1   tablespoon non-GMO soy or sunflower lecithin
½   teaspoon Ceylon cinnamon
⅛   teaspoon cloves

In a blender, blend the water, protein powder, spinach, and pumpkin until smooth.

Add the other ingredients.

Stream in the oil while the blender is running.

PHASES 2 AND 3; MAKES 1 SERVING.

Morning Sunshine Smoothie

Brighten your morning with this delicious smoothie boasting three of the healthiest fruits on the planet. Among its many attributes, pineapple is the only source of bromelain, a plant compound that aids in reducing inflammation, enhances immune system function, and helps your gut by stimulating better digestion. Add to this the cancer-fighting antioxidants of the berries, and you'll be starting your day off right.

8   ounces water or Fat Flush Cran-Water (Chapter 12)
1   scoop vanilla protein powder
    Small handful of kale
¼   cup frozen pineapple
¼   cup frozen strawberries
¼   cup frozen blueberries
1   tablespoon flaxseed oil
1   tablespoon ground flax seeds
1   scoop powdered probiotic
1   tablespoon non-GMO soy or sunflower lecithin
    Dash of turmeric
    Ice cubes (optional)

In a blender, blend the water, protein powder, kale, and fruit until smooth.
Add the other ingredients.
Stream in the oil while the blender is running.

PHASES 2 AND 3; MAKES 1 SERVING.

Take It to the Tropics Smoothie

This smoothie is like a little tropical vacation for your taste buds!

8   ounces water or Fat Flush Cran-Water (Chapter 12)
1   scoop vanilla protein powder
      Small handful of romaine lettuce
¼   cup frozen pineapple chunks
½   small, frozen banana
1   tablespoon coconut oil
1   scoop powdered probiotic
1   tablespoon non-GMO soy or sunflower lecithin
      Dash of Ceylon cinnamon
      Ice cubes (optional)

In a blender, blend the water, protein powder, lettuce, and fruit until smooth.
Add the other ingredients.
Stream in the oil while the blender is running.

PHASES 2 AND 3; MAKES 1 SERVING.

Mango Magic Smoothie

Mangoes are not only delicious; they have been found to have an alkalizing effect on the body, help with weight loss, and even fight many kinds of cancer. So go ahead and make some magic!

1   cup unsweetened, organic almond milk
1   scoop green powder
1   scoop vanilla protein powder
1   mango
1   tablespoon ground hemp seeds
1   scoop powdered probiotic
1   tablespoon non-GMO soy or sunflower lecithin
1   teaspoon dried mint leaves or 1 tablespoon fresh
    Ice cubes (optional)

In a blender, blend the almond milk, green powder, protein powder, and mango until smooth.
Add the other ingredients.
Stream in the oil while the blender is running.

PHASE 3; MAKES 1 SERVING.

Kiwi Pear Smoothie

This unusual pairing of tender fruits provides a delightfully fresh treat for your palate.

8   ounces water
1   scoop vanilla protein powder
     Small handful of romaine lettuce
½   kiwi
½   pear
1   tablespoon coconut oil
1   tablespoon hemp seeds
1   scoop powdered probiotic
1   tablespoon non-GMO soy or sunflower lecithin
     Dash of cardamom
     Ice cubes (optional)

In a blender, blend the water, protein powder, lettuce, and fruit until smooth.
Add the other ingredients.
Stream in the oil while the blender is running.

PHASE 3; MAKES 1 SERVING.

EGGS 'N' SUCH

Eggs are either hidden ingredients or front and center in these Fat Flush quick-and-easy breakfasts.

Raspberry Breakfast "Cookies"

Who knew weight loss could taste this good? Thanks to Charli Sorenson, one of my Fat Flush emeritus moderators, for coming up with this gem, which is a big favorite with our online Facebook Fat Flush Nation.

1   scoop protein powder
1   egg
½   teaspoon Ceylon cinnamon
     Dash of ground cloves
⅛   teaspoon SweetLeaf Stevia or to taste
¼   cup fresh raspberries, mashed
6   whole raspberries, shaken with SweetLeaf Stevia in a small Ziploc bag
     Olive oil or paper liners

Preheat the oven to 300°F.

Mix all the ingredients except the raspberries (both the mashed and the whole berries) and olive oil in a blender until smooth.

Pour into a mixing bowl, fold in the mashed berries, and stir well.

Using a muffin pan, lightly coat each of the six cups with olive oil, or use paper liners if you prefer.

Pour the batter evenly into the six cups (about ¼ full).

Top each "cookie" with a stevia-coated raspberry.

Bake for 15 minutes or until set.

ALL PHASES; MAKES 6 COOKIES.

Spaghetti Squash Pancakes

For a sweet or savory breakfast treat, these simple pancakes can't be beat.

2   cups cooked spaghetti squash
2   eggs
     Ground Ceylon cinnamon to taste
     Lakanto Monkfruit Sweetener to taste
     Avocado oil spray

In a medium bowl, combine the cooked spaghetti squash with the egg, cinnamon, and monk fruit sweetener.

Heat a griddle pan that has been lightly coated with avocado oil spray.

Ladle the squash mixture into the pan in portions of about 2 tablespoons per pancake and cook until small bubbles form on the surface.

Flip the pancakes over and continue cooking until almost "dry."

Repeat with the remaining batter.

Variations

• Very tasty topped with fresh berries!
• For a savory treat, replace the cinnamon and sweetener with herbs such as minced fresh cilantro, parsley, or mint.

ALL PHASES; MAKES 4 SERVINGS.

Bountiful Berry Breakfast Crepes

For a special breakfast treat, try these elegant and healthy crepes. It may take a little practice to make the crepes just right, but they're so worth it. They're sure to become a family favorite!

Crepe Batter:

2   eggs
1   scoop protein powder
½   teaspoon Ceylon cinnamon

Filling:

1   cup frozen berries
1   tablespoon water
1   tablespoon coconut oil
¼   teaspoon Lakanto Monkfruit Sweetener or to taste
    Avocado oil spray

To make the crepe batter, blend the eggs, protein powder, and cinnamon together until smooth (the batter will be thin).

For the filling, place the frozen berries in a small bowl and mix with the water.

Puree the softened berries, coconut oil, and monk fruit sweetener with a wand mixer or mini–food processor; set aside.

Lightly coat a crepe pan (or small frying pan) with the avocado oil spray; place the pan over medium heat.

When the pan is hot (a drop of water will sizzle), pour a couple of tablespoons of batter into the pan, tilting quickly to cover the surface, cooking until the bottom is golden brown (about two minutes), and then cooking briefly on the other side.

Continue making crepes until all the batter is used.

Place 2 to 3 tablespoons of berry puree along one edge of the crepe and roll up, arranging seam side down on the plate.

Pour the remaining berry puree over the top of the rolled crepes.

Variation

- If you're on phase 3, or you want to make them extra special for family and friends, try mixing ½ cup of organic ricotta cheese into the berry filling. Then add a dollop of whipped cream on top with a dusting of Ceylon cinnamon.

ALL PHASES; MAKES ABOUT 4 CREPES.

Blueberry Delight Breakfast Pudding

Make this delicious treat the night before and give yourself something to look forward to in the morning!

    Avocado oil spray
4   large eggs
1   scoop vanilla protein powder
1   teaspoon Lakanto Monkfruit Sweetener
3   cups cooked spaghetti squash, drained well
1   cup fresh or frozen blueberries

Preheat the oven to 350°F.

Lightly coat a pie pan with the avocado oil spray.

Mix the eggs on low speed in a blender.

Add the protein powder and monk fruit sweetener; blend well on low speed.

Add the spaghetti squash; blend on high speed until thick and creamy.

Spread the blueberries into the pan.

Pour in the spaghetti squash mixture.

Bake for 25 to 30 minutes or until set.

Chill.

TIP

This recipe can be doubled—the family doesn't need to know the secret squash ingredient!

Variations

- Cherries or apples make delicious substitutions for the blueberries.
- Or if you prefer, omit the fruit completely and add a little cinnamon.

ALL PHASES; MAKES 2 SERVINGS.

Avocado Egg in Hole

The avocado contains more potassium than a banana, is loaded with fiber, is filled with vitamins, and brims with healthy fats. Who could ask for more first thing in the morning?

1   avocado, halved and pitted
1   egg, beaten
     Garlic powder
     Cumin

Place the halves face up on a muffin tin so they won't tip over.
Pour the beaten egg into each hole (one egg fills two halves).
Sprinkle with the garlic powder and cumin.
Bake at 350°F for 15 to 20 minutes or until done.

> **TIP**
> If the pit is too small, scoop out a bit of the avocado to make the hole deeper before adding the egg. Tell the kids you're making "avocado eyes" for breakfast. They may be intrigued enough to gobble them right up!

ALL PHASES; MAKES 2 SERVINGS.

Fresh Veggie Frittata

Take advantage of the freshest organic veggies from your local farmers market or home garden to make this filling frittata.

1   tablespoon coconut oil
2   garlic cloves, crushed
½   cup scallions, chopped
½   cup Italian (flat-leaf) parsley, chopped
1   tablespoon cilantro, chopped
¼   cup fresh asparagus, diced
¼   cup spinach
¼   cup plum tomatoes, chopped
6   eggs
    Cayenne to taste

Preheat the broiler.

On top of the stove, heat the oil in a medium ovenproof skillet with a lid.

Add the garlic to the skillet and sauté until softened.

Add the scallions, parsley, cilantro, asparagus, spinach, and tomatoes and sauté until crisp-tender.

Remove the skillet from the heat.

In a medium bowl, blend together the eggs and cayenne.

Turn the heat to low; pour the egg mixture into the skillet, stirring well.

Cover and cook about 3 minutes or until the egg mixture begins to come away from the sides of the pan.

Place the skillet under the preheated broiler.

Broil for an additional minute or until the frittata is set and lightly browned.

Cut into 4 wedges and serve.

Variation

•   Other vegetables to try are artichokes, eggplant, mushroom, bell pepper, and zucchini.

ALL PHASES; MAKES 4 SERVINGS.

Eggs Florentine à la Cumin

The cumin in this recipe imparts a nutty taste and Middle Eastern touch. And, of course, the spinach in the recipe is so good for you because it is brimming with heart-smart folic acid.

1   cup chopped spinach, fresh or thawed, drained and patted dry
¼   cup red pepper, chopped
1   garlic clove, minced
     Pinch of cumin
2   tablespoons bone broth
2   eggs, lightly beaten

In a skillet over medium heat, sauté the spinach, red pepper, garlic, and cumin in the broth.
Pour the eggs over the spinach and pepper mixture.
Reduce the heat to low, cover, and cook until the eggs are set.

Variation
•   For phase 3, top with 1 tablespoon of freshly grated Parmesan cheese.

ALL PHASES; MAKES 1 SERVING.

Zesty Mushroom and Asparagus Open Omelet

This is an old standby that I have modified for Fat Flush. The dried mustard gives this dish just the kick it needs.

4	eggs
½	cup steamed asparagus, chopped and drained
½	cup sliced mushrooms
1	teaspoon purified water
½	teaspoon dried mustard
½	tablespoon fresh parsley, finely minced
½	teaspoon onion powder

Beat the eggs in a bowl and stir in the remaining ingredients.

Pour the egg mixture into a preheated skillet and cook over medium heat.

As the mixture sets, lift the edges and tilt the skillet, so that the uncooked egg flows underneath and sets.

When the underside is set (about 2 minutes), turn over with a spatula.

Cook until the bottom is set and turns golden brown.

Serve immediately.

Variation

- For phase 3, top with 2 tablespoons of freshly grated Parmesan or Romano cheese.

ALL PHASES; MAKES 2 SERVINGS.

Tofu Scrambler

Perfect for vegetarian Fat Flushers, the turmeric gives this dish the traditional color of real scrambled eggs.

½   cup mushrooms
3   tablespoons scallions, chopped
½   garlic clove, minced
1   tablespoon chives, chopped
3   tablespoons bone broth
1   pound soft tofu, drained, rinsed, and squeezed until lightly crumbled
     Pinch of turmeric
2   tablespoons fresh parsley, chopped, for garnish

In a large skillet over medium heat, sauté the mushrooms, scallions, garlic, and chives in the broth until tender.

Add in the tofu and turmeric; then scramble until the tofu resembles scrambled eggs, about 3 minutes.

Garnish with parsley and serve while hot.

ALL PHASES; MAKES 4 SERVINGS.

Laced Artichoke Egg Bake

I like to serve this dish for company. Everyone is always surprised that something so tasty is so very Fat Flush friendly.

2	tablespoons butter
2	tablespoons scallions, chopped
1	tablespoon fresh parsley, chopped
2	teaspoons fresh basil, chopped
8	artichoke hearts, quartered, rinsed, and dried
4	large eggs
4	tablespoons grated Parmesan cheese

Preheat the oven to 400°F.

Rub the butter onto the bottom and sides of four ramekins.

Sprinkle each with the scallions and herbs.

Place 2 artichoke hearts in each dish.

Crack 1 egg into each dish.

Sprinkle with the cheese and bake for about 9 minutes or until the eggs set.

PHASE 3; MAKES 2 SERVINGS (2 RAMEKINS EACH).

Oat and Honey Chilled Chia Pudding

Make this comforting pudding the night before and give each family member his or her own jar in the morning. (Or make a batch for yourself and keep extra servings in the fridge.)

4   (16-ounce) canning jars with lids
2   cups organic old-fashioned oats
4   tablespoons chia seeds
4   tablespoons raw honey
2⅔ cups unsweetened almond milk
1   teaspoon organic pure almond extract

Add to each jar: ½ cup of oats, 1 tablespoon of chia seeds, 1 tablespoon of honey, ⅔ cup of almond milk, and ¼ teaspoon of almond extract.

Cover; shake well to combine.

Refrigerate overnight.

> **TIP**
> This is a really fun recipe for the kids to make too!

PHASE 3 SPECIAL OCCASION; MAKES 4 SERVINGS.

Protein-Packed Pancakes with Berry Coulis

Saturday-morning pancakes are elevated here to a protein-packed, antioxidant-rich treat that kids (old and young) will love.

Batter:

½   cup organic, old-fashioned oats
2   eggs
⅓   cup organic ricotta cheese
1   tablespoon ground flax seeds
2   teaspoons aluminum-free baking powder
1   teaspoon organic pure vanilla extract
¼   teaspoon cardamom
1   teaspoon Lakanto Monkfruit Sweetener
     Avocado oil spray

Coulis:

¼   cup blueberries
¼   cup raspberries
2   tablespoons fresh-squeezed orange juice

Place the oats in a blender and pulse until powdered.

Add the eggs, ricotta cheese, flax seeds, baking powder, vanilla, cardamom, and sweetener.

Blend until smooth.

If the batter is too thick, add 1 tablespoon of water at a time until the desired consistency is reached.

Heat the griddle to 325°F and spritz with the avocado oil spray.

Ladle 1 heaping tablespoon of batter per pancake and cook until bubbles form on the surface and around the edges, about 2 minutes.

Flip and cook until golden, about 2 more minutes.

To make the coulis, combine the berries and orange juice in the blender and process until blended but still a little chunky

Drizzle over the pancakes.

> **TIP**
> **Recipe can be doubled!**

PHASE 3; MAKES 4 SERVINGS.

Eggs Tex-Mex

So easy, so fast, so good.

2   eggs
1   egg white
     Cayenne to taste
1   ounce Monterey Jack cheese, grated

Whisk the eggs and cayenne.

Cook in a medium skillet over medium heat.

Add the cheese and serve.

Variations

Experiment with various herb and spice combos:
- For an Asian flavor, mix in a pinch of ginger, coriander, and cayenne.
- For an Indian flavor, mix in a pinch of cumin, turmeric, and coriander.
- For a Greek flavor, mix in a squeeze of lemon and a pinch of oregano.
- For a French flavor, add a drop of white wine, a pinch of tarragon, and 1 crushed garlic clove.

PHASE 3; MAKES 1 SERVING.

Simple Sweet Potato Hash

When you need something a little heartier for breakfast, this healthy hash delivers.

1 tablespoon avocado oil
½ pound nitrate-free turkey bacon, diced
½ cup onion, chopped
1 large red bell pepper, cut into thin strips
2 pounds sweet potatoes, peeled and chopped into small cubes
½ teaspoon sea salt
1 tablespoon fresh thyme leaves, chopped, or 1 teaspoon dried thyme

Heat a heavy skillet over medium heat.

Add the avocado oil and turkey bacon. (If the turkey bacon is a little fatty, add the oil after crisping.)

Stir and cook until the bacon begins to crisp.

Add the onion and red bell pepper.

Stir and cook until the veggies soften.

Add the sweet potatoes and sea salt.

Cook, stirring occasionally, until the potatoes become tender and browned.

Sprinkle in the thyme leaves.

Variation

• Crack an egg, one for each portion, on top of the hash when the potatoes are almost done. Cover and cook until desired doneness.

PHASE 3; MAKES 6 SERVINGS.

CEREAL

Overnight Oatmeal

This is a great way to cook oatmeal—or brown rice—for those wintry, cold mornings. Cooking on low heat or in an oven at 200°F overnight retains optimum mineral values since minerals are easily destroyed at high temperatures. Enjoy in the morning!

1   cup steel-cut oats
5   cups purified water

Bring the water to a boil in a small pan.

Combine the oats and the water in a small Crock-Pot or slow cooker on low heat.

Cover and cook on low heat overnight or until done.

Variations

•   Add 1 tablespoon of flaxseed oil to the oatmeal after cooking and right before serving, or how about a tablespoon or two of Olive Flaxy Spread (Chapter 10).

•   For a phase 3 special occasion, add a spoonful of mixed dried fruits like dates, figs, and apricots. Or sweeten instead with a tablespoon of date sugar or honey.

PHASE 3; MAKES 1 SERVING.

Cinna Berry Oatmeal with Toasted Walnuts

Elevate your oatmeal to new heights with this nutritious rendition of an oldie but goodie breakfast!

1   cup water
⅛   teaspoon sea salt (optional)
½   cup old-fashioned oats
½   teaspoon Lakanto Monkfruit Sweetener or to taste
¼   cup fresh chopped cranberries or other seasonally available fruit
1   tablespoon chopped toasted walnuts

To toast the walnuts:

Heat the oven to 350°F.

Spread the walnuts in a single layer on a baking sheet.

Toast for 5 to 10 minutes, stirring occasionally, just until beginning to brown (walnuts brown quickly, so keep an eye on them!).

To make the oatmeal:

Heat the water (and the salt, if using) in a small saucepan; bring to a rolling boil.

Stir in the oats, monk fruit sweetener, and cranberries (if using other berries, save them for topping).

Reduce the heat to low, and cook 5 minutes, stirring occasionally.

Cover, remove from the heat, and let stand 2 to 3 minutes.

Pour the oatmeal into a serving bowl; top with the walnuts.

TIP

You can easily multiply the servings for as many mouths as you need to feed.

PHASE 3; MAKES 1 SERVING.

6 Lunch or Dinner Entrées

Quick and easy but oh so tasty, wholesome, and Fat Flush friendly. That's the theme for the lunch and dinner entrées in this chapter. I have included packable or work-friendly lunches like Artichoke Chicken Salad to Go and Taco Tuesday (or Any Day) Salad, as well as quick-fix entrées (who said that egg dishes like the Artichoke Frittata are just for breakfast?), main-course salads, casseroles, and one-dish skillet meals that provide comfort food with a bit of flair—the Fat Flush way.

What's more, these recipes provide you and your family with protein power. And having protein power means your energy levels stay high longer, your blood sugar levels stay in balance, your immune system is strengthened, and the healing process is bolstered. Most importantly, your body's fat-burning and detoxing capabilities are stimulated.

You'll find scrumptious poultry dishes like Tex-Mex Turkey Jicama Tostadas and Lemon Garlic Rosemary Cornish Hens. And I've purposely included quite a few entrées made with beef and lamb (like Beefy Mushroom Burgers and special occasion Lamb Chops Glazed with Apricot Preserves). This is not by accident. These protein-rich foods are some of our best sources of both zinc and L-carnitine—two important nutrients that are lacking in most diets and essential for healing, hormonal balance, and fat burning.

And there's succulent seafood! What lurks beneath the sea? Omega-rich treasures galore! Eating two or more seafood meals a week can do a great deal to boost your omega-3 levels as well as slim your figure. And that translates to better health. The fattier fish (good fat, that is) are salmon, tuna, herring, anchovies, trout, mackerel, and whitefish. But don't dismiss their other compadres, such as shrimp, halibut, cod, flounder, crab, catfish, or snapper. They all do their part in the bigger equation of helping you and your family enjoy a healthier, more nutritious lifestyle.

Vegetarian and vegan Fat Flushers, you too will find many protein-rich entrées to delight the palate, such as Gingery Garlic Tempeh, Avocado Tofu Ceviche, and Quinoa "Risotto" with Caramelized Onions. Onions, leeks, shallots, scallions (or green onions), and garlic figure prominently in the entrée section. The onion family is a rich source of sulfur-based compounds and antioxidants, which are cleansing for the liver, anti-inflammatory, and helpful in bringing cholesterol levels down. Garlic, that lovely "stinking rose," contains similar sulfur-based compounds and is believed to contain potent antibiotic, antifungal, and antiparasitic properties.

I know you will enjoy the new selection of slow-cooker meals—they take care of themselves all day and greet you with heavenly aromas when you come home hungry and ready to eat. The easy seafood offerings, kebabs, and main-dish salads in this section are designed to provide you with some delicious main courses that take minimal time in the oven, on the grill, or in the skillet.

FAT FLUSH SECRET TIP

For phase 3 special occasions, you can make many chicken, fish, or lamb dishes unique by using a nut crust! In one small bowl, combine 3 or more tablespoons of ground flax seeds seasoned with your favorite herbs. In another bowl, place ¼ cup of Dijon mustard. And in a third bowl, place ½ cup of finely chopped toasted pumpkin seeds, sunflower seeds, walnuts, almonds, or macadamia nuts. Dip each breast, fillet, or chop in the flaxseed mixture, then the mustard, and finally the nut mixture to coat. Cook over medium-low heat in a skillet until cooked through.

RECIPES IN THIS CHAPTER   PAGE

RECIPES IN THIS CHAPTER

EASY-PACKED LUNCHES

The following recipes make it a snap to stay on the Fat Flush track when you need a healthy lunch to go. It can be tempting to grab whatever's quick and close by on a busy day. Why not set yourself up for success by being prepared with healthy choices! During the workweek, do yourself a favor by making a habit of fixing your lunch the night before. Throw one of these mouth-watering salads together while you're already in the kitchen fixing dinner or packing lunches for the kids. Then just grab it from the fridge on your way out the door in the morning. Here are some tips to help set yourself up as a lunch-to-go pro:

- Invest in a set of glass to-go containers with plastic lids.
- Get an insulated lunch bag to take cold salads or smoothies along.
- Keep bags of prechopped organic lettuce and other veggies in the fridge.
- Buy organic frozen veggies like green beans that you can toss in the container with your salad the night before—they'll slowly thaw out while keeping your salad colder longer.
- When cooking chicken or beef entrées like Lemon Chicken on the Grill or Sassy Beef and Vegetable Kebabs, make extra and save out a portion of protein to use in one of the following salads for lunch the next day.
- Prepackaged and frozen grilled chicken strips and cooked shrimp are great to keep in the freezer to use in a pinch for to-go salads. Just be sure to read the labels and avoid products with any added sugar, salt, or preservatives.

Spinach and Shrimp Salad

Mix this oh-so-simple salad in a container with a lid the night before; then grab it out of the fridge in the morning on your way to work.

1   cup spinach, rinsed and patted dry
½   cup cherry tomatoes, halved
¼   cup red onion, sliced
2   tablespoons hearts of palm, canned or bottled, rinsed and chopped
3   olives, diced
4   ounces cooked shrimp

Combine all the ingredients in a bowl and toss gently with a dressing (Chapter 9).

> **TIP**
> You can buy precooked shrimp in the meat or frozen foods section of your grocery store. Toss the frozen shrimp into your lunch salad the night before— it will help keep your salad cold and will be thawed enough to eat by lunchtime.

ALL PHASES; MAKES 1 SERVING.

Taco Tuesday (or Any Day) Salad

This healthy Mexican-flavored salad is so good, you won't even miss the tortilla!

1   cup romaine lettuce, chopped
½   cup cooked chicken, shredded
¼   cup red bell pepper, chopped
2   scallions, chopped
½   cup tomato, chopped
2   tablespoons organic salsa
¼   avocado, sliced
1   tablespoon cilantro, chopped
     Juice of ½ lime
     Dash of cumin

Layer the first 8 ingredients in a container.
Squeeze the lime juice over the top.
Sprinkle with the cumin.

Variation
- For phase 3, add ½ cup of organic, non-GMO, frozen corn kernels or ½ cup of black beans.

ALL PHASES; MAKES 1 SERVING.

Stuffed Avocado with Tuna Salad

This is a great, easy way to bring your lunch to work. Avocados are not only excellent sources of good fat that may help you to absorb nutrients from other food; they also contain almost 20 essential vitamins and minerals as well as beneficial compounds like lutein and zeaxanthin for eye health. The turmeric is delightfully aromatic and therapeutically supports liver function and acts as an anti-inflammatory. Serve with leafy greens and a drizzle of lemon juice.

1   (6-ounce) can tuna in water, rinsed and drained
1   tablespoon flaxseed oil
¼   cup celery, finely chopped
2   tablespoons onion, finely minced
½   teaspoon turmeric
1   medium avocado
    Juice of 1 lemon

Mix the tuna, flaxseed oil, celery, onion, and turmeric together.
Cut the avocado in half lengthwise and remove the pit.
Scoop out the flesh, reserving the hull.
Dice the avocado flesh and mix into the tuna mixture.
Sprinkle the lemon juice over all and spoon the mixture into the avocado hull.

Variations
- Replace the tuna with salmon, sardines, or mackerel.
- Replace the avocado with a red pepper or tomato, seeded and with the top removed.
- For phase 3, how about a couple of tablespoons of chopped walnuts for crunch?

PHASES 2 AND 3; MAKES 1 SERVING.

Thai-Time Steak Salad

Take advantage of the tasty mix of health-enhancing herbs and spices in this hearty salad.

¼   teaspoon turmeric
¼   teaspoon cinnamon
¼   teaspoon coriander
¼   teaspoon cumin
2   ounces cooked steak, sliced
2   cups mixed organic salad greens
½   teaspoon fresh ginger, minced
1   tablespoon shallots, diced
¼   avocado, sliced
¼   cup cilantro, chopped
    Juice of ½ lime
1   tablespoon hemp seeds

Combine the four spices in a bowl.
Sprinkle over the steak slices.
In a to-go bowl, toss the salad greens, ginger, and shallots.
Place the steak slices on top.
Garnish with the avocado and cilantro.
Squeeze the lime juice over the salad.
Sprinkle the hemp seeds over the top.

Variation
•   For phase 3, drizzle 1 tablespoon of toasted sesame oil over the salad.

ALL PHASES; MAKES 1 SERVING.

Artichoke Chicken Salad to Go

With its natural combination of fresh flavors, this salad is a to-go favorite!

2   cups romaine lettuce, chopped
½   cup green beans
2   sliced artichoke hearts
2   tablespoons almonds, sliced or chopped
4   ounces cooked chicken, sliced

Combine all the ingredients in a to-go container, and toss with Nutty Avocado Dressing (Chapter 9).

PHASE 3; MAKES 1 SERVING.

Creamy Lemon-Lime Crab Salad

A quickie all-in-one lunch, sweet crab meat is delectable with Creamy Lemon-Lime Yogurt Dressing. Please note that for those following the Fat Flushing food combination rules from The New Fat Flush Plan for phase 3, I consider yogurt (if it is made from whole milk and not nonfat) a dairy fat similar to butter, cream, and sour cream, and so yogurt combines with other protein foods.

1   pound crab, cooked and flaked
3   tablespoons lime juice
½   cup celery, chopped
1¼ cups Creamy Lemon-Lime Yogurt Dressing (Chapter 9)
4   cups mixed salad greens, shredded
2   tablespoons scallions, finely chopped

Combine all the ingredients, except the scallions, in a salad bowl.
Mix well and serve.
Garnish with the scallions.

PHASE 3; MAKES 4 SERVINGS.

SLOW-COOKER MEALS

Slow-Cooker Beef Stew

No time to fuss when you come home from work? Then pop this into your slow cooker or Crock-Pot before you leave for work in the morning, and you will have a comforting stew as your reward. Slow cooking over low heat makes the stew meat as tender as butter (or should I say flaxseed oil?).

1½ pounds stew meat, lean and trimmed of all visible fat, cut into chunks
4   Roma tomatoes, cut into chunks
2   scallions, thinly sliced
1   teaspoon Fat Flush Curry Seasoning (Chapter 10)
1   teaspoon cayenne
1   small head cauliflower, cut into florets
1   small head broccoli, cut into florets
1   carrot, grated
1   cup purified water

Mix all the ingredients in a 3½-quart or larger slow cooker.

Cover and cook on low for 6 to 8 hours until the beef is cooked through and the vegetables are tender.

Variations
- For phase 2, add 1 small sweet potato.
- For phase 3, replace 1 cup of water with 1 cup of sherry.

ALL PHASES; MAKES 4 SERVINGS.

No-Sweat Slow-Cooker Salsa Chicken

Nothing could be easier than throwing this together in the morning and coming home to enjoy it at the end of the day.

1   (6-pound) organic, free-range chicken, neck and giblets removed
1   (16-ounce) jar organic salsa
2   avocados, sliced

Rinse the chicken and pat dry. Place in the slow cooker.

Pour the whole jar of salsa over the chicken. Cover with the lid.

Cook on low 6 to 8 hours.

Transfer the chicken to a cutting board, carve, and spoon the salsa over each
    serving.

Top with the avocado slices.

Variation

•   If you're on phase 3, enjoy a dollop of organic sour cream on top!

ALL PHASES; MAKES 6 SERVINGS.

Ultimate Beef Brisket with Vegetables and Gravy

This brisket will be fall-off-your-fork tender and flavorful after cooking all day while you're away.

1   (3-pound) beef brisket, trimmed
2   cups bone broth
1   large onion stuck with 3 whole cloves
3   large carrots, cut into chunks
4   celery stalks with leaves, cut into 1-inch pieces
1   cup cauliflower florets
1   bay leaf
3   garlic cloves, minced
½   small head of cabbage, quartered
½   teaspoon cayenne

In a large skillet, sear the beef brisket over medium heat until browned.
Pour off the fat and place the brisket in the slow cooker.
Add the broth, onion, carrots, celery, cauliflower, bay leaf, and garlic.
Sprinkle the cabbage with the cayenne; then add to the pot.
Cover and cook on low for 8 to 10 hours.
Transfer the brisket to a serving platter.

Gravy:

Remove the bay leaf.
Mash the vegetables into the meat broth.
Bring to a boil and reduce to the desired consistency.
To serve, slice the cooked brisket in 1-inch slices.
Spoon the gravy over the brisket.

Variation
• For phases 2 and 3, add 1 large sweet potato, cut into chunks.

ALL PHASES; MAKES 4 SERVINGS.

Slow-Cooker Salmon with Pomegranate Glaze

This succulent salmon recipe is easy to prepare but has a definite gourmet flair. A spinach salad with shaved fennel makes a perfect accompaniment.

2   cups unsweetened pomegranate juice
1   tablespoon yacon syrup
1   teaspoon ground allspice
4   (6-ounce) salmon fillets
     Sea salt to taste (optional)
2   leeks, white part only, sliced

In a slow cooker combine the pomegranate juice, yacon syrup, and allspice.

Cover and cook on high for 30 minutes.

Cut a piece of parchment paper about 6 inches longer and wider than the slow cooker (you can use the lid as a guide).

Place the salmon fillets on the parchment paper; sprinkle with the sea salt and sliced leeks.

Set the parchment paper with the salmon into the slow cooker on top of the pomegranate mixture, leaving enough paper up the sides to lift the salmon out when done.

Cover and continue to cook on high for 20 to 30 minutes until the salmon is done.

Lift the parchment paper with the cooked salmon out of the slow cooker.

Place the fillets on a plate, and spoon the pomegranate glaze over the top.

PHASE 3; MAKES 4 SERVINGS.

Slow-Cooker Lamb and Portobello Risotto

This is an aromatic and filling all-in-one meal with a gourmet touch. Try topping it off with a dollop of Minty Dill Pesto (Chapter 10).

1   pound boneless leg of lamb, cut into bite-sized pieces
¼   teaspoon sea salt
½   teaspoon smoked paprika
     Avocado oil spray
½   cup shallots, peeled and chopped
1   pound baby portobello mushrooms, sliced
3   cloves garlic, minced
3   tablespoons fresh rosemary leaves
1   tablespoon fresh thyme leaves or 1 teaspoon dried
1   cup brown rice, rinsed
3   cups organic chicken broth
2   teaspoons lemon zest
2   cups baby arugula
1   cup baby spinach

Season the lamb with the sea salt and smoked paprika.

Spray a large skillet with the avocado oil; heat to medium.

Brown the lamb for 1 to 2 minutes per side.

Place in the slow cooker.

Add the shallots, mushrooms, garlic, 2 tablespoons of the rosemary, thyme, rice, and chicken broth.

Stir, cover, and cook on low for 6 to 8 hours.

Gently stir in the remaining rosemary, lemon zest, arugula, and spinach.

Let rest until the greens are just wilted, 5 to 10 minutes, and serve.

PHASE 3; MAKES 4 SERVINGS.

Slow-Cooker Curried Chicken

This tender chicken is smothered in a spice-rich, mouthwatering curry sauce.

Spice Rub:

1   teaspoon each ground cardamom, cumin, coriander, and sea salt
½   teaspoon each ground Ceylon cinnamon, turmeric, and cloves

Chicken:

6   organic, free-range chicken breasts, boneless and skinless
1   large Vidalia (or other sweet variety) onion, sliced and separated
    into rings
3   carrots, thinly sliced
2   sweet potatoes, peeled and cut into chunks
1   can water chestnuts, drained and rinsed
2   cups organic chicken broth
½   cup coconut milk
1½ tablespoons curry powder
1   tablespoon lemon juice
2   tablespoons fresh ginger, grated
1   clove garlic, minced
2   cups broccoli florets, chopped

Mix the spice-rub ingredients together in a small bowl.

Wash the chicken and pat dry.

Thoroughly coat the chicken with the spice rub; cover and refrigerate for 1 hour.

Place the onion in the bottom of the slow cooker.

Add the carrots, sweet potatoes, and water chestnuts.

In a small bowl, mix together the chicken broth, coconut milk, curry powder,
    lemon juice, sea salt, ginger, and garlic.

Pour half the liquid over the veggies in the slow cooker.

Add the chicken and gently pour the rest of the liquid over the top.

Cook on high for 4 hours or low for 6 hours, adding the broccoli for the last
    15 minutes.

Remove the chicken to a large bowl.

Skim any fat from the surface of the sauce, and spoon it and the vegetables
    over the chicken.

PHASE 3; MAKES 6 SERVINGS.

MAIN-DISH SALADS, CASSEROLES, AND ONE-DISH SKILLET MEALS

Artichoke Frittata

This is an easy-to-cook entrée when you don't feel like having heavy proteins at night or at lunch, for that matter. Artichokes contain silymarin — an antioxidant known to help protect the liver from toxic substances.

2   small leeks, sliced, white part only
1   garlic clove, minced
2   scallions, sliced
¼   cup bone broth
    Dried dill to taste
2   tablespoons water
4   eggs, lightly beaten
1   (3½-ounce) can artichoke hearts, rinsed and sliced
6   black olives, pitted and minced
2   tablespoons cilantro, chopped
1   teaspoon fresh lemon juice

In a medium skillet, sauté the leeks, garlic, scallions, and broth until the leeks are soft.

Spread evenly over the bottom of the skillet.

Mix the dill and water with the eggs and pour into the skillet.

Arrange the artichoke slices and olives on top of the egg mixture.

Sprinkle with the cilantro and cook over low heat until the egg mixture is set, about 8 minutes, shaking the skillet occasionally.

Cover the skillet handle and place the skillet under the broiler until the mixture is lightly brown, about 2 minutes.

Cut into wedges and drizzle with the lemon juice.

Variations
*   A bit of Homemade Salsa (Chapter 10) may be used as a topping.
*   For phase 3, add salt to taste.

ALL PHASES; MAKES 2 SERVINGS.

Baked Chicken and Artichoke Casserole

This is a comforting one-dish meal that's sure to please.

2   (5-ounce) chicken breasts, boneless and skinless
1   cup bone broth
½   medium red onion, diced
1   red bell pepper, chopped
1   (8-ounce) can artichoke hearts, rinsed and drained
4   garlic cloves, minced
6   black olives, chopped
     Juice of 1 lemon
1   (8-ounce) can no-salt–no-sugar-added tomato sauce
     Handful of fresh cilantro, chopped

Preheat the oven to 350°F.

In a medium pot, place the chicken breasts and broth and simmer.

Poach the chicken until tender.

When cooked, shred the chicken into bite-sized pieces.

Place the chicken, onion, red bell pepper, artichoke hearts, garlic, olives, and
    lemon juice in a medium casserole dish and mix well.

Cover and bake in the oven for 45 minutes.

Stir the tomato sauce into the casserole and return to the oven for 20 minutes
    uncovered.

Mix in the cilantro and serve.

Variations

- For phases 2 and 3, try replacing the cilantro with a tablespoon of fresh
  basil for a Mediterranean feel.
- For phase 3, stir in 1 tablespoon of sherry during the last 10 minutes of
  cooking.

ALL PHASES; MAKES 2 SERVINGS.

Chicken Stir-Fry with a Touch of Turmeric

A key ingredient in Indian dishes, turmeric is a wonderful Fat Flush seasoning because it helps to tone the liver, is a blood sugar regulator, and is especially high in beta-carotene, a nutrient known to support skin health. Its musky warm aroma is very inviting.

¼   cup no-salt-added chicken broth or 1-2-3 Chicken Broth
     (Chapter 11)
1   medium onion, cut into ½-inch slices
1   cup mushrooms, sliced
1   pound chicken breast, boned, skinned, and cut into strips
½   cup water chestnuts
2   cups broccoli florets
2   cups cauliflower florets
1   teaspoon ground turmeric
1   teaspoon ground cumin

In a large skillet, heat the broth over medium heat.

Add the onion and cook until soft, about 3 to 5 minutes.

Add the mushrooms and cook until soft, about another 1 minute.

Add the chicken and cook an additional 5 minutes.

Finally, add the water chestnuts, broccoli, cauliflower, and spices.

Cook until tender, another 6 minutes.

Variations
- You may use turkey instead of chicken.
- For phase 3, add ⅛ teaspoon of ground saffron over the top with a squeeze of lime.

ALL PHASES; MAKES 4 SERVINGS.

Fat Flush Shepherd's Pie

Here's a delicious classic that works well with Kari's Marvelously Mashed Cauliflower.

1   pound lean ground beef
1   medium onion, chopped
4   garlic cloves, minced
1   green pepper, chopped
8   ounces mushrooms, sliced
1   teaspoon cayenne
½   teaspoon onion powder
½   teaspoon garlic powder
2   small carrots, grated
12 black olives, pitted and chopped
    Handful of fresh cilantro, chopped
1   (8-ounce) can no-salt–no-sugar-added tomato sauce
1   (14½-ounce) can no-salt–no sugar-added diced tomatoes
2   cups mashed cauliflower, as prepared in Kari's Marvelously Mashed
    Cauliflower (Chapter 7)

Preheat the oven to 350°F.

In a large skillet, brown the ground beef, onion, and garlic.

When the beef is nearly done, add the green pepper, mushrooms, cayenne, onion powder, and garlic powder. When the beef is no longer pink, transfer to a large casserole dish.

Add the carrots, olives, cilantro, tomato sauce, and diced tomatoes to the casserole dish and mix well.

Spread the mashed cauliflower over the top.

Bake in the oven for 30 minutes.

Place under the broiler for 3 minutes or until browned on top.

Variations

- Ground turkey may be used instead of beef.
- For phase 3, add ½ teaspoon of salt to the casserole mixture before baking.

ALL PHASES; MAKES 4 SERVINGS.

Hearty Mushroom Chili

You won't be missing the beans with this chili. The mushrooms are a great bean substitute and provide lots of healthy B vitamins, which are so good for the nervous system and the skin. Accompany with a nice leafy green salad and a Fat Flush dressing of your choice.

1 pound lean ground beef
1 cup onions, chopped
4 garlic cloves, minced
1 green pepper, chopped
1 pound mushrooms, sliced
12 black olives, chopped
1 (28-ounce) can no-salt–no sugar-added tomato puree
2 (14½-ounce) cans no-salt–no sugar-added diced tomatoes
1 tablespoon ground fennel
1 teaspoon ground cumin
1 teaspoon garlic powder
1 teaspoon onion powder
   Cayenne to taste
   Juice of 1 lime
   Fresh cilantro for garnish

In a large pot over medium heat, place the beef, onions, and garlic and brown until the beef is nearly done.

Add the green pepper and mushrooms and cook until the beef is no longer pink.

Stir in the remaining ingredients except the cilantro.

Bring to a boil, reduce the heat, and simmer for at least 1 hour.

Garnish with the cilantro just before serving.

TIP

Freezes well.

Variation
•   For phase 3, add ½ teaspoon of salt to the seasonings.

ALL PHASES; MAKES 4 SERVINGS.

Garlicky Herbed Chicken Thighs

If you love garlic, you'll really enjoy this delicious, tender chicken recipe! Serve alongside Kari's Marvelously Mashed Cauliflower (Chapter 7) and a green salad.

12	cloves garlic, peeled and smashed
6	shallots, peeled and quartered
2	carrots, sliced
1	pound crimini mushrooms, halved
6	(or a dozen if they're very small) organic, free-range chicken thighs, boneless and skinless
1	teaspoon turmeric
1	teaspoon dry mustard
2	tablespoons each, chopped fresh herbs: rosemary, thyme, sage, and marjoram
1	cup organic chicken broth

Place the garlic in the slow cooker and top with the shallots, carrots, and mushrooms.

Rinse the chicken thighs and pat dry.

Sprinkle the thighs with turmeric and dry mustard.

Set the thighs on top of the veggies.

Add the herbs and chicken broth.

Cook on low for 6 hours.

PHASES 2 AND 3; MAKES 6 SERVINGS.

Greek-Inspired Shrimp Salad

This mixed salad has a definite Mediterranean flair. It's easy to throw together and looks beautiful on the plate. Perfect with Greek Style Ranch (Chapter 9).

1   cup romaine lettuce
1   cup spinach
½   cup grape tomatoes, halved lengthwise
½   red onion, sliced
1   English cucumber, sliced
¼   cup Kalamata olives, rinsed, drained, and diced
8   ounces shrimp, cooked and peeled

Combine all the ingredients in a bowl.
Toss with dressing.

Variation
• For phase 3, add ½ cup of feta cheese.

ALL PHASES; MAKES 2 SERVINGS.

Grilled Steak Salad with Horseradish Dressing

Cool buttery lettuce topped with warm grilled steak just hits the spot on a hot summer night. The piquant horseradish dressing finishes it off perfectly.

1½	pounds skirt steak, cut crosswise into 4 pieces
1	teaspoon ground cumin
½	teaspoon ground turmeric
½	teaspoon garlic powder
1	tablespoon prepared horseradish (I like Bubbie's!)
1	scallion, chopped
2	tablespoons extra virgin olive oil
2	tablespoons apple cider vinegar
1	teaspoon Dijon mustard
½	cup daikon radish, thinly sliced
½	cup snap peas, sliced
1	head Bibb lettuce, torn into bite-sized pieces

Heat the grill or a heavy skillet on medium-high heat.

Season the steak with the cumin, turmeric, and garlic powder and cook to desired doneness.

Let the steak rest on a cutting board for 10 minutes while preparing the salad.

In a small bowl, combine the horseradish, scallion, and 1 tablespoon each of the olive oil and apple cider vinegar.

Set aside.

In a large bowl, whisk the Dijon mustard with the remaining oil and vinegar.

Add the radishes, snap peas, and lettuce and toss gently.

Divide the salad evenly onto four plates, slice each piece of steak into strips, and set the steak strips on top of the salad.

Spoon the horseradish vinaigrette over the steak.

ALL PHASES; MAKES 4 SERVINGS.

The Best Grilled Chicken Salad

This bountiful salad is great for lunch or a light dinner.

4   cups fresh spinach leaves, torn
2   cups green or red leaf lettuce, romaine, or baby greens, torn
2   tablespoons parsley, chopped
2   tablespoons rosemary, chopped
2   tablespoons basil, chopped
2   tablespoons cilantro, chopped
2   tablespoons chives, chopped
1   cucumber, peeled and diced
1   red bell pepper, cut into strips
1   yellow bell pepper, cut into strips
½   cup cherry tomatoes, halved
4   slices red onion, separated into rings
¼   cup apple cider vinegar
2   tablespoons flaxseed oil
    Juice of 2 limes
    Juice of 1 lemon
1   pound grilled chicken breast, chilled and diced

Combine all the ingredients except the chicken in a large bowl and toss until
    evenly mixed.
Arrange the chicken on top of the salad.

ALL PHASES; MAKES 4 SERVINGS.

Shrimp Nicoise Salad

A fresh and beautiful salad for a light lunch or dinner.

Salad:

8   cups mixed leafy greens (Boston, romaine, baby spinach, etc.), torn
4   scallions, sliced, or fresh chives
2   cups fresh green beans, steamed and chilled
4   hard-boiled eggs, quartered
1   cup black olives, halved
1   cup cherry tomatoes, halved
1   pound medium shrimp, fresh or frozen, cooked, peeled, and
    deveined

Dressing:

¼   cup apple cider vinegar
½   teaspoon dry mustard
½   teaspoon garlic powder
¼   teaspoon dried dillweed
    Pinch of salt
¼   cup flaxseed oil
    Lemon wedges for garnish

Decoratively arrange all the salad ingredients (except the shrimp) on a plate.
Whisk together the dressing ingredients; drizzle over the salad.
Top with the shrimp and garnish with the lemon wedges.

Variation

• You can replace the fresh or frozen shrimp with four (6-ounce) cans of
  shrimp, rinsed and drained.

ALL PHASES; MAKES 4 SERVINGS.

Mexican Salad

The cumin, cayenne, and garlic give this all-in-one salad a south of the border flair.

1 pound flank steak, thinly sliced
2 tablespoons bone broth
1 onion, chopped
4 garlic cloves, minced
2 teaspoons ground cumin
1 teaspoon cayenne
¼ cup no-salt–no-sugar-added tomato sauce
2 tablespoons tomato paste
1 tablespoon apple cider vinegar
   Sea salt to taste
8 cups leafy greens (romaine, spinach, mixed lettuces)
3 scallions, sliced
2 tomatoes, chopped
¼ cup black olives
   Baked tortilla chips or blue corn chips

In a skillet, brown the flank steak over medium heat.
Cook until the steak is almost cooked through.
Add the broth.
Add the onion and garlic and cook for 2 minutes.
Add the cumin, cayenne, tomato sauce, tomato paste, vinegar, and salt.
Heat until lightly bubbly, reduce the heat, and simmer for 10 to 15 minutes.
Place 2 cups of the greens per serving on a plate.
Top with the beef mixture, scallions, tomatoes, and olives.
Serve with a side of chips.

TIP
For phases 1 and 2, omit the salt and chips.

PHASE 3; MAKES 4 SERVINGS.

VEGETARIAN AND VEGAN FRIENDLY

Tofu-Veggie Stir-Sauté

Try this vegetarian dish as a change from meat.

¼   cup no-salt-added vegetable broth or 1-2-3 Vegetable Broth
     (Chapter 11)
2   garlic cloves, minced
2   cups broccoli florets
1   red pepper, cut into 1-inch squares
1   cup asparagus, cut into 1-inch lengths
1   cup zucchini, halved and cut into ½-inch slices
1   carrot, thinly sliced
1   leek, cut into ¼-inch slices
1   tomato, cut into small cubes
1   pound firm tofu, washed, drained, and cut into 1-inch cubes

In a large skillet, heat the broth over medium heat.

Add the garlic and sauté for 1 minute.

Add the broccoli, red pepper, asparagus, zucchini, and carrot and stir-sauté
    until crisp-tender.

Add the leek and the tomato and stir-sauté for 2 minutes.

Add the tofu and stir-sauté until the tofu is heated through.

Variation
• For phase 3, add salt to season or 2 tablespoons of tamari.

ALL PHASES; MAKES 4 SERVINGS.

Avocado Tofu Ceviche

This fresh and tasty vegetarian entrée is high in protein and rich antioxidants.

    Juice of 6 limes
1   garlic clove, minced
3   tablespoons parsley, minced
3   tablespoons cilantro, minced
½   teaspoon sea salt (optional)
½   pound tofu, cut into 1-inch slices
1   cup cherry tomatoes (optional)
2   onions, thinly sliced
2   avocados, halved

Mix the lime juice, garlic, parsley, cilantro, and salt, if using.

Pour over the tofu slices and marinate for 30 minutes or more.

Pour off the excess juice, and add the tomatoes, if using, and the onions.

Mix and serve in the avocado halves.

ALL PHASES; MAKES 4 SERVINGS.

Gingery Garlic Tempeh

This entrée will be a satisfying standby for our vegan and vegetarian Fat Flushers, but it's so simple and delicious that everyone will want to give it a try! It's especially nice with a side of brown rice and Carrots and Snow Peas with Parsley (Chapter 7).

16 ounces tempeh
2   tablespoons low-sodium, wheat-free tamari
1   tablespoon yacon syrup or to taste
2   cloves garlic, crushed
2   teaspoons fresh ginger, grated
    Toasted sesame seed oil
½   cup scallions, chopped

Steam the tempeh for 10 minutes (a metal vegetable steamer in a lidded saucepan over boiling water works well for this).

Set aside.

After it cools, slice into 4 portions.

Whisk the tamari, yacon syrup, garlic, and ginger together and pour over the tempeh.

Marinate in the refrigerator for 2 hours.

Lightly oil a skillet with the sesame seed oil.

Cook the tempeh on medium heat for about 3 minutes.

Flip it over and brush with the marinade, cooking until golden brown, about 5 minutes.

Top with the chopped scallions.

PHASE 3; MAKES 4 SERVINGS.

Butternut Squash Stuffed with Quinoa and Cashews

This vegetarian dish is chock-full of protein, healthy fats, and vitamin-rich veggies. Start off with a cup of hot Shiitake Mushroom Soup (Chapter 11) and you'll be warm and satisfied all evening.

2	small butternut squash
¼	cup water
¼	cups vegetable broth
1	cup mushrooms, chopped
1	cup spinach, chopped
¼	cup shallots, diced
1	teaspoon dried thyme
¼	teaspoon dried sage
½	cup cashews
1	cup cooked quinoa

Cut the squash in half lengthwise.

Scoop out the seeds.

Pour the water into a rimmed baking sheet.

Place the squash on the baking sheet, with the cut side down.

Bake at 375° for 35 minutes.

Heat a skillet to medium heat.

Add ¼ cup of the vegetable broth.

Stir in the mushrooms, spinach, shallots, thyme, sage, and cashews.

Stir until the veggies are softened.

Mix the cooked quinoa into the veggies.

With a fork, loosen the flesh of the butternut squash, making more room around the hole where the seeds were removed.

Spoon the quinoa mixture into the squash.

Pop the stuffed squash back into the oven for 10 minutes until heated through.

PHASE 3; MAKES 4 SERVINGS.

Lentil and Quinoa Pasta with Mushroom Sauce

Lentils and quinoa provide the protein, while the veggies and mushrooms make a delicious, savory sauce.

1   garlic clove, minced
½   onion, finely chopped
1   stalk celery, finely chopped
1   carrot, finely chopped
2   tablespoons extra virgin olive oil
1½   pounds tomatoes, fresh or canned, whole peeled
1   cup mushrooms, coarsely sliced
1   cup lentils, cooked and drained
¼   teaspoon salt (optional)
1   pound lentil and quinoa pasta (Ancient Harvest), cooked and
       drained

Sauté the garlic, onion, celery, and carrots in the oil.
Add the tomatoes and simmer for 20 minutes.
Add the mushrooms and lentils and simmer 20 minutes longer.
Add the salt, if using.
Toss with the cooked pasta.

PHASE 3; MAKES 6 SERVINGS.

Tempeh Chili

Sometimes a bowl of chili just fits the bill, and this vegetarian recipe pays up big time!

2   (8-ounce) packages tempeh
2   (14-ounce) cans organic diced tomatoes (Muir Glen)
1   medium onion, diced
3 to 4 stalks celery, diced
4 to 6 garlic cloves, minced
1   tablespoon cumin
1   teaspoon ground coriander
1   teaspoon oregano
¼   teaspoon garlic powder
⅛   teaspoon ground cloves
¼   teaspoon cayenne or to taste
¼   teaspoon powdered jalapeño chili or to taste
½   teaspoon salt (optional)
3   tablespoons apple cider vinegar
½   cup chopped cilantro
2   tablespoons dried parsley
½ to 1 cup vegetable broth
8   ounces mushrooms, diced
      Dash of SweetLeaf Stevia, if needed

Combine all the ingredients except the mushrooms and stevia in a large soup pot over medium heat.

Bring to a boil; reduce the heat, and simmer, covered, for about 45 minutes or until the vegetables are fork-tender.

Add the mushrooms and simmer an additional 10 minutes.

Taste and adjust the spices as needed.

If the chili tastes too spicy or sour, add a dash of stevia.

PHASE 3; MAKES 4 TO 6 SERVINGS.

Sweet-and-Sour Tempeh

When you're in the mood for Asian food, this sweet-and-sour sensation is a wonderful alternative to sugar- and MSG-laden alternatives.

¼   cup water
¼   cup low-sodium, wheat-free tamari
½   teaspoon ground coriander
1   garlic clove, minced
2   packages tempeh, cut into 1-inch cubes
¼   cup arrowroot

Preheat the oven to 350°F.
In a small bowl, mix the water, tamari, coriander, and garlic.
Dip the tempeh into the mixture; then drain and coat with the arrowroot.
Bake for 20 minutes.

Sweet and Sour Sauce

Makes about 1 cup.

1   onion, finely chopped
1   tablespoon toasted sesame oil
1¼   cups water
2½   tablespoons barley malt (or rice malt)
4   tablespoons low-sodium, wheat-free tamari (or soy sauce)
1   tablespoon rice vinegar
1   tablespoon tahini
1   teaspoon grated ginger
2   scallions, finely chopped
2   teaspoons kuzu diluted in 2 tablespoons cold water

Sauté the onion in the oil for 5 minutes.
Add the water, malt, tamari, vinegar, tahini, ginger, and scallions.
Bring to a boil.
Thicken with the kuzu and serve over the tempeh.

Variation

- Instead of tempeh, you can use tofu, chicken, or turkey.

PHASE 3; MAKES 4 SERVINGS.

Quinoa "Risotto" with Caramelized Onions

Quinoa is a nutritional powerhouse. It's high in protein and fiber, it's rich in vitamins and minerals, and it happens to be one of the only plant foods that contain all nine essential amino acids.

2   tablespoons extra virgin olive oil
1   red bell pepper, diced
2   cups sweet onions, sliced very thin
      Bone broth (chicken) or vegetable broth, as needed
      Sea salt to taste
1½ cups quinoa, rinsed and drained
2½ cups water
½   teaspoon sea salt

Heat 1 tablespoon of the oil in a large nonstick skillet.

Add the peppers and the onions; cook over low heat, stirring frequently, until the peppers are soft and the onions are golden, about 25 minutes (add a little broth as needed to keep the onions from sticking to the pan).

Season with the salt; keep warm.

Heat the remaining tablespoon of oil in a large saucepan.

Add the quinoa; cook over medium-high heat, stirring, until lightly browned, about 7 to 8 minutes.

Add the 2½ cups of water and the ½ teaspoon of sea salt; bring to a boil.

Cover tightly; simmer until the water has been absorbed and the quinoa is thoroughly cooked, about 15 minutes.

Fluff with a fork; stir in the warm peppers and onions.

PHASES 2 AND 3; MAKES 6 TO 8 SERVINGS.

Mung Bean Dal

A traditional Indian comfort food, Dal is usually made with lentils. This mung bean version is a delicious twist on a particularly satisfying dish.

1   tablespoon sesame oil
½   teaspoon cinnamon
½   teaspoon cumin
1   onion, minced
3   cups mung beans
1   strip kombu
12 cups water
3   cups basmati rice or brown rice, for serving
¼   teaspoon sea salt (optional)
6   cilantro sprigs for garnish
6   slices fresh lemon for garnish

Heat the oil in a soup pot.

Sauté the cinnamon, cumin, and onion.

Add the beans, kombu, and water.

Cook for 45 to 60 minutes.

Add the salt, if using.

Serve over basmati or brown rice, garnished with the cilantro and lemon slices.

Variation
• Use chickpeas instead of mung beans.

PHASE 3; MAKES 6 SERVINGS.

FISH AND SEAFOOD

Simply Baked Fish

Fat Flushers find this recipe easy and fast. It lends itself beautifully to any white fish.

1   (5-ounce) fish fillet (halibut, cod, grouper, flounder)
4   tablespoons lemon juice
1   clove garlic, minced
1   tablespoon fresh parsley, chopped
1   teaspoon gingerroot, grated
    Lemon wedges for garnish

Preheat the oven to 350°F.

Place all the ingredients in a bowl; mix well, making sure the fillets are evenly coated with spices.

Let stand for 15 minutes.

Place the fish in a shallow pan and bake for about 12 minutes or until the fish is flaky.

Baste occasionally with the marinade.

Garnish with a lemon wedge.

Serve immediately.

Variations
• For phase 2, substitute cilantro or garlic for the gingerroot.
• For phase 3, substitute thyme for the gingerroot and add a pinch of salt to taste.

ALL PHASES; MAKES 1 SERVING.

Gingerly Grilled Salmon

Ginger goes well with any fish, but it has a special affinity for salmon.

4   tablespoons bone broth
1   bay leaf, finely chopped
5   garlic cloves, minced
4   (5 ounce) salmon fillets
1   tablespoon apple cider vinegar
⅛   teaspoon ground ginger
10 black olives, chopped
1   tomato, chopped
½   red onion, sliced

Place 2 tablespoons of the broth plus the bay leaf and garlic in a small bowl.

In a glass baking dish, coat the fish with the spices and arrange the coated fish in a single layer in the dish. Cover and refrigerate for at least 2 hours or overnight.

Whisk the remaining broth, vinegar, and ginger in a medium bowl.

Add the olives, tomato, and red onion.

Set aside.

Preheat the broiler.

Broil (or grill) the salmon for about 9 minutes or until the salmon is opaque in the center.

Transfer to serving plates and top with the olives, tomato, and onion.

ALL PHASES; MAKES 4 SERVINGS.

Salmon Cakes

These cakes are certainly savory just the way they are. However, when you move on to phase 3, try them with Gingered Asparagus (Chapter 7) and a tablespoon or two of Minty Dill Pesto (Chapter10) for a special flavor and natural digestive-aid treat.

8   ounces cooked salmon fillet, skinned
¼   cup scallions, finely chopped
2   teaspoons fresh dill
2   garlic cloves, minced
     Splash of fresh lemon juice
1   egg, beaten

Preheat the oven to 350°F.
Place the salmon in a large bowl and separate with a fork.
Mix in the scallions, dill, garlic, lemon juice, and egg.
Shape the mixture into two patties, about ¾ inch thick.
Place the patties in a baking dish or on a baking sheet and put in the oven.
Bake for about 15 minutes or until golden brown and cooked through.

ALL PHASES; MAKES 2 SERVINGS.

Seafood Kebabs

Seafood Kebabs are Fat Flush favorites for parties and cookouts. This recipe calls for 8 skewers.

1   pound white fish (cod, sole, or flounder), cut into 1-inch cubes
    Juice of 2 lemons
1   tablespoon no-salt-added vegetable broth or 1-2-3 Vegetable
    Broth (Chapter 11)
3   tablespoons fresh parsley, chopped
1   teaspoon fresh ginger, grated, or dash of dried ginger
2   garlic cloves, minced
6   baby zucchinis, each cut into four chunks
16 button mushrooms
8   cherry tomatoes

In a large bowl, marinate the fish with the lemon juice, broth, parsley, ginger, and garlic; cover and refrigerate for 1 hour, turning the fish over every 20 minutes.

Preheat the broiler for 5 minutes on high.

Remove the fish from the marinade.

Using skewers, thread the fish, zucchini pieces, mushrooms, and tomatoes alternately.

Grill or broil for about 10 minutes, turning occasionally, until the fish is cooked through.

Variation

• For phase 3, you may add a splash of dry vermouth to the marinade.

ALL PHASES; MAKES 4 SERVINGS.

Shrimp-Stuffed Portobello Mushrooms

The shrimp and portobello mushrooms are a meaty combination that pro-vides satiety and satisfaction.

2   celery stalks, chopped
2   scallions, chopped
4   button mushrooms, chopped
2   garlic cloves, chopped
4   tablespoons bone broth
8   ounces of shrimp, cooked, peeled, and deveined
6   black olives, chopped
1   Roma tomato, chopped
4   tablespoons no-salt-no-sugar-added tomato sauce
     Pinch of cayenne
     Juice of ½ lemon
1   tablespoon fresh cilantro, chopped
6   portobello mushroom caps (approximately 4 inches in diameter),
     with underside brown gills removed

Preheat the oven to 400°F.

In a skillet over medium heat, sauté the celery, scallions, button mushrooms, and garlic in 2 tablespoons of broth for 8 to 10 minutes or until soft, adding more broth as needed.

Place the sautéed veggies in a food processor with the cooked shrimp and all the remaining ingredients except the portobello caps.

Pulse the processor about 10 times until the mixture is finely chopped.

Place spoonfuls of the mixture on the underside of the portobello mush-rooms.

Bake on a baking sheet for 30 minutes.

Serve immediately.

ALL PHASES; MAKES 2 SERVINGS (3 CAPS APIECE).

Marinated Fish in Jicama Soft Taco Shells

These fish tacos are swimming in flavor and feature a new twist on the traditional taco shell.

Marinade and Fish:

⅓ cup extra virgin olive oil
½ cup cilantro, chopped
1 teaspoon ground cumin
1 jalapeño, seeded and chopped
Zest of 1 large or 2 small limes (reserve juice)
1 teaspoon sea salt
1½ pounds white fish like sole or bass fillets

Jicama Soft Tortillas and Fillings:

1 cup tomato, diced
½ cup scallions, sliced
1 jalapeño, seeded and chopped
1 avocado, peeled, seeded, and diced
½ cup cilantro, chopped
2 medium jicamas

Step 1:

Combine the marinade ingredients in a blender and process until a paste is formed.

Add the paste to a bowl, coat the fish in the paste, and let the fish marinate for 20 minutes.

Preheat the oven to 375°F.

Remove the fish from the bowl and place on a parchment-lined baking sheet and bake for 10 minutes.

Step 2:

Gently toss the tomato, scallions, jalapeño, avocado, and cilantro together in a bowl and drizzle with the reserved lime juice.

Step 3:

Peel the jicamas and carefully slice into thin rounds with a mandolin or sharp
kitchen knife.

Place the jicama rounds in a steamer basket over boiling water for about 3
minutes or until they become flexible.

Step 4:

Fold each jicama round in half. Fill with the fish, add the topping mix, and
enjoy!

ALL PHASES; MAKES 4 SERVINGS.

Salmon Fillet Infused with Herbs and Spices

You can't go wrong with this combination of savory herbs and satisfying salmon! Double the recipe and have enough leftover fish to make Simple Salmon Patties (the recipe follows later in the chapter) for lunch the next day.

1   pound salmon fillet
     Mixed greens or spinach leaves, for serving

Marinade:

2   tablespoons apple cider vinegar
1   tablespoon avocado oil
1   garlic clove, minced
½   teaspoon dry mustard
½   teaspoon coriander
½   teaspoon cumin
1   tablespoon fresh lemon juice
2   tablespoons Italian (flat) parsley, chopped
1   tablespoon dill, chopped

Combine the marinade ingredients in a blender or mini–food processor and pour into a large plastic bag with a zipper closure.

Add the salmon fillet, turning to coat.

Refrigerate no more than 2 hours, turning occasionally.

Preheat the oven to 375°F.

Lightly coat a 9- by 13-inch baking pan with the avocado oil spray.

Place the salmon in the baking dish and cover with the marinade.

Bake the salmon about 25 minutes or until almost cooked through.

Broil 1 to 2 minutes just until the salmon flakes and a golden herb crust starts to form (watch carefully to ensure it doesn't burn).

Serve hot or chilled over mixed greens or fresh spinach leaves.

Variation

• For phase 3, add 1 tablespoon of raw honey to the marinade.

ALL PHASES; MAKES 4 SERVINGS.

Spicy Tuna Croquettes

Jalapeño, high in vitamin C and joint-loving capsaicin, adds a touch of spice to these simple croquettes. Instead of the usual bread crumbs, leftover baked sweet potato adds richness and helps the croquettes hold their shape.

Avocado oil spray
2   (5-ounce) cans albacore tuna, drained
4   scallions, chopped
2   tablespoons fresh cilantro, finely minced
1   cup mashed, oven-baked sweet potato
2   large eggs
1   tablespoon jalapeño, minced
Zest of ½ lemon
2   lemons, cut into wedges

Preheat the oven to 350°F.

Spray a baking sheet with the avocado oil.

Combine all the ingredients (except for the lemon wedges) in a large bowl.

Mix well and form into four small loaf-shaped croquettes.

Place on the prepared baking sheet and bake for 10 minutes; flip over and bake for 10 more minutes.

Serve with the fresh lemon wedges.

TIP

This recipe can easily be doubled or tripled.

Variation

• If you'd like an egg-free version, substitute flax seeds for the eggs. Just mix 1 tablespoon of ground flax seeds with 2 tablespoons of water—per egg— and let the mixture sit in the fridge for 10 minutes before adding it to the recipe.

PHASES 2 AND 3; MAKES 2 SERVINGS.

Lemon-Almond–Crusted Trout Fillets

This fresh fish recipe is really a catch! It combines the classic flavors of lemon, garlic, and parsley with crunchy almonds and health-boosting coconut oil to enhance the flavor of the trout.

1   tablespoon coconut oil
4   trout fillets
    Zest and juice of 1 lemon
1   cup roasted almonds, chopped
1   tablespoon fresh thyme, chopped
¼   cup parsley, chopped
1   clove garlic, minced
¼   teaspoon sea salt
1   lemon, cut into wedges

Preheat the oven to 350°F.

Coat the bottom of a baking dish with a little bit of the coconut oil.

Set the trout fillets in the baking dish and brush with the remainder of the coconut oil.

In a small bowl, combine the zest and juice of 1 lemon, almonds, thyme, parsley, garlic, and sea salt.

Pat the mixture firmly onto the tops of the trout fillets.

Bake for about 10 minutes or until the fish flakes easily with a fork.

Garnish with the fresh lemon wedges.

PHASE 3; MAKES 4 SERVINGS.

Saucy Cucumber Basil Halibut

Unlike many of the other recipes in which you may substitute dried herbs for fresh, the basil really needs to be fresh in this fish dish. The pungent taste of fresh basil truly sets off the whole recipe and makes the dish a refreshing entrée for a summery kind of day.

4   (5-ounce) halibut fillets
    Juice of ½ lemon
1   pound cucumber, skinned and grated
1   cup plain, whole-milk yogurt
1½ teaspoons fresh lemon juice
3   teaspoons fresh basil, chopped

Preheat the oven to 300°F.

Place the fillets in a baking dish or on a nonstick baking sheet.

Squeeze the lemon over the top of the fish.

Bake, uncovered, for about 10 to 15 minutes (depending upon the thickness of the fish) or until the fish is cooked and flakes easily with a fork.

While the fish is in the oven, place the cucumber, yogurt, lemon juice, and basil in a large skillet to make the sauce.

Cook over low heat until the sauce is hot, making sure that the sauce doesn't boil.

Serve the fish topped with sauce.

Variation
•   As an alternative to the fresh basil, 1 teaspoon of dried oregano or dill will give this dish some zip.

PHASE 3; MAKES 4 SERVINGS.

Blackened Red Snapper

Drawn from colorful Cajun cuisine, this mouthwatering fish is great alongside another Southern star, Dilly Okra (Chapter 7).

1	tablespoon paprika
½	teaspoon onion powder
1	teaspoon cayenne
½	teaspoon dried thyme
½	teaspoon dried oregano
½	teaspoon dried basil
½	teaspoon sea salt (optional)
6	(5-ounce) red snapper fillets, about 1 inch thick
5	tablespoons extra virgin olive oil
6	lemon wedges for garnish

Combine the spices, herbs, and salt, if using, on a platter.

Place a cast-iron skillet over medium heat until very hot.

Dip the red snapper in the oil and coat with the spice mixture.

Place the fish in the hot skillet for 1 minute.

Turn and char the other side.

Remove from the pan.

Serve garnished with the lemon wedges.

PHASE 3; MAKES 6 SERVINGS.

Simple Salmon Patties

These are great for a simple dinner or lunch entrée. Sprinkle with freshly snipped chives for a fun twist and restaurant-worthy presentation.

	Extra virgin olive oil cooking spray
1	pound salmon fillet, cooked, or 1 pound canned salmon, drained well
½	medium sweet onion, minced
¼	cup celery, minced
2	tablespoons dillweed, minced
2	tablespoons Italian (flat) parsley, minced
1	garlic clove, minced
1	tablespoon fresh lemon juice or fresh lime juice
2	eggs, beaten
2	teaspoons Dijon mustard
½	cup flax crackers, crumbled

Preheat the oven to 350°F.

Lightly coat a baking sheet with the cooking spray.

In a large bowl, flake the salmon with a fork.

Combine with the remaining ingredients.

Shape the mixture into 8 patties and place the patties on a baking sheet.

Bake for 20 to 25 minutes or until nicely browned and cooked through.

TIP

This freezes and reheats well.

PHASE 3; MAKES 4 SERVINGS.

POULTRY

Limey Chicken

The coriander imparts a curry-like flavor. Coriander is a marvelous spice that is from the seed of the cilantro plant. Serve with a fresh garden salad.

Juice of 2 limes
1   garlic clove, minced
½   teaspoon dried ginger
½   teaspoon coriander
4   (5-ounce) chicken thighs or breasts, skinned
Lemon slices for garnish

Preheat the oven to 350°F.
In a small bowl, combine the lime juice, garlic, ginger, and coriander.
Rub the mixture onto the chicken.
Place the chicken in a casserole dish or baking pan and cover.
Bake about 45 minutes or until tender.
Serve hot, garnished with the lemon slices.

Variation
•   For phase 3, you may add ½ teaspoon of salt to the spice mixture.

ALL PHASES; MAKES 4 SERVINGS.

Chicken with Dill

This is as easy as can be. I have used this recipe many times when I have come home from work. I put it all together even before I take my coat off.

3   garlic cloves, minced
2   (5-ounce) chicken breasts, boned, skinned, and halved
½   teaspoon dried dill
¼   cup fresh lemon juice
½   cup bone broth

Preheat the oven to 350°F.

Rub the garlic on the chicken.

Place the chicken in a baking dish and sprinkle with the dill and lemon juice.

Pour the broth over the chicken.

Bake for 45 minutes or until the chicken is cooked through.

ALL PHASES; MAKES 2 SERVINGS.

Tangy Chicken with Tomatillos

Tomatillos, most commonly used in salsas, have a sweet-and-sour flavor that provides this dish with a most memorable and tangy taste. Kari's Marvelously Mashed Cauliflower is an integral component of this taste sensation, which, I predict, will become one of your most requested entrées. Many thanks to Kari Wheaton, who created this recipe for me.

4   (5-ounce) chicken breasts, skinned, boned, and cubed
1½ teaspoons ground cumin
½   teaspoon cayenne
1   teaspoon garlic powder
¼   cup bone broth
1   cup onion, chopped
4   garlic cloves, minced
4   cups tomatillos, chopped
2   cups mashed cauliflower, as prepared in Kari's Marvelously Mashed
    Cauliflower (Chapter 7)
2   cups cherry tomatoes, halved
1   cup fresh cilantro, chopped

In a medium bowl, combine the chicken breasts, cumin, cayenne, and garlic powder, making sure to evenly coat the chicken with the spices.

In a large skillet on medium heat, heat ⅛ cup of the broth, add the chicken mixture, and sauté for 5 minutes.

Remove from the skillet onto a plate and set aside.

Heat the remaining broth in the skillet on medium heat and add the onion and garlic cloves, sautéing about 2 minutes until tender.

Add the tomatillos and sauté for another 2 minutes.

Add the mashed cauliflower and the chicken mixture back to the skillet, cover, and cook for 10 minutes or until the chicken is thoroughly cooked.

Add the tomatoes and cilantro, cover, and cook for 2 minutes and serve.

ALL PHASES; MAKES 4 SERVINGS.

Lightly Spiced Chicken Wraps

A great lunch for taking to work and is actually easier than it sounds. You can pack the chicken and cabbage mixtures in baggies and microwave these as needed to serve over the romaine lettuce leaves.

2   (5-ounce) chicken breasts, skinned, boned, and halved
1   teaspoon ground cumin
½   teaspoon cayenne
½   teaspoon cinnamon
2   teaspoons plus 1 tablespoon fresh ginger, minced
1   tablespoon fresh parsley, chopped
3   garlic cloves, minced and divided
2   tablespoons apple cider vinegar
½   cup no-salt-added chicken broth
⅛   teaspoon SweetLeaf Stevia (optional)
1   jalapeño, minced (optional)
3   scallions, sliced
1   medium onion, chopped
1   green pepper, sliced
1   carrot, shredded
6   cups napa cabbage, thinly sliced
1   cup cilantro, chopped
1   tablespoon flaxseed oil
    Juice of 1 lime
    Romaine lettuce leaves

Place the chicken breasts in a plastic bag with the cumin, cayenne, cinnamon, 2 teaspoons of ginger, parsley, and 1 clove of garlic.

Seal the bag and place in the fridge.

Let the spices coat the chicken and be absorbed for at least 1 hour or overnight.

Preheat the oven to 350°F.

Remove the chicken from the bag, place in a baking dish, and bake for about 30 minutes or until cooked through.

In a small bowl, make a dressing by combining the vinegar, broth, stevia, remaining ginger, remaining garlic cloves, and jalapeño.

In a large saucepan, combine the dressing with the scallions, onion, and green pepper and sauté for 2 to 3 minutes.

Add the carrot and cabbage and cook for an additional 5 minutes.

Remove from the heat and toss in the cilantro, flaxseed oil, and lime juice.

Slice the chicken breasts into thin strips and serve on the romaine lettuce leaves with the cabbage mixture.

Variations

- Use ½ pound of flank steak instead of the chicken.
- Or how about substituting turkey breasts for the chicken?
- For phase 2, you might replace the cumin, cayenne, and cinnamon with 2 teaspoons of Chinese 5-spice powder for an exotic touch.
- For phase 2, add ½ teaspoon of dried dill to the spices.
- For phase 3, try adding a pinch of sea salt.

ALL PHASES; MAKES 2 SERVINGS.

Roast Turkey with Lemon, Garlic, and Fennel

Turkey is a great staple for the whole week. Turkey slices can be used as quick snacks and placed in bone broth for turkey soup. The lemon, garlic, and fennel help with digestion to make this bird Fat Flush friendly. (Save a couple cups of leftover turkey to make TexMex Turkey Jicama Tostadas, the next recipe after this one.)

     Zest and juice of 1 lemon
2   garlic cloves, minced
2   teaspoons ground fennel
3   tablespoons bone broth
1   (5- to 6-pound) whole turkey breast
2   fresh lemons, halved

Preheat the oven to 425°F.

In a bowl, mix the lemon zest, lemon juice, garlic, fennel, and broth.

Rub the turkey with the herb mixture and place the halved lemons on top.

Place the turkey in a roasting pan and roast for 20 minutes.

Lower the oven to 325° and roast the turkey for another 1¾ hours, basting with pan drippings.

When done, the juices from the thickest part of the turkey should run clear.

Remove from the oven and cool for 20 minutes before carving.

Variations

- For phases 2 and 3, serve with Pureed Sweet Potatoes (Chapter 7).
- For phase 3, try adding ½ teaspoon each of thyme, sage, and marjoram, plus a dash of salt.

ALL PHASES; MAKES 8 TO 10 SERVINGS.

Tex-Mex Turkey Jicama Tostadas

Crunchy sliced jicama rounds replace corn tortillas in this unique take on the traditional tostada.

1   jicama
½   cup turkey bone broth
4   green onions, chopped
2   cloves garlic, minced
1   teaspoon powdered cumin
2   cups turkey, cooked and shredded
1   bell pepper, chopped
1   small red onion, chopped
1   cup tomato, diced
1   avocado, sliced
    Jalapeños, fresh, canned, or bottled, to taste

Peel the jicama and carefully cut into eight ¼-inch round slices. Set aside.

Heat 2 tablespoons of the bone broth in a large skillet on medium heat. Add the green onions, garlic, and cumin powder and stir until softened and aromatic.

Add the shredded turkey and the remaining bone broth. Stir and heat through.

Place two jicama rounds on each plate. Top each with ¼ cup of the turkey mixture.

Dress each tostada with the bell pepper, red onion, tomato, avocado, and jalapeños.

Variations

• Instead of shredded turkey, use cooked ground turkey, shredded beef, or ground beef.
• For phase 3, add shredded cheese and a dollop of organic sour cream.

ALL PHASES; MAKES 4 SERVINGS.

Dijon Turkey Cutlets

Serve with Cinnamony Apple Sauce (Chapter 13) and a baby green salad with one of the Fat Flush dressings (Chapter 9).

4   (5-ounce) turkey cutlets
1   garlic clove, minced
1   cup almond meal
1   teaspoon fresh parsley, chopped
1   tablespoon Dijon mustard
    Avocado oil spray

Pound the turkey cutlets to ¼-inch thickness.

Mix the garlic, almond meal, and parsley together in a separate bowl and set aside.

Using a pastry brush, coat both sides of each cutlet with mustard.

Then dip the cutlets into the almond meal mixture, coating each side.

Coat a skillet with the avocado oil spray and heat to medium.

Add the coated cutlets and cook until golden brown, about 2 to 3 minutes per side.

Remove and serve warm.

PHASES 2 AND 3; MAKES 4 SERVINGS.

Rosemary Cloves Grilled Chicken with Yogurt Sauce

Here's a special phase 3 dish that is very aromatic, thanks to the ground cloves.

1   cup plain, whole-milk yogurt
⅓   cup lemon juice
½   teaspoon ground cloves
2   garlic cloves, minced
4   (5-ounce) chicken breasts, boned and skinned
2   cups bone broth
1   teaspoon dried rosemary, crushed
1   tablespoon fresh parsley, chopped

In a medium bowl, place the yogurt, lemon juice, cloves, garlic, and chicken; cover and let marinate refrigerated for at least 2 hours or overnight.

Place the broth and rosemary in a medium saucepan over high heat and boil until the broth is reduced and thickened.

Cool and set aside.

Preheat the broiler, or light a gas or charcoal grill.

Remove the chicken from the marinade and broil for 8 to 10 minutes or place on the grill for 10 to 15 minutes, turning occasionally.

Reheat the reduced chicken broth in a small saucepan and add parsley.

Transfer to a small bowl for serving.

Remove the chicken from the broiler or grill and serve with the warm sauce.

PHASE 3; MAKES 4 SERVINGS.

Lemon Garlic Rosemary Cornish Hens

These little beauties are simple to make. Yet they look so spectacular, your guests will think you slaved over them for hours. Often called "Cornish game hens," they are actually a small breed of broiler chicken with nothing "gamey" about them. You can find them in the frozen meat section of most grocery stores. Serve with a mixed green salad.

2   Cornish game hens, giblets removed
1   tablespoon olive oil
    Sea salt (optional)
    Paprika, to taste
8   sprigs fresh rosemary
1   lemon, cut into wedges
6   cloves garlic, peeled

Preheat the oven to 425°F.

Rinse the hens and pat dry.

Rub the olive oil over the skin and inside the cavities.

Sprinkle a little sea salt and paprika inside the cavities and over the skin.

Place 2 sprigs of rosemary, half the lemon slices, and 3 garlic cloves inside each bird.

Roast the hens on a rack in a shallow roasting pan in the preheated oven for 15 minutes.

Reduce the heat to 350° and continue roasting for 30 minutes or until an internal meat thermometer registers 180°.

Let rest 10 minutes.

Remove the stuffing and slice the hens in half lengthwise.

Place half of each hen, skin side up, on a plate and garnish with the fresh lemon wedges and rosemary sprigs.

PHASE 3; MAKES 4 SERVINGS.

Chicken Cacciatore

Enjoy this classic dish with a Fat Flush twist!

1   pound chicken breast halves, boneless and skinless
    Sea salt (optional)
1   tablespoon extra virgin olive oil
1   large onion, coarsely chopped
1   cup dried porcini mushrooms, reconstituted in 1 cup hot water
1   medium green bell pepper, coarsely chopped
1   medium red bell pepper, coarsely chopped
1   cup button mushrooms, sliced
5   garlic cloves, minced
1   (16-ounce) can organic tomato puree (Muir Glen)
2   tablespoons dry white wine, organic and sulfite free
½   cup Italian (flat) parsley, minced
2   teaspoons dried basil
1   teaspoon dried oregano
1   tablespoon kuzu, dissolved in 2 tablespoons water
    Hot cooked spaghetti squash, for serving

Season the chicken breasts lightly with the sea salt, if using.

Heat the extra virgin olive oil in a large nonstick skillet over medium-high heat.

Add the chicken and sauté, turning once, until lightly browned, about 3 minutes.

Remove the chicken and set aside.

Remove the porcini mushrooms from the water and keep the water.

Add the onion to the skillet with ½ cup of the porcini water.

Cook, stirring occasionally, until the onion is softened, about 2 to 3 minutes.

Add the peppers, porcini mushrooms, button mushrooms, and garlic and cook 3 minutes longer.

Add the tomatoes and stir, breaking up the tomatoes with a spoon.

Add the wine, parsley, basil, and oregano.

Add the remaining porcini water as needed.

Cut the chicken into strips and return the strips to the skillet, along with any pan juices that have collected.

Reduce the heat to medium-low and simmer, uncovered, stirring occasionally, until the chicken is just cooked through, about 5 minutes.

Add the kuzu to the chicken mixture, stirring until thickened.

Serve over the hot spaghetti squash.

TIP

You can double the recipe and freeze the leftover portions.

PHASE 3; MAKES 4 SERVINGS.

Lemon Chicken on the Grill

This recipe never fails to please when it's BBQ time! Make it even better by serving alongside Simply Grilled Mushrooms and Onions (Chapter 7).

8   chicken thighs, skinless
3   tablespoons parsley, chopped
2   tablespoons cilantro, chopped
1½ teaspoons grated lemon zest
     Lemon slices, for garnish

Marinade:

3   tablespoons yacon syrup
2   garlic cloves, mashed
2   scallions, sliced
½   teaspoon coriander
¼   teaspoon ginger
     Salt to taste
⅛   teaspoon cayenne or to taste
¼   cup fresh lemon juice
1½ teaspoons grated lemon zest

Prepare the grill for medium heat.

In a small bowl, whisk together the marinade ingredients.

Pour the marinade into a plastic bag with a zipper closure.

Add the thighs to the marinade and refrigerate for at least 30 minutes or overnight, shaking the bag occasionally to evenly distribute the marinade.

Place the thighs on the preheated grill.

Grill the thighs for 20 minutes, brushing periodically with the marinade until the thighs are thoroughly cooked and the juices run clear when the chicken is pierced with a fork.

Sprinkle with the parsley, cilantro, and lemon zest.

Garnish with the lemon slices.

TIP
Serve with assorted grilled vegetables.

Variation

- The chicken thighs can also be baked on a baking sheet (lightly coated with extra virgin olive oil spray) in a 400°F oven. Bake about 30 minutes, brushing the chicken periodically with the marinade, until the thighs are thoroughly cooked and the juices run clear when the thighs are pierced with a fork.

PHASE 3; MAKES 4 SERVINGS.

Tasty Holiday Chicken

This fragrant recipe is a rich, filling meal all by itself. Make it even better by starting with a simple tossed green salad and your favorite Fat Flush dressing (Chapter 9).

3	tablespoons sesame oil
½	teaspoon grated ginger
½	teaspoon coriander
½	teaspoon cardamom
½	teaspoon cumin
3	whole chicken breasts, skinned and halved
1	onion, sliced
2	carrots, sliced
1	cup cauliflower florets
1	cup green beans, cut into pieces 1 inch long
2	cups water
¼	teaspoon sea salt (optional)
1	large butternut squash, cooked and pureed

Heat the oil in a skillet.

Sauté the ginger, coriander, cardamom, and cumin in the oil.

Add the chicken, onion, and carrots.

Sauté until the chicken is golden and the onions are translucent.

Add the cauliflower, beans, water, and salt, if using.

Cover and cook 15 more minutes.

Add the pureed squash and cook 5 minutes longer.

PHASE 3; MAKES 6 SERVINGS.

BEEF, VEAL, AND LAMB

Burgers with Herbs

Sometimes you're just in the mood for a good burger—Fat Flush style!

1½ pounds lean ground beef
1   tablespoon dried mustard
2   garlic cloves, minced
1   teaspoon cayenne
1   tablespoon fresh cilantro, chopped

Preheat the broiler.

Combine all the ingredients and shape into patties.

Place the patties on a broiling pan and broil until done.

Variations
- For phase 2, add ½ teaspoon of mint to replace the cayenne.
- For phase 3, substitute dried horseradish for the mustard.

ALL PHASES; MAKES 4 SERVINGS.

Frankly Flank

Flank steak is a relatively inexpensive and versatile cut of beef. Prepare it simply as in this recipe, or amp it up by tenderizing it in one of Teresa's Lifestyle Marinades for All Seasons. (Chapter 10). Either way, be sure to let it rest for about 10 minutes after cooking and slice it crosswise into strips before serving.

1½ pounds lean flank steak
1   teaspoon onion powder
1   teaspoon garlic powder
1   teaspoon dried mustard

Preheat the broiler.

Place the flank steak on the broiling pan.

Sprinkle the onion powder, garlic powder, and dried mustard on the top of the steak.

Broil for about 4 to 5 minutes on each side until done.

Variations

- For phase 3, marinate in ½ cup of sherry with 2 small minced garlic cloves and ¼ teaspoon of ground ginger before broiling.
- For phase 3 special occasions, marinate in a sherry, garlic, and ginger mixture with ½ teaspoon of low-sodium, wheat-free tamari.

ALL PHASES; MAKES 4 SERVINGS.

Beef Stroganoff

A gourmet treat, this dish can be served with I Can't Believe It Isn't Garlicky Mashed Potatoes (Chapter 7).

3   cups button mushrooms, sliced
1   cup shiitake mushrooms, sliced
1   large onion, sliced
3   garlic cloves, minced
2   tablespoons plus 1 (14-ounce) can no-salt-added beef broth
1   pound flank steak, thinly sliced
2   tablespoons Fat Flush Catsup (Chapter 10)
½   teaspoon garlic powder
     Tofu Sour Cream (see below in this recipe)
1   medium spaghetti squash, as prepared in Fat Flush Spaghetti with Meat Sauce (given later in this chapter)

In a large skillet over medium heat, sauté the button and shiitake mushrooms, onion, and garlic cloves in 2 tablespoons of broth for 8 minutes or until the onions are soft.

Remove the mushroom-onion mixture from the skillet and set aside.

Lightly brown the flank steak in the skillet for approximately 5 minutes.

Add the remaining broth, catsup, and garlic powder, cover, and simmer for 10 minutes.

Return the mushroom-onion mixture to the skillet, add the Tofu Sour Cream, mix well, bring to a boil, and cook for 1 minute.

Serve over the cooked spaghetti squash.

Tofu Sour Cream

1   (12-ounce) block silken, firm tofu
     Juice of 1 lemon
1   teaspoon apple cider vinegar
12 black olives

Place all the ingredients in a blender and blend until smooth.

Variations

- You may substitute mashed cauliflower for the spaghetti squash.
- For phase 3, after you've added the garlic powder, add ½ teaspoon of salt to the Beef Stroganoff.
- For phase 3, add a pinch of cardamom to the Tofu Sour Cream.

ALL PHASES; MAKES 4 SERVINGS.

Stuffed Cabbage

Here's a stuffed cabbage with a unique gingery flavor. Ginger is a warming herb, and its pungent, peppery taste stimulates digestion and increases circulation.

8   large cabbage leaves, washed
¼   cup leek, finely chopped
1   teaspoon fresh ginger, grated, or pinch of dried ginger
½   pound ground lean beef
2   garlic cloves, minced
1   egg, lightly beaten
8   toothpicks
2   cups bone broth
2   tablespoons fresh parsley, chopped

In a large pot, cook the cabbage in boiling water until the leaves are soft enough to be used as wrapping.

Gently remove the cabbage from the hot water with a slotted spoon, refresh in cold water, and dry.

In a medium skillet, sauté the leek, ginger, beef, and garlic until the beef is cooked through.

Add the egg to the meat and mix thoroughly for the filling.

Divide the filling into 8 portions, placing each portion in the middle of a cabbage leaf.

Fold the two opposite sides of the leaf over the filling and roll up tightly, securing with toothpicks.

Arrange the cabbage rolls in the skillet, add broth, and simmer for 20 minutes.

Sprinkle with the parsley.

ALL PHASES; MAKES 2 SERVINGS.

Fragrant Fat Flush Meatballs

The fennel—which is so good for your digestion—is the high note in these Fat Flush Meatballs. This dish is terrific over a medley of steamed veggies like zucchini, snow peas, summer squash, and string beans, or serve with Roasted Peppers with Garlic (Chapter 7).

1   pound lean ground beef
½   cup cauliflower, diced
1½ cups purified water
⅓   cup onion, chopped
1   garlic clove, minced
1   (15-ounce) can no-salt-added tomato sauce (Muir Glen)
½   teaspoon ground fennel
¼   teaspoon SweetLeaf Stevia

Preheat the oven to 350°F.

Mix the beef, cauliflower, ½ cup of water, onion, and garlic together.

Shape into meatballs and place in a baking dish.

In a separate bowl, stir the tomato sauce, 1 cup of water, fennel, and stevia.

Pour over the meatballs.

Cover and bake for 45 minutes.

Remove the cover and bake for an additional 10 to 15 minutes or until done.

ALL PHASES; MAKES 4 SERVINGS.

Fat Flush Spaghetti with Meat Sauce

A wildly popular favorite, here's how to put spaghetti and meat sauce together the Fat Flush way.

1   medium spaghetti squash
1   pound lean ground beef
½   onion, chopped
1   cup mushrooms, sliced
1   (16-ounce) can tomato puree (Muir Glen)
1   teaspoon ground fennel
¼   teaspoon SweetLeaf Stevia
2   garlic cloves, crushed

Preheat the oven to 350°F.

Cut the spaghetti squash in half lengthwise and scoop out the seeds.

Place the cut side down on a baking sheet and bake for 30 minutes.

When the spaghetti squash is cooked, use a fork to remove the flesh that forms the spaghetti-like strands.

While the squash is cooking, mix the beef, onion, and mushrooms together in a skillet.

Cook over medium heat until done.

While the meat is cooking, put the tomato puree, fennel, stevia, and garlic in a 2-quart saucepan. Simmer over medium heat for 20 minutes.

When the meat is cooked, add to the sauce.

Toss the spaghetti strands with the sauce and serve.

Variations
- Substitute Fragrant Fat Flush Meatballs (the recipe is given earlier in this chapter) for the meat sauce.
- Substitute zoodles (spiralized zucchini) for the spaghetti squash.
- For phase 3 add ½ teaspoon oregano and ½ teaspoon basil to the spices.

ALL PHASES; MAKES 4 SERVINGS.

Veal Medallions with Mushrooms and Garlic

This is good enough for company and yet simple, fast, and healthy.

1   pound veal medallions, pounded to ⅛-inch thickness
½   cup bone broth
1   large onion, chopped
2   cups mushrooms, sliced
2   garlic cloves, minced

Brown the veal in the broth in a skillet.

Remove the veal from the skillet and set aside.

Sauté the onions, mushrooms, and garlic in the remaining broth in the same skillet until tender.

Return the veal to the skillet with the onions, mushrooms, and garlic mixture and heat through for about 1 minute or until done.

Serve immediately.

ALL PHASES; MAKES 4 SERVINGS.

Pot Roast with Sweet Potatoes and Vegetables

There's just something so homey and comforting about a good pot roast in the oven or slow cooker!

½   cup organic beef bone broth
4   pounds boneless chuck roast or brisket
3   large onions, sliced
4   garlic cloves, sliced
    Salt to taste
    Cayenne to taste
½   cup organic crushed tomatoes (Muir Glen)
1   bay leaf
    Water as needed
2   medium sweet potatoes, peeled and cut into chunks
4   medium carrots, peeled and cut into chunks
½   pound button mushrooms, quartered

Heat the bone broth in a Dutch oven.

Braise the chuck roast or brisket until well browned on both sides; remove.

Lay half the sliced onions and garlic in the Dutch oven; place the meat on top.

Season with the salt and cayenne.

Place the remaining onions and garlic on top of the meat and add the crushed tomatoes and bay leaf and enough water to just reach the top of the meat.

Bring to a boil, reduce the heat to low, and cover.

Simmer about 2 hours (adding additional water as needed) or until the meat starts to feel tender when pierced with a fork.

Remove the meat; let cool slightly.

Add the sweet potatoes, carrots, and mushrooms to the pot; place the meat on top of the vegetables; cover.

Continue to simmer, adding small amounts of water as needed, for an additional 1 to 2 hours or until the meat is tender enough to cut with a fork.

Remove the meat; let rest 20 minutes; slice thinly.

Arrange the meat on a platter with the vegetables (remove the bay leaf), passing the gravy separately (see tip below).

> **T I P**
>
> For a rich aromatic gravy, puree half the vegetables and gravy in a blender and stir into the remaining portion.

Variation (slow cooker)

- Rub the meat with sea salt and cayenne. Brown the meat in 1½ table-spoons of avocado oil in a heavy skillet; put in vegetables, a bay leaf, and crushed tomatoes (optional) and continue cooking on high for about 2 hours or until the meat is tender. Remove the bay leaf.

PHASES 2 AND 3; MAKES 8 SERVINGS.

Lamb Kebabs

*A good friend created this recipe and says that asparagus with Citrus Vinai-
grette (Chapter 9) is a tasty companion.*

½   cup apple cider vinegar
¼   teaspoon cayenne
1½ teaspoons dried oregano, crushed
½   teaspoon dried rosemary, crushed
½   cup onion, minced
1   garlic clove, minced
1½ pounds lamb, trimmed and cut into 1½-inch cubes
8   whole mushrooms
1   medium red pepper, seeded and cut into 8 pieces
8   small, whole boiling onions, parboiled
4   skewers

In a medium bowl, combine the vinegar, cayenne, oregano, rosemary, onion,
   and garlic for a marinade and mix well.

Add the lamb, making sure to coat evenly with the marinade.

Cover and let marinate in the refrigerator overnight.

Remove the lamb from the marinade.

Make kebabs by alternating the lamb with the mushrooms, red peppers, and
   onions on the skewers.

Cook over the grill or barbecue for 15 to 20 minutes, turning the skewers
   repeatedly, until the meat is done and nicely browned.

PHASES 2 AND 3; MAKES 4 SERVINGS.

My Mother's Meatloaf

This dish is great for the family and for freezing. My mother, Edith, who fol-lowed the Fat Flushing principles for almost 20 years, told me that the dried horseradish is the special ingredient in this recipe. Pungent and stimulating, horseradish is also a great source of both potassium and iron. It can increase circulation and perspiration, acting as a diuretic. Serve with I Can't Believe It Isn't Garlicky Mashed Potatoes (Chapter 7).

1   tablespoon olive oil
2   pounds lean ground beef
1   cup Toasted Nuts (Chapter 10)
¾   cup onions, chopped
1   teaspoon dried oregano
1   tablespoon dried horseradish
1   teaspoon dried mustard
½   cup Fat Flush Catsup (Chapter 10)
2   eggs, beaten

Preheat the oven to 350°F.

Grease an 8- by 4-inch loaf pan with the olive oil.

In a large bowl, mix the beef, toasted nuts, onions, oregano, horseradish, mustard, catsup, and eggs together.

Shape into a loaf and place in the loaf pan.

Bake for 1¼ hours or until done.

PHASE 3; MAKES 8 SERVINGS.

Lamb Chops Glazed with Apricot Preserves

This dish is so simple, it is sinful. Just sit back and let the compliments roll in.

8   baby lamb chops, trimmed of all visible fat
8   tablespoons unsweetened apricot preserves
½   teaspoon ground ginger

Preheat the broiler.

Place the chops on the broiling pan.

In a small bowl, mix the apricot preserves with the ginger.

Spread ½ the mixture over the top of the chops.

Broil for 5 minutes, turn, and spread the remaining mixture over the other side.

Broil another 5 minutes or until cooked through.

Variations

• Substitute unsweetened peach preserves for the apricot preserves and add a dash of cinnamon.

• In place of the preserves and ginger, try marinating the lamb chops in ⅓ cup of unsweetened pineapple juice and ½ tablespoon of Fat Flush Curry Seasoning (Chapter 10) and then broiling.

PHASE 3; MAKES 4 SERVINGS.

Beefy Mushroom Burgers

Finely chopped mushrooms help hold these juicy burgers together while adding a rich, woodsy flavor boost for the best burgers ever!

12 ounces crimini mushrooms
1   pound ground beef
1   clove garlic, minced
1   tablespoon low-sodium, wheat-free tamari
    Avocado oil spray

Place the mushrooms in a blender or food processor and pulse until very finely chopped.

Combine the mushrooms, ground beef, garlic, and tamari in a bowl and mix well.

Form into four ½-inch-thick patties.

Spray a large skillet with avocado oil and heat to medium-high.

Cook about 5 minutes per side or to desired doneness.

PHASE 3; MAKES 4 SERVINGS.

Sassy Beef and Vegetable Kebabs

After marinating in this marvelous sauce for up to 4 hours, the beef is a tender companion for the veggies in these tasty kebabs.

Marinade:

4   garlic cloves, crushed
2   scallions, chopped
1   tablespoon low-sodium, wheat-free tamari
1   tablespoon coconut vinegar
1   tablespoon fresh lime juice
1   teaspoon tahini
1   teaspoon Dijon mustard
1   tablespoon toasted sesame seed oil
1½ tablespoons grated ginger
2   teaspoons toasted sesame seeds

Kebabs:

1   pound lean boneless beef sirloin, cut into 1½-inch cubes
1   onion, cut into chunks
1   green bell pepper, cut into chunks
1   red bell pepper, cut into chunks
1   large zucchini, cut into 1-inch slices
1   large yellow squash, cut into 1-inch slices
     Cherry tomatoes
     Button mushrooms

Glaze:

2   tablespoons yacon syrup
1   tablespoon low-sodium, wheat-free tamari

Prepare the grill for medium-high heat.

Combine all the marinade ingredients in a plastic bag with a zipper closure.

Add the beef and marinate for 2 to 4 hours, shaking the bag occasionally to distribute the marinade evenly.

Drain the beef, reserving the marinade.

Thread the beef and vegetables onto skewers.

Grill about 10 minutes, basting frequently with the reserved marinade and turning the skewers often to ensure even cooking.

Mix the glaze ingredients together; baste the skewers and continue grilling about 5 minutes or until the beef is cooked through and the vegetables are lightly charred.

PHASE 3; MAKES 4 SERVINGS.

Middle Eastern Lamb Loaf

The mix of rich spices makes this loaf special. Serve with Sweet Potato Delight and Gingered Asparagus (both recipes are in Chapter 7).

2   pounds ground lamb
4   garlic cloves, minced
1   medium onion, chopped
2   tablespoons red bell pepper, minced
2   tablespoons green bell pepper, minced
1   egg
¼   cup Flaxseed Crackers (Chapter 8), crumbled
3   tablespoons cilantro, chopped
3   tablespoons parsley, chopped
2   tablespoons cumin
2   tablespoons coriander
2   teaspoons cinnamon
2   tablespoons ginger, chopped
     Avocado oil spray

Preheat the oven to 375°F.

Combine all the ingredients in a large bowl.

Shape into a loaf.

Place on a broiling pan that has been lightly coated with avocado oil spray.

Bake for 45 minutes or until cooked through.

Variation

• Place half the lamb mixture on the pan and cover with 1 (10-ounce) package of frozen chopped spinach that has been defrosted and squeezed dry. Top with the other half of the lamb mixture, pressing firmly to seal. Bake as directed.

PHASE 3; MAKES 4 SERVINGS.

Savory Beef Satay

This recipe is perfect for dinner parties or quiet nights in.

2   tablespoons low-sodium, wheat-free tamari
2   tablespoons apple cider vinegar
1   tablespoon organic honey
1   tablespoon fresh ginger, chopped
¼   cup green onion, chopped
2   cloves garlic, minced
2   pounds beef sirloin (from pasture-raised cows)
2   large organic bell peppers, cut into 1-inch pieces
1   fresh pineapple, cubed
½   cup organic peanut butter
1½ cups no-salt-added organic chicken broth
    Cayenne to taste

Mix the tamari, apple cider vinegar, honey, ginger, green onion, and garlic in a medium-sized bowl. Pour ⅓ cup into a shallow dish and set aside the remainder.

Remove the beef from the freezer and cut against the grain. Add the slices to the ⅓ cup of marinade. Cover and refrigerate for at least 30 minutes or up to 4 hours.

Soak the skewers for 40 minutes.

Alternate the beef, bell peppers, and pineapple on the skewers, arranging so that the slices lie flat.

On medium heat, grill the skewers for about 5 to 6 minutes on each side.

Add the peanut butter, broth, and cayenne to the marinade that you set aside. Heat on medium, but do not boil. Serve as a dipping sauce.

PHASE 3 SPECIAL OCCASION; MAKES 8 SKEWERS.

7 Vegetables

Rainbow-colored vegetables play a major role in Fat Flush—the more vibrant the pigment, the more antioxidants and bioflavonoids to support total health and vitality. In fact over 5,000 antioxidants are found in plant foods. Many plant foods contain specific health-enhancing phytonutrients, such as sulforaphane (broccoli and broccoli sprouts), flavonoids (carrots, cabbage, and tomatoes), and sulfites (onions and garlic). The Fat Flush vegetable recipes are also rich in chlorophyll-rich, purifying leafy greens (spinach, kale, and arugula) that power up the plate with natural sources of folate, which is critical for the nervous system and helps to repair DNA from your head to your toes.

Keep in mind that yellow-green selections include peas (phases 2 and 3) and non-GMO corn (phase 3), which are vision all-stars, containing lutein to protect vision and zeaxanthin, an antioxidant proved to prevent cataracts and macular degeneration.

You will find yellow-orange selections like phase 2 acorn squash, sweet potatoes, and carrots bursting with carotenoids for healthy skin and strong adrenal glands.

And there are many dishes featuring red tomatoes, a tasty source of lycopene, the red compound that is a powerful aid for prostate and breast health.

The white-green vegetable choices such as onions, garlic, mushrooms, endives, leeks, and celery provide allicin and flavonoids to help detoxify on a cellular level while protecting cells and strengthening immunity.

Whether served as a side salad or a delightful companion to an entrée, each of our recipes will help fortify your family's health. They're loaded with fiber, vitamins, and minerals that give them their antioxidant power to halt disease in its tracks. Consequently, adding these wonderful ingredients isn't just for taste appeal, but for health appeal as well. So have fun and paint your plates with a rainbow of healthy colors, choosing from broccoli, carrots, brussels sprouts, cabbage, kale, string beans, eggplant, peppers, and so many delicious others. These tasty side dishes are also a terrific way to get your kids running to the dinner table for those all-too-important omega-rich foods they need for their developing brains. A vegetable focus will also translate into a shrinking waistline!

Veggies are best stored in the refrigerator, in a separate bin from fresh fruits. Many fruits, like pears and apples, for instance, produce a ripening gas called ethylene that can alter the taste of vegetables.

And one more thing: be sure to check out the yummy Jicama Slaw, Fresh Spinach Sauté, Gingered Asparagus, and Shiitake Snow Peas Stir-Fry recipes. Vegetables never tasted so good!

THE HEIRLOOM REVIVAL

When it comes to color, there is nothing more visually vital than heirloom vegetables. These veggies (and fruits, by the way) are making their way back onto America's tables. These are specialty vegetables with all their original genetic characteristics intact as were veggies before modern agriculture replaced them with hybrids that were designed to have a longer shelf life, were easier to ship, and were easier to process through machine harvesting.

The heirlooms are definitely more colorful and packed with higher nutritional values. Some kinds of heirloom corn, for example, are true powerhouses of protein—providing nearly three times the amount of protein of today's hybrid corn. Some kinds of heirloom apples are richer sources of vitamin C than your typical orange.

Today heirlooms can be found in upscale grocery stores, in farmers markets, and on roadside stands. Or you can grow your own from seeds, which are available in health food stores, at upscale grocery stores, or from seed supply companies on the Internet. The main reason for this renaissance, however, probably has nothing to do with nutrition or health. The taste of these heirlooms is simply out of this world.

Whether you are enjoying fresh, organic, or heirloom produce, the rule of thumb is simply this: if fresh or frozen is unavailable, then the next best is canned or jarred with no added salt. First and foremost, look for the words "no salt added" and "no sugar added" on the label for both canned and jarred veggies. When it comes to other additives or preservatives (such as EDTA, ascorbic acid, and citric acid, for example), the least amount the better, although these have no known toxicity.

By the way, many companies now offer triple-washed and precut fresh greens in plastic bags. So now there's really no excuse for not eating your greens, because it doesn't get any easier than prewashed and ready cut! Spinach, chard, kale, collards, and turnip and mustard greens are a great source of folic acid and nondairy calcium on Fat Flush, as you may remember from *The Fat Flush Plan*.

From a practical standpoint, the best cooking news about vegetables is this: with a small, stainless-steel steamer, you can have maximum taste with a minimum of effort. The veggies can be crisply tender or firm and crunchy. When veggies are cooked this way, on average they take only 10 to 15 minutes. Of course, the tougher ones, like artichokes, take longer.

So before you delve any further, take a look below at our Fat Flush Vegetable Steaming Guide. I know you will enjoy experimenting with the herbs and herb blends that can be used for each and every phase of the plan. Many of these herbs can single-handedly or in combination take an ordinary veggie from simple to sublime in minutes.

THE 3:1 HERB RATIO

Remember that when seasoning your veggies (or even main dishes, for that matter) with herbs, the basic ratio for fresh to dried is 3:1. In other words, for dill you would replace 3 teaspoons (or 1 tablespoon) of fresh dill with 1 teaspoon of dried dill.

Any vegetable can be further accented with a drizzle of flaxseed oil, a baste of chicken, beef, or veggie broth, lemon juice, and herbs for phases 1 and 2. For phase 3, you can widen your taste horizons with a drizzle of olive, grape seed, or sesame oil for lifestyle eating and enjoyment. In phase 3, you can further experiment by adding some crunch in the form of toasted pine nuts, almonds, walnuts, filberts, and pumpkin and sunflower seeds to your vibrant vegetables—whether sautéed or steamed.

INSIDER TIPS

- When steaming veggies, use purified water. After the veggies are steamed, you can save this nutrient-rich water and add it to your ready-made or homemade broths for extra vitamins, minerals, and flavor.

- If steaming is not your thing, how about roasting your veggies in a hot oven. Roasting helps to potentize flavors in phase 2 and 3 favorites (think sweet potatoes) because the natural sugars caramelize.

THE FAT FLUSH VEGETABLE STEAMING GUIDE

VEGETABLE	STEAMING TIME
ARTICHOKES	
Globe, whole	45 minutes
INSIDER TIP	*Delicious with a sprinkling of lemon juice, basil, or thyme.*
ASPARAGUS	
Whole	7–12 minutes
Tips	6–10 minutes
INSIDER TIP	*Bring out the flavor with lemon zest, parsley, tarragon, or mustard.*
BEANS	
Green, wax, or yellow	8–12 minutes
INSIDER TIP	*Flavor with a dash of coriander, basil, or garlic.*
BEETS	
Whole	20–25 minutes
¼-inch slices	3–5 minutes
INSIDER TIP	*A bit of cloves, ginger, or bay leaf really enhances the flavor.*
BROCCOLI	
Stalks, split	8–10 minutes
INSIDER TIP	*Try some mustard, garlic, or tarragon to heighten the taste.*
BRUSSELS SPROUTS	8–12 minutes
INSIDER TIP	*Delicious with garlic, basil, sage, or thyme.*
CABBAGE	
Green, quartered	5–7 minutes
Green or red, shredded	3 minutes
INSIDER TIP	*Turmeric, mustard, or oregano will tickle your taste buds.*

Vegetable	Steaming time
CARROTS	
Whole	15–20 minutes
¼-inch slices	8–12 minutes
INSIDER TIP	*Please your palate with a sprinkling of dill, ginger, mint, or nutmeg.*
CAULIFLOWER	
Whole	20–25 minutes
Florets	7–10 minutes
INSIDER TIP	*Try a sprinkling of cumin, rosemary, or marjoram.*
CELERY	
Whole	8–12 minutes
Diced	3–7 minutes
INSIDER TIP	*Celery by itself acts as a spice to bring out the flavor of other veggies.*
CORN	
On the cob	5–8 minutes
Kernels	3–5 minutes
INSIDER TIP	*Add sweet basil. Sweet basil and cayenne powder can perk things up.*
EGGPLANT	
Sliced	8–10 minutes
INSIDER TIP	*Delicious with garlic, oregano, basil, or marjoram.*
KALE	3–7 minutes
INSIDER TIP	*Garlic and lemon are perky taste enhancers.*
KOHLRABI	
Whole	10–15 minutes
Sliced	3–7 minutes
INSIDER TIP	*Similar to kale, kohlrabi goes well with garlic and lemon.*

Vegetable	Steaming time
OKRA	
Whole	10–12 minutes
Sliced	3–6 minutes
INSIDER TIP	*Try a sprinkling of dill or basil to heighten taste.*
ONIONS	5–8 minutes
INSIDER TIP	*Delicious with a sprinkling of cumin, oregano, thyme, or nutmeg.*
SNOW PEAS	3–5 minutes
INSIDER TIP	*There is nothing like minced garlic or crushed mint to bring out the flavor.*
SPINACH	3–5 minutes
INSIDER TIP	*Try with garlic, basil, nutmeg, or marjoram for a taste treat.*
SQUASH, YELLOW	
Whole	15–25 minutes
¼-inch slices	8–10 minutes
INSIDER TIP	*Great with a sprinkling of cloves, fennel, ginger, or nutmeg.*
SWISS CHARD	3–5 minutes
INSIDER TIP	*Try with a garlic clove, lemon zest, or fennel.*
TOMATOES	
Whole	5–8 minutes
½-inch slices	3–5 minutes
INSIDER TIP	*Fennel, anise, basil, and oregano are all a tomato's best friend.*
ZUCCHINI	
Whole	8–12 minutes
¼-inch slices	3–6 minutes
INSIDER TIP	*Garlic or basil brings out the flavor.*

Spinach Toss

A lovely side salad for any Fat Flush entrée of your choice, spinach not only is a terrific source of eye-nourishing lutein but is rich in potassium as well.

4   cups fresh spinach, shredded
1   cup jicama, cut into thin strips
½   cup mushrooms, sliced
2   tablespoons flaxseed oil
1   tablespoon lemon juice
⅛   teaspoon garlic powder

In a large salad bowl, combine the spinach, jicama, and mushrooms and toss
    lightly.
Mix the flaxseed oil, lemon juice, and garlic powder in a jar, cover, and shake
    well.
Pour the dressing over the salad and toss lightly.

ALL PHASES; MAKES 4 SERVINGS.

Jicama Slaw

Jicama is definitely a Fat Flush favorite! It is a crunchy alternative to cabbage and tastes similar to water chestnuts—only sweeter. Jicama is quite delicious when served raw. This slaw is perfect for packing with lunches. It's a terrific side with any fish dish, but my choice would be Spicy Tuna Croquettes (Chapter 6).

12	ounces jicama, peeled and cut into thin strips
1	red onion, thinly sliced
1	carrot, grated
1	cucumber, cut into thin strips
1	cup parsley, chopped
½	cup apple cider vinegar
½	teaspoon dill
3	tablespoons flaxseed oil
3	garlic cloves, minced
	Juice of 1 lemon

In a large bowl, place the jicama, onion, carrot, and cucumber and set aside.

In a jar, put the parsley, vinegar, dill, flaxseed oil, garlic, and lemon juice and shake well.

Pour the dressing over the jicama mix and toss lightly.

Variations

- Add ½ sliced whole fennel bulb for an intriguing taste sensation and substitute lime juice for the lemon.
- For phase 3, try adding toasted pumpkin seeds or sunflower seeds to the slaw.

ALL PHASES; MAKES 4 SERVINGS.

Simply Grilled Mushrooms and Onions

This is a wonderful side dish to accent the beef entrées or even a hearty burger. In fact, I like this dish as a topping for my scrambled eggs.

¼   cup bone broth
8   ounces mushrooms, sliced
3   onions, sliced
1   garlic clove, minced
1   teaspoon lemon juice

In a medium skillet, heat the broth over medium-high heat.
Add the mushrooms, onions, and garlic.
Cook until the onions are translucent and tender.
Add the lemon juice.
Serve.

ALL PHASES; MAKES 2 SERVINGS.

Carrot Burdock Stir-Sauté

This is a very therapeutic as well as tasty dish. In Asian medicine the burdock is a revered blood cleanser and blood builder. It is found in many mainstream grocery stores, health food stores, and Asian markets. This dish is also good for your reproductive system.

4   tablespoons bone broth
2   medium burdocks, cut into shavings
4   small carrots, cut into shavings
    Dash of dried ginger
    Fresh parsley for garnish

In a large skillet, heat the broth over medium-high heat.

Sauté the burdocks, carrots, and ginger for about 4 minutes or until crisp-tender.

Serve warm and garnish with the fresh parsley.

Variation
•   For special occasions, add ¼ teaspoon of tamari.

ALL PHASES; MAKES 4 SERVINGS.

Dilly Okra

I am a big fan of okra. Lightly steamed (see the Fat Flush Steaming Guide above), it can be eaten just like green beans, and it makes a wonderful natural thickener for stews and soups. Plus, it has the added health benefits of easing constipation and lubricating the intestinal tract. Serve with Simply Baked Fish (Chapter 6).

1½ cups okra, cut into ½-inch lengths and steamed
½   cup tomatoes, chopped
1   teaspoon dried dill

Put the okra, tomatoes, and dill in a pot and simmer for 5 minutes.

ALL PHASES; MAKES 4 SERVINGS.

Glorious Greens

Many people don't realize that green, leafy veggies really are rich in magnesium! Choose from kale, collards, spinach, chard, arugula, and escarole. These glorious greens will do any entrée proud, and the more bitter the green, the better it is for liver and gallbladder support.

2	pounds assorted greens, trimmed and cleaned
2	cups water
¼	cup bone broth
1	onion, sliced
2	garlic cloves, minced
	Juice of 1 lemon
4	tablespoons flaxseed oil

Place the greens in a pot and add water to cover.

Bring to a quick boil and then lower the heat; simmer, cooking the greens until barely tender, about 5 to 8 minutes depending upon the toughness of the greens.

Drain, chop, and set aside.

Heat the broth in a saucepan and sauté the onion and garlic over low heat until tender.

Quickly add the greens to the saucepan, reducing the heat to low, and cook the greens until tender.

Dish the greens into a bowl; add the lemon juice and flaxseed oil and toss.

Serve warm or at room temperature.

ALL PHASES; MAKES 4 SERVINGS.

Roasted Peppers with Garlic

Like the Simply Grilled Mushrooms and Onions (see earlier in the chapter), I personally enjoy this dish with eggs. I know you will enjoy it with the Artichoke Frittata (Chapter 6).

4   large bell peppers (combination of colors), halved, seeded, and membranes removed
8   garlic cloves
2   cups boiled water
1   tablespoon flaxseed oil
½   cup parsley, chopped
½   cup scallions, chopped

Preheat the broiler.

Broil the peppers on a parchment-covered baking sheet, turning constantly until the skin has browned.

Remove the peppers and set aside in a paper bag for about 15 minutes.

Peel the skin from the peppers and cut into long, thin strips.

Dry thoroughly with paper towels.

Place the garlic in a bowl with the boiled water for 15 minutes.

Cool and remove the skins.

Place the garlic, oil, parsley, and scallions in a blender and blend to make a paste.

Toss the paste with the peppers and refrigerate for 1 hour before serving.

ALL PHASES; MAKES 4 SERVINGS.

Brussels Sprouts with Curry

Brussels sprouts really did originate in Brussels, Belgium. They contribute many disease-fighting chemicals to the diet and are a fair source of beta-carotene, which is so helpful for immunity. They go well with just about any fish, meat, or poultry entrée. They are also the "new" kale and can be enjoyed in a multitude of ways—roasted with cauliflower steaks or as various toppings. They are also available without the outside leaves, prepackaged.

1   pound brussels sprouts, trimmed of outside leaves
1   cup bone broth
1   medium onion, finely chopped
2   teaspoons Fat Flush Curry Seasoning (Chapter 10)

Put all the ingredients into a medium-sized pot.

Bring to a quick boil and then simmer for about 15 minutes or until the liquid cooks down.

As the liquid starts to thicken, gently coat the brussels sprouts with the liquid, being sure to glaze on all sides.

Serve warm.

Variation

- Instead of the brussels sprouts, try other members of the cancer-fighting cruciferous food family like broccoli, cauliflower, and cabbage.

ALL PHASES; MAKES 4 SERVINGS.

I Can't Believe It Isn't Garlicky Mashed Potatoes

The cauliflower is the special ingredient here, and you won't even miss pota-
toes if you are on phase 1 or 2. Mashing these "potatoes" with the peppers in a
food processor (or blender) yields a pretty "confetti" effect—a perfect company
dish! Serve with Beef Stroganoff or My Mother's Meatloaf (both recipes are
found in Chapter 6).

1   small onion, chopped
½   red pepper, chopped
½   yellow pepper, chopped
¼   cup bone broth
1   tablespoon bone broth
2   cups cooked cauliflower, diced
¼   teaspoon dried dill
½   teaspoon garlic, minced

In a skillet, sauté the onion, red pepper, and yellow pepper in ¼ cup broth for
about 5 minutes over medium heat.

Add the cauliflower and toss until heated through.

Add the dill and garlic.

Transfer to a food processor (or blender) and puree, adding the additional
tablespoon of broth to achieve a smooth consistency.

Serve hot.

ALL PHASES; MAKES 2 TO 3 SERVINGS.

Kari's Marvelously Mashed Cauliflower

This recipe has become the Fat Flush answer to mashed potatoes and white rice. It appears as an accompaniment to several of the entrées like Fat Flush Shepherd's Pie (Chapter 6).

1   medium head cauliflower, cut into florets
1   cup purified water
2   garlic cloves, minced
1   teaspoon fresh chives, chopped
½   teaspoon onion powder
½   teaspoon fresh parsley, chopped
1   tablespoon bone broth

Put the cauliflower and water in a medium pot and bring to a quick boil.

Lower the heat to simmer; cover.

Cook for an additional 12 minutes or until soft.

Drain, transfer the cauliflower to a bowl, and mash.

Blend in the garlic, chives, onion powder, parsley, and broth with the mashed cauliflower.

Serve hot.

ALL PHASES; MAKES 2 SERVINGS.

Asparagus with Flaxy Lemon-Herb Dressing

A potent natural diuretic, asparagus is a source of carotenoids and vitamin E.
Serve with broiled lamb chops or Lamb Kebabs (Chapter 6).

1   pound asparagus spears, trimmed
     Juice and zest of 1 lemon
¼   cup flaxseed oil
¼   cup apple cider vinegar
1   garlic clove, minced
1   tablespoon each, chopped chives, chopped fresh dill, and chopped
     fresh parsley

Blanch the asparagus spears in a large pot of boiling water for 5 minutes or
    until tender but not mushy.

Plunge the spears in ice water to cool quickly, then drain.

Add the remaining ingredients in a small bowl and whisk together for the
    dressing.

Drizzle the lemon-flaxseed dressing over the asparagus before serving.

Variation
•   For true parsley lovers, you may use 2 tablespoons of parsley to replace
     the chives and dill.

ALL PHASES; MAKES 4 SERVINGS.

Green Beans with Garlic and Spice

Green beans are delightfully flavorful when enhanced with garlic, turmeric, cumin, cayenne, or jalapeños (for those who like to turn up the heat). Serve as a side dish with lamb or beef.

1   cup bone broth
3   garlic cloves, thinly sliced
2   small jalapeño peppers, seeds removed, minced (optional)
1   teaspoon turmeric
2   teaspoons cumin
⅛   teaspoon cayenne
1   pound whole green beans, trimmed
     Lemon juice for drizzling

Heat ½ cup of the broth in a pan.

Add the garlic, jalapeños (if using), turmeric, cumin, and cayenne and cook until the garlic turns golden, about 3 minutes.

Add the green beans and the remaining ½ cup of broth and stir well.

Cover and cook over medium heat, stirring occasionally for 5 to 6 minutes or until the beans are tender.

Drizzle with the lemon juice and serve.

Variation

• You can add 1 package of frozen pearl onions, thawed, to give a sophisticated flair.

ALL PHASES; MAKES 4 SERVINGS.

Leeks with Garlic and Mustard

This simple dish cannot go wrong when paired with poultry, beef, or veal.

1   cup bone broth
4   leeks, washed and cut in half lengthwise, then into ¼-inch strips at
     a diagonal
1   garlic clove, chopped
1   tablespoon fresh parsley, chopped
2   tablespoons apple cider vinegar
½   teaspoon dried mustard

Bring the broth to a boil in a nonstick skillet on medium-high heat.

Add the leeks and garlic to the broth, cover, and simmer until the leeks are
     tender, about 10 to 12 minutes.

Remove from the heat, drain, transfer to a large bowl, and stir in the parsley,
     vinegar, and dried mustard.

Variation

• Try this dish tossed with chopped hard-boiled eggs for a quick starter to
  a lunch or dinner.

ALL PHASES; MAKES 4 SERVINGS.

Gingered Asparagus

This warming veggie dish goes well with salmon—especially Salmon Cakes (Chapter 6).

1   pound asparagus spears, washed and dried
2   teaspoons fresh ginger, grated
2   garlic cloves, minced
2   teaspoons fresh parsley, chopped
¼   cup bone broth
2   teaspoons fresh lemon juice
1   tablespoon flaxseed oil (optional)

In a medium-sized bowl, toss the asparagus with the ginger, garlic, and parsley and let stand for 20 minutes or longer.

Bring the broth to a quick boil in a nonstick skillet.

Add the asparagus and herbs to the broth, lower the heat, and sauté for 12 minutes, turning the asparagus occasionally until the spears are just tender.

Remove onto a serving dish and drizzle with the lemon juice and flaxseed oil, if using.

Variation
•   Add 1 teaspoon dried mint to the seasonings.

ALL PHASES; MAKES 4 SERVINGS.

Carrots and Snow Peas with Parsley

Carrots and snow peas team up to provide an interesting flavor twist with Gingery Garlic Tempeh (Chapter 6).

2   garlic cloves, minced
4   carrots, cut into thin strips
2   tablespoons bone broth
¼   pound snow peas, strings removed from both sides
1   tablespoon fresh parsley, chopped

Sauté the garlic and carrots in broth in a nonstick skillet for 7 to 10 minutes.
Add the snow peas and cook for about 2 minutes or until crisp-tender.
Remove from the heat.
Stir in the parsley and serve.

Variation

• For phase 3, use 1 tablespoon of fresh basil to replace the fresh parsley.

ALL PHASES; MAKES 4 SERVINGS.

Shiitake Snow Peas Stir-Fry

This simple, fresh stir-fry is a great side dish to complement beef, chicken, fish, or tofu entrées.

½   cup bone broth
1   cup shiitake mushrooms, sliced
1   cup snow peas
1   cup red peppers, sliced into strips
1   large leek, white part chopped
   Dash of ground ginger
   Dash of turmeric

Heat a skillet on medium-high and add the bone broth.

When the bone broth starts to sizzle, add the veggies and stir until the leek pieces and mushrooms are soft and the snow peas and red peppers are crisp-tender.

The broth will cook down as you stir. Remove from the heat and sprinkle with a dash of ginger and turmeric.

TIP

Bone broth is a nutritious substitute for oils when stir-frying, making it friendly for all Fat Flushers.

Variation

• If you're on phase 3, you may want to throw in a few cashews and drizzle a little toasted sesame seed oil on top.

ALL PHASES; MAKES 4 SERVINGS.

Sweet 'n' Sour Cucumber and Red Onion Salad

Cukes are one of our only vegetable sources of silica—refreshing and bone strengthening at the same time.

3   large cucumbers, peeled and halved lengthwise
1   red onion, sliced
4   heirloom tomatoes, quartered
1   lemon, juiced
2   tablespoons apple cider vinegar
    SweetLeaf Stevia, to taste
    Dillweed, chopped
    Italian (flat) parsley, chopped

Combine all the ingredients in a nonmetal container.
Cover and refrigerate about 6 hours, stirring occasionally.

ALL PHASES; MAKES 4 SERVINGS.

Spinach-Stuffed Portobello Mushrooms

A great starter or party hors d'oeuvres.

      Avocado oil spray
4   large portobello mushrooms, stems removed
2   garlic cloves, minced
¼   cup onion, finely diced
½   red bell pepper, chopped
½   yellow bell pepper, chopped
½   pound frozen chopped spinach, defrosted and squeezed dry
1   tablespoon avocado oil
¼   cup freshly grated Parmesan cheese (optional)
¼   cup Flaxseed Crackers (Chapter 8), crumbled
1   tablespoon fresh Italian (flat) parsley
      Sea salt to taste
      Dash of cayenne
      Flaxseed oil

Preheat the oven to 375°F.

Coat a large baking sheet with a light misting of avocado oil spray.

Blot the portobello caps dry.

Sauté the garlic, onion, peppers, and spinach in the avocado oil.

Stir in the remaining ingredients (except the flaxseed oil), and sauté for a few minutes more.

Mound the stuffing inside the mushroom caps, pressing firmly.

Place the stuffed mushroom caps on a baking pan; bake for 15 minutes.

Broil for 1 minute or until golden brown.

Arrange on a platter and drizzle with the flaxseed oil.

PHASES 2 AND 3; MAKES 4 SERVINGS.

Chilled Asparagus with Roasted Bell Pepper Sauce

A delicious cool crunch on a hot day.

1   pound thin asparagus, trimmed and steamed
1   red bell pepper
1   yellow bell pepper
¼   cup extra virgin olive oil
1   garlic clove, minced
1   tablespoon Dijon mustard
1   tablespoon Italian (flat) parsley, chopped
     Juice of ½ lemon
½   cup toasted pine nuts

Arrange the steamed asparagus on a decorative platter; chill.

Place the peppers on a baking sheet to char under the broiler, or use tongs to char over a gas flame until blackened.

Let the peppers sit 10 to 15 minutes inside a paper bag; then peel, seed, and chop coarsely.

Puree the olive oil, garlic, mustard, parsley, and lemon juice in a blender until smooth.

Drizzle the sauce over the asparagus and top with the toasted pine nuts.

Serve immediately or refrigerate up to 4 hours.

PHASES 2 AND 3; MAKES 4 SERVINGS.

Spaghetti Squash with Vegetables and Spring Herbs

The snow peas add a delightful crunch to this perennial favorite.

2   tablespoons avocado oil
4   garlic cloves, crushed
2   cups hot cooked spaghetti squash
2   scallions, thinly sliced diagonally
¼   cup snow peas, sliced diagonally
¼   cup steamed carrots, diced
¼   cup steamed green beans, sliced diagonally
2   teaspoons thyme, minced
2   tablespoons Italian (flat) parsley, minced
1   tablespoon chives, snipped
    Sea salt to taste (optional)
    Cayenne to taste
    Additional fresh herbs, minced, for garnish

Heat 1 tablespoon of the avocado oil in a large skillet over medium heat.

Stir in the garlic and sauté for 2 minutes, stirring constantly, until the garlic begins to turn golden (be careful not to let the garlic get darker).

Stir in the cooked spaghetti squash, remaining tablespoon of avocado oil, scallions, snow peas, carrots, green beans, thyme, parsley, and chives, cooking just until heated through.

Season with the salt, if using, and cayenne to taste.

Garnish with the additional minced fresh herbs.

Variation

• Top with a sprinkling of freshly grated Parmesan cheese.

PHASES 2 AND 3; MAKES 4 SERVINGS.

Pureed Sweet Potatoes

Vegetable purees are a great way to add color-packed antioxidants to the plate. They are easy to make, and your guests will be impressed. This basic puree recipe can be used for any vegetable, but the ones that work the best are brussels sprouts, asparagus, eggplant, and red pepper for phase 1, rutabagas, yams, and butternut squash for phase 2, and chestnuts for phase 3. I like this dish with Roast Turkey with Lemon, Garlic, and Fennel (Chapter 6).

2   small sweet potatoes, skinned, baked, and mashed
½   cup bone broth
⅛   teaspoon ground cumin
       Fresh parsley sprigs for garnish

Puree the sweet potatoes, broth, and cumin in a blender.
Garnish with the parsley sprigs.

Variation
•   For phase 3, a dash of nutmeg would be divine.

PHASES 2 AND 3; MAKES 2 SERVINGS.

Favorite Israeli Salad

In Israel, I enjoyed this for breakfast every day!

1   red bell pepper, seeded and diced
1   green bell pepper, seeded and diced
2   cucumbers, peeled, seeded, and diced
4   heirloom tomatoes, diced
3   scallions, white and green parts, thinly sliced
½   cup Italian (flat) parsley, chopped
     Juice of 2 lemons
¼   cup extra virgin olive oil
     Sea salt to taste
3   heads romaine lettuce, chopped

Combine the bell peppers, cucumbers, tomatoes, scallions, and parsley in a large bowl.

In a small bowl, whisk together the lemon juice, extra virgin olive oil, and salt.

Pour half the dressing over the salad and toss until all the ingredients are well combined.

Refrigerate for at least 1 hour to allow the flavors to blend.

Toss the remaining dressing over the romaine leaves; then top the romaine with the marinated vegetables.

PHASE 3; MAKES 4 SERVINGS.

Green Beans Oregano

The health-enhancing oregano in this dish will increase antioxidant levels 3 to 20 times more than other herbs. And Green Beans Oregano is simple and tasty, too.

1   pound green beans, sliced
½   cup purified water
½   teaspoon dried oregano

In a heavy saucepan, place the green beans and water.

Add the oregano and cook uncovered until the beans are crisp-tender, about 12 minutes.

Drain well and serve.

PHASE 3; MAKES 4 SERVINGS.

Summer Confetti Salad

A light salad to complement any main dish.

8 to 10 endive leaves, chopped
1   avocado, pitted, peeled, and cubed
1   cup cooked organic non-GMO corn
1   red bell pepper, diced
1   green bell pepper, diced
    Juice of 1 lemon
3   tablespoons avocado oil
    Sea salt to taste

Combine the first 5 ingredients in a salad bowl.
Drizzle with a dressing of lemon juice, avocado oil, and salt.
Toss, and enjoy!

PHASE 3; MAKES 6 SERVINGS.

Tabbouleh Salad

Quinoa replaces the traditional bulgur wheat in this yummy rendition. Goes well with a vegan main.

1   cup Italian (flat) parsley, chopped
3   stalks celery, finely chopped
½   cup capers
½   cup finely chopped basil
3   cups cooked quinoa
     Juice of 2 lemons
3   tablespoons extra virgin olive oil
1½ tablespoons low-sodium, wheat-free tamari
⅛   teaspoons cayenne
6   mint leaves, finely chopped, for garnish

Mix the parsley, celery, capers, and basil in a large bowl; combine with the
    quinoa.
Whisk the lemon juice, oil, tamari, and cayenne and drizzle over the salad,
    stirring to fully mix.
Add salad mixture to grain and toss.
Marinate for 30 minutes.
Serve chilled, garnished with the mint.

PHASE 3; MAKES 6 SERVINGS.

Moroccan Carrot Salad

Exotic and fragrant, this salad adds a touch of the Orient to any chicken dish, like Garlicky Herbed Chicken Thighs (Chapter 6).

1	pound organic carrots, washed and sliced into rounds
1	garlic clove, smashed
4	cups water
½	teaspoon sea salt (optional)
½	teaspoon paprika
½	teaspoon ground cumin
⅛	teaspoon cinnamon
	Juice of 2 lemons
2	tablespoons extra virgin olive oil
1	tablespoon parsley, chopped, for garnish

In a medium saucepan, add the carrots, garlic, and water.

Bring to a boil and simmer for about 20 minutes.

Drain the water and discard the garlic.

Combine the salt (if using), paprika, cumin, cinnamon, lemon juice, and oil.

Blend well and toss with the carrots.

Garnish with the parsley.

PHASE 3; MAKES 6 SERVINGS.

Orient Express Salad

Shirataki noodles take center stage to provide a gluten- and grain-free pasta for everybody's palate.

1   (1-pound) package shirataki noodles
1   cup carrots, grated
1   package firm tofu, cut into thin strips
1   cup diced scallions
1   cup red cabbage, chopped and cooked
½   cup slivered almonds
3   tablespoons sesame oil
3   tablespoons apple cider vinegar
¼   teaspoon salt (optional)

Rinse noodles and combine the noodles with the carrots, tofu, scallions, cabbage, almonds, and cilantro.

Drizzle with the oil and vinegar and add the salt, if using.

Serve either warm or chilled.

Variations

• Can substitute or add 1 cup sea palm fronds. Prepare by first washing, soaking, and boiling until soft. Add to the noodles.

PHASE 3; MAKES 6 SERVINGS.

Fresh Spinach Sauté

Folate-rich spinach is a winning side on everyone's plate.

1   tablespoon extra virgin olive oil
3   garlic cloves, crushed
1   pound fresh spinach, washed and trimmed
    Sea salt to taste
    Dash of cayenne
    Juice of 1 lemon
2   tablespoons toasted pine nuts

Heat the extra virgin olive oil in a large skillet; sauté the garlic just until slightly golden.

Add the spinach a handful at a time and gently sauté until the leaves just begin to wilt and the spinach is coated with the olive oil and garlic, about 2 minutes.

Remove from the heat; sprinkle with the salt and cayenne.

Drizzle the fresh lemon juice over the spinach and toss gently with the toasted pine nuts.

PHASE 3; MAKES 2 SERVINGS.

Red Cabbage with Chestnuts

*This cabbage dish can be served hot or cold with the Artichoke Frittata
(Chapter 6).*

2   tablespoons onion, diced
¼   cup bone broth
4   cups red cabbage, shredded
¼   cup apple cider vinegar
     Pinch of turmeric
12   chestnuts, roasted and peeled, or reconstituted from dried

Sauté the onions in the broth over medium heat in a nonstick skillet.

Add the cabbage, vinegar, and turmeric, and mix gently.

Cover, lower the heat, and simmer until the cabbage is tender, about 20 minutes, stirring occasionally.

Blend in the chestnuts; cook through another 5 minutes.

Serve hot or cold.

PHASE 3; MAKES 4 SERVINGS.

Sweet Potato Delight

This is easy and deceptively rich. It goes great with turkey.

4   small sweet potatoes, baked
⅓   cup unsweetened pineapple juice
1   egg, beaten
¼   teaspoon ground cloves
¼   teaspoon ground cinnamon
¼   teaspoon ground nutmeg

Preheat the oven to 350°F.

Peel the sweet potatoes (or leave the skin on if you prefer).

Mash and blend in the pineapple juice.

Add in the egg and spices and beat until foamy.

Pour into a greased casserole dish.

Bake for about 35 minutes.

Variations

- Top with shredded coconut.
- Top with toasted, ground flax seeds.

PHASE 3 SPECIAL OCCASION; MAKES 4 SERVINGS.

Burdock Carrot Kimpira

A great stir-fry to break up fat and cleanse the blood.

1   tablespoon extra virgin olive oil
1   teaspoon toasted sesame oil
4   medium carrots, scrubbed and cut into shavings
2   medium burdock roots, scrubbed and cut into shavings
½   teaspoon low-sodium, wheat-free tamari

Heat the olive oil and sesame oil in a heavy skillet.
Sauté the carrots and burdock roots for a few minutes.
Add the tamari.

PHASE 3 SPECIAL OCCASION; MAKES 6 SERVINGS.

8 Snacks

Fat Flush snacks are not just an afterthought. They are every bit as important as regular meals because they keep blood sugar levels steady. In fact, as many of you already know from *The New Fat Flush Plan*, you must eat about every 3 hours to keep blood sugar levels steady, in order to avoid the overproduction of the fat-promoting hormone insulin at your next meal. When you crave something crunchy, you'll find great options here, like Fat Flush Chickpea Peanuts and Crispy Potato Skins. If your sweet tooth is calling, recipes like Sunny Day Muffins and Playful Papaya Kiwi Smoothie Bowl will surely satisfy. Many of these recipes, like Artichoke and Black Olive Canapés, can be popped in the fridge to take out for quick snacks or used as appetizers or hors d'oeuvres. You'll also be delighted to find healthy snack suggestions the whole family can make together and enjoy, like Fat Flush Petite Pizza and Fat Flush Nutty Mix.

In addition to the fresh Fat Flush fruits for each phase and the snack recipes that follow, consider trying these easy snack ideas to satisfy the between-meal munchies:

SPEEDY SNACKS FOR ALL PHASES

- Precut veggies such as zucchini, broccoli and cauliflower florets, string beans, radishes, baby asparagus spears, snow peas, and carrots in an apple cider vinegar–flaxseed oil marinade
- 1 steamed artichoke dipped in Homemade Salsa (Chapter 10)
- Jicama rounds sprinkled with fresh lime juice and a dash of cayenne
- Celery sticks and red pepper slices
- Chicken broth with chopped spinach or escarole, sprinkled with ground or milled flax seeds
- Red and yellow cherry and pear tomatoes with a squeeze of lemon
- Button mushrooms with a dash of garlic powder and onion powder
- Artichoke hearts with black olives
- Sliced cucumbers with apple cider vinegar and dill
- Fennel stalks with lemon juice

- Beef broth soup with sliced mushrooms and onions
- Sliced apple or nectarine rolled in toasted ground or milled flax seeds with cinnamon
- Red, yellow, green, and orange bell peppers cut into strips
- Snow peas split open and spread with tofu and toasted ground or milled flax seeds
- Water chestnuts sprinkled with fresh lemon juice and a dash of ground ginger
- Cascadian Farms Reduced Sodium Kosher Dill Pickles (rinsed well under running water)
- Stuffed celery ribs with mashed tofu, garlic powder, onion powder, and a dash of cayenne

PHASES 2 AND 3

- 1 Fat Flush Tortilla with chopped eggs, onions, and flaxseed oil
- 1 small yam sprinkled with toasted ground or milled flax seeds
- ½ cup baked butternut or acorn squash slices with cinnamon
- Sliced tomato with flaxseed oil, oregano, and basil

PHASE 3

- 2 tablespoons toasted pumpkin seeds with a dash of cumin, coriander, and turmeric
- 1 tablespoon almond butter with cantaloupe chunks
- 1 tablespoon peanut butter on apple slices
- ½ mashed avocado with lemon juice, ½ teaspoon dried dill, and a handful of blue corn chips
- 1 cup plain yogurt with ½ cup mixed melon chunks and chopped walnuts
- 1 cup plain yogurt with pomegranate seeds and slivered almonds
- 1 slice Swiss cheese with sliced tomatoes
- Endive leaves with 1 ounce sliced cheddar cheese
- 3 cups air-popped popcorn with flaxseed oil
- 1 small ear of corn on the cob with flaxseed oil
- 1 baked corn tortilla with Homemade Salsa (Chapter 10)
- ½ banana rolled in toasted ground or milled flax seeds with cardamom
- Frozen grapes (to freeze, simply pop fresh grapes into an airtight container and freeze until solid)
- Frozen banana with dash of cinnamon (to freeze, peel a ripe banana and pop into an airtight container, freezing until solid)
- Snow peas split open and spread with ½ cup cottage cheese and a dash of Fat Flush Curry Seasoning (Chapter 10)
- ½ cup ricotta cheese blended with ½ teaspoon lemon zest and 1 teaspoon Flora-Key

- Blanched baby squash hollowed out and stuffed with a fresh dill and cream cheese mixture

SPECIAL OCCASION

- 1 cup yogurt with ½ to 1 teaspoon blackstrap molasses, ¼ teaspoon vanilla extract, and 1 tablespoon toasted ground or milled flax seeds
- 1 cup soup made with coconut milk, sliced mushrooms, scallions, and lime
- 1 cup plain yogurt with 1 teaspoon honey, 3 tablespoons chia seeds, and ½ banana
- 1 fig stuffed with goat cheese and broiled
- Kiwi slices rolled in toasted ground flax seeds and sprinkled with unsweetened shredded coconut
- 1 cup berries with whipped cream sweetened with Stevia Plus
- ½ grapefruit dabbed with 1 teaspoon honey and broiled for 3 minutes

Flaxseed Crackers

These versatile crackers are a Fat Flush standby, and for good reason. They go well with just about any topping and are great for when you need a little crunchiness.

1   cup ground flax seeds
4   teaspoons Flavored Fat Flush Blend (Chapter 10)
½   cup 1-2-3 Vegetable Broth (Chapter 11)

Preheat the oven to 275°F.

In a large bowl, mix the dry ingredients.

Add the broth and let sit for 1 to 2 minutes.

Stir the mixture with a fork until the seeds start sticking together, about 5 minutes.

Spoon the mixture onto a cookie sheet lined with parchment paper and cover with wax paper.

Using a rolling pin or drinking glass, roll the mixture flat and out toward the edges of the cookie sheet; remove and discard the top wax paper.

Score the dough lightly into 16 crackers, using a pizza cutter or fork.

Bake the cracker mix for 1 to 1½ hours, until the crackers lift off the cookie sheet and crack apart easily.

Variation

• Try using any of your favorite seasoning mixtures.

ALL PHASES; MAKES 16 SERVINGS.

Chia Crackers

These crackers will satisfy when your sweet tooth comes knocking. They're great with toppings but are so nice to nibble on plain with a cup of hot tea.

Chia Gel:

⅓   cup chia seeds
2   cups water

Crackers:

¾   cup chia seeds
2   packets SweetLeaf Stevia or 1 to 2 teaspoons Lakanto Monkfruit
     Sweetener
1   tablespoon ground cinnamon
½   teaspoon ground ginger
½   cup Chia Gel (above)

To make the Chia Gel:

Combine the chia seeds and water in a container with a lid.

Cover and shake for 45 seconds.

Let the mixture rest for 1 minute and shake again.

Let the mixture rest for 15 minutes before using.

Store the leftover Chia Gel in the refrigerator for up to 2 weeks.

To make the crackers:

Preheat the oven to 275°F.

In a medium-size bowl, combine the chia seeds, stevia or monk fruit sweet-
     ener, and spices.

Add the Chia Gel, stirring until well mixed and the seeds start to form a ball
     (about 5 minutes).

Line the baking sheet with parchment paper.

Spoon the chia seed mixture onto the baking sheet.

Cover with another sheet of parchment paper.

Using a drinking glass or rolling pin, roll the mixture flat and out to the sides
     of the baking sheet.

When the mixture is evenly distributed, remove and discard the top parch-
     ment paper.

Score the dough lightly into 16 crackers, using a pizza cutter or fork.

Bake for 45 minutes to 1 hour or until the crackers pull away from the parchment paper and separate easily.

Store the crackers in an airtight container at room temperature.

ALL PHASES; MAKES 16 SERVINGS.

Crunchy Cumin and Lime Jicama Wedges

This simple recipe makes a slightly sweet and savory snack for when you just need something crunchy.

1   cup sliced jicama
1   lime
¼   teaspoon ground cumin
     Dash of sea salt (optional)

Look for a firm, healthy jicama with smooth skin.

Peel the skin with a vegetable peeler or sharp paring knife.

Cut the jicama in half, lay the halves on the flat-cut end, and slice crosswise into thin wedges.

Squeeze the lime juice over the wedges and sprinkle with the cumin and a pinch of sea salt.

ALL PHASES; MAKES 1 SERVING.

Artichoke and Black Olive Canapés

A rustic Italian-style combo—simple yet so satisfying. Close your eyes, pop a canapé in your mouth, and pretend you're sitting on a balcony in the Tuscan countryside.

1   (14-oz) can or (12-oz) jar artichoke hearts
12   black olives
1   cucumber

Rinse the artichoke hearts and olives in a sieve under cold running water to remove any excess salt or oil.

Roughly chop and combine in a bowl.

Slice the cucumber into rounds and top each with a spoonful of the mixture.

ALL PHASES; MAKES 4 SERVINGS.

Cherry Tomato Medley

The fresh, cheerful colors of this simple high-antioxidant snack will brighten your day.

1   cup red and yellow cherry tomatoes, halved
¼   cup scallions, sliced
1   clove garlic, chopped
     Juice of 1 lime
1   tablespoon fresh basil leaves, chopped
1   teaspoon cumin

Toss the ingredients together in a bowl and enjoy.

ALL PHASES; MAKES 1 SERVING.

Fat Flush Pickles

One of my premiere Fat Flush secrets is this: when you crave something sweet, satisfy that craving with something sour. And what could be better than these easy homemade pickles. These are great snacks—you can actually eat all of them in one sitting if you like, and they can be used sliced in salads and to accompany burgers.

8   cucumbers, cut into spears
1   cup apple cider vinegar
1   garlic clove, minced
2   teaspoons fresh dill
    Dash of turmeric

In a medium bowl, blend cucumbers, vinegar, garlic, dill, and turmeric. Cover; refrigerate for at least 6 hours and enjoy.

ALL PHASES; MAKES 4 SERVINGS.

Spinach-Stuffed Mushrooms

These little snacks are easy to pack and take on the go, but they also make very nice appetizers for any gathering.

Avocado oil spray
1   (10-ounce) package frozen spinach, thawed and drained
1   egg yolk
1   garlic clove, minced
12 large white mushrooms, cleaned and stemmed

Heat the oven to 350°F.

Spray a small baking sheet with the avocado oil.

In a large bowl, mix the spinach, egg yolk, and garlic.

Stuff each mushroom with the spinach mixture and place on a baking sheet.

Bake for 15 to 25 minutes or until the mixture is firm to the touch.

Serve hot.

Variation

- For phase 3, add ½ teaspoon of nutmeg and ¼ cup of chopped walnuts to the stuffing mix.

ALL PHASES; MAKES 4 SERVINGS.

Peppy Mushrooms

This is a quick-fix nibble that will keep in the fridge for days.

¼   cup apple cider vinegar
2   tablespoons flaxseed oil
½   teaspoon cayenne
¼   teaspoon ground cloves
¼   teaspoon ground cumin
      Dash of coriander
1   pound small button mushrooms, stems removed

In a small bowl, combine everything but the mushrooms.
Pour the mixture over the mushrooms, cover, and refrigerate overnight.
When ready to serve, drain and put toothpicks in the mushrooms.

ALL PHASES; MAKES 4 SERVINGS.

Crabby Quiche Cups

These mini-quiches are so satisfying as snacks, and they make impressive hors d'oeuvres as well. They would be a very nice prelude to any seafood entrée, such as Gingerly Grilled Salmon (Chapter 6).

	Avocado oil spray
4	eggs
	Zest of 1 lime
	Juice of ½ lime
2	scallions, thinly sliced
1	(6-ounce) can crab meat, well rinsed and drained
1	tablespoon fresh chives, chopped
1	Roma tomato, finely diced

Preheat the oven to 425°F.

Spray two 12-cup mini-muffin pans with avocado oil.

Whisk all the ingredients together.

Fill each mini-muffin cup ¾ full with the mixture.

Bake for 15 minutes or until lightly golden.

ALL PHASES; MAKES 2 TO 4 SERVINGS.

Fruity Kebabs

Grilling isn't just for veggies, as you will soon see and savor. Grilled fruits make for interesting appetizers, sensational starters, and succulent tidbits for hors d'oeuvres.

1   apple, cored and cut into chunks
     Avocado oil spray
     Bamboo skewers
     Dash of ground cloves

Preheat the grill to medium-high, coating the racks with the avocado oil spray.

Season the apple chunks with the cloves.

Thread the apple chunks onto the skewers and place on the grill racks, turning until the fruit is hot and streaked with brown, about 5 to 7 minutes.

Variations

- You may replace the apple with a peach or a nectarine.
- For phases 2 and 3, you may replace the apple with ½ cup of pineapple chunks. Drizzle with a bit of coconut oil and add a dash of dried mint. Use the same grilling time.
- For phase 3, you may also try a combo of honeydew and cantaloupe chunks, drizzled with coconut or macadamia oil, but reduce the grilling time to about 3 minutes.
- For Phase 3, mango and papaya would work very nicely, too. Grilling time with these fruits is about 4 minutes.

ALL PHASES; MAKES 1 SERVING.

Yummy Yam Chips

The kids will love these crunchy, high-energy chips! Yams are rich in B-complex vitamins and a good source of fiber.

2   small yams, cut into ⅛-inch slices
½   teaspoon dried parsley
½   teaspoon dried oregano
½   teaspoon onion powder
     Avocado oil spray

Preheat the oven to 300°F.

In a self-sealing plastic bag, place the yam slices, herbs, and onion powder.

Shake to coat.

Remove the yam slices from the bag and place them on a baking sheet sprayed with the avocado oil.

Bake for about 45 minutes or until the yam slices are slightly golden and crispy, making sure to turn at least once during the cooking process and taking care not to burn the yam slices.

Variations

- It is okay to substitute sweet potatoes for the yams.
- Try changing the flavor mix by substituting sweeter spices such as ground anise and fennel for the Italian herbs.
- Sprinkle with a dash of cayenne for another kick.
- Substitute ¼ teaspoon of cinnamon and 1 packet of Stevia Plus for the Italian herbs for a sweet treat.
- Substitute ¼ teaspoon of onion powder, ¼ teaspoon of ginger, and ¼ teaspoon of cumin for a new savory twist.
- For phase 3, sprinkle with sea salt to taste.

PHASES 2 AND 3; MAKES 2 SERVINGS.

Quinoa Crisps

These savory crisps are loaded with nutrition and taste great too!

¾ cup water

⅓ cup chia seeds

¾ cup cooked, cooled quinoa

⅓ cup hemp seeds

½ teaspoon dried mustard

½ teaspoon cumin

¼ teaspoon cayenne

Preheat the oven to 325°F and line a large baking sheet with parchment paper.

Mix the water and chia seeds together in a bowl and let stand 5 minutes until thickened.

Mix in the quinoa, hemp seeds, and spices and let stand for 5 more minutes.

Spread the mixture onto the prepared pan and shape into a rectangle about ¼ inch thick.

Bake for 30 minutes and then remove from the oven.

Lift the parchment paper onto a cutting board, and using a sharp knife or pizza cutter, cut the mixture into 20 squares.

With a spatula, turn each square over on the parchment paper and place back on the pan.

Bake for 25 to 30 minutes longer until golden around the edges and set at the center.

Transfer the sheet to a wire rack and let the crackers cool completely before storing in an airtight container.

PHASES 2 AND 3; MAKES 10 SERVINGS OF 2 CRACKERS EACH.

Sunny Day Muffins

These scrumptious muffins are practically a meal in themselves, and they make a more than satisfying snack any time of the day. The kids will love them too!

1	cup ground flax seeds
½	cup ground walnuts
¾	cup vanilla protein powder
2	teaspoons aluminum-free baking powder
1	teaspoon baking soda
1½	teaspoons cinnamon
⅛	teaspoon ginger
¼	teaspoon salt
4	teaspoons macadamia nut oil
2	large eggs
¼	cup yacon syrup
2	teaspoons vanilla extract
⅓	cup grated zucchini
⅓	cup grated carrot
¼	cup Granny Smith apple or other baking apple, finely chopped
⅔	cup ricotta cheese
½	cup walnuts, chopped (optional)
2	tablespoons raisins or finely chopped cranberries (optional)
	Drizzle of honey (optional)

Preheat the oven to 350°F.

Using one 12-cup regular muffin pan or three 12-cup mini-muffin pans, lightly coat the muffin cups with extra virgin olive oil spray.

In a small bowl, whisk together the flax seeds, walnuts, protein powder, baking powder, baking soda, cinnamon, ginger, and salt.

Set aside.

In a large mixing bowl, mix together the macadamia nut oil, eggs, yacon syrup, vanilla, zucchini, carrot, apple, and ricotta.

Fold the flaxseed mixture into the egg mixture.

Fold in the chopped walnuts, if using, and the raisins or cranberries, if using.

Divide the batter evenly into the muffin cups (cups will be almost full).

Bake 18 to 20 minutes or until a toothpick inserted into the middle of a muffin comes out clean.

Let cool; store in the refrigerator.

Serve with a drizzle of honey, if desired.

 TIP

These muffins freeze very well.

PHASE 3; MAKES 12 SERVINGS OF 1 LARGE OR 3 MINI-MUFFINS EACH.

Crispy Potato Skins

I bet you thought potato skins were forever off-limits on Fat Flush. The most nutritious part of the potato is right beneath the skin. High levels of vital trace minerals such as selenium, chromium, manganese, and potassium can be found there, not to mention vitamin C. Just make sure to remove any sprouts or greenish color from the skins before you bake. I find that organic potatoes are less likely to contain these undesirable elements. Crispy Potato Skins can be topped with Paradise Salsa (Chapter 10).

4   large potatoes, well scrubbed, for baking
     Avocado oil spray

Preheat the oven to 400°F.

Pierce the potatoes with a fork and bake for about 1 hour or until the potatoes are done inside.

Remove and let cool.

Scoop out the white inside part of the potato and transfer the skins to a nonstick baking sheet sprayed with the avocado oil.

Place the skins back in the oven for another 12 minutes or until they are crispy.

TIP

To make this approved for phase 2, substitute sweet potatoes for the baking potatoes.

Variation

• Top with Minty Dill Pesto or Basil Pesto (both recipes are in Chapter 10).

PHASE 3; MAKES 4 SERVINGS.

Fat Flush Nutty Mix

This is a good make-ahead snack when you need some crunch. I personally add a tablespoon or two of this basic mix to plain yogurt or cottage cheese. Nuts are a great source of essential and healthy fatty acids and provide extra vitamin E, fiber, and satiety at snack times.

2	tablespoons butter
½	cup almonds
½	cup pecans
½	cup walnuts
½	cup pumpkin seeds
¼	teaspoon cayenne
⅛	teaspoon ground Ceylon cinnamon
⅛	teaspoon ground ginger

Melt the butter in a medium skillet over medium heat.

Add all the ingredients to the skillet, stirring constantly to blend and making sure to coat the nuts evenly with the spices.

Cook until the nut mixture is lightly golden brown and toasted, about 6 minutes.

Remove from the heat and let cool. Store in an airtight container.

Variation

• For a special occasion, add in ¼ cup of raisins or a mixture of ¼ cup of chopped, dried apricots, dates, and/or figs.

PHASE 3; MAKES 6 SERVINGS.

Fat Flush Chickpea Peanuts

These are quite addictive, so be careful on the quantities. This is a great snack for the kids, by the way.

1   (15-ounce) can chickpeas, rinsed well and drained
1   tablespoon sesame oil
¼   teaspoon ground ginger
¼   teaspoon ground coriander
¼   teaspoon ground cumin
     Avocado oil spray

Preheat the oven to 400°F.

In a bowl, mix the chickpeas with the oil and spices.

Place on a baking sheet sprayed with the avocado oil.

Bake about ½ hour or until the chickpeas are golden and crunchy.

Variation

• You may substitute olive oil for the sesame oil and add ¼ teaspoon of sea
  salt.

PHASE 3; MAKES 4 SERVINGS.

Fat Flush Petite Pizza

This easy-to-make, guilt-free pizza snack is surprisingly satisfying and filling.

¼ cup red onion, sliced
¼ cup mushrooms, sliced
2 bell peppers, sliced
¼ cup bone broth
1 Ezekiel 4:9 Sprouted Tortilla
   Dash of dried oregano
4 tablespoons no-salt–no-sugar-added tomato sauce
   Dash of garlic powder
   Dash of ground fennel
4 tablespoons Romano cheese

Preheat the oven to 350°F.

Sauté the onions, mushrooms, and peppers in the bone broth until the liquid is evaporated and the veggies are tender and caramelized.

Place the sprouted tortilla on a baking sheet.

Add the oregano to the tomato sauce and spread the sauce on the tortilla.

Sprinkle with the garlic powder and fennel.

Add the cheese.

Bake for about 8 minutes or until the cheese is melted.

Variation

• Slice a medium-size eggplant into rounds and use as a "crust" for the toppings. Bake as above.

PHASE 3; MAKES 1 SERVING.

Turkey Bacon Asparagus Spears

These make wonderful appetizers as well as tasty snacks. Try them dipped in Cumin and Curry Aioli (Chapter 10).

4   strips nitrate-free turkey bacon
8   large asparagus spears

Preheat the oven to 400°F.

Cut each strip of bacon in half lengthwise.

Trim the tough ends from the asparagus.

Wrap a strip of bacon in a spiral around each asparagus spear, tucking in the ends.

Place on a baking sheet and bake until the bacon is crispy, about 20 minutes.

PHASE 3; MAKES 4 SERVINGS.

Going Bananas Smoothie Bowl

½   cup almond milk
1   scoop vanilla protein powder
½   frozen banana, cut into chunks
½   avocado, diced
½   cup spinach
1   teaspoon coconut oil

Toppings:

½   cup organic, all-natural granola
1   tablespoon shredded unsweetened coconut
     Handful of sliced almonds

Put the smoothie ingredients in a blender and process until smooth and creamy.

Pour into a bowl and add the toppings.

PHASE 3; MAKES 1 SERVING.

Mango Macadamia Madness Smoothie Bowl

Turmeric is incredibly anti-inflammatory and can help lower cholesterol, plus it's an antioxidant, wound healer, digestive stimulant, and liver detoxifier.

½ cup organic almond milk
1 scoop vanilla protein powder
2 teaspoons macadamia nut oil
½ cup frozen mango chunks
½ cup frozen pineapple chunks
¼ teaspoon ground turmeric

Toppings:
1 tablespoon unsweetened shredded coconut or shaved fresh
coconut
Handful of macadamia nuts, chopped

Put the smoothie ingredients in a blender and process until smooth and creamy.

Pour into a bowl and add the toppings.

PHASE 3; MAKES 1 SERVING.

The Cayenne Mocha Smoothie Bowl

Spice up your morning with this delicious bowl of protein-packed rich flavors.

¼ cup almond milk

6 ounces organic firm tofu

2 tablespoons raw cashew butter

4 teaspoons raw cacao powder or unsweetened cocoa powder

1 shot organic espresso, chilled, or 1½ teaspoons organic instant coffee granules

½ teaspoon pure vanilla extract

½ cup ice

Pinch of sea salt

1 teaspoon SweetLeaf Stevia or Lakanto Monkfruit Sweetener

¼ teaspoon cardamom

⅛ teaspoon cayenne or to taste

Toppings:

Handful of raw cashews, chopped

1 tablespoon organic hemp seeds

1 tablespoon unsweetened shredded coconut or shaved fresh coconut

Handful of macadamia nuts, chopped

Put the smoothie ingredients in a blender and process until smooth and creamy.

Pour into a bowl and add the toppings.

PHASE 3; MAKES 1 SERVING.

Playful Papaya Kiwi Smoothie Bowl

The delicious papaya is low in calories, contains a huge amount of vitamin C (144 percent of the recommended daily dose), and is also full of fiber, antioxidants, and minerals. This superstar fruit also boasts several enzymes including papain, which is an excellent digestive aid and anti-inflammatory.

¼   cup organic almond milk
1   scoop vanilla protein powder
½   cup frozen papaya chunks
1   tablespoon coconut oil
½   cup romaine lettuce
½   cup ice, optional

Toppings:

½   cup organic granola
1   small kiwi, sliced
1   tablespoon toasted sunflower seeds

Put the smoothie ingredients in a blender and process until smooth and
   creamy.
Pour into a bowl and add the toppings.

PHASE 3; MAKES 1 SERVING.

9 Dressings

Dressings can wake up simple proteins, salads, veggie side dishes, and fruity desserts and transform them into true gourmet delights. You will find flaxseed oil predominating in many of these dressings because it is a staple in all three phases. But unlike other oils, flaxseed oil needs a lot more TLC when it comes to storage. It is supersensitive to heat, air, and light, so keep it in the fridge. Flaxseed oil's nutty flavor is enhanced with aromatic Fat Flush herbs as well as a bit of lemon, lime, or apple cider vinegar to aid digestion. Most of these dressings are so easy and fast that you can make them fresh on a daily basis.

By the way, you'll find that mustard is a frequent ingredient in these dressings—not only because it has a pungent bite, but because dried mustard has the ability to raise metabolism. (One teaspoon of dried mustard has a 25 percent metabolism-raising effect.)

The Basic Fat Flush Salad Dressing

Not just for salads, this dressing can be drizzled over steamed veggies. When drizzled over cooked vegetables, the flaxseed oil takes on a buttery taste. (Please see the Fat Flush Vegetable Steaming Guide in Chapter 7 for some varied veggie ideas.)

4   tablespoons flaxseed oil
2   tablespoons apple cider vinegar
2   tablespoons fresh lemon juice
1   teaspoon fresh parsley, chopped

Put all the ingredients in a small jar, cover, and shake vigorously until mixed. Use immediately or refrigerate for up to 4 days.

Variations
- Add ½ to 1 teaspoon of ground fennel, ground anise, ground coriander, or ground cumin.
- For phase 3, add ½ to 1 teaspoon of dried tarragon, basil, oregano, rosemary, dried thyme, or saffron.

ALL PHASES; MAKES ABOUT ⅔ CUP.

Cilantro-Lime Vinaigrette

This vinaigrette may be used to quickly add zip to any simple tuna, salmon, or shrimp dish. Add more veggies as a side to this dish, and you have lunch or dinner in minutes.

½   cup scallions, chopped
2   tablespoons fresh lime juice
2   tablespoons fresh cilantro, chopped
½   teaspoon dried mustard
2   tablespoons flaxseed oil

Combine the scallions, lime juice, cilantro, and mustard in a medium bowl. Whisk in the flaxseed oil.
Use immediately or refrigerate in a small jar for up to 4 days.

ALL PHASES; MAKES ABOUT ½ CUP.

Pass the Flax Dressing

I like this drizzled onto greens—kale, turnip greens, watercress, or escarole.

4   tablespoons flaxseed oil
3   tablespoons fresh lemon juice
2   garlic cloves, minced
1   teaspoon fresh parsley, chopped
½   teaspoon dried mustard

Place all the ingredients in a small jar, cover, and shake vigorously until mixed.

Use immediately or refrigerate in a small jar for up to 1 week.

Variations

- Add a grated cucumber, chopped chives, and dash of cayenne for a kick.
- For phase 3, turn this into a sautéing liquid by substituting olive oil for the flaxseed oil.

ALL PHASES; MAKES ABOUT ½ CUP.

Fat Flush French Dressing

Here's a dressing you can prepare several days ahead of time. The Fat Flush Catsup is an integral ingredient in this dressing. Please keep this dressing refrigerated after you use it because of the fragility of the flaxseed oil. This is a perfect fancy dressing for company. Try drizzling it over plain old baked chicken or fish for an epicurean delight.

1   cup flaxseed oil
½   cup Fat Flush Catsup (Chapter 10)
1   teaspoon SweetLeaf Stevia
⅓   cup apple cider vinegar
½   teaspoon dried mustard
2   garlic cloves, minced

Place all the ingredients in a blender and mix well.

Transfer to a small covered jar and use immediately or store in the fridge for up to 1 week.

ALL PHASES; MAKES ABOUT 1¾ CUP.

Emerald Greens Dressing

This is great with leafy greens, chopped fresh veggies, or any of the Fat Flush seafood entrées.

4   tablespoons flaxseed oil
1   tablespoon apple cider vinegar
4   tablespoons green bell pepper, chopped
½   teaspoon dried dill
1   tablespoon fresh parsley, chopped
1   tablespoon onion, chopped

Place all the ingredients in a small jar and shake vigorously until mixed. Use immediately or store in the fridge for up to 4 days.

ALL PHASES; MAKES ABOUT ⅔ CUP.

Cranberry Lover's Salad Dressing

Not just for Thanksgiving—let the antioxidant power of cranberry support good health year round!

½   cup flaxseed oil
2   tablespoons apple cider vinegar
½   cup Fat Flush Cran-Water (Chapter 12)
¼   teaspoon dry mustard
¼   teaspoon minced garlic
¼   teaspoon ginger or turmeric
¼   teaspoon cinnamon
     Juice of ½ lime or to taste
½   teaspoon SweetLeaf Stevia

Process all the ingredients in a blender or mini–food processor.
Use immediately or cover and refrigerate.

> **TIP**
> You can substitute 1 tablespoon of unsweetened cranberry juice concentrate mixed with 3½ ounces of water for the cran-water.

ALL PHASES; MAKE 4 SERVINGS.

Raspberry Vinaigrette

The Fat Flush version of the tasty staple. Experience the sweetness of summer all year long, especially on fruity desserts.

½   cup raspberries, fresh or frozen
¼ to ½ cup water
2   tablespoons flaxseed oil
1½ tablespoons apple cider vinegar
     Dash of SweetLeaf Stevia

Process all the ingredients in a blender or mini–food processor; strain if the seeds are not desired.

Use immediately or refrigerate in an airtight container.

ALL PHASES; MAKES ABOUT 1 CUP.

Garlicky Avocado Dressing

Avocado makes a velvety smooth dressing for just about everything.

2   small avocados, peeled, pitted, and mashed
2   garlic cloves, minced
4   tablespoons fresh lemon juice
4   tablespoons flaxseed oil

Put all the ingredients together in a bowl and mix well.
Use immediately or store in the fridge for up to 4 days.

ALL PHASES; MAKES ABOUT 1½ CUPS.

Nutty Avocado Dressing

Avocados, with their buttery smooth consistency, make delicious dressings for both vegetable salads and fruit salads. Here I have added some omega-rich crunch with the pumpkin seeds. The avocado picks up the flavor of the foods it is combined with.

2   ripe avocados, peeled, pitted, and mashed
4   tablespoons toasted pumpkin seeds, chopped
2   tablespoons lime juice

Mix all the ingredients together in a small bowl until well blended. Use immediately or store in the fridge for up to 4 days.

PHASE 3; MAKES 1½ CUPS.

Cinnamon Yogurt Dressing

This is a great dress-up for simple fruit desserts. Why not enjoy it over Baked Cranberry Apples (Chapter 13) or Spiced Vanilla Peaches (Chapter 13)?

1   cup Greek yogurt
½   teaspoon vanilla extract
½   teaspoon SweetLeaf Stevia
     Lemon zest
¼   teaspoon ground Ceylon cinnamon
     Pinch of ground nutmeg

Mix all the ingredients together in a bowl and chill.
Store in the fridge for up to 1 week.

PHASE 3; MAKES ABOUT 1 CUP.

California Guacamole Dressing

I especially like this over main-dish salads featuring shrimp, crab, or scallops. It also makes a great dip.

1   avocado, sliced
½   red onion, sliced
1   tablespoon fresh lemon juice
1   tablespoon fresh cilantro, chopped
1   garlic clove, minced
2   tablespoons olive oil
2   tablespoons apple cider vinegar
1½ tomatoes, chopped

Place all the ingredients, except ½ chopped tomato, in a blender and blend until smooth.

Pour into a small bowl and mix in the remaining chopped tomato.

PHASE 3: MAKES ABOUT 1 CUP.

Asian Ginger Dressing

Adds a special finishing touch to baby greens salad topped with shrimp.

3   garlic cloves, minced
2   tablespoons ginger, minced
¾   cup toasted sesame oil
⅓   cup apple cider vinegar
½   cup low-sodium, wheat-free tamari
½   teaspoon SweetLeaf Stevia
¼   cup water

Process all the ingredients in a blender or mini–food processor.
Use immediately or pour into a container, cover, and refrigerate.

PHASE 3; MAKES 8 SERVINGS.

Light Miso Tahini Dressing

Not only for dressing up your salad. Try this on steamed veggies or sautés, too!

3 tablespoons tahini
1½ tablespoons light miso
1½ tablespoons apple cider vinegar
¼ teaspoon Lakanto Monkfruit Sweetener
½ teaspoon toasted sesame oil
¼ cup water or more

Blend all the ingredients well.

Add more water for a more liquid dressing, if desired.

PHASE 3; MAKES 6 SERVINGS.

Citrus Vinaigrette

Bright, crisp flavor pairs well with chicken or fish.

Juice of ½ grapefruit
Juice of 1 lemon
¼ cup avocado oil
1 teaspoon chia seeds
½ teaspoon ginger
¼ teaspoon sea salt

Whisk all the ingredients together and let sit for 15 minutes before whisking again and serving.

PHASE 3; MAKES ABOUT 1 CUP.

Walnut Pesto Vinaigrette

Rich flavors with a detoxifying punch!

1   cup basil leaves
1   cup arugula leaves
⅓   cup apple cider vinegar
½   cup walnuts
3   tablespoons shallots, chopped
½   cup macadamia nut oil
    Sea salt to taste

Pulse all the ingredients in a blender or food processor until the desired consistency.

PHASE 3; MAKES 3 CUPS.

Mellow Yellow Vinaigrette

Enjoy the anti-inflammatory benefits of this tasty dressing!

    Juice of 2 lemons
1   teaspoon turmeric
1   teaspoon cumin
¼   teaspoon red pepper flakes
¼   teaspoon cinnamon
¼   cup avocado oil

Whisk all the ingredients together until fully mixed.

PHASE 3; MAKES 1 CUP.

Roasted Red Vinaigrette

This fiery dressing is deep and complex in flavor, and it's delicious on a steak salad!

1   (6-ounce) can fire-roasted tomatoes
½   cup roasted red peppers
1   clove garlic, chopped
½   teaspoon chili powder
2   tablespoons apple cider vinegar
¼   cup extra virgin olive oil

Combine all the ingredients, puree, and then serve.

PHASE 3; MAKES 2 CUPS.

Rosemary-Revelry Vinaigrette

Use as a dressing or an aromatic marinade for chicken.

1   tablespoon Dijon mustard
1½ tablespoons apple cider vinegar
1   tablespoon lemon juice
½   cup avocado oil
2   tablespoons minced shallots
1   teaspoon fresh minced rosemary

Combine the ingredients in a jar and seal the lid shut.
Shake vigorously; then serve.

PHASE 3; MAKES 1 CUP.

Creamy Italian Dressing

Toss hearty greens and chopped vegetables in this rich and creamy dressing!

½ cup apple cider vinegar
1 tablespoon Italian seasoning
1 clove minced garlic
6 tablespoons Parmesan cheese, grated
2 tablespoons Macadamia Mayo (Chapter 10)
½ cup avocado oil

Puree the ingredients in a blender or food processor and serve.

PHASE 3; MAKES 3 CUPS.

Sweet Orange-Tarragon Dressing

Light, delicate flavors complement fish and chicken over baby greens.

4   sprigs fresh tarragon
2   tablespoons raw apple cider vinegar
     Juice of ½ orange
1   teaspoon Lakanto Monkfruit Sweetener or SweetLeaf Stevia
¼   cup olive oil
     Sea salt to taste

Muddle the tarragon in the apple cider vinegar; then whisk the remaining
    ingredients together.

PHASE 3; MAKES 1 CUP.

Coco-Almond-Thyme

Magnificent tossed over carrot and cabbage slaw!

⅓ cup unsweetened almond butter
1   clove minced garlic
    Juice of 1 lemon
2   tablespoons coconut oil
1   tablespoon yacon syrup
1   teaspoon minced thyme
2   tablespoons hot water

Combine the ingredients in a jar with a tight-fitting lid.
Seal; then shake until mixed.

PHASE 3; MAKES 1 CUP.

Greek-Style Ranch

Healthy twist on a long-loved classic.

1   avocado
½   cup organic buttermilk
3   tablespoons plain Greek yogurt
3   tablespoons apple cider vinegar
2   cloves garlic
     Juice of ½ lemon
1   tablespoon each, chopped fresh chives, parsley, and dill

In a blender or food processor, blend until smooth.

PHASE 3; MAKES 2 CUPS.

Roasted Red Pepper Dressing

Layer over slices of roasted eggplant for Mediterranean magic!

1   cup roasted red peppers
3   tablespoons apple cider vinegar
1   clove garlic
½   teaspoon smoked paprika
2   tablespoons fresh parsley, chopped
¼   cup macadamia nut oil

Put all the ingredients in a blender or food processor; pulse until smooth.

PHASE 3; MAKES ABOUT 1½ CUPS.

Creamy Lemon-Lime Yogurt Dressing

Using yogurt instead of flaxseed, olive, sesame, or grape seed oil in dressings allows you to use these flavorful oils instead for drizzling or cooking. The Creamy Lemon-Lime Yogurt Dressing goes well with the Creamy Lemon-Lime Crab Salad (Chapter 6).

1	cup plain Greek yogurt
1	tablespoon fresh lemon juice
1	tablespoon fresh lime juice
½	teaspoon dried mustard
1	small onion, grated
1	teaspoon dried basil
⅛	teaspoon cayenne
1	garlic clove, minced

Combine all the ingredients in a bowl.

Cover and refrigerate for at least 30 minutes before serving.

May be stored in the fridge for up to 1 week.

PHASE 3; MAKES ABOUT 1¼ CUPS.

Thai Carrot Zinger

Serve over zucchini noodles (zoodles) for an exotic delight!

1   cup carrots, peeled
1   tablespoon ginger, grated
2   teaspoons Lakanto Monkfruit Sweetener
2   tablespoons apple cider vinegar
3   tablespoons sesame oil
2   tablespoons full-fat coconut milk
2   tablespoons low-sodium, wheat-free tamari
    Juice of 1 lime

In a blender or food processor, blend all the ingredients until smooth.

PHASE 3 SPECIAL OCCASION; MAKES 2 CUPS.

10 Condiments, Sauces, and Spices

This section truly represents the spice of life. Here you will find perfect toppings, coatings, seasonings, accompaniments, dips, and spreads for Fat Flush breakfast foods, entrées, veggies, snacks, and sweet indulgences. The bold flavors and creative twists on classic recipes (Toasted Sesame Guacamole anyone?) say it all. You will find our Macadamia Mayo with macadamia nut oil good on absolutely everything. I guess you can say that's also true of the salsas, sauces, and pestos, too!

Adding these unusual condiments to your meals, as you probably know by now, isn't just for taste appeal but for health. I am sure you will want to try your own hand at being adventurous with these various condiments. For example, you can roll and coat all kinds of Fat Flush fruits and veggies with the omega-rich toasted and ground flax seeds or hemp seeds for heart-smart, fiber-filled crunch appeal. You can also dress up veggies (eggplant, squash, okra) and fish, poultry, beef, and tofu with coconut or nut and seed crust.

I think that you will find that even a single addition of one of the condiments can perk up a meal. I personally enjoy the Fat Flush Curry Seasoning or West Indian Seasoning when I need a zesty lift for my dips and sauces. I especially like the Minty Dill Pesto on plain tuna or salmon when I don't have time to fuss.

If you make up condiments ahead of time, you can always use them as easy snacks between meals. Between lunch and dinner, I typically grab a handful of Toasted Nuts (though not until phase 3) to keep me going before supper and have even been known to relish the Homemade Salsa as a between-meal pick-me-up.

Just wait until you taste our Avocado-Cilantro Dip, mouthwatering Beet Hummus, and Tangy Tapenade made with walnuts, black olives, and capers; and there is our titillating array of pestos and salsas, such as Paradise Salsa blended with ginger and fresh mint. Or you can go for a dip and grab your favorite veggies (the kids love jicama sticks) and plunge into one of our delectable crowd-pleasers like Chunky Spinach and Artichoke Dip.

No doubt you will notice some new Fat Flush–friendly flavoring enhancements like smoky paprika. This delightful phase 3 spice is one I became enamored of back during my Pritikin days. It was the favorite go-to perker-upper of the cooking school director. I hope you will become a fan as well.

SEEDS AND NUTS

Toasted Superseeds

Toasted and ground flax seeds are a perfect Fat Flush add-on for smoothies, soups, veggies, and Greek yogurt and provide a crunchy coating for cut-up fruit.

1   cup whole flax seeds

Preheat the oven to 250°F.
Spread the flax seeds on a baking sheet and place in the oven.
Bake for 15 to 20 minutes until crispy.
Grind in a flaxseed or coffee grinder.
Store in the fridge or freezer.

Variations
• For all phases, season with a dash of onion powder, garlic powder, cayenne, or Fat Flush Curry Seasoning (recipe given later in this chapter).
• Or try blending cloves, Ceylon cinnamon, and anise for a sweeter touch.
• For phase 3, add a dash of cardamom to the flax seeds.

ALL PHASES; MAKES ABOUT 1 CUP.

Toasted Nuts

Crunchy, flavorful, and high in the amazing omegas, crushed nuts do double duty as a bread crumb substitute and a crust for fish and chicken. Here's the best way to prepare them for good digestion and good taste.

1   cup soaked nuts, raw almonds, filberts, pecans, peanuts, pistachios, or macadamia nuts

Preheat the oven to 250°F.
Spread the nuts on the baking sheet.
Place in the oven and bake for about 15 to 20 minutes or until golden.
Store in the fridge or freezer.

TIP

Nuts and seeds last longer when they are stored in the fridge or in a dry, cool place away from light. They can also be stored in the freezer for about a year in an airtight container.

PHASE 3; MAKES 1 CUP.

SEASONINGS

Fat Flush Curry Seasoning

Here's a tasty and creative way to blend the flavor factors of the thermogenic spices with their fat-burning powers. The Fat Flush Curry Seasoning is great for waking up veggies and simply broiled chicken, fish, and seafood.

4   tablespoons ground coriander
1   tablespoon ground cumin
1   tablespoon dried fennel
1   tablespoon cayenne
1   tablespoon ground cinnamon
1½ teaspoons ground turmeric
5   whole cloves

Crush all the ingredients together using a mortar and pestle or grind together in a food processor until fine.

Store in an airtight container in the refrigerator or in a cool, dry place away from heat and moisture.

Variation

• For phase 3, add 3 ground cardamom seeds to the mix for extra flavor.

ALL PHASES; MAKES APPROXIMATELY ½ CUP.

Fat Flush West Indian Seasoning

Here's a variation of the mixes popular in the islands of the West Indies. This rendition really spices up seafood, meats of all kinds, and poultry. You can be as creative as you like according to your taste preferences. This one is a bit hot. You can make this fresh weekly and change the ingredients for more or less heat.

4	scallions, chopped
½	cup lime juice, freshly squeezed
½	cup fresh parsley, chopped finely
1	garlic clove, minced
1	teaspoon cayenne

Place all the ingredients in a food processor or blender.

Process until finely chopped.

Transfer to a storage container.

Cover and refrigerate.

Variation
- For phase 3, add 2 teaspoons of dried thyme or rosemary to the recipe and enjoy.

ALL PHASES; MAKES ABOUT 1 CUP.

Flavored Fat Flush Blend

Add Eastern flair to tofu, chicken, or seafood with this Asian-inspired spice blend. Turmeric and cumin signal a self-destruct message to fat cells.

3   tablespoons ground ginger
3   tablespoons ground cardamom
2   tablespoons turmeric
2   tablespoons ground cumin
2   tablespoons ground allspice
2   teaspoons cayenne pepper
2   teaspoons sea salt
1   teaspoon dried mustard

Combine the ingredients.

PHASE 3; MAKES ABOUT ¾ CUP.

CONDIMENTS

Fat Flush Catsup

This recipe, which first appeared in The Fat Flush Plan, *is not just for grown-ups. My nephews use this catsup on almost everything—from scrambled eggs to burgers to meatloaf and veggies such as carrots and broccoli. It is a primary ingredient in the Fat Flush French Dressing (Chapter 9) and Fat Flush Cocktail Sauce (later in this chapter).*

2   tablespoons tomato puree (Muir Glen)
1½ teaspoons apple cider vinegar
⅛   teaspoon SweetLeaf Stevia
½   teaspoon garlic, finely minced
      Pinch of cayenne

Place all the ingredients in a small bowl and whisk until well blended. Keep refrigerated.

ALL PHASES; MAKES 1 SERVING.

Fat Flush Mayo

A beloved staple the Fat Flush way—with all of the taste and none of the guilt.

1   garlic clove
2   egg yolks
2   tablespoons lemon juice
½   teaspoon dried mustard
2   tablespoons apple cider vinegar
1   cup flaxseed oil

Combine the garlic, egg yolks, lemon juice, mustard, and vinegar in a food processor or blender.

With the machine running, slowly drizzle in the oil until the mixture thickens into mayonnaise.

Keep refrigerated.

Variation
*   For Fresh Herbed Mayonnaise, mix ½ cup of minced fresh green herbs (dill, cilantro, parsley, etc.). Thin with a few drop of filtered water, if desired.

ALL PHASES; MAKES 4 SERVINGS.

Macadamia Mayo

This delicious twist will become a fixture at your table.

1   egg
1   tablespoon lemon juice, freshly squeezed
¼   teaspoon ground mustard seed
1   cup macadamia nut oil
    Sea salt to taste

In a blender or food processor, blend the egg, lemon juice, and mustard seed.

Slowly add the oil, 1 tablespoon at a time, continuing to blend.

When the oil has all emulsified and you have a creamy mayonnaise, add in the salt.

Keep in a jar in the fridge. This mayo will last about a week.

PHASE 3; MAKES 4 SERVINGS.

Cumin and Curry Aioli

This makes a delicious accompaniment to beef, lamb, or fish recipes such as Simple Salmon Patties (Chapter 6).

2   garlic cloves, minced and smashed
1   large egg yolk
2   teaspoons lemon juice, freshly squeezed
½   teaspoon Dijon mustard
¼   cup extra virgin olive oil
1   teaspoon dried cumin
1   teaspoon curry powder

Peel and mince the garlic cloves; then smash with the flat edge of a kitchen knife until they form a paste.

In a bowl, whisk together the egg yolk, lemon juice, and mustard until well combined.

Whisking continuously, add the olive oil, very slowly, in a continuous stream until all the olive oil is incorporated and the mixture is emulsified.

Whisk in the garlic paste, cumin, and curry powder.

PHASE 3; MAKES ABOUT ½ CUP OR SIX 1-TABLESPOON SERVINGS.

SAUCES

Fat Flush Cocktail Sauce

This is a nice way to dress up seafood appetizers. The Fat Flush Catsup plays an important part in this saucy blend.

2   tablespoons Fat Flush Catsup (recipe given earlier in chapter)
1   teaspoon lemon or lime juice, freshly squeezed
¼   teaspoon dried mustard
1   teaspoon fresh cilantro, finely chopped
3   pinches cayenne to taste

Prepare the Fat Flush Catsup as directed.
Add the lemon or lime juice, mustard, cilantro, and cayenne.
Whisk until well blended.

ALL PHASES; MAKES 1 SERVING.

Pico de Gallo Sauce

The perfecting pairing to any south-of-the-border selection, this sauce also serves up nicely as a condiment for grilled beef and broiled fish.

1½ pounds fresh tomatoes, seeded and finely chopped
1   large red onion, finely chopped
2   jalapeños, seeded and minced (optional)
¼   cup fresh cilantro, chopped
3   tablespoons fresh lime juice
4   tablespoons bone broth

In a small bowl, mix all the ingredients until well blended.
Cover and let sit for at least 1 hour before serving.

ALL PHASES; MAKES ABOUT 1 CUP.

Hearty Barbecue Sauce

This is great for basting plain meats, poultry, and fish on the grill or in the oven.

½ cup onion, finely chopped

2   garlic cloves, minced

2   tablespoons plus ¼ cup bone broth

¼ cup apple cider vinegar

1   teaspoon onion powder

½ teaspoon SweetLeaf Stevia

1   (8-ounce) can tomato puree (Muir Glen)

1   teaspoon cayenne or to taste

1   teaspoon diced jalapeño or to taste (optional)

Sauté the onion and garlic in 2 tablespoons of the broth until tender.

Add the remaining broth, vinegar, onion powder, stevia, tomato puree, cayenne, and jalapeño.

Bring to a boil, reduce the heat, and simmer for about 30 minutes.

Cool and store in the fridge.

ALL PHASES; MAKES 1 CUP.

Quick Cran-Raspberry Sauce

Tasty in yogurt for phase 3!

½   cup cranberries, fresh or frozen, thawed
½   cup raspberries
½   teaspoon orange zest
¾   teaspoon SweetLeaf Stevia

Place all the ingredients in a blender and blend until smooth.
Heat in a saucepan for about 2 minutes or until hot.

ALL PHASES; MAKES 1 SERVING.

Teresa's Lifestyle Marinade for All Seasons

A good marinade can elevate a simple steak or chicken breast from ho-hum to simply divine. Start with this basic recipe; then experiment with Fat Flush– friendly ingredients until you find your favorite combinations. Works equally well with beef, chicken, turkey, lamb, fish, or even vegetables.

½ cup coconut oil
¼ cup apple cider vinegar
1 teaspoon each, cumin, dried mustard, and ginger
1 tablespoon each of fresh aromatic herbs, garlic, parsley, and
    cilantro

Mix the ingredients; pour into a resealable plastic bag or glass dish with a lid. Add meat, fish, or vegetables and let the marinade sit in the refrigerator, turning occasionally.

TIPS

- Marinating times for beef, chicken, and lamb: 2 to 24 hours; for fish: 30 minutes to 1 hour max; for veggies: 30 minutes max.

- The basic marinade recipe covers two servings but can easily be doubled or tripled for more servings.

Variations

- For phase 3, substitute avocado, olive, macadamia, or sesame oil for the coconut oil. Or you can substitute coconut vinegar, lemon juice, lime juice, or special occasion wine for the apple cider vinegar.
- Substitute spices and herbs to suit each Fat Flush phase.
- For phase 2, try a Tropical Take, yummy with chicken: ½ cup of coconut oil, ¼ cup of coconut vinegar, ½ cup of crushed pineapple, 1 teaspoon of onion powder, and 1 tablespoon of chopped garlic.
- For phase 3, make a Mediterranean Medley, especially good with lamb: ½ cup of olive oil, ¼ cup of lemon juice, 1 teaspoon of dried mustard, 1 teaspoon of sea salt, 1 tablespoon of smashed garlic cloves, and 1 tablespoon of rosemary.

- For phase 3, create an Asian Infusion, wonderful with seafood: ½ cup of toasted sesame seed oil, ¼ cup of lemon juice, 1 teaspoon of sea salt, 1 tablespoon each of grated fresh ginger, chopped scallions, and sliced garlic.
- For phase 3, prepare Bohemian Vibes, delightful with mixed veggies: ½ cup of macadamia oil, ¼ cup of lime juice, 1 teaspoon of sea salt, 1 tablespoon each of fresh thyme leaves, diced chilies, and orange zest.

ALL PHASES; MAKES 2 SERVINGS.

Lemon Caper Sauce

A delicious addition to drizzle on roasted chicken and vegetables—picatta style!

¼ cup lemon juice

1½ teaspoons Dijon mustard

3 garlic cloves, pressed

½ cup olive oil

3 tablespoons red bell pepper, minced

½ cup capers, drained

⅛ teaspoon dried parsley

⅛ teaspoon sea salt or to taste

Use a blender to combine the lemon juice, mustard, and garlic.

With the blender on low speed, slowly add the olive oil, pouring in a thin stream until the sauce begins to emulsify, 1 to 2 minutes.

Transfer to a serving dish and stir in the red bell pepper, capers, parsley, and sea salt.

PHASE 3; MAKES 1½ CUPS.

Greek Tzatziki Sauce

*This sauce may easily double as a snack. I especially enjoy it over a chopped
parsley, olive, onion, and tomato salad.*

½   cucumber, peeled, seeded, and diced
1   cup plain Greek yogurt
1   tablespoon fresh parsley, chopped
1   tablespoon fresh dill or basil, chopped

Place all the ingredients in a small bowl, mix well, cover, and chill for 3 to 4
    hours before serving.

Variation
•   Try adding ½ teaspoon dried oregano with the parsley and dill or basil.

PHASE 3; MAKES ABOUT 1½ CUPS.

Minty Dill Pesto

Rather than an ordinary pesto, why not try a pesto made the Fat Flush way? The three herbs I have combined here offer a new flavor experience. In this recipe, the fresh dill, mint, and basil are much more flavorful than the dried herbs. This is divine on any kind of white fish (cod, sole, haddock, or halibut), and I personally enjoy spooning this onto fresh green vegetables, especially broccoli and kale. The Minty Dill Pesto goes well with Salmon Cakes (Chapter 6).

2   tablespoons walnuts, chopped
2   garlic cloves, minced
2   tablespoons fresh dill, chopped
1   tablespoon fresh mint, chopped
2   tablespoons fresh basil, chopped
4   tablespoons flaxseed oil

Place all the ingredients in a blender or food processor and blend until pureed.

PHASE 3; MAKES 4 SERVINGS.

Basil Pesto

This classic dressing enhances just about everything it touches. I love it the best on a medley of colorful and fresh vegetables. It's a good way to get the kids to eat their veggies.

¼   cup fresh basil, chopped
⅛   cup grated Parmesan cheese
⅛   cup flaxseed oil
2   garlic cloves, minced
⅛   cup pine nuts
⅛   cup olive oil

Place all the ingredients in a blender and blend until smooth.

PHASE 3; MAKES 4 SERVINGS.

Walnut Miso Sauce

Drizzle over steamed vegetables for a microbiome-nourishing flavor boost.

1   cup chopped walnuts
3   tablespoons light miso
2   tablespoons apple cider vinegar
2   tablespoons Dijon mustard
3   tablespoons water

Blend all the ingredients in a blender or food processor.

PHASE 3; MAKES 1 CUP.

Thai Sesame Peanut Sauce

A rich and exotic way to dress up any dish!

⅔ cup organic creamy peanut butter
½ cup canned coconut milk
1   tablespoon lime juice
1   tablespoon sesame oil
1   tablespoon low-sodium, wheat-free tamari
2   teaspoons fresh ginger, grated
1   garlic clove, chopped
    Fresh cilantro for garnish (optional)

Combine all the ingredients, except the cilantro, in a blender and pulse until smooth.

Garnish with the cilantro if desired.

PHASE 3; MAKES 1¼ CUPS.

Sweet and Savory BBQ Rub

Upgrade your barbeque with intensely bold flavors.

¼   cup Lakanto Monkfruit Sweetener
¼   cup smoked paprika
2   tablespoons chili powder
1   tablespoon garlic powder
2   teaspoons sea salt
½   teaspoon cinnamon

Combine the ingredients, adjusting the amounts or omitting ingredients to your liking.

Store in an airtight container.

PHASE 3; MAKES ABOUT ½ TO ¾ CUP OF THE SPICE RUB.

DIPS AND SUCH

Chunky Spinach and Artichoke Dip

I like mushroom caps as dippers for this energizing and liver-lovin' accompaniment!

1   (14-ounce) can artichokes, drained, rinsed, and coarsely chopped
2   (10-ounce) packages frozen spinach, defrosted and squeezed dry
⅓ cup red bell pepper, finely chopped
1   (3-ounce) can water chestnuts, coarsely chopped
1   tablespoon Fat Flush Mayo (recipe given earlier in chapter)
1   tablespoon fresh lemon juice
½   teaspoon dried dillweed
2 to 3 roasted garlic cloves, mashed
    Cayenne to taste

Combine all the ingredients in a small bowl; mix well.
Cover and chill.

Variation
•   For a cheesy taste in phase 3, add 2 tablespoons of freshly grated
    Parmesan cheese.

ALL PHASES; MAKES 4 SERVINGS.

Homemade Salsa

I like this with cut-up jicama, snow peas, and cucumber. In phase 3, of course, a handful of corn chips hits the spot. The Homemade Salsa is lovely with the Artichoke Frittata (Chapter 6).

⅛ cup fresh cilantro, finely minced
¼ cup green pepper, finely minced
2 garlic cloves, finely minced
1 (14½-ounce) can no-salt–no sugar-added diced tomatoes, drained
   Juice of ½ lime
6 scallions (white parts only), finely diced
2 tablespoons apple cider vinegar

In a medium bowl, mix all the ingredients until well blended.
Refrigerate a few hours or overnight.

ALL PHASES; MAKES ABOUT 2 CUPS.

Avocado-Cilantro Dip

Family won't eat veggies? Serve this tasty dip with some crunchy jicama, carrots, cucumbers, or celery cut into sticks. Then stand back and watch those veggies disappear!

1   large ripe avocado, peeled, pitted, and diced
¼   cup scallions, finely chopped
¼   cup fresh cilantro, stemmed
1   tablespoon fresh lemon juice
2   medium tomatoes, seeded and finely chopped
½   teaspoon ground cumin
     Hot sauce
     Sea salt to taste
1   tablespoon flaxseed oil

Place the avocado in a large bowl and mash.

Blend in the scallions, cilantro, lemon juice, tomatoes, cumin, hot sauce, and salt.

Pour in the oil and blend, using a wooden spoon.

Serve with veggie dippers.

ALL PHASES; MAKES 1 TO 2 CUPS.

Beet Hummus

A beautiful rosy color is a welcome twist on this classic dip—not to mention the digestive benefits! Try serving with cauliflower florets.

1   (15-ounce) can chickpeas, drained
1 to 2 beets, roasted and peeled
4   garlic cloves, minced
    Juice of 1 lemon plus juice for drizzling
2   tablespoons extra virgin olive oil plus olive oil for drizzling
1   teaspoon sea salt
    Cayenne to taste (optional)

Coarsely puree the chickpeas, beets, garlic, lemon juice, 2 tablespoons of the olive oil, and salt together to the desired consistency.

To serve, top with a drizzle of the olive oil and lemon juice; sprinkle with the cayenne, if desired.

TIP
Make this a phase 3 by reducing the olive oil to 1 tablespoon and adding 1 tablespoon of tahini.

PHASES 2 AND 3; MAKES ABOUT 1¼ CUPS.

Cauliflower Garlic Hummus

Roasted cauliflower replaces the traditional chickpeas in this tasty dip. Serve it with fresh, crispy vegetable slices or Flaxseed Crackers (Chapter 8).

1   head cauliflower
⅓   cup sesame seed oil
⅓   cup organic tahini
3   garlic cloves, peeled
¼   cup lemon juice
1   teaspoon sea salt or to taste
½   teaspoon smoked paprika plus dash of paprika for sprinkling
1 to 2 tablespoons water as needed

Preheat the oven to 425°.

Break the cauliflower into pieces and coat with about 1 tablespoon of the sesame oil.

Place the cauliflower on a baking sheet and roast until caramelized, about 20 minutes.

After the cauliflower cools, add it and the remaining ingredients to a food processor and process until the desired consistency, adding water if needed.

Spoon into a bowl and sprinkle with the dash of smoked paprika.

PHASE 3; MAKES 4 SERVINGS.

Zesty Avocado Dip

The avocado is a vegetarian source of protein, potassium, and vitamin E. Its high content of the heart-smart monounsaturated omega-9 fatty acids makes this a fruit that's safe to eat. This dip is perfect with such veggies as snow peas, jicama, and endive leaves.

1 small ripe avocado, peeled, pitted, and mashed
¼ cup scallions, finely chopped
¼ cup cilantro, chopped
1 tablespoon lemon juice, freshly squeezed
2 tomatoes, seeded and finely chopped
½ teaspoon ground cumin
½ teaspoon cayenne
1 tablespoon flaxseed oil

Place all the ingredients in a large bowl and blend well.
Serve with veggies for dipping.

> **TIP**
> Thinned down with a bit of water to the desired consistency, this zesty dip can double as a salad dressing.

Variations
- You may substitute olive oil for the flaxseed oil.
- Or try adding the seeds of ½ or 1 small pomegranate for a taste treat.

PHASE 3; MAKES ABOUT 1 CUP.

Fat Flush Yogurt Dip

This basic yogurt dip goes well with pungent veggies for dipping, like radishes (especially daikon, which is good for breaking down fat) and yellow, green, and red fresh pepper strips.

1   cup plain, whole-milk yogurt
2   tablespoons fresh lemon juice
¼   cup leek, minced
1   teaspoon dried dill

Combine all the ingredients.
Chill.

Variations

- Replace the leek with scallions and add ½ teaspoon of dried horseradish.
- For a curry-type flavor, replace the leek and dill with ¼ teaspoon of ground cumin and ¼ teaspoon of ground turmeric.
- For garlic lovers, replace the leek and dill with 2 mashed garlic cloves.

PHASE 3; MAKES ABOUT 1 CUP.

Tangy Tapenade

Try this flavorful blend with grilled poultry or fish, or with a hamburger . . . or, of course, with raw veggies.

¼ cup black olives, chopped
⅛ cup capers, drained
¼ cup walnuts, chopped
½ cup fresh basil, chopped
2 large garlic cloves, pressed
½ cup extra virgin olive oil
2 tablespoons fresh lemon juice
  Salt and pepper to taste

Combine all the ingredients in a food processor and pulse, lightly blending (do not puree).
Transfer to a small bowl and refrigerate until serving.

PHASE 3; MAKES 1 CUP.

Baba Ghanoush

Flavor-packed appetizer fit for entertaining. Serve with fresh-cut vegetables. I especially love it for dipping raw zucchini spears!

1	medium eggplant
1	medium yellow onion
1	tablespoon extra virgin olive oil
5	garlic cloves, mashed
¼	teaspoon salt
¼	cup tahini
1	teaspoon turmeric
1	tablespoon cumin
1	teaspoon cayenne or to taste
3	tablespoons fresh lemon juice
	Chopped tomatoes as a topping
	Chopped black olives as a topping
	Extra virgin olive oil or flaxseed oil (optional)

Prick the skin of the eggplant with a fork and then roast the eggplant over an open flame or in a 450°F oven until the skin darkens and collapses; let cool.

Remove the skin and chop the flesh.

Sauté the onion in the extra virgin olive oil until the onion is lightly browned.

Add the garlic and salt; sauté for 1 minute.

Add the eggplant and continue sautéing for about 3 minutes or until the liquid is reduced.

Add the tahini, turmeric, cumin, cayenne, and lemon juice, mashing well.

Taste the mixture and adjust the seasonings.

Top with the tomatoes and olives.

When ready to serve, drizzle with the extra virgin olive oil, if desired.

PHASE 3; MAKES 4 SERVINGS.

Bean Pâté

Serve with tortillas or crackers. In fact, Flaxseed Crackers (Chapter 8) are the perfect mate for this party pâté.

4   cups adzuki beans, cooked and drained
1   tablespoon light miso
¼   teaspoon cayenne pepper
2   tablespoons apple cider vinegar
2   tablespoons extra virgin olive oil
1   garlic clove, minced
1   teaspoon dried thyme
1   teaspoon dried oregano

Blend all the ingredients in a blender or food processor.

PHASE 3; MAKES 4 CUPS.

Toasted Sesame Guacamole

This good-for-you guacamole with an Asian twist is fun and easy to make! Try it with strips of red, yellow, and green peppers for a great snack.

3   large avocados
1   leek, white portion, chopped
1   teaspoon fresh lime juice
½   teaspoon low-sodium, wheat-free tamari sauce
½   teaspoon toasted sesame oil
2   teaspoons toasted sesame seeds
2   tablespoons cilantro, chopped
     Sea salt to taste

Toasted sesame seeds:

Heat a heavy skillet on medium heat.

Pour in a layer of sesame seeds.

Stir constantly until the seeds turn lightly golden and release their warm, nutty aroma.

Set aside to cool.

Guacamole:

Halve, pit, and scoop out the avocados into a bowl.

Mash with a fork until the desired consistency.

Stir in the leek, lime juice, tamari, sesame oil, sesame seeds, and cilantro and season with the sea salt.

> **TIPS**
>
> • It's nice to make extra toasted sesame seeds to have on hand while you're at it. Just store what you don't use in a glass container in the refrigerator.
>
> • To save for later, press a piece of parchment or waxed paper flush on the top of the guacamole to help keep it from turning brown, and refrigerate. It's best to be eaten within 24 hours.

PHASE 3; MAKES 6 SERVINGS.

Paradise Salsa

A zesty treat you can make in one easy step. Serve it with any of your favorite grilled dishes.

½ papaya, peeled, pitted, and cut into small cubes
½ red bell pepper, slivered
5 tablespoons fresh lime juice
1 teaspoon fresh ginger, grated
½ teaspoon crushed red pepper flakes
1 teaspoon fresh mint, chopped
2 tablespoons coconut oil
Sea salt to taste

Mix all the ingredients in a bowl and marinate for at least 2 hours.

PHASE 3; MAKES 1¼ CUPS.

SPREADS

Olive Flaxy Spread

This is a quickie spread that makes a terrific snack as a dip for vegetables between meals. It is also an instant topping to finish off grilled chicken, fish, or beef. I personally enjoy this with the Crispy Potato Skins (Chapter 8).

1 cup black olives, rinsed and pitted
1 tablespoon flaxseed oil
1 tablespoon fresh lemon juice
2 small garlic cloves, minced

Place all the ingredients in a blender or food processor and chop finely.

Variation
• For phase 3, substitute olive oil for the flaxseed oil and add a dash of salt.

ALL PHASES; MAKES 4 SERVINGS.

Zingy Tofu Drizzle

Dress up your salad with a little extra protein! This makes a great sauce to drizzle over cooked vegetables, or use as a tasty dip with artichokes or raw veggies.

1	package silken tofu
2	tablespoons fresh lemon juice
2	tablespoons Dijon mustard
2	tablespoons flaxseed oil
2	tablespoons minced dillweed
½	teaspoon salt (optional)

Combine all the ingredients in a blender or food processor and puree until creamy.

ALL PHASES; MAKES ABOUT 1 CUP.

Dilled Butter Spread

Here's a variation on the flaxy spread theme—but this time without the flax! This spread is delicious as an add-on to all steamed veggies and is wonderful with fish, especially salmon.

½   cup (1 stick) butter, softened to room temperature
½   cup fresh dill, chopped, or about ⅛ cup dried and crushed dill

In a small bowl, blend together the butter and dill until creamy and smooth. Cover and chill for a couple of hours to bring out the flavor.

PHASE 3; MAKES ABOUT 1 CUP.

Flaxy Syrup

When you need a sweet topping, this one comes in handy, especially for the kids.

4 tablespoons maple syrup
4 tablespoons flaxseed oil

Blend together and store in fridge.

Variation
• Adding spices like ground cloves, anise, cinnamon, or nutmeg can hit the spot.

PHASE 3 SPECIAL OCCASION; MAKES 4 SERVINGS.

11 Stocks and Soups

SOUP'S ON!

Fat Flush soups are so soothing, nourishing, and filling, and as they say, good for the soul! Many of these soups, such as Teresa's Terrific Turkey Meatball Soup, are a meal in themselves. Others, like Roasted Cauliflower Tandoori Soup, are great for lunch or as a first course for a special supper. I've even been known to have a nourishing soup like Velvety Cool Avocado Puree for breakfast!

The Fat Flush broths (especially the new bone broth) that were featured in *The New Fat Flush Plan* are so essential to phases 1 and 2 cooking that they are repeated here your convenience. As many Fat Flushers already know, the broths are a marvelous substitute for oils and poaching liquids, they keep foods moist, and they pick up the delicate flavors of herbs and spices. Bone broth helps heal leaky gut and provides collagen for the skin, hair, and nails and lots of minerals for the bones.

I always use bone broth instead of water for imparting a unique flavor to all grain-like seeds like quinoa, oatmeal (even), and of course brown rice for phases 2 and 3.

INSIDER TIPS

- You may want to freeze broths in an ice cube tray for convenience; 1 tablespoon of broth is equivalent to 1 cube of broth. Frozen stock should keep in the freezer for up to about 3 months.

- Use cold water for making a soup—especially broth. This allows the nutrients from the chicken and chicken pieces or beef and bones to absorb into the soup rather than be sealed into the meat and bones.

- Cool the soup before putting it in the fridge. This saves wear and tear on the refrigerator motor, which can work overtime to cool down extra-hot foods that are placed in the fridge.

- If the soup is frozen, first thaw it out to room temperature and then reheat it. This preserves the flavor.

- Soup is a great way to fill yourself up before going out to a party or special occasion, where you just know you will be tempted with non–Fat Flush foods.

EASY SOUPS

Soups are a perfect candidate for a quick meal because they can be made ahead and frozen. With the exception of the Gingery Egg Drop Soup that is best fresh, the soups here can be made ahead and frozen.

When it comes to freezing soups, first let the soup cool to room temperature and then freeze it in jars or containers, making sure to leave a couple of inches at the top because the liquid will expand when frozen. Also, seal tightly so the soups do not lose their flavor.

Fat Flush Bone Broth

This simple bone broth truly is the backbone of many Fat Flush recipes. Filled to the brim with nutrient-rich benefits, it can help to restore joint health, treat leaky gut syndrome, boost your immune system, and even reduce unsightly cellulite.

2   quarts filtered water
3   pounds bone-in chicken or beef shank with bone
3   tablespoons apple cider vinegar
2   cups daikon radish, grated
1   large onion, cut into 1-inch pieces
3   stalks celery, cut into 1-inch pieces
4   fresh parsley sprigs
2   bay leaves

Place all the ingredients in a large pot and bring to a boil.

Reduce the heat, cover, and simmer for about 45 minutes or until the chicken or beef is done.

Strain and discard the vegetables, bones, and bay leaves; save the chicken or beef for another recipe.

Refrigerate the broth and use within 3 days, or freeze.

ALL PHASES; MAKES 4 SERVINGS.

1-2-3 Vegetable Broth

This makes a rich vegetable broth that is great to sip by itself and is equally great as a base for other soups and dishes.

2   quarts purified water
1   large onion, cut into 1-inch pieces
3   celery stalks, cut into 1-inch pieces
1   carrot, cut into 1-inch pieces
1   bunch scallions, chopped
8   garlic cloves, minced
8   fresh parsley sprigs
8   ounces mushrooms, cut into ½-inch slices
2   bay leaves

Place all the ingredients in a large pot and bring to a boil.

Reduce the heat and simmer uncovered for about 1 hour.

Strain and discard the vegetables and bay leaves.

Refrigerate and use within 3 days, or freeze.

Variation
• For phases 2 and 3, you may sweeten the pot by adding 1 small sweet potato, cubed.

ALL PHASES; MAKES 4 SERVINGS.

1-2-3 Chicken Broth

This broth is delicious as a clear soup all by itself as a meal starter or as a snack. And it can be used as a cooking stock for so many other dishes. To remove any fat, chill the broth and skim off the fat, which will rise to the top.

2   quarts purified water
3   pounds chicken pieces with bones
3   tablespoons apple cider vinegar
1   large onion, cut into 1-inch pieces
3   celery stalks, cut into 1-inch pieces
1   carrot, cut into 1-inch pieces
4   sprigs fresh parsley
2   bay leaves

Place all the ingredients in a large pot and bring to a boil.

Reduce the heat, cover, and simmer for about 45 minutes or until the chicken is done.

Strain and discard the vegetables, bones, and bay leaves and save the chicken for another dish.

Refrigerate the broth and use within 3 days, or freeze.

Variations
*   For phases 2 and 3, add 1 small sweet potato, cubed, to the pot.
*   To make a rich, brown sauce, leave the onion skin on.

ALL PHASES; MAKES 4 SERVINGS.

1-2-3 Beef Broth

Similar to the vegetable and chicken broths, this broth can be used for sautéing other foods or by itself as a light soup. To remove any fat, chill the broth and skim off the fat, which will rise to the top.

3   pounds beef shank bones
1   large onion, cut into 1-inch pieces
2   quarts purified water
3   tablespoons apple cider vinegar
3   celery stalks, cut into 1-inch pieces
1   carrot, cut into 1-inch pieces
4   fresh parsley sprigs
4   garlic cloves, minced
2   bay leaves

Preheat the oven to 450°F.

Place the bones and onion in a roasting pan.

Bake for 30 minutes or until the bones are browned.

Remove from the oven.

Place the bones and onion in a large stockpot.

Add the water, vinegar, celery, carrot, parsley, garlic, and bay leaves to the stockpot and bring to a boil.

Reduce the heat, cover, and simmer for 3 hours.

Strain and discard the vegetables and bones and save the meat for later use or another recipe.

Refrigerate the broth and use within 3 days, or freeze.

Variations
- For phases 2 and 3, add 1 small sweet potato, cubed.
- To make a rich, brown sauce, leave the onion skin on.

ALL PHASES; MAKES 4 SERVINGS.

Harvest Bone Broth (Slow Cooker)

*This is a great way to make a hearty, healthy bone broth. Allowing it to sim-
mer all day or overnight in the slow cooker helps to bring the maximum nutrients into the broth.*

2   carrots, roughly chopped
2   organic celery stalks, roughly chopped, leaves included
1   medium organic onion, roughly chopped
8   organic garlic cloves
3½ to 4 pounds of beef bones, especially knuckles
4   bay leaves
     Sea salt to taste
2   tablespoons apple cider vinegar
4   quarts purified water

Place the veggies in a slow cooker.

Add the beef bones.

Tuck in the bay leaves.

Sprinkle with the sea salt.

Drizzle the apple cider vinegar on the beef bones.

Add garlic cloves.

Cover with the 4 quarts of purified water.

Cook on the low setting for at least 8 to 10 hours or overnight.

Strain the broth and refrigerate overnight.

Remove any layer of fat that has risen to the surface.

Store in the fridge for up to 3 days, or freeze up to several months.

TIP

**Freeze in 1-cup portions to heat and drink or add to soups and stews as
needed.**

ALL PHASES; MAKES 16 ONE-CUP SERVINGS.

Cucumber Dill Soup

This is a refreshing, hydrating soup anytime and makes a great first course for Simply Baked Fish (Chapter 6).

6   cucumbers, peeled and cut into 1½-inch slices
4   cups water
3   tablespoons minced dillweed
2   tablespoons grated lemon zest
    Juice of 1 lemon
6   dillweed sprigs for garnish
6   lemon slices for garnish

Place the cucumbers in a soup pot with the water, dillweed, and lemon zest.
Cover and simmer until the cucumbers are soft.
Puree in a blender or food processor with the lemon juice.
Garnish with the dillweed sprigs and lemon slices.

ALL PHASES; MAKES 6 SERVINGS.

Summertime Gazpacho

Gazpacho is an iconic summer soup for good reason—it's just brimming with antioxidants and bursting with fresh flavors. Make a batch to serve with Mexican Salad (Chapter 6) for a summer south-of-the-border lunch or dinner.

1   bunch celery, trimmed and chopped
6   Kirby cucumbers, chopped, or 3 large cucumbers, peeled and chopped
3   red bell peppers, chopped
2   green bell peppers, chopped
2   yellow bell peppers, chopped
1   small red onion, chopped
4   large ripe tomatoes, chopped
1   (28-ounce) can diced tomatoes (Muir Glen)
1   (28-ounce) can tomato puree (Muir Glen)
     Juice of 6 lemons plus additional for serving (optional)
     Juice of 4 limes plus additional for serving (optional)
1   bunch Italian (flat) parsley, minced, reserving some for garnish
¼   cup apple cider vinegar or to taste plus additional for serving (optional)
     Cayenne to taste

Combine the chopped celery, cucumbers, peppers, onion, and fresh tomatoes in a large bowl.

Stir in the diced canned tomatoes and canned tomato puree.

Puree ⅓ to ½ of the mixture (in batches) in a blender or food processor; blend until the gazpacho reaches the desired consistency.

Return the blended portion to the remaining gazpacho in the bowl; stir in the lemon and lime juices, most of the parsley, apple cider vinegar, and cayenne.

Chill.

Before serving, enhance the flavor by adding more lemon and lime juices, apple cider vinegar, and cayenne, if desired.

Sprinkle with the reserved minced parsley.

Serve cold.

> **T I P**
>
> **If possible, refrigerate the gazpacho overnight to let the flavors develop.**

ALL PHASES; MAKES 12 SERVINGS.

Roasted Ratatouille Soup

Roasting the vegetables before adding to the broth gives this rustic soup a richer flavor. It goes well with just about any entrée, especially beef or lamb dishes. Try it with Middle Eastern Lamb Loaf (Chapter 6).

	Avocado oil spray
1	large eggplant, diced
2	medium zucchinis, diced
2	large red bell peppers, diced
1	teaspoon avocado oil
2	large leeks, diced
2	large garlic cloves, minced
⅛	teaspoon cayenne
1	teaspoon fennel seed
1	teaspoon Italian seasoning
3	cups plum tomatoes, diced
4	cups 1-2-3 Chicken Broth (recipe given earlier in this chapter)
½	cup chopped basil plus extra for garnish

Arrange the oven racks in the bottom third of the oven.

Preheat the oven to 450°F.

Line two rimmed baking sheets with parchment paper and mist with the avocado oil spray.

Spread the eggplant on one baking sheet and the zucchini and bell peppers on the second one.

Roast in the oven, stirring and rotating the pans half way through, until lightly browned, 35 to 40 minutes.

While the vegetables roast, heat the oil in a large soup pot over medium-low heat.

Add the leeks and cook, stirring frequently, until very soft, about 10 minutes.

Add the garlic, cayenne, fennel seed, and Italian seasoning; cook, stirring a few more times, about 1 minute.

Add the tomatoes and broth to the pot; stir and bring to a boil over high heat.

Reduce the heat to low; simmer, uncovered, 10 to 15 minutes.

Add the roasted vegetables; stir and cook for the flavors to meld, about 5 minutes.

Stir in the basil.

ALL PHASES; SERVES 8.

Heirloom Tomato Soup to Love

This fresh tomato soup is so much better than anything you could buy in a can!
Try it with the Artichoke Frittata (Chapter 6) for a great lunch or easy dinner.

5½ cups 1-2-3 Chicken or Vegetable Broth
    (recipes given earlier in this chapter)
1   small onion, chopped
4   garlic cloves, minced
1   cup celery, chopped
    About 5 to 6 large fresh tomatoes, diced, enough to make 4 cups,
    or 2 (28-ounce) cans diced tomatoes (Muir Glen)
2   tablespoons parsley, chopped
1   bay leaf
¼   cup basil, chopped
    Salt to taste
    Cayenne to taste
    Additional herbs and spices, as desired

Heat a soup pot or Dutch oven on medium and add ¼ cup of the broth.

Sauté the onion, garlic, and celery until softened.

  Add the rest of the broth, fresh or canned tomatoes, parsley, bay leaf, basil, salt, and cayenne.

Add other herbs and spices as desired.

Cover and simmer for 30 minutes to 1 hour, being careful the soup does not spill over.

Remove the bay leaf and serve.

TIP

For a complete meal, stir 2 cups of cooked shrimp or chicken into the soup for the last 5 minutes of cooking.

Variation

• For phase 3, make Cream of Tomato Soup by adding 1 can of coconut cream or 1 ½ to 2 cups of cream when adding the rest of the broth.

ALL PHASES; MAKES 4 SERVINGS.

Grandma's Chicken "Un-Noodle" Soup

This soup is perfect for a sick day or any family meal—and just as comforting as you remember.

12 cups homemade 1-2-3 Chicken Broth or Fat Flush Bone Broth
    (recipes given earlier in this chapter)
1   bay leaf
4   garlic cloves, crushed
½   teaspoon cumin
1   cup celery, chopped
1   cup onion, chopped
3   cups cooked chicken, diced
2   cups cooked spaghetti squash
1   tablespoon chives, minced, for garnish

In a large saucepan or Dutch oven, combine the broth, bay leaf, garlic, and cumin. Bring to a boil; add the celery and onion.

Cover and reduce the heat to medium; simmer for 15 minutes.

Stir in the chicken and spaghetti squash.

Cook an additional 15 minutes or until the soup is thoroughly heated.

Remove the bay leaf.

Garnish with the chives.

Variations

- Substitute zucchini noodles for the spaghetti squash. Slice or spiralize 4 medium zucchinis and stir into the soup during the last 5 minutes of cooking.
- For phase 3, if a thicker soup is desired, mix 2 teaspoons of arrowroot powder into ½ cup of the broth; stir into the soup. After the soup has simmered for 15 minutes, stir in 1 small cooked mashed sweet potato. Cook an additional 5 minutes and then stir in the chicken and spaghetti squash.

ALL PHASES; MAKES 8 SERVINGS.

Gingery Egg Drop Soup

There are many variations of this satisfying soup. You can use chopped cilantro or parsley to replace the scallions

½   teaspoon fresh gingerroot, grated
1   cup no-salt-added chicken broth or 1-2-3 Chicken Broth
     (recipe given earlier in this chapter)
1   egg, beaten
2   tablespoons scallions, chopped, for garnish

In a medium saucepan, add the grated gingerroot to the chicken broth and
     bring to a boil.
Reduce the heat to simmer.
Pour the egg into the broth slowly, stirring constantly to create egg shreds.
Garnish with the scallions.

ALL PHASES; MAKES 1 SERVING.

Rose's Fat Flush Soup

This is a tasty Fat Flush standby created by Rose Grandy, "Lady Rose," from our original Fat Flush Messaging Board! Many Fat Flushers have used this "meal-in-a-soup" to keep themselves fueled up and filled up throughout the day.

	Olive oil
1	pound ground beef or turkey
16	ounces tomato puree (Muir Glen)
16	ounces purified water
½	onion, chopped
1	cup spinach
1	cup green beans, chopped
2	garlic cloves, minced
½	medium green pepper, chopped
½	medium red pepper, chopped
1	celery stalk, chopped
1	bay leaf
1	tablespoon fresh parsley, chopped

In olive oil, brown the meat in a skillet over medium heat until it is no longer pink.

Drain the fat.

Place the browned meat and the rest of the ingredients in a large pot.

Cook over low-medium heat for about 1 hour.

Remove the bay leaf and serve hot.

Variation
• Substitute cooked, diced chicken for the beef.

ALL PHASES; MAKES 4 SERVINGS.

Very Veggie Soup

Did you know that carrots, celery, and parsley are considered higher-sodium vegetables? They impart a naturally salty (and satisfying) flavor to this soup, without any added salt. Along with potassium, sodium is required for the proper functioning of our nerves and the contraction of our muscles (like the heart, our hardest-working muscle). Fluid balance, electrolyte balance, and pH (acid-alkaline) balance depend upon sodium.

2   cups 1-2-3 Vegetable Broth (recipe given earlier in this chapter)
1   zucchini, sliced
2   carrots, sliced
1   celery stalk, sliced
½   tablespoon fresh parsley or coriander for garnish

Combine the broth, zucchini, carrots, and celery in a medium-sized pot.
Bring to a boil.
Reduce the heat, cover, and simmer for 20 minutes or until the vegetables are tender.
Puree the soup in a blender.
Garnish with the parsley or coriander.

Variation
•   For a chunkier texture, omit the pureeing.

ALL PHASES; MAKES 2 SERVINGS.

Hot and Sour Shrimp and Vegetable Soup

This is an all-in-one meal when you don't have time for side dishes.

5   cups no-salt-added chicken broth or 1-2-3 Chicken Broth
     (recipe given earlier in this chapter)
¼   cup apple cider vinegar
½   teaspoon SweetLeaf Stevia
¼   teaspoon cayenne
¼   teaspoon ground ginger
1   pound raw shrimp, peeled and deveined
1½   cups radishes, sliced
1½   cups spinach, shredded
⅔   cup scallions, sliced
1   cup enoki mushrooms for garnish (optional)

Bring the broth to a boil in a large soup pot.

Stir in the vinegar, stevia, cayenne, and ginger.

Add the shrimp and cook until the shrimp turn pink and curl, about 3 to 4
    minutes.

Remove from the heat.

Stir in the radishes, spinach, and scallions.

Cover and let stand 2 to 3 minutes before serving.

Garnish with the enoki mushrooms, if desired.

ALL PHASES; MAKES 4 SERVINGS.

Creamy Red Pepper Soup

Red pepper is a great source of vitamin C and provides a touch of natural sweetness to this soup.

1   large red pepper, chopped
2   small leeks (white part only), chopped
½   cup onion, chopped
2   teaspoons fresh dill, chopped
½   teaspoon chives, chopped
¼   teaspoon onion powder
3   tablespoons plus 2 cups 1-2-3 Chicken Broth (recipe given earlier in this chapter)
3   tablespoons fresh cilantro, chopped
1   cup silken tofu

Combine the red pepper, leeks, onion, dill, chives, onion powder, and 3 tablespoons of the chicken broth in a medium-size pot.

Sauté over medium heat for 8 to 10 minutes or until tender, adding more broth if needed.

Add the remaining broth, bring to a boil, lower the heat, and simmer for 20 minutes.

Remove from the heat and let stand for 10 minutes.

After cooled, puree in a blender with the cilantro and tofu.

Return to the pot and warm before serving.

ALL PHASES; MAKES 2 SERVINGS.

Tofu Shrimp Soup

A meal in one, like Rose's Fat Flush Soup, this soup is very filling and nourishing.

1   tablespoon fresh ginger, chopped
3   garlic cloves, minced
2   tablespoons plus 4 cups 1-2-3 Chicken Broth
     (recipe given earlier in this chapter)
1   cup carrots, sliced
1   cup broccoli florets
1   cup water chestnuts, sliced
1   cup mushrooms, sliced
½   cup bamboo shoots, sliced
2   tablespoons apple cider vinegar
1   pound firm tofu, cut into 1-inch cubes
1   pound shrimp, peeled and deveined
2   cups mustard greens, cut roughly
¼   cup parsley, chopped
2   tablespoons scallions, chopped

In a large pot, sauté the ginger and garlic in 2 tablespoons of the broth for 2 minutes.

Add the remaining broth, carrots, broccoli, water chestnuts, mushrooms, bamboo shoots, and vinegar and bring to a boil.

Cook until crisp-tender.

Add the tofu and shrimp.

Reduce the heat and simmer until the shrimp is cooked, about 3 to 5 minutes.

Add the mustard greens, cooking until the greens are lightly cooked but still crisp.

Sprinkle the soup with parsley and scallions.

Serve right away or freeze.

ALL PHASES; MAKES 4 SERVINGS.

Velvety Cool Avocado Puree

This is a delightful cold soup for hot summer days. I even like this soup for breakfast any day.

3   avocados, diced
3   cups Fat Flush Bone Broth (recipe given earlier in this chapter)
3   tablespoons fresh lemon or lime juice
⅓   cup fresh cilantro leaves
1   teaspoon ground cumin
1   teaspoon turmeric
¼   teaspoon cayenne pepper
1   teaspoon lemon or lime zest for garnish

Combine the ingredients, except the zest, in a blender and process until smooth.

Cover and refrigerate for 2 hours or until completely chilled.

Pour the soup into serving bowls and top with the lemon or lime zest.

ALL PHASES; MAKES 4 SERVINGS.

Moroccan Butternut Bisque

This spice-rich soup turns out rich and creamy without even using a drop of cream. It goes very nicely with Lamb Kebabs or Sassy Beef and Vegetable Kebabs (both recipes are in Chapter 6).

1	teaspoon coconut oil
2	cups leek, diced
3	cups carrot, diced
1	teaspoon fresh ginger, minced
2	garlic cloves, minced
1	tablespoon coriander
2	teaspoons cumin
1	teaspoon Ceylon cinnamon
	Pinch of cayenne
8	cups butternut squash, peeled and cubed
4	cups 1-2-3 Chicken Broth (recipe given earlier in this chapter)
2	tablespoons chives, chopped, for garnish
6	fresh parsley sprigs for garnish

Heat the oil in a large soup pot or Dutch oven over medium heat.

Add the leeks and carrots and cook, stirring frequently, until softened, about 10 minutes.

Add the ginger, garlic, coriander, cumin, Ceylon cinnamon, and cayenne and cook, stirring for about 1 minute.

Add the butternut squash and broth; increase the heat and bring to a boil.

Reduce the heat to medium-low and simmer, uncovered, until the squash is tender, about 30 minutes.

Puree, in batches, in a blender.

Garnish with the chives and parsley.

TIP

For phase 3, stir in 1 tablespoon of orange juice after pureeing.

PHASES 2 AND 3; MAKES 8 SERVINGS.

Tomato-Quinoa Soup

Fennel gives this soup a lick of mild licorice-like flavor. It goes well with Lemon Chicken on the Grill (Chapter 6).

1	cup quinoa
2	tablespoons coconut oil
2	medium shallots, diced
2	garlic cloves, minced
1	tablespoon fennel seeds
2	cans no-salt–no-sugar-added whole peeled tomatoes (Muir Glen)
2	cups 1-2-3 Chicken or Vegetable broth (recipe given earlier in this chapter)
¼	cup toasted pumpkin seeds for garnish
1	tablespoon fresh chives, snipped, for garnish
½	teaspoon cayenne for garnish

Cook the quinoa according to the directions on the package.

In a large saucepan, heat the coconut oil and add shallots, garlic, and fennel seeds.

Cook, stirring occasionally until the vegetables begin to soften, about 4 to 6 minutes.

Add the tomatoes and broth and heat to just before a boil; then reduce the heat and simmer for 15 minutes, stirring occasionally.

Puree in a blender, in batches, and return to the saucepan.

Divide the cooked quinoa into 4 bowls and ladle the soup over the top.

Garnish with the toasted pumpkin seeds, chives, and cayenne.

To toast the pumpkin seeds:

Heat a heavy skillet on medium heat.

Pour in the pumpkin seeds and stir until most of them are lightly browned. (They'll make a popping sound while toasting.)

PHASES 2 AND 3; MAKES 4 SERVINGS.

Chilled Red-Velvet Borscht

Beets are just chock-full of essential nutrients and so beneficial for helping to reduce water retention and promote detoxification. This beautiful borscht is refreshing on a warm day.

5   medium fresh beets
5   cups no-salt-added-broth
1   tablespoon coconut oil
2   tablespoons lemon juice
2   teaspoons coconut vinegar
3   leeks, chopped
2   garlic cloves, minced
2   cups English cucumber, diced
2   tablespoons fresh dill, chopped, plus 1 tablespoon for garnish

Cook the beets in a pot of boiling water until tender, 30 to 40 minutes.

Remove the beets and set aside to cool.

Strain the cooking liquid and set it aside to cool.

Add 1½ cups of the beet cooking liquid, broth, coconut oil, lemon juice, and coconut vinegar to a large bowl and whisk together.

Peel the cooled beets and dice.

Add the beets, leeks, garlic, cucumber, and 2 tablespoons of the dill to the bowl and mix well.

Cover and chill in the refrigerator for 4 hours or overnight.

Divide the remaining tablespoon of dill and sprinkle on top of each serving.

PHASES 2 AND 3; MAKES 6 SERVINGS.

Shiitake Mushroom Soup

Mushrooms are a source of energy-producing B vitamins and immune-boosting zinc. They also contain glutamic acid, another source of energy. The tofu provides a creamy consistency and a boost of protein. This hearty mushroom soup with an Asian flair is delicious served alongside Gingerly Grilled Salmon (Chapter 6).

1   teaspoon toasted sesame oil
1   tablespoon minced ginger
2   garlic cloves, minced
½   teaspoon cayenne or to taste plus a dash for garnish (optional)
4   cups 1-2-3 Chicken Broth (recipe given earlier in this chapter)
2   cups water
2   tablespoons low-sodium, wheat-free tamari
1   (8-ounce) package sliced cremini mushrooms
4   cups sliced shiitake mushrooms
1   (8-ounce) can sliced water chestnuts, drained
4   baby bok choy, coarsely chopped
1   cup matchstick-cut carrots plus extra for garnish
1   cup snow peas
½   cup chopped scallions plus extra for garnish
½   cup chopped cilantro plus extra for garnish
1   tablespoon fresh lime juice

Heat the oil in a large soup pot over low heat.

Add the ginger, garlic, and cayenne; cook, stirring frequently, 1 to 2 minutes.

Add the broth, water, and tamari; stir and bring to a boil over high heat.

Reduce the heat to low and add the mushrooms and water chestnuts; simmer, covered, for 15 minutes.

Add the bok choy, carrots, and snow peas; stir and cook until the vegetables are tender, about 5 minutes.

Stir in the scallions, cilantro, and lime juice.

Serve garnished with carrots, scallions, and cilantro and a dash of cayenne, if
desired.

TIP

For a special occasion, add 1 tablespoon of fish sauce with the tamari.

PHASE 3; MAKES 8 SERVINGS.

Teresa's Terrific Turkey Meatball Soup

Nutrient-rich mushrooms replace the usual bread crumbs in these tender meatballs. Slightly bitter, nutty-tasting escarole infuses the soup with healthful antioxidants. It's great accompanied by a Bibb lettuce salad and any Fat Flush dressing (Chapter 9).

1   pound ground turkey
1   egg
1   cup baby portobello mushrooms, minced
2   shallots, minced
2   garlic cloves, minced
½   cup Italian (flat) parsley, finely chopped
1   teaspoon dry mustard
     Avocado oil spray
2   leeks, thinly sliced
8   cups 1-2-3 Chicken Broth (recipe given earlier in this chapter)
1   tablespoon fresh thyme leaves
½   tablespoon fresh rosemary leaves
1   bunch escarole (about ¾ pound), coarsely chopped

Combine the ground turkey, egg, mushrooms, shallots, half the garlic, parsley, and dry mustard in a large bowl and mix with your hands until the ingredients are well combined.

Form into 24 meatballs, about the size of golf balls.

Heat a large skillet to medium, spray with the avocado oil, and cook the meatballs until golden brown and cooked through, about 5 minutes.

Heat a large soup pan or Dutch oven over medium heat, spray with the avocado oil, add the leeks and remaining garlic, and cook until soft and translucent, 3 to 5 minutes.

Add the chicken broth and simmer about 5 minutes.

Stir in the thyme, rosemary, meatballs, and escarole and return to a simmer until heated through.

PHASE 3; MAKES 4 TO 6 SERVINGS.

Roasted Cauliflower Tandoori Soup

Inspired by Indian cuisine, the spices in this soup in combination with the caramelized flavor of the roasted cauliflower will warm you to your toes.

8　cups cauliflower, cut into bite-sized florets, divided into 4 cups for roasting and 4 cups added raw
　　Avocado oil spray
2　teaspoons plus ½ teaspoon curry powder
1　teaspoon coconut oil
2　cups shallots, diced
1　teaspoon fresh garlic, minced
1　teaspoon fresh ginger, minced
1　teaspoon dried mustard
1　teaspoon cumin seed
½　teaspoon coriander
4　cups 1-2-3 Chicken Broth (recipe given earlier in this chapter)
1　(14-ounce) can salt-free–sugar-free diced tomatoes (Muir Glen), drained
2　cups green beans, cut into bite-size pieces
1　tablespoon fresh lime juice
2　tablespoons fresh basil, chopped (optional)

Preheat the oven to 450°F.

Line a baking sheet with parchment paper.

Place 4 cups of the cauliflower in a large bowl and coat with the avocado spray; toss with 2 teaspoons of the curry powder.

Spread the cauliflower on a prepared pan; roast, stirring once halfway through, about 30 minutes.

While the cauliflower roasts, heat the coconut oil in a large soup pot.

Add the shallots and cook, stirring often, until slightly softened, about 5 minutes.

Add the garlic, ginger, mustard, cumin seeds, coriander, and remaining ½ teaspoon of the curry powder and cook, stirring frequently, about 1 minute.

Add the remaining 4 cups of the raw cauliflower florets and broth to the pot; increase the heat to high and bring to a boil.

Reduce the heat to medium-low; simmer, uncovered, until the cauliflower is very soft, 15 to 20 minutes.

Puree the soup in batches in a blender, or puree it in the pot with a hand immersion blender.

Stir in the tomatoes and green beans and cook, uncovered, until the green beans are tender, 5 to 7 minutes.

Stir in the lime juice and roasted cauliflower; sprinkle with the basil, if desired.

PHASE 3; MAKES 8 SERVINGS.

Escarole and Bean Soup

This is a snap to make thanks to the canned beans. Serve it with Quinoa Crisps (Chapter 8) and a green salad.

Avocado oil spray
1   tablespoon avocado oil
2   garlic cloves, sliced
¼   cup scallions, diced
1   teaspoon cumin
¼   teaspoon cayenne or to taste
1   small head escarole, leaves torn into 2-inch pieces (about 12 cups)
1   (15½-ounce) can organic red kidney beans, rinsed and drained
1   (15½-ounce) can organic chickpeas, rinsed and drained
4   cups 1-2-3 Chicken Broth (recipe given earlier in this chapter)
2   cups purified water
1   avocado, peeled, pitted, and sliced into wedges for topping
     Lemon wedges for serving

Heat a medium saucepan over medium heat and coat with avocado oil spray.

Add the garlic, scallions, cumin, and cayenne, stirring, 1 minute.

Stir in the escarole and cook just until wilted, about 2 minutes.

Add the kidney beans, chickpeas, broth, and 2 cups of water and bring to a simmer.

Cook until heated through, about 3 minutes.

Top with the avocado slices and avocado oil, and serve with the lemon wedges.

PHASE 3; MAKES 4 SERVINGS.

12 Beverages

There are many creative and secret ways (without cheating!) to adapt the Fat Flush principles to healthy and thirst-quenching beverages. Certain herbal teas, as you will discover in this chapter, can be made from the Fat Flushing herbs and spices allowed in each phase. These special teas do not take the place, of course, of the recommended cran-water, lemon and water, or plain water in the daily protocols in each of the three phases, but they can be used as delightfully fragrant and satisfying additions—about 1 to 2 cups per day, if you wish, between meals and snacks.

Fat Flush Cran-Water

This foundational fat-flushing beverage helps melt away stubborn cellulite and release fluid from waterlogged tissues while detoxifying the liver and cleansing the lymphatic system.

8   ounces 100% unsweetened cranberry juice or 3 tablespoons concentrate

56   ounces plain filtered water or 64 ounces if using cranberry concentrate

In a 64-ounce (½-gallon) bottle, stir together the cranberry juice or concentrate with the water.

> **TIP**
> Allergic to cranberry juice? Omit the cranberry juice and add 4 tablespoons of unfiltered apple cider vinegar or coconut vinegar to 64 ounces of plain filtered water.

ALL PHASES; MAKES 64 OUNCES.

Cinnamon-Cranberry Tea

Rose Grandy created this unusual beverage. Simply subtract ¼ cup (or 2 ounces) of unsweetened cranberry juice from your daily allotment, use it here instead, and you have Cinnamon-Cranberry Tea.

¼   cup unsweetened cranberry juice
¾   cup purified water
½   teaspoon ground Ceylon cinnamon

Combine the cranberry juice and water in a small saucepan.
Bring to a quick boil.
Reduce the heat and stir in the cinnamon.
Serve warm.

ALL PHASES; MAKES 1 SERVING.

Fat Flush Lemonade

On a warm summer day, there is nothing like real lemonade. Here is the Fat Flush version that you can enjoy and even serve to your company. The lemonade should take the place of the hot water and lemon in all three phases and can be enjoyed twice a day as a treat.

¼   cup lemon juice, freshly squeezed
¼   teaspoon SweetLeaf Stevia or to taste
2   cups chilled, purified water

Combine all the ingredients and stir until the stevia is completely dissolved. Serve chilled.

Variations

- You can substitute ¼ cup of freshly squeezed lime juice for the lemon juice to make a limeade.
- Or you might substitute ¼ cup of unsweetened cranberry juice for the lemon juice for a "cranade."

ALL PHASES; MAKES 2 SERVINGS.

Fennel Tea

Fennel is an excellent herb for relieving gas and indigestion. Used by mothers for years to control infant colic, fennel has a licorice-like taste that lends itself well to teas for adults.

1   teaspoon whole fennel seeds
1   pint purified water

Place the seeds in the water in a small saucepan.
Boil for about 15 to 20 minutes.
Strain and enjoy hot or cold.

ALL PHASES; MAKES 1 SERVING.

Parsley Tea

Parsley is a great natural diuretic, high in potassium and other alkalinizing minerals. This tea is very helpful for relief of painful urination.

1   teaspoon fresh parsley
1   pint purified water

Place the parsley in the water in a small saucepan.
Bring to a simmer for about 15 minutes.
Strain and enjoy, hot or cold.

ALL PHASES; MAKES 1 SERVING.

Metabolism Cocktail

A great way to boost your metabolism and nourish your gut while sipping away any afternoon slump.

1   large tomato
⅓   cup lime or lemon juice, freshly squeezed
½   cup filtered water
     Handful of fresh parsley
     Handful of fresh cilantro
1   green onion, chopped
1   garlic clove, crushed
⅛   teaspoon cayenne or to taste
2   teaspoons extra virgin olive oil
½   teaspoon Eden Seaweed Gomasio
½   teaspoon turmeric
1   teaspoon Flora-Key
1   tablespoon chia seeds
6   ice cubes

Combine all the ingredients in a blender until the desired consistency is reached.

ALL PHASES; MAKES 1 SERVING.

Calming Ginger Tea

Ginger is wonderfully soothing for the digestive system and can help your body to absorb all the healthy nutrients that you're eating on the Fat Flush plan. It's great for calming an upset tummy too!

3½ cups water
1-inch piece fresh ginger, sliced into thin rounds (about 1 tablespoon)
6   cloves
     SweetLeaf Stevia to taste
1   teaspoon Ceylon cinnamon
     Slice of lemon

Combine the water, ginger, and cloves in a small pot.

Bring to a boil and simmer for 10 minutes.

Remove from the heat.

Steep the tea for 10 minutes.

Remove the ginger and cloves.

Stir in the stevia and sprinkle with the cinnamon.

Drink hot or cold, served with the slice of lemon.

Store the extra tea in an airtight container in the refrigerator.

ALL PHASES; MAKES 2 SERVINGS.

Bahama Splash

This sweet and tangy punch would be great to serve at any gathering.

½ cup unsweetened cranberry juice
  Juice of 1 lime
  Juice of ½ grapefruit
3½ cups water
  Handful of ice cubes
  SweetLeaf Stevia to taste
1 tablespoon chopped fresh mint (optional)
  Fresh mint sprigs for garnish

Place all the ingredients, except the chopped mint and mint sprigs, in a blender and blend until smooth.

Stir in the chopped mint, if using. Pour into tall glasses; garnish with the mint sprigs.

ALL PHASES; MAKES ABOUT 1 QUART.

Gazpacho Cooler

This is a great pick-me-up on a sunny afternoon. Or make up a pitcher to serve alongside zesty Mexican Salad (Chapter 6).

1   medium cucumber, peeled and diced
2   tablespoons celery, chopped
1   tablespoon red onion, chopped
2   teaspoons apple cider vinegar
2   tablespoons fresh lemon juice
2   tablespoons fresh lime juice
     Salt to taste
     Cayenne to taste
4   cups 1-2-3 Vegetable Broth (Chapter 11)
     Crushed ice
4   small celery stalks for garnish

In a blender on high speed, lightly puree the cucumber, celery, onion, vinegar, lemon and lime juices, salt, and cayenne.

Combine the vegetable broth and the cucumber mixture in a large pitcher.

Chill for 1 hour.

Pour into tall glasses over the crushed ice.

Serve with the celery stalk stirrers.

ALL PHASES; MAKES 4 SERVINGS.

Peppermint Tea

Very refreshing, peppermint tea is cleansing of and calming to the nervous system.

1 teaspoon fresh peppermint
1 pint purified water

Place the peppermint in the water in a small saucepan.
Bring to a simmer for about 15 minutes.
Strain and enjoy, hot or cold.

Variation
• You can use spearmint as a substitute for the peppermint.

PHASES 2 AND 3; MAKES 1 SERVING.

Hot Cocoa

Bet you thought you'd never see this one in a Fat Flush cookbook. The cream is very satisfying and actually quite good for the nervous system.

1   rounded tablespoon cocoa powder
1½ teaspoons vanilla extract
¼   teaspoon SweetLeaf Stevia
¾   cup purified water
¼   cup cream

Combine all the ingredients in a small saucepan.
Whisk together until the cocoa is blended.
Heat until just simmering.
Serve hot.

PHASE 3 SPECIAL OCCASION; MAKES 1 SERVING.

Hot Carob

If you are allergic to cocoa or want to avoid it because of its high copper content, why not try carob?

1 rounded tablespoon carob
1½ teaspoons vanilla
¼ teaspoon SweetLeaf Stevia
¾ cup purified water
¼ cup cream

Combine all the ingredients in a small saucepan.
Whisk together until the carob is blended.
Heat until just simmering.
Serve hot.

PHASE 3 SPECIAL OCCASION; MAKES 1 SERVING.

Bedtime Toddy

A comforting and delicious way to wind down before bed.

1   cup almond milk
½   teaspoon ground turmeric
⅛   teaspoon ground ginger
     Dash cardamom
⅛   teaspoon Ceylon cinnamon

Over medium heat, combine all the ingredients, whisking slightly.
Bring to a boil.
Simmer on low for another 3 minutes.

PHASE 3; MAKES 1 SERVING.

13 Nourishing Sweets and Indulgences

Naturally, the best desserts of all are those that Mother Nature provides. However, you will be impressed that the treats in this section make it so easy to get the sugar out and still satisfy anybody's sweet tooth on the New Fat Flush Plan. Whether as a dessert or a snack, you will be pleasantly surprised at how satisfying these naturally sweetened recipes really are. Cinnamon is used frequently in these easy desserts because it helps to regulate blood sugar levels. Many of the desserts, like Cinnamony Applesauce and the Fat Flush Cheesecake, use the sweetener SweetLeaf Stevia or Lakanto Monkfruit Sweetener (made from non-GMO erythritol and monk fruit). As many of you already know from *The New Fat Flush Plan*, neither stevia nor Lakanto raises blood sugar or fuels yeast overgrowth.

For special occasions or for a healthful dessert option for the family, you will find that some recipes in this section do use minimal amounts of more traditional sweeteners. For instance, date sugar is in the Apple Crisp, and honey can be found in the Lemony Almond Cookies. The newest smart sweetener, yacon syrup, is included in recipes such as Crustless Custard-Pumpkin Pie. The other treats are great healthy desserts for the kids anytime and for you too when you feel like having a comfort food.

What you won't see in this section are any desserts made with fructose—the sugar that is predominant in certain fruit juices and that has been found to have many health drawbacks if consumed excessively. It can decrease satiety hormones like leptin and raise hunger, increasing ghrelin while elevating artery-clogging LDL cholesterol levels, raising uric acid levels in the blood, and boosting triglyceride levels more than any other type of sugar. The fructose that naturally occurs in most whole fruits, however, is combined with both fiber and minerals that balance out fructose's negative health effects when it is consumed only as an isolated sweetener or as apple juice concentrate, for example.

Before we begin, please keep in mind that many of the desserts herein contain meringue (stiffly beaten egg whites). If you are intolerant to eggs or concerned about gallbladder health, it is best to skip the meringue desserts entirely. For those who can tolerate the incredible egg, the following are just a few pointers from the get-go to get you in the meringue mood. These pointers will greatly help you to get the meringues to hold their shape:

- When the recipe calls for egg whites, you will be making meringues out of them.
- Take the eggs out of the fridge at least ½ hour before you start. Egg whites at room temperature produce a fluffier and faster whip than do cold egg whites.
- The best kinds of bowls to use for making meringues are glass or metal.
- The frothiness or volume of the meringue may be reduced if the bowls are not clean, so take a damp cloth with a bit of apple cider vinegar and wipe them thoroughly to cut any residue.
- You will know when the meringues are ready when the egg whites become shiny and do not slip and slide in your bowl.
- To test if your meringues are at their peak (no pun intended), try turning the bowl upside down. If the meringues cling to the bowl, they are ready for prime time.
- Cream of tartar is a marvelous meringue stabilizer and is good for you, too. Cream of tartar is made from grapes, is a decent source of potassium, and, according to folk medicine, is a natural blood cleanser. This ingredient fits the Fat Flush criteria, now doesn't it?
- Make sure you watch the meringues carefully because they can burn easily. Go for a lightly golden color.
- Do keep in mind that meringues made without sugar are not as crispy as those made with sugar. The Fat Flush–style meringues will not have the same texture as those made with sugar.

RECIPES IN THIS CHAPTER   PAGE

Cinnamony Applesauce

This aromatic applesauce recipe lends itself to many varieties of apples such as the ones listed below. You may also use Golden Delicious, Gala, Jonathan, Pippin, or Winesap. I like Cinnamony Applesauce after one of the poultry entrées, especially Dijon Turkey Cutlets or Tasty Holiday Chicken (both recipes are in Chapter 6).

1   apple (Rome Beauty, Granny Smith, or McIntosh), peeled, cored, and sliced
¼   teaspoon SweetLeaf Stevia or Lakanto Monkfruit Sweetener to taste (optional)
½   teaspoon Ceylon cinnamon

Preheat the oven to 300°F.
Arrange the apple slices in a small baking dish.
Sprinkle with the stevia or Lakanto, if desired, and cinnamon and cover.
Bake for 15 minutes.
Mash when cooked and serve hot or cold.

Variations
- For a change of pace, substitute cherries (omit the cinnamon), berries, or a peach for the apple.
- Try a touch (just a touch) of cloves.
- For phase 3, add a drop of vanilla extract and a dash of allspice and nutmeg.

ALL PHASES; MAKES 1 SERVING.

Baked Cranberry Apples

Here's your basic baked apple recipe with some uniquely Fat Flush–friendly fillings.

½ cup cranberries, fresh or frozen, thawed
1 teaspoon Flora-Key or SweetLeaf Stevia or Lakanto Monkfruit Sweetener
1 teaspoon Ceylon cinnamon
4 medium apples (Rome Beauty, McIntosh, or Golden Delicious), cored and pared
3 to 4 tablespoons purified water

Preheat the oven to 350°F.

In a small bowl, blend the cranberries, Flora-Key or stevia or Lakanto, and cinnamon.

Stuff the apples with the cranberry mixture.

Place in a shallow baking dish, add the water in the baking dish with the fruit, and cover.

Baste the fruit with the liquid from the baking dish during cooking and bake for about 30 to 40 minutes.

Variations
- Chopped walnuts or pecans, grated lemon or orange zest, nutmeg, cloves, and allspice are tasty phase 3 variations as well.
- For a special occasion, top with a tablespoon of Fat Flush Whipped Cream (the recipe is given at the end of the chapter).
- For a phase 3 special occasion, you can transform this recipe into Baked Cranberry Raisin Apples by adding 1 tablespoon of raisins to each apple and a dash of nutmeg, too.

ALL PHASES; MAKES 4 SERVINGS.

Blueberry Mousse

You really can enjoy some treats on phases 1 and 2. This Blueberry Mousse proves it.

1   cup blueberries
1   teaspoon Flora-Key, SweetLeaf Stevia, or Lakanto Monkfruit
     Sweetener to taste
1   egg white
     Pinch of cream of tartar

Place the blueberries and Flora-Key, stevia, or Lakanto in a blender and puree until smooth.

Beat the egg white with cream of tartar until stiff peaks form.

Stir ¼ of the egg white into the blueberry mixture to "lighten."

Gently fold in the remaining egg white.

Pour into a small freezer container with a lid and freeze until firm.

Partially defrost for 10 minutes and serve.

Variation
•   Whip one block of silken tofu and add for an extra-creamy treat.

ALL PHASES; MAKES 1 SERVING.

Spiced Vanilla Peaches

This is a personal, all-time favorite.

4   peaches, peeled, pitted, and halved
1   tablespoon purified water
1   teaspoon allspice
16 drops vanilla extract

Preheat the oven to 350°F.

Place the peaches and water in a baking dish.

Sprinkle the peaches with allspice and drizzle each peach half with 3 drops of
    vanilla extract.

Cover and bake for about 20 minutes.

Serve warm.

Variations

- Fresh plums, nectarines, Bartlett pears, and apples may be substituted for
  the peaches, and any of these is also delightful with a dash of allspice and
  a touch of vanilla.
- Serve with Lemon-Almond-Crusted Trout Fillets (Chapter 6) for a gourmet
  ending to a flavorful meal.

ALL PHASES; MAKES 4 SERVINGS.

Razzle Dazzle Sorbet

The special ingredient in this sorbet is bananas. They give this dessert a consistency almost like ice cream. Do note that this sorbet provides 1½ fruit servings per person, so adjust additional fruit intake accordingly.

2   cups raspberries, fresh or frozen
2   bananas, sliced
1   teaspoon Flora-Key, SweetLeaf Stevia, or Lakanto Monkfruit
     Sweetener
½   teaspoon fresh lemon juice

Place all the ingredients in a blender or food processor and blend until
    smooth.
Place in plastic containers or ice-cube trays and freeze at least 2 hours.
Take out the partially frozen mixture and stir well to break up the ice crystals.
Return to the freezer to freeze completely.
Let the sorbet stand 15 minutes at room temperature before serving.

Variations

- Any type of berry can be used in place of the raspberries. Blueberries are
  especially good and very high in a health-promoting and brain-boosting
  substance called anthocyanin—an antioxidant belonging to the flavonoid
  family.
- For a phase 3 special occasion, substitute 1 tablespoon of honey for the
  stevia or Lakanto.

PHASES 2 AND 3; MAKES 4 SERVINGS.

Apple Crisp

The oat flour in this recipe is especially light and sweet. Healthier than wheat flour, oat flour is lower on the glycemic index than regular flour. If you can't find oat flour in your health food store or grocery, you can always make it at home by grinding rolled oats in your food processor until you get a flour con-sistency. This crisp is good hot or cold and is a perfect accompaniment to just about any Fat Flush entrée.

⅔   cup date sugar
½   cup oat flour
½   cup old-fashioned rolled oats
⅓   cup butter, softened
1   teaspoon Ceylon cinnamon
1   teaspoon nutmeg
3   medium apples (Granny Smith, Golden Delicious, or Rome Beauty), cored, peeled, and sliced

Preheat the oven to 375°F.

In a bowl, mix the date sugar, flour, oats, butter, cinnamon, and nutmeg together.

Add the apple slices and toss lightly.

Pour into an 8-inch-square, nonstick baking pan.

Bake for about 30 minutes or until the apples are soft.

Variations

• Add a cup of cooked cranberries for added color and antioxidant power.
• Top with 4 tablespoons of raisins.

PHASE 3 SPECIAL OCCASION; MAKES 4 SERVINGS.

Apple, Cranberry, and Pear Crisp

Nutty and filling with tigernut flour—which is naturally sweet—even the kids will love this.

Extra virgin olive oil spray

Filling:

2   baking apples (Granny Smith, Gala, etc.), peeled, cored, and sliced
2   pears, peeled, cored, and sliced
½   cup cranberries, fresh or frozen
1   tablespoon tigernut flour
½   teaspoon SweetLeaf Stevia or Lakanto Monkfruit Sweetener
2   tablespoons fresh lemon juice

Crust:

⅓   cup tigernut flour
1   scoop vanilla protein powder
1½ teaspoons SweetLeaf Stevia or Lakanto Monkfruit Sweetener
½ to 1 teaspoon Ceylon cinnamon
2   tablespoons butter, chilled
½   cup steel-cut oats, soaked in ½ cup hot water until softened
¼   cup chopped walnuts

Preheat the oven to 375°F.

Coat an 8- by 8-inch baking dish with the extra virgin olive oil spray.

In a medium bowl, mix the apples, pears, and cranberries.

In a small bowl, combine the 1 tablespoon of tigernut flour and the stevia or Lakanto.

Stir in the lemon juice, mixing until the stevia or Lakanto is dissolved.

Pour over the fruit and toss until well coated.

In a separate bowl, combine the ⅓ cup of tigernut flour, vanilla protein powder, 1½ teaspoons of stevia or Lakanto, and cinnamon.

Cut in the butter, using a pastry blender or 2 knives, until only small lumps remain.

Stir in the soaked oats.

The oat-flour mixture should resemble a thick paste (stir in a small amount of additional water if needed).

Fold in the walnuts.

Pour the fruit mixture into the prepared pan and spread the crust mixture over the top.

Bake 45 minutes or until brown and crispy on top.

For a pretty finish, place under the broiler for the last minute, watching carefully.

Remove; let cool for 10 minutes before serving.

PHASE 3; MAKES 8 SERVINGS.

Crunchy Flaxy Almond Apples

Good for the whole family and a great snack.

2   apples, cut into wedges and cored
2   tablespoons ground flax seeds
2   tablespoons crushed toasted slice almonds
     SweetLeaf Stevia or Lakanto Monkfruit Sweetener to taste
     Ceylon Cinnamon to taste

Place all the ingredients in a plastic bag with a zipper closure; shake well, coating all the apples with the flaxseed mixture.

Divide onto plates and serve.

PHASE 3; MAKES 2 SERVINGS.

Winter Fruits with Coconut Maple Sauce

I like this not only in the winter but in the spring, summer, and fall, too.

2   cinnamon sticks
1   tablespoon kuzu, dissolved in 1 tablespoon cold water
¼   cup natural unheated honey
1   cup coconut milk
1½ teaspoons maple extract
6   cups assorted fresh fruit
     Ceylon cinnamon (optional)

In a medium saucepan, combine the cinnamon sticks, dissolved kuzu, and honey.

Quickly stir in the coconut milk.

Cook over medium heat, stirring constantly, until the mixture begins to boil and thicken slightly.

Remove the cinnamon sticks.

Remove the sauce from the heat; stir in the maple extract.

Chill the sauce for at least 2 hours.

Alternate layers of fruits and sauce in parfait glasses or bowls.

Garnish with a sprinkle of cinnamon if desired.

Sauce may also be served warmed.

> **TIP**
> Fruits that go well with this sauce are apples, bananas, pears, grapefruit, grapes, pomegranates, and cranberries.

PHASE 3 SPECIAL OCCASION; MAKES 6 SERVINGS.

Fat Flush Cheesecake

Deprive yourself no more! This simple but luscious cheesecake was created by Ellen Buier, who added bananas to give it that creamy texture we adore. With the Quick Cran-Raspberry Sauce (Chapter 10), this is simply divine.

1   pound 2 percent cottage cheese
1   cup mashed ripe banana
½   teaspoon SweetLeaf Stevia or Lakanto Monkfruit Sweetener
     Juice of 1 lemon
4   eggs
½   teaspoon vanilla extract

Preheat the oven to 350°F.

Place the cottage cheese in a blender and blend until smooth.

Add the mashed banana, lemon juice, and stevia or Lakanto and blend until mixed.

Beat the eggs one at a time and add to the mixture, blending well after each addition.

Stir in the vanilla extract.

Pour the mixture into a lightly greased (use butter), 8-inch springform cake pan.

Bake for 35 minutes.

Remove from the oven and loosen the cake from the sides of the pan with a knife.

Cool and then chill for several hours or overnight before serving.

Variation

• Add a splash of rum before pouring the mixture into the cake pan for baking.

PHASE 3; MAKES 8 SERVINGS.

Delightful Pumpkin Pie

Not just for Thanksgiving, canned pumpkin is often a mixture of squashes—a welcome dessert 12 months a year.

Crust:

- ½   cup almond meal
- ¼   cup almond flour
- 1   teaspoon SweetLeaf Stevia or Lakanto Monkfruit Sweetener
- 1   egg
- 2   tablespoons butter, melted

Filling:

- ¼   cup natural unheated honey
- ¼   cup pure maple syrup
- ¼   cup date sugar
- 12   ounces cream cheese, at room temperature
- ½   cup coconut milk
- 2   cups unsweetened canned pumpkin
- 2   eggs
- ½   teaspoon Ceylon cinnamon
- ½   teaspoon ginger
- ¼   teaspoon nutmeg
- ¼   teaspoon mace
- ¼   teaspoon allspice
- ⅛   teaspoon cloves
- 1   teaspoon vanilla extract
      Fat Flush Whipped Cream (recipe given at end of chapter) for garnish (optional)

Preheat the oven to 350°F.

In a small bowl, combine the almond meal and almond flour with the stevia or Lakanto.

Beat the egg with the melted butter and pour into the almond mixture; stir well.

Press evenly into a 9- or 10-inch pie plate. As the mixture may be sticky, cover with a layer of plastic wrap while pressing, then discard the wrap.

Bake the crust about 12 minutes or until it just starts to brown; let cool.

Fold the honey, maple syrup, and date sugar into the cream cheese.

Add the coconut milk, pumpkin, and eggs.

Stir in the spices and vanilla and mix until smooth.

Pour the filling into the nut crust and bake 1 hour or until a toothpick inserted into the center of the pie comes out clean.

Let cool for 1 hour (the pie can be served chilled if desired).

Garnish with a dollop of whipped cream if desired.

Refrigerate the leftover pie.

PHASE 3; MAKES 8 SERVINGS.

Crustless Custard-Pumpkin Pie

Yes, Virginia, there is a Fat Flush–style pumpkin pie. High in beta-carotene, this pumpkin pie is sweetened with honey, molasses, and SweetLeaf Stevia or Lakanto. With the traditional pumpkin pie spices of ginger, nutmeg, and cloves, your family or guests may not even know this dessert is 100 percent sugar-free! Serve with Roast Turkey with Lemon, Garlic, and Fennel (Chapter 6).

1   (15-ounce) can pumpkin
2   tablespoons honey
2   teaspoons molasses or yacon syrup
1   teaspoon Ceylon cinnamon
1   egg yolk
⅛   teaspoon ginger
⅛   teaspoon nutmeg
¼   teaspoon cloves
¼   teaspoon SweetLeaf Stevia or Lakanto Monkfruit Sweetener
2   egg whites
      Pinch of cream of tartar

Preheat the oven to 350°F.

In a bowl, thoroughly blend together all the ingredients except the egg whites and cream of tartar.

Place the egg whites in a large bowl, add the cream of tartar, and beat until the mixture forms soft peaks.

Fold the pumpkin mixture into the egg whites and pour into a lightly greased (use butter) 9-inch pie plate.

Bake for 45 minutes to 1 hour or until a toothpick comes out clean.

Cool before serving.

Variation

• Top with Fat Flush Whipped Cream or Creamy Nutty Dessert Topping (both recipes are given at the end of the chapter).

PHASE 3 SPECIAL OCCASION; MAKES 8 SERVINGS.

Chocolate Fat Flush Ice Cream

A childhood favorite that's still delicious.

1   scoop chocolate protein powder
¼   cup purified cold water

In a small bowl, blend the protein powder and water.

Pour into a freezer container and freeze until ready to serve.

Variations

- Piña colada–flavored whey-based protein powder and tropical twist–flavored whey-based protein powder can alternate with the chocolate for special occasions.
- Top with 1 teaspoon of toasted walnuts and shredded, unsweetened coconut.

PHASE 3; MAKES 1 SERVING.

Coconut Ice Cream

This is so scrumptious anytime, and it makes a perfect ending to a fish entrée like Saucy Cucumber Basil Halibut (Chapter 6).

1   tablespoon SweetLeaf Stevia or Lakanto Monkfruit Sweetener
2   egg yolks
2   cans organic coconut milk
½   cup organic honey or maple syrup
2   teaspoons vanilla extract
    Cinnamon to taste (optional)

Whisk together the stevia or Lakanto and egg yolks, add the remaining ingredients, and continue to whisk.

On medium heat, warm the mixture in a pot, stirring constantly, until thickened to a consistency that lightly coats your spoon. Do not let the mixture boil.

Pour the contents into a bowl and place in the refrigerator.

Once chilled, process in an ice cream maker, put in the freezer, and serve when firm.

PHASE 3; MAKES 4 TO 6 SERVINGS.

Mad About Mango Sorbet

This is a lovely light dessert after a meal of beef, veal, or lamb that is surprisingly satisfying without the sugar.

3   cups mango, cubed
2   teaspoons almond extract
1   teaspoon Flora-Key, SweetLeaf Stevia, or Lakanto Monkfruit
     Sweetener
½   teaspoon fresh lemon juice

Place all the ingredients in a blender or food processor and blend until
    smooth.
Freeze in plastic containers or ice-cube trays for about 2 hours.
Take out the partially frozen fruit and stir well to break up the ice crystals.
Return to the freezer and freeze completely.
Let stand at room temperature 15 minutes before serving.

Variation
*   This sorbet can be made with other types of fruit and flavorings. Try
    substituting pears for the mango and adding ¼ teaspoon of powdered
    gingerroot.

PHASE 3; MAKES 4 SERVINGS.

Fresh Cranberry Sorbet

Wonderfully fresh and fragrant, this sorbet is delightful any time of year, but especially nice at holiday time after a full meal.

2   cups fresh cranberries
¼   cup fresh orange juice
1   tablespoon grated orange zest
3½ cups water
½   cup natural unheated honey
1   tablespoon fresh lemon juice
1   tablespoon kuzu

Place the cranberries, orange juice, and zest and 1½ cups of the water in a medium saucepan; cook over medium heat until the berries pop, 5 to 7 minutes.

Coarsely mash the berries.

Add the honey, lemon juice, kuzu, and remaining 2 cups of water.

Simmer, stirring often, until the mixture forms into a syrup-like consistency, about 1 hour.

Let cool.

Pour into a freezer-safe container with an airtight lid.

Freeze overnight.

The next day, stir with a fork periodically to keep ice crystals from forming.

This sorbet will keep in the freezer for 2 to 3 weeks.

Variation

• Pour the cooled cranberry mixture into the bowl of an ice cream maker; process according to the manufacturer's directions. Serve immediately or freeze.

PHASE 3 SPECIAL OCCASION; MAKES 6 SERVINGS.

Fruity Yogurt Freeze

Taste what a touch of yogurt can do! The kids will really enjoy these treats. They won't even know that what they're eating is healthy.

2   cups strawberries, raspberries, or pineapple (or a mix of all)
4   tablespoons plain whole-milk yogurt
¼ to ½ teaspoon Flora-Key, SweetLeaf Stevia, or Lakanto Monkfruit
      Sweetener to taste

Place the berries, yogurt, and Flora-Key, stevia, or Lakanto in a blender and
      blend until smooth.
Pour into Popsicle molds or small paper cups with Popsicle sticks and freeze
      until solid.

Variation

• Top with 2 tablespoons of coconut, toasted almonds, or toasted sunflower seeds.

PHASE 3; MAKES 2 SERVINGS.

Strawberry-Banana Freeze

If Fruity Yogurt Freeze (see the previous recipe) is for kids, then Strawberry-Banana Freeze definitely has "grown-up" written all over it. This is simple and fast. (Don't forget that ½ banana equals 1 fruit, so with this treat, you will be using all your fruit allotments for the day.)

½ banana
1 cup strawberries
1 cup plain, whole-milk yogurt
¼ to ½ teaspoon Flora-Key, SweetLeaf Stevia, or Lakanto Monkfruit
    Sweetener to taste
    Dash of cardamom

Place all the ingredients except the cardamom in a food processor or blender
    and puree until smooth.
Pour into ice-cube trays and freeze until solid, at least 3 hours.
Serve frozen with a dash of cardamom.

Variation
• Top with toasted, chopped walnuts.

Phase 3; makes 1 serving.

Coconut Citrus Frozen Yogurt

This doubles as a snack between meals.

2   tablespoons kuzu
2   tablespoons fresh lime juice
2   tablespoons fresh lemon juice
½   cup unheated raw honey
½   cup coconut milk
1   teaspoon vanilla extract
1   teaspoon SweetLeaf Stevia or Lakanto Monkfruit Sweetener
1   egg
     Grated zest of 1 lemon
     Grated zest of 1 lime
1   cup plain Greek yogurt
½   cup unsweetened coconut

Dissolve the kuzu in the lime and lemon juices.

In a saucepan over medium heat, mix the juice mixture, honey, coconut milk, vanilla, and stevia or Lakanto.

Bring to a boil, stirring often.

When the mixture thickens, remove from the heat; let cool slightly.

In a small bowl, beat the egg with the lemon and lime zests.

Return the juice mixture to low heat, stirring constantly.

Slowly whisk in the egg mixture.

Simmer, stirring constantly, for 2 minutes.

Chill 10 minutes in the refrigerator.

Fold in the yogurt and coconut.

Pour into an ice cream machine and process according to the manufacturer's directions.

Serve immediately.

TIPS

- The texture of this frozen yogurt is best when it is served immediately.

- You can make the recipe without an ice cream maker. After mixing the ingredients, place in a freezer-safe container with an airtight lid. Stir every hour for 3 to 4 hours until the mixture reaches the texture of sorbet.

PHASE 3 SPECIAL OCCASION; MAKES 6 SERVINGS.

Frozen Berry Mousse

A delicious treat that will look beautiful on your table.

2   cups strawberries (or berries of your choice)
¼   cup unsweetened apple juice
2   egg whites
     Pinch of cream of tartar

In a blender or food processor, puree the berries with the apple juice.

Transfer the puree to a bowl.

In another bowl, beat the egg whites with the cream of tartar until the egg whites form soft peaks.

Fold into the puree mixture, blending well.

Freeze until firm around the edges; then stir once again and place back in the freezer until firm throughout.

Variation
• Instead of the strawberries, try blueberries with 1 teaspoon of lemon zest.

PHASE 3 SPECIAL OCCASION; MAKES 4 SERVINGS.

Lovely Lemon Mousse

A zesty treat that is lovely to serve at a small mid-day gathering.

3   large ripe avocados (soft to touch, but not mushy)
    Juice of 4 lemons
3   tablespoons maple syrup or yacon syrup
4   small or 3 large frozen bananas
    Blackberries (optional)
    Lemon zest (optional)
    SweetLeaf Stevia or Lakanto Monkfruit Sweetener to taste
    (optional)

Mix the avocados, lemon juice, syrup, and bananas in a food processor until
    creamy in consistency.
Serve with the blackberries and a sprinkling of lemon zest and/or sweetener.

PHASE 3; MAKES 4 SERVINGS.

Silky Swirled Pudding

Refreshing and just the right touch of sweetness to crown every meal.

4 ounces silken tofu, drained
4 ounces firm tofu, drained (Mori-Nu brand is preferable)
1 tablespoon pure maple syrup
1 teaspoon vanilla extract
¼ teaspoon almond extract
2 tablespoons unsweetened raspberry preserves
2 tablespoons unsweetened peach preserves
½ teaspoon SweetLeaf Stevia or Lakanto Monkfruit Sweetener
½ teaspoon grated lime zest
2 tablespoons fresh raspberries for garnish
2 tablespoons fresh blackberries for garnish
2 tablespoons sliced fresh strawberries for garnish

In a blender on high speed, whip the silken and firm tofu until smooth.

Add the maple syrup, sweetener, and extracts and continue blending until thick and creamy.

Using a small teaspoon, carefully swirl in the raspberry preserves with a backward motion. Repeat with the peach preserves. Use the edge of the spoon to swirl the preserves throughout the pudding without mixing thoroughly.

Divide the pudding into 4 glass bowls, garnish with the fresh berries, and serve immediately.

TIP
Because tofu continuously releases liquid, this recipe is not suitable for storing in the refrigerator to be served at a later time.

PHASE 3 SPECIAL OCCASION; MAKES 4 SERVINGS.

Creamy Cinnamon-Chocolate Pudding

Oh so delicious and satisfying!

1   large ripe avocado (soft to touch, but not mushy)
3   tablespoons raw almond butter or no-salt-added peanut butter
½   cup chocolate protein powder
½   cup unsweetened coconut milk
1   teaspoon vanilla extract
    Pinch of Ceylon cinnamon
    Pinch of sea salt
    SweetLeaf Stevia or Lakanto Monkfruit Sweetener to taste
    Chia seeds to taste

Mash the avocado and almond or peanut butter in a bowl until smooth.

In a blender, mix in the remaining ingredients, except the chia seeds, and mix until smooth.

Refrigerate for 30 minutes.

Sprinkle with the chia seeds before serving.

Variation

• Top with a dollop of Fat Flush Whipped Cream (the recipe is given at the end of the chapter) or coconut cream and a sprinkle of cardamom.

PHASE 3; MAKES 2 TO 4 SERVINGS.

Pecan Chia Pudding

This is like having a decadent slice of pecan pie in a jar—without a trace of guilt.

1½ cups unsweetened almond milk
⅓   cup chia seeds
3   tablespoons maple syrup plus additional for drizzling
1   teaspoon vanilla extract
½   cup pecans, chopped

Combine the ingredients and divide into 4 jars; cover with lids and refrigerate overnight.

Before serving, stir 2 tablespoons of the chopped pecans into each and drizzle with maple syrup.

PHASE 3; MAKES 4 SERVINGS.

Honey Pear Overnight Chia

This is a fun and refreshing treat to keep in the fridge. Makes a great after-school or work snack, too.

4   (16-ounce) jars
1   cup organic oats
4   teaspoons chia seeds
4   teaspoons organic honey
2⅔ cups no-sugar-added coconut or almond milk
1   cup pears, sliced

In each jar add ¼ cup of oats, 1 teaspoon of chia seeds, 1 teaspoon of honey, and ⅔ cup of coconut or almond milk.

Add lids and shake each jar until the contents are fully combined.

Remove the lids, add ¼ cup of the pears to each jar, gently mix, again add the lids, and refrigerate overnight.

PHASE 3; MAKES 4 SERVINGS.

Fat Flush Fudge

A healthy and guilt-free indulgence!

½   cup cashew butter
¼   cup coconut oil
3   tablespoons carob powder
3   tablespoons Lakanto Monkfruit Sweetener
½   teaspoon vanilla extract
¼   cup organic cashews, chopped

Line a baking pan with parchment paper.

Add the first five ingredients to a medium-sized bowl and mix until just combined.

Stir in the cashews.

Spread the mixture evenly in the pan.

Freeze for 30 to 60 minutes or until firm.

Remove from the freezer and cut into 12 squares.

PHASE 3; MAKES 12 SERVINGS.

Lemony Almond Cookies

These are flourless cookies made with ground almonds. They are a bit soft right out of the oven, but they harden up when cooled down. These are best stored in an airtight container.

2	egg whites
	Pinch of cream of tartar
2	tablespoons honey
½	teaspoon vanilla extract
1	tablespoon lemon zest
1	cup almonds, ground

Preheat the oven to 250°F.

Beat the egg whites with the cream of tartar until stiff white peaks form.

Gradually beat in the honey, vanilla, and lemon zest.

Gently fold in the almonds.

Drop 1 tablespoonful of batter at a time on a lightly greased (use butter) regular cookie sheet, spacing about 2 inches apart.

Bake for about 30 minutes.

Variation
• Try roasted, ground pumpkin seeds instead of the almonds and omit the lemon zest.

PHASE 3 SPECIAL OCCASION; MAKES 12 SERVINGS.

Almond Tigernut Cookies

Tigernuts are not really nuts. They're actually small root vegetables, or tubers, that our ancestors enjoyed. These cookies are made with tigernut flour—a versatile, gluten-free, nut-free, and dairy-free alternative to wheat flours. It has a sweet and nutty flavor all its own and combines well with nut butters.

3   tablespoons purified water
1   tablespoon ground flax seeds
½   cup tigernut flour
½   cup almond butter
¼   cup yacon syrup or raw honey
1   teaspoon aluminum-free baking powder
¼   cup unsweetened carob chips

Preheat the oven to 350°F.

Line a baking sheet with parchment paper.

Mix the water and ground flax seeds in a small bowl and refrigerate for 10 minutes.

In a medium bowl, mix the flour, almond butter, yacon syrup or honey, and baking powder.

Stir in the flaxseed-and-water mixture.

Add the carob chips and stir until combined.

Spoon the dough (about 1 large teaspoonful each) onto a cookie sheet; this should make a dozen cookies.

Bake 10 to 15 minutes or until slightly brown.

Let cool for 10 minutes.

PHASE 3; MAKES 12 SERVINGS.

My Mother's Meringue Kisses

Ever since I was a little girl, I've enjoyed these melt-in-your-mouth cookie fluffs. Of course, in those days my mother didn't know that sugar was bad (and neither did I). And I've tried and tried with my test kitchen to get these to work with SweetLeaf Stevia or Lakanto. No luck. So here are those meringue kisses from yesteryear updated to Fat Flush standards, but alas, you will have to delay your reward until you reach phase 3.

4   egg whites
¼   teaspoon cream of tartar
1   tablespoon honey
1   teaspoon vanilla extract
    Nonstick cooking spray

Preheat the oven to 250°F.

As you beat the egg whites, add the cream of tartar.

Combine the honey and vanilla.

Add to the egg whites as the whites begin to stiffen and form soft peaks.

Spray a cookie sheet with nonstick cooking spray.

Place 8 meringue mounds on the cookie sheet and make indentations with the back of a spoon.

Bake in the oven for about 1¼ hours or until the meringues become crispy.

Turn off the oven, but let the meringues remain in the oven to cool.

When crispy, remove from the oven and store in a covered container.

Variation

• Turn the kisses into meringue nests by topping with some Quick Cran-Raspberry Sauce (Chapter 10). Serve by filling with toasted, chopped pecans (or any toasted nut or seed of your choice) and unsweetened coconut shreds.

PHASE 3 SPECIAL OCCASION; MAKES 8 SERVINGS.

Berry Beautiful Meringues

Light and airy, great for a tea party in the middle of a wintry afternoon.

Shells:

3   large egg whites
⅛   teaspoon salt
½   teaspoon cream of tartar
¼   teaspoon almond extract
1   tablespoon natural unheated honey

Garnish:

1   cup heavy whipping cream
1½ tablespoons natural unheated honey
     Ceylon cinnamon

Filling:

1   cup fresh strawberries, sliced
1   cup fresh raspberries
1   cup fresh blackberries

Preheat the oven to 235°F.

Line a baking sheet with baking parchment.

With an electric mixer on high speed, beat the egg whites until foamy.

Sprinkle the salt and cream of tartar evenly over the egg whites, add the almond extract, and beat until soft peaks form.

Slowly drizzle the 1 tablespoon of honey over the egg whites, beating until stiff peaks form.

Drop 8 portions of the meringue onto the parchment.

With the back of the spoon, carefully smooth the centers while pushing toward the edge, forming a well.

Bake 1 hour; turn the oven off.

Let cool in the oven with the door closed.

Gently remove the meringues from the parchment.

Whip the cream and the 1½ tablespoons of honey to form stiff peaks.

Carefully spoon the berries into the meringue shells.

Top each with a dollop of whipped cream and sprinkle with cinnamon.

Arrange on a decorative plate; serve immediately.

PHASE 3 SPECIAL OCCASION; MAKES 8 SERVINGS.

Creamy Nutty Dessert Topping

This makes a delicious dairy alternative topping for any dessert.

1   cup raw unsalted cashews, macadamia nuts, or almonds
1   cup plus ½ cup purified water
2   tablespoons pure maple syrup, yacon syrup, or raw honey
1   teaspoon pure vanilla extract
    Pinch of sea salt

Fill a jar with the nuts and purified water and soak for 2 hours or overnight.

Drain the nuts and discard the soaking water.

In a blender, add the ½ cup purified water, nuts, sweetener, vanilla, and sea salt and blend on high until well combined and creamy.

Place the mixture in a container with a lid and chill in the refrigerator for a few hours or overnight.

TIP

Make ahead and store in the refrigerator for up to 5 days.

PHASE 3; MAKES 1¼ CUP.

Fat Flush Whipped Cream

Once you've made it to phase 3, you'll occasionally want to reward yourself with a dollop of whipped cream to top a special dessert. And now that you've gotten the sugar out, you'll notice that many foods, like pure, organic milk and cream, have a subtle sweetness all on their own. The addition of almond extract combined with the natural sweetness of the cream makes a just-right topping.

1 pint organic heavy whipping cream
1 teaspoon almond extract

Chill a glass or stainless-steel bowl in the refrigerator.

Pour in the whipping cream and whip on medium speed with a mixer.

When the cream starts to thicken, add the almond extract and continue to whip until soft peaks form.

> **TIP**
>
> If you're nondairy, you can use coconut cream instead. Follow the same directions; just be aware that the consistency will be slightly denser. You can buy organic coconut cream or scoop the cream off the top of a can of organic coconut milk. I like it just the way nature made it—unsweetened—with just an added sprinkle of cardamom on top. But if you really need that extra sweetness, add a teaspoon of SweetLeaf Stevia or Lakanto Monkfruit Sweetener with the almond extract.

PHASE 3 SPECIAL OCCASION; MAKES 2 CUPS.

Resources and Support

ONLINE SUPPORT

Please visit http://www.fatflush.com and http://www.annlouise.com for complete support on your Fat Flush journey and new lifestyle. Visitors to my website and subscribers to my e-mail list never miss my latest blogs and are the first to know about news and upcoming events. Plus you can stay up-to-date with my latest online webinars, articles, and radio and television appearances. Also, do join our Fat Flush community on Facebook at http://www.facebook.com/groups/fatflushcommunity/ for a 24/7 connection with other members, Fat Flush–friendly recipes, diet and exercise tips, testimonials, and motivation. The folks in this group are immeasurably generous in their support, advice, and knowledge!

UNI KEY HEALTH SYSTEMS

Uni Key Health Systems has been my go-to distributor for many supplements and test kits for over 25 years. It was founded in 1992 by James Templeton, a cancer survivor who used alternative medicine to heal himself and has since dedicated his life to helping others find the root causes of disease. Uni Key Health proudly provides high-quality, natural nutritional supplements, vitamins, and health information for diet and detox, weight loss, cleansing, antiaging, energy, hormonal balance, and skin care. I have been a spokesperson and formulator for Uni Key Health Systems for over 20 years.

181 West Commerce Drive
Hayden Lake, ID 83835
800.888.4353
http://www.unikeyhealth.com

Fat Flush–Compatible Supplements Available from Uni Key

- Bile Builder
- Carlson Fish Oil and Softgels
- CLA-1000
- Dandelion Root Tea
- Fat Flush Body Protein
- Fat Flush Whey Protein
- Flora-Key
- GLA-90
- Liver-Lovin Formula
- Mag-Key
- Melatonin 3 mg
- Omega Nutrition Cold Milled Flax Seeds
- Omega Nutrition Flaxseed Oil and Softgels
- ProgestaKey
- Super-GI Cleanse
- SweetLeaf Stevia
- Weight Loss Formula
- Whole Chia Seeds
- Y-C Cleanse

Also Available from Uni Key

- **Earthing products.** Reconnect to the earth's natural healing electrons with products designed to ground yourself for better sleep, increased endurance, enhanced energy, and overall balance.
- **Salivary hormone test.** Unlike blood tests, which do not measure bioavailable hormone activity, saliva testing is considered to be the most accurate measure of free, bioavailable hormonal activity. This personal hormone evaluation can be used to profile up to six hormones: estradiol, estriol, progesterone, testosterone, DHEA, and cortisol. Your personal results and a personal letter of recommendation from my office are mailed directly to your home.
- **Tissue mineral analysis.** This test uses a small sample of hair cut from the back of your head. The analysis includes a full report, up to 20 pages, which graphically shows the levels of 32 major minerals and 6 toxic metals in the body. Each mineral is fully evaluated in terms of its relationship with other minerals, which is a key to glandular function and metabolism rate. This report provides information on the effect of vitamin deficiency and excesses. There is also a complete discussion regarding environmental influences and disease tendencies based upon mineral levels and ratios. A list of recommended food choices and supplements, based on the individual findings, is included at the end of the report.

- Water filtration. Purify your water to protect against harmful chemicals and toxins, parasites like giardia and amoeba, chloromines, and heavy metals. A free water quality consultation with a filtration expert is also available.

ADDITIONAL PRODUCTS

ASEA Global
6550 South Millrock Drive, Suite 100
Salt Lake City, UT 84121
http://www.aseaglobal.com

Over time, due to aging, stress, and environmental toxins, our bodies lose the ability to function at optimum levels. ASEA Redox Supplement is composed of the same life-sustaining molecules that exist in the human body, suspended in a pristine saline solution. It works at the cellular level to enhance function and assist your body's natural efforts to maximize energy and vitality.

Index

About the Author

Ann Louise Gittleman, PhD, CNS, is undisputedly the First Lady of Nutrition. As a nutritional visionary and health pioneer, she has fearlessly stood on the front lines of diet and detox, the environment, and women's health. *Self* magazine describes her as one of the Top Ten Notable Nutritionists in the United States, and thousands of nutritionists, health coaches, and practitioners have benefited from her work.

Years before the Paleo, ketogenic, and vegan diet trends, in her first book, *Beyond Pritikin* (1988), Ann Louise was the very first to proclaim that obesity and diabetes were caused by a lack of the right type of fat and an excess of the wrong kind of carbohydrates, including gluten-rich grain. She was also the first nutritionist to write about the perils of gluten and discuss the blood-type theory in 1996, boldly stating, in her book *Your Body Knows Best*, that one diet may not be right for everyone.

She has also been a tireless crusader for women by offering natural solutions to menopause and perimenopausal symptoms, decades before anybody else, in her award-winning *Super Nutrition for Women*, as well as *Super Nutrition for Menopause* and her *New York Times* bestseller *Before the Change*.

She then revolutionized dieting in the first edition of *The Fat Flush Plan*—an international bestseller—by proclaiming that the liver was the body's primary fat-burning organ (and detoxifier).

Most recently, she led the charge against the hidden hazards of cell phones, iPads, smart meters, and WiFi in her groundbreaking book *Zapped*.

She has appeared on *20/20*, *Dr. Phil*, *The View*, *Good Morning America*, *Extra!*, *FitTV*, and *The Early Show*. In addition, her work has been featured on ABC, CNN, PBS, CBS, NBC, MSNBC, CBN, Fox News, and the BBC.

She has served as a celebrity spokesperson and formula developer for many of the leading companies in the health foods and network marketing industry. Her work has been featured in a myriad of national publications including *Time*, *Newsweek*, *Glamour*, and the *New York Times*.

ENGAGING HEALTH

Today she continues to dedicate herself to carving out new landmarks in functional and integrative medicine with her latest e-book, *Eat Fat, Lose Weight*. She is a popular speaker on Internet summits and is actively involved with videos and her blog. Her expert advice often appears in *First for Women* magazine, where she was the nutrition columnist for more than 10 years.

In 2016 Ann Louise was presented with the Humanitarian Award from the Cancer Control Society. She currently sits on the Advisory Board for the International Institute for Building-Biology & Ecology, the Nutritional Therapy Association, Inc., and Clear Passage, Inc.

Connect with Ann Louise at www.annlouise.com, www.fatflush.com, and facebook.com/annlouisegittleman.

Books from Award-Winning Pioneer Nutritionalist Ann Louise Gittleman, PH.D, C.N.S.